# ALSO BY JOEL SHEPHERD

*Crossover*
*A Cassandra Kresnov Novel*

*Breakaway*
*A Cassandra Kresnov Novel*

Published 2007 by Pyr®, an imprint of Prometheus Books

Inquiries should be addressed to
Pyr
59 John Glenn Drive
Amherst, New York 14228–2119
VOICE: 716–691–0133, ext. 210
FAX: 716–691–0137
WWW.PYRSF.COM

11  10  09  08  07      5  4  3  2  1

Library of Congress Cataloging-in-Publication Data

Shepherd, Joel, 1974–
    Killswitch : a Cassandra Kresnov novel / Joel Shepherd.
        p. cm.
    "The third Cassandra Kresnov novel"—T.p. verso.
    Originally published: Sydney, Australia : Voyager, an imprint of HarperCollins
Publishers, 2004.
    ISBN 978–1–59102–598–6 (trade pbk.)
    1. Kresnov, Cassandra (Fictitious character)—Fiction. 2. Androids—Fiction. I. Title.

PR9619.4.S54K55 2007
823'.92—dc22

2007033803

Printed in the United States of America on acid-free paper

# KILLSWITCH
## JOEL SHEPHERD
### A CASSANDRA KRESNOV NOVEL

an Imprint of Prometheus Books
Amherst, NY

*To Stephanie,*
*for having faith*

# CHAPTER I

The day was turning out nothing like Sandy had planned. But she was getting used to that.

"What kind of sabotage?" She was seated in the command chair of a brand-spanking-new A-9 assault flyer. Past the pilot's head, the bubble canopy afforded her a decent aerial view of gleaming, sunlit Tanusha. She listened to the reply over her headset with little surprise. "No, don't bother Secretary Grey, I'll have the President's ear personally in a few minutes. Get me Captain Reichardt as soon as he's available."

She deactivated, and swivelled her command chair away from the bank of multiple screens to tap the pilot, Gabone, on the helmet.

"How are you finding the interface?" she asked him.

"It still makes me a little dizzy, Commander," Gabone replied.

"Don't push it, it takes a while to adjust, even for me."

"I'll be okay," Gabone replied with confidence, casually flipping a few switches on the compact control panel, tipping them into a gentle starboard bank. "It's worth anything to have this much firepower."

Sandy gazed at the Presidential convoy, strung out before them in single file above the vast, sprawling cityscape of Tanusha. Gabone's view, she knew, would be overlaid with target highlights and trajectory-prediction graphics, time-accelerated in the pilot and weapon officers' brains by the fancy interface with the flyer's computer systems. About her, the A-9's cramped, streamlined hull packed enough precision weaponry to take out the entire convoy in several seconds, had its crew chosen to. Just two years ago, such weaponry had been unheard of in Tanushan skies. But two years in Tanusha had been a long time indeed.

Sandy monitored her screens, her own mental interface scanning across vast swathes of metropolitan info-network with much greater ease than Gabone, or any other regular human, could ever experience. The patterns she saw across Tanusha were familiar—the Callayan Defence Force sweepers flying in wide and forward defensive patterns, as always the case when the President or another similarly ranked foreign dignitary moved. The usual security walls about the approaching Parliament grounds, and the distant Gordon Spaceport. Several security hotspots where ongoing operations warranted extra cover. One such caught her eye, emanating from a particularly high volume of traffic. A further brief scan showed her several ambulances had been called. Velan Mall, a major shopping and entertainment centre . . . she zoomed further into the schematic within her internal vision. Sim Craze, the establishment was called. A further scan of the local established tac-net registered a lot of civilian com traffic, lots of alarmed voices. Evidently something had perturbed the locals.

She restrained a faint smile, dialing into the tac-net with her command signature fully visible, hardly surprised that *someone* had ended up in an ambulance, considering who was in charge. Her query got a familiar reply.

*"Hi, smartarse, I hope you're happy."* Vanessa's voice sounded a little strange, muffled. Sandy frowned.

"Are you eating? You sound like you're talking with your mouth full."

*"That's 'cause my nose is busted!"*

"You got hit?"

*"What, that surprises you? They're goddamn Fleet marines, you blonde bimbo. They didn't want to leave quietly and we're not all indestructible like you, in case you hadn't noticed . . ."*

"Ricey, I'm sorry." She injected a note of winsome apology into her voice . . . oh, the little subtleties she'd learned in her short life as a civilian. "I sent you because you're the best, and I thought they might have better manners than trying to flatten a cute little button like you."

*"Yeah, well their squad sergeant was a cute little button herself, so chivalry was out of the question."*

"What's the score?"

*"She'll be okay once they wire her jaw back into place. Two of the others will need a leg reconstruction and a new left elbow respectively, young Chanderpaul got a little overexcited. I think a week on training sims will calm him down."*

"Never fault enthusiasm."

*"It was six against four, I wasn't in a sporting mood. With those numbers it wasn't called for."*

"Well, okay, nice work, get back to Medical and get your nose fixed."

*"Gee, where would I be without your sage advice? Thank you for royally ruining my day."*

"Oh go on, you've been itching to pick a fight with some Fleet knuckleheads for weeks."

*"When I want a busted nose, I'll ask for one."*

The connection went blank. Sandy sighed, and wondered for the ten thousandth time if she'd ever have the quiet, peaceful life she'd once dreamed of.

The assault flyer followed the Presidential convoy down over the grassy green Parliament grounds, Alpha Team security aircars fanning out ahead as the main cluster came in toward the huge, red-brown structure of domes and arches. Sandy had flown this approach route many times in the past two years, but still it gave her a shiver of deadly memories. If she strained her vision toward the Rear Wing, she knew she would see a memorial garden where a service carpark used to be, colourful native plants and flowers in profusion about the shattered wreck of an Alpha Team aircar, the names of seventy-two dead inscribed into one red-brown Parliament wall. Sandy's uplinks locked into the Parliament tac-net, the entire regional airspace monitored and scanned by the millisecond, the full span clearly visible across her internal vision. The CDF assault flyer and the convoy vehicles broad-casted friendly frequencies clearly into that hair-triggered airspace, their electronic signature and careful human monitoring the only things preventing them from being instantly blasted from the sky by the weapon emplacements strategically located about the grounds.

Sandy began unhooking herself from the command connections and undoing the chair straps as the flyer came in behind the Alpha Team formation, the East Wing rooftop landing pads approaching ahead, small beside the looming central dome.

"I'm clear," she told Gabone, securing her ops headset and removing her rifle from rack storage behind the chair. "Wait for me at holding point five, you're too conspicuous up here."

"*Commander,*" came the weapon officer's voice from the front cockpit seat, "*we have a large group of journalists by the platform. That's not in accordance with . . .*"

"I know, I saw them. Don't get bored waiting, this isn't a drill."

The rear fuselage doors cracked open, bringing a rush of wind and light into the cramped flyer interior. Sandy one-armed the rifle and made her way along the aisle on past the empty trooper berths in the back. The rooftop pads appeared below as the doors flared fully outward, and she stepped out before touchdown, taking the impact comfortably with a half-spin, slowing from a run to a walk as Gabone poured on the power with a roar of fan blades. The flyer lifted away from the Parliament roof, banking to avoid the huge central dome above Parliament's main chambers. Sandy walked in the dissipating rush of slipstream, rifle ready, aware that no few of the Alpha Team security were staring as she came.

There were six armoured black aircars down on the pads, gull doors open, and men in suits with weapons gathered strategically about. Beyond, in the cordoned section of the rooftop behind a series of leafy plant boxes, a cluster of perhaps twenty journalists were waiting—no cameras, Sandy saw, just voice recorders and other communication or computer gear, camera access, like most things, being highly restricted within Parliament grounds these days.

President Neiland, accompanied by several of her closest advisors amidst the immediate "body security," was walking toward the waiting media with an evident announcement on her mind. Sandy shook her head in exasperation, and spun a slow three-sixty as she walked, visually scanning the broad grounds, across the multiple wings to the giant Corinthian pillars of the Senate, allowing her subconscious to soak up the detail and seek possible clues. Nothing registered, and she strode firmly between the aircars and suited security toward the gathering cluster on the pad's edge. No one stopped her, and she put a hand on the President's shoulder just as she was about to start speaking.

"Ms. President, security has red-zoned all outdoor spaces for now, we really should get you inside."

"Just a moment, Sandy, this won't take long . . ."

"No, Ms. President. Now."

Neiland stared at her, anger flashing in steely blue eyes within a pale, handsome face. Her red hair was bound up with fashionable pins and a comb, Sandy noted. Evidently she'd been intending to make an impressive appearance before the media, lack of cameras or otherwise. But it took more to intimidate a combat GI than angry eyes and a fancy title. Neiland covered the anger fast, all too aware of the audience. And, supremely professional politician that she was, turned it quickly into an exasperated smile and roll-of-the-eyes at the journalists.

"Very tenacious, isn't she?" The journalists smiled.

And one of them took the opportunity to ask, "Commander, what's the alarm this time?"

"No comment," Sandy told him. And increased the pressure on Neiland's shoulder by a fraction. Neiland got the message in a hurry— often the case, when Sandy started squeezing.

"Look, we can continue this inside . . . if that's okay with you, Commander?" She said it with a smile, but Sandy wasn't fooled.

"Sure."

The contingent began to move, Sandy falling into place behind the President, where Alpha Chief Mitchel was walking. She took the opportunity to throw him a very dirty look. Further along, Vice-Chief Tan noticed, and gave a nod of agreement to her, with evident exasperation of his own, even as Mitchel tried to ignore her.

"I don't care who started squeezing your balls," she said to Mitchel later in the hall outside the room Neiland's advisors had requisitioned for the impromptu press briefing. Mitchel evidently wanted to be elsewhere, but Sandy had his back to the wall and wasn't about to lose the advantage. When the second-in-command of the Callayan Defence Force gave a lecture, even the head of the President's personal security was obliged to stand and take it . . . unless, of course, he was itching to get "promoted" to training and recruitment. Sandy kept her expression hard, her eyes unblinking, her stare as direct as she could make it. She knew Mitchel was no pushover, either as a man or as a security operative, but still he looked a little nervous. "Where her security is in question, you take orders from no one. Your own fucking procedures say that you must follow every red-zone precaution, no exceptions. Since when do you start getting picky?"

"It was a weak report, Commander," Mitchel retorted, with all the stubbornness that his hard jaw and sharp eyes suggested he could muster. "It was one witness, some scant information, no corroboration . . ."

"You are *not* an Intelligence agent. We've got an entire division of specialists whose job it is to make those decisions. Your job is to do what you're told, and to implement their recommendations. Do I make myself clear?"

"You," Mitchel bit out in retort, "are not my superior."

"No, I'm much worse. I'm the President's *senior* security advisor. My next report, in that capacity, will be on the alarming spread of political influence upon the promotions and policies within Alpha Team and other specialist security agencies. You don't bend the rules for *anyone,* not the Speaker, not the Majority Whip, not Ms. Red-haired God Almighty herself. Another breach, and I'll see that you lose your job. It's that simple."

Vice-Chief Tan was standing nearby, well in earshot of Alpha-standard hearing enhancements. Sandy refrained from giving him an acknowledgement—dividing Alpha Team by setting second-in-command against the Chief would be very dangerous. She walked to a clear space of corridor instead and waited with weapon at cross-arms for the President's media briefing to finish, completely annoyed at how politics interfered with *everything* in this environment. Especially those things where it least belonged.

One of the President's key advisors, Sudasarno, intercepted her before she could devote full attention to her remote links.

"Sandy, what was the red-zone for?" Sandy barely raised an eyebrow at the nickname—she'd been in constant contact with the President and her personal staff for the last two years, and felt they'd earned the informality. Until the shit hit the electro-turbine, anyhow.

"Small matter of a missing rocket launcher," Sandy replied with no small irony. "Self-guided, several kilometres range, just the kind of thing that might penetrate the defence grid and blow her and her little knot of favourite journalists into very small pieces."

"From our own stockpile?" Sudasarno asked with a pained look.

"Production line, actually."

"Shit . . ." The advisor's Indonesian features were pained, necktie loosened, his dark hair uncharacteristically rumpled. "We only started making that stuff since we started the CDF . . ."

"Plenty of weapons got in through the smuggling routes before . . . so these are indigenous, big deal."

"It doesn't look good."

"That's your problem, not mine," she told him patiently. "I've told everyone what we need to keep our stockpiles safe, somehow the recommendations keep getting blocked in parts."

"We're suddenly an arms producer, Sandy. Callay's never done that before, just two years ago we weren't even allowed to have armed forces independent from the Fleet. We're not good at all this stuff yet. Who stole the launcher?"

Sandy shook her head. "My source doesn't know."

Sudasarno gave her a wary, knowing look. "Yeah, well tell your *source* he'd better have some leads soon, because the press are going to be asking why you dragged the President away from an interview like that."

"Because certain political influences interfered with her supposedly politically invulnerable security." She fixed Sudasarno with a mild, firm stare. Sudasarno sighed, and stared momentarily off into space, in profound frustration.

"It never gets any easier around here, does it?"

Sandy restrained a faint smile. "Shit, you're telling me?"

Alpha Team were moving past them then, the door opening behind and Neiland emerging, flanked by several other advisors.

"Sandy," said the President, "with me, if you please."

Sandy fell in beside the elegant, long-legged President, pondering not for the first time the contrast in styles they made, herself shorter and broad shouldered in khaki-green CDF fatigues. The President's heels clacked as they walked. Sandy's boots barely squeaked.

"Damn it, Sandy," the President said in a low voice, temper still plain in her voice, "*never* do that in front of the media. Do I make myself clear?"

"Ms. President, *never* put pressure on your Alpha Chief to break with protocol for your day-to-day convenience. Do I make *myself* clear?"

"Fuck it all," the President muttered, "I *knew* there had to be a downside to making you Commander." Sandy raised an eyebrow—the President's swear words were usually limited to the tamer variety. If the f-word was in use, things were bad.

"There's a rocket launcher missing," Sudasarno explained from the President's other side. Neiland sighed.

"Another one? I swear, Sandy, soon these crazies will be better armed than you are."

"Unlikely. What was so important about that rooftop that it couldn't wait a few minutes, anyway?"

"Sudie has evidence that some of my political opponents are misusing the building's info-net."

The lead Alphas turned a corner. The next hallway was wider with tiled patterns on the floor. Well-dressed Parliament staff made way as the Presidential procession passed by, a common enough sight in these corridors lately. Sandy frowned.

"Eavesdropping?" she asked, with a glance across at Sudasarno, who shrugged.

"Some information turned up in their possession that we don't see any other way for them to have," he explained. Them, of course, being the President's political enemies. Who these days were too numerous and varied to count. Sandy thought about it for a moment.

"Ms. President, talk to me. I'm not your enemy. Coordinate with me in advance and we'll clear a location and keep it private so no one has advance warning, terrorists or Progress Party alike."

Neiland sighed, as if releasing stored tension. "Thank you, Sandy. I should have thought ahead, I've just . . . I've just been so damn busy. What else has been going on?"

"Another nine hospitalisations from fights with Fleet marines on leave from orbit . . ."

"Oh fuck," said the President, wearily. Sandy nearly smiled.

"I wish they would just fuck," she replied, "that's usually the main pastime of grunts on leave. But the populace is giving them a hard time, apparently."

"Damn it, we have a renegade mob of Fleet loyalists threatening to blockade our fucking stations, what do they expect?"

"We should have cancelled leave," said Sudasarno.

"Would have caused another stink," Sandy replied. "We've enough stinks with the Fleet already. The good news is that five of those hospitalisations are marines—one from a very angry kung fu blackbelt citizen, and the other four courtesy just now of Major Rice and some friends."

"Why am I not surprised?" said Neiland. "Anything else?"

"Someone sabotaged the *Mekong*, took out the regulator controls for the thruster injection."

Neiland actually stopped, and all Alpha Team stopped with her, plus Sandy, Sudasarno and the other advisors. The President stared at the CDF commander for a long moment.

"Seriously?" Sandy gave her a mock-reproachful tilt of the head. Neiland took a deep breath. "Damn. Captain Reichardt is not going to be happy."

"There's going to be a lot of captains leaning his way that will be unhappy."

"That's all we need," muttered the President. "A fucking civil war between competing Fleet factions in orbit."

"Ms. President, I've never heard you use such bad language so frequently."

"Oh, stick it up your arse."

The splendour of the Grand Congressional Hearings Chamber had not yet entirely worn off for Sandy. She sat in her usual place at the central bench, surveying the now-familiar line of faces that looked down on her from the two rows of grand benches opposite—the Union and Progress Party congressors. To her right, also as usual, sat Mahudmita Rafasan, in a typically elegant sari, scanning through various notes on her comp-slate at rapid speed. Audience members in their hundreds shuffled and murmured at the back of the chamber, the collective sound echoing off the chamber's high, arching dome. Chandeliers gleamed within that vast mosque-style space and the dome's tiled patterns and midlevel arches were marvellous to behold.

Chairman Khaled Hassan rang the little bell on the desk before him, and announced the proceedings open. Barely had he finished when Congressor Augustino, from the Union side of the benches, launched into action.

"Commander Kresnov, I believe your weapon is in contravention of the standing orders of this Chamber—section 142, I believe—stating that no weapons shall be allowed into the Chamber that are not in the possession of authorised security agents."

Sandy leaned slightly forward to her desktop microphone, to make sure her voice carried upon the speakers throughout the Chamber. "I'm second-in-command of the Callayan Defence Force, Mr. Augustino. How much more authorised would you like me to get?"

There was a murmur of laughter through the audience behind, and noticeable smiles upon the faces of various Congressors. Sandy's assault rifle, of course, lay upon the desk to her left hand—precisely where it belonged, in Sandy's estimation. But Augustino, she knew, wasn't the slightest bit interested in the Chamber's standing orders. He had bigger fish to fry. Sandy-sized fish.

"Mr. Chairman," said the conservative Congressor, "I'd like to register my complaint at this latest breach from the Commander. In her various appearances within this Chamber she has never failed to treat the Chamber standing orders with anything less than contempt. I think we can see another clear instance of this attitude here today."

Khaled Hassan looked concerned, stroking his long white beard. And gave Sandy a patient look, inviting her to respond. Sandy smiled at him. She liked Hassan. Among politicians, it was a luxury she did not often allow herself to indulge in.

"Mr. Chairman, I'm a busy girl, I have a lot of official functions I'm trying to perform simultaneously. Foremost among them, I'm trying to get this novel experiment we call the Callayan Defence Force off the ground, in the face of some fairly stiff opposition from obvious sources. I also occasionally get out on official security duties, such as today, when I noticed the President's arrival time would be approximately that of my own, and in light of some recent security alerts I decided to provide the usual CDF escort personally. Thus the weapon, as I am here in dual capacities. Don't worry, the safety is on, and I am fairly well practised in its use."

That got another laugh from behind. Typically, when confronted by politicians in such a setting making clearly inflammatory, opportunistic attacks before the global media, a person would be advised to remain calm, straight-faced and professional—and so allow the attacker's unprofessionalism to backfire, in the eyes of those watching. Various political advisors and publicists, however, had decided that where she was concerned, too much professionalism was a bad thing.

They'd done polling, apparently. And had concluded that what scared people most about her, as a combat GI, was the image of a deadpan, unemotional, human-shaped killing machine. Smile, they'd told her. Be off-the-cuff. Keep it light, where ever possible. Oh, and try to do that while still reassuring the population that you're perfectly well qualified to hold your present position. The two requests couldn't have been more contradictory—she couldn't be cheerful and caring while demonstrating her proficiency at managing the planet's most lethal combat force. But, as in all impossible political situations, she tried . . . because of course, there was no other choice.

"Before we move on to procedural matters regarding the CDF, Commander," began Congressor Selvadurai, another Union Party rep, "I'd like to get your response to the recent violent incidents between members of the Federation Fleet and the Tanushan public. Do you think that your inflammatory remarks regarding the nature of the Fleet presence about Callay at this moment have anything to do with the bad blood that evidently exists here?"

Sandy gazed at the Union rep, calm and unblinking. "Which inflammatory remarks would they be, Congressor Selvadurai?"

"You remarked that the Fleet presence about Callay was in fact a de facto blockade intending to intimidate Callay and other Federation worlds into granting concessions to Fleet hardliners."

"I did say that it was a de facto blockade," Sandy replied, "and in doing so, I was merely echoing remarks made by many others in this building and beyond, including my own President. If you check my exact words, you'll find that I did not speculate as to the intent of the blockade. That is not my place."

"But it is your place to provoke hostile feeling toward the Fleet within sections of the Callayan population by mischaracterising its actions in this manner?"

At Sandy's elbow, Mahudmita Rafasan gave a snort of exasperation. Sandy spoke before things got ugly.

"Look, Congressor, we have a situation in orbit right now, I'm sure we're all only too well aware of that. It is not my intention here today, nor at any other time, to make statements that may inflame the situation, or make things worse. But clearly the presence of leading elements of the Fifth Fleet at our various orbital facilities is unhelpful at best, and provocative at worst. The Fifth's actions are not sanctioned by Federation law, nor by Fleet operating procedure under any circumstances that I am aware of . . ."

"Fleet Admiral Duong of the Fifth has stated many times, Commander," interrupted Congressor Selvadurai, "that the present state of political flux on Callay places us in a precarious situation vis-à-vis our security. The leaders of approximately a quarter of the entire Federation are presently here, negotiating with our own President Neiland plus Earth's senior representative in Secretary General Benale, to hammer out the new rules and workings of the Federation Grand Council now that it is just a year from being relocated permanently to our planet. We have indigenous and off-world extremist and other groups all focusing upon this world as the centre of their concerns. Our local security is improved but remains imperfect at best, and the degree of weaponry and sophisticated network technology available to these various sources of instability is truly alarming. Would you not say, Commander, that under these circumstances, Fleet Admiral Duong is perfectly correct to state that Callay's security is in question, and in need of assistance?"

"Congressor, as second-in-command of the CDF, I've stated many times that we'll take all the genuine help we can get. We've had many offers of assistance from friendly worlds who supported us in the referendum, who are staunch supporters of the relocation, and we truly welcome their contributions. We are strengthening our various security operations on the ground, Parliament and other dedicated security groups are vastly advanced on where they were two years ago, and the CDF gives us the extra punch we may need if faced with heavier weaponry than the police, the Callayan Security Agency or aligned security have the capability to handle. What we are *not* at risk from is an assault with warships from orbit. Or if we are, then I would suggest that (a) the Fleet should inform us immediately so we can make preparations, and (b) that they'd be an awful lot more effective defending us against that assault if they were to position themselves somewhere mid-system as is customary when defending against inbound attackers. They certainly won't do any good snuggled up to our space stations with their noses clamped in dock."

"Commander," cut in Congressor Augustino, "we are at serious risk of being flooded by waves of militants, terrorists, foreign agents and sophisticated weaponry from around the Federation and beyond . . ." That's right, Sandy thought, never miss a chance to raise the spectre of the League. ". . . and you don't think it's a good idea for our overworked station staff and customs to receive some help filtering all this inbound traffic?"

Sandy restrained an exasperated smile. "Sir, the Fleet are soldiers. Damn good ones, but soldiers nonetheless. They blow stuff up. Or they hold onto facilities to stop other people from blowing stuff up. They're not customs officers, they're not criminal investigators, they don't have access to files on wanted persons, have limited experience in counter-smuggling, and wouldn't know what the hell to do with any of this information if they received it. We have professionals up there in orbit right now, doing the jobs for which they are specifically equipped and trained, to the best of their considerable abilities.

"The one thing Callay is not yet particularly good at is security and the application of military or paramilitary force, although we are improving fast. The one thing we are *remarkably* good at is commerce. The customs requirements you are speaking of are a matter of bureau-cratic commerce, Congressors—there have been plenty of restrictions on certain items of trade for a long time now, both for security, and commercial and legislative reasons. The commercial system has gotten pretty good at it, and now that the circumstances have changed to expand the number of prohibited items and persons, they've adapted marvellously. It's a job for civilian workers in overalls or suits and ties. It's *not*, and I'll stress this, *not* a job for grunts with guns in armour.

I've been a grunt myself, and by many measurements I still am. I recall that nothing irritated me more than being called upon to perform civilian tasks for which I and my people were neither equipped nor trained. Not only did I consider that unfair on us, I considered it unfair on the people we were attempting to serve.

"We didn't ask for Fleet help, and we don't need it. In fact, I'm having great difficulty getting a straight answer on exactly who *did* order the Fleet out here. And even more difficulty getting an answer on why there are also elements of the Third Fleet here as well, in the temporary command of Captain Reichardt of the warship *Mekong*, who are not participating in the activities of the Fifth, nor appear to be answerable to their leader in Admiral Duong. It's obvious to all of us that the Fleet are not united on the question of the relocation. From my perspective in the CDF, such divisions only make the local security environment more precarious, not less. I personally would much prefer that they held their private disagreements well away from Callay, and let us all get on with our jobs."

At Sandy's side, Mahudmita Rafasan gave her a slightly bewildered, worried look. The look she'd given on various occasions before, when the newly appointed CDF Commander had overstepped the official line, and said things that weren't polite. Well, screw it, she thought to herself, it was only one small faction that would be annoyed at her voicing such sentiments, anyhow. They happened to include the President . . . so that was a problem. But not rocking the boat was a part of any Presidential job description. There were many others, whom the President was presently resisting, who thought she should throw the book at Admiral Duong and his hardline captains. Federation law was on their side after all, whatever the increasingly isolated, alienated Earth majority thought about it . . .

"Commander Kresnov," Congressor Augustino said angrily. "The great and honourable Federation Fleet is far too great an institution to be so easily divided, as you and various media scaremongers have been suggesting! It is only thanks to the heroic sacrifices made by the men and women of the Fleet that the war against the League was won, and all humanity saved from rampant techno-liberalism and political fragmentation and disintegration! I for one do not think that it is either right or fitting for a public figure in a position such as your own to be belittling that achievement, nor the honour and unity of the Fleet today!"

The only problem, Sandy continued her previous line of thought, was that the most outspokenly conservative wing of Callayan politics were all within the President's own Union Party, like Augustino and Selvadurai. They were loud because they could afford to be. Praising the Fleet's heroism was, she recalled Vanessa recently remarking, something of a motherhood statement—you praised it, and everyone nodded and applauded, and opponents could not possibly raise voices in protest because what politician could be against motherhood, and expect to win an election? The Fleet had until very recently been a sacred cow in Callayan politics. And she barely managed to restrain a smile at the memory of what her favourite media personality, Rami Rahim, had remarked just the other night on that subject—no longer a sacred cow, the Fleet was now more of a sacred goat. A mangy one with a limp, fleas and a bad case of flatulence. Any more incidents, and it might not be more than a sacred rat. Or one of those small winged insects that tried to bite beneath your collar at outdoor parties every summer . . .

"Congressors," she said, in the calm and unhurried manner she assumed in the presence of people she didn't respect, "since this part of my brief is to keep you all informed as to the ongoing security situation regarding the CDF, I think this could be a good time to overstep my bounds a little and relate to you the most recent news of all from orbit. Apparently the warship *Mekong*, commanded by Captain Reichardt of the Third Fleet, has been sabotaged."

There was a deathly silence from the benches. Busy politicians simply weren't in the loop for that kind of information . . . doubtless this was the first they'd heard. From the audience seats behind the ornately carved partition, there came a shifting and murmuring. Particularly from that part of the seating reserved for media.

"It happened at dock," Sandy continued, "and was only reported to me half an hour ago. I have never been shipcrew, ships to me were just a means of transport when I was a grunt, so I don't claim to be an expert on the matter, but from what I do know, such sabotage had to be carried out by someone with considerable expertise."

"This was targeted sabotage?" asked Congressor Zhou, leaning forward on her bench with an expression of great concern. One of the Union Party right wing, and thus a staunch ally of Neiland's. Sandy nodded. "Targeted to do what?"

"To disable the engines, possibly to force *Mekong* to conduct an extensive overhaul. It could have taken them out of action for weeks . . . although thankfully the problem was detected in the last systems check by *Mekong*'s engineers, preventing serious damage. Given the security of any warship at dock, during times of war or peace, it seems unlikely that the person responsible could have been anyone other than a member of the Fleet . . . particularly when you account for the expertise involved.

"My job in the CDF is to maintain Callay's security. This task will become exceedingly difficult if we have warring Fleet factions docked to our stations in a state of political stand-off, without any clear idea of lines of command. I am particularly concerned about this, considering the present disorganisation in the Grand Council. There appears to be no effective civilian oversight at present to direct the Fleet in its actions. Fleet HQ is running the show entirely on its own, except that Fleet HQ appears to be divided.

"Furthermore, since the Grand Council began downsizing the Fleet following the conclusion of the war three years ago, we've seen clear evidence of a kind of political stacking going on within certain parts of the Fleet structure—particularly within the Fifth Fleet. As ships from other units have been mothballed, their crews are broken up and the most hardline, pro-Earth officers have been moved into the Fifth, filling gaps left by the departure of long-serving officers from other parts of the Federation who finally had a chance to go home. The Fleet has been warned of this development many times in the past, as has the Grand Council, but no action has been taken. And now we have Fifth Fleet marines on leave in Tanusha who seem more interested in picking fights with the local populace than they do with relaxing and having fun, as crews usually do during downtime.

"Ladies and gentlemen . . . I'm CDF. I have big guns and professional soldiers at my disposal. I can't deal with civil disturbances. I can't stop them blowing up into bigger political issues that inflame passions on all sides and only make the present state of negotiations far more precarious. These are political issues. Your issues. I can only sit here before you today, and ask that you recognise the increasing threat to Callayan security that these factors, in combination, create today."

Ten minutes later, in response to an invitation, Sandy entered the waiting room to Senator Lautrec's office. A man seated upon one of the stylish leather chairs, to the left of the Senator's doors, caught her immediate attention. The man smiled as he saw her, and rose cordially to his feet, a hand extended in welcome, perfect white teeth flashing within a handsome African face.

"Commander." His tone was deep, cultured, and very self-assured. Sandy stepped across and took the offered hand, eyeing Major Mustafa Ramoja up and down, warily. He looked good in his civvie suit. Although she'd often thought that attractive African men and women would look good in anything. No other race seemed to have that luxury. Not that Ramoja, a GI like herself, belonged to an actual race any more than she was the genuine, pale European she appeared to be. "Nice speech. How long until Krishnaswali chews your ear off for that one?"

"As soon as I step in his door," Sandy replied, still warily. "They let you out of your cage. Why?"

Ramoja only smiled, well used to her casual provocations. "The Vice-Ambassador is inside. Senior Embassy staff are allowed to have GIs as bodyguards now. I appointed myself, naturally."

"Naturally. I'm sure all your friends in the CSA were real thrilled to hear that." Ramoja's smile grew broader, and he nodded across the room. Sandy looked, and saw a man and a woman reading from comp-slates, trying to look inconspicuous. Groomed and clipped with athletic poise, and uplinked into some seriously encrypted network feeds, Sandy's uplinks informed her, they weren't about to fool anyone.

"I call them Number One, and Number Two," Ramoja said smugly. "They vary, of course. Don't worry, I shan't hurt them. They're very well behaved." The two CSA agents could easily overhear, but remained expressionless.

Ramoja's very existence had been a revelation to her, just two years before. A GI with a higher designation than her own. Until that moment, she had not been aware that there *were* such GIs in existence . . . although that assumption seemed fairly naive, in hindsight. He'd been commissioned by the League's Internal Security Organisation, the ISO, based upon her own, somewhat controversial design, and the success it had attained. Well, before she'd proven a failure by defecting, anyway. Now, he was the ISO's pointman on Callay, running out of the very heavily watched and defended League Embassy in downtown Tanusha. An enclave full of very capable League GIs, right in the heart of Tanusha, made no local officials happy. And in that particular piece of anti-GI xenophobia, Sandy was right there with them.

"Can I ask what business you have with Senator Lautrec?" Ramoja asked now, with a charming smile.

"You can," said Sandy.

"More troubles with weapons procurement?"

"We're having an affair," Sandy said flatly.

"He's one hundred and three."

"Doesn't look a day over seventy-five. The wrinkles grow on you."

"That would be the only thing."

"And what would the Vice-Ambassador's visit be in aid of?" Sandy returned.

Ramoja made a vague gesture. "League Ambassadors are very popular these days. They get around."

"So does herpes."

"An amazingly resistant little virus." Nothing, and no diversionary tactic, would ever leave Ramoja short of something to say. "Today's strains would kill a pretechnology human rather quickly, I understand, so resistant they've become to everything we throw at them."

Sandy made a face. "They have the galaxy's most unstoppable delivery mechanism. STDs have always been the hardest bugs to kill. They spread so easily."

Ramoja's eyes flicked toward the office doors. "On top of centurian senators' desks, one would believe."

"The Afghan carpet, actually." She shrugged. "It's easier on his back."

Ramoja smiled broadly. He'd been smiling quite a lot, lately, within the parameters of his usual clipped formality. As far as Sandy was aware, Tanusha was Ramoja's first truly civilian posting. And it seemed to be working its spell on even him. There came voices from inside the Senator's office, and the door handle turned—an aide emerging first, as the conversation wound up within. Sandy gave the major a bright smile.

"Well, it was entertaining as always," she told him. "Until the next time."

"Cassandra," Ramoja intervened before she could move through the door. She looked at him, expectantly wary. "I have a request to make."

"Yes?"

Ramoja looked slightly pained. Or perhaps bemused, it was often difficult to tell. "As a personal favour to me," he said, "do you think you could please refrain from asking Rhian too many questions regarding Embassy scheduling and activities?"

And Sandy found that it was her turn to smile. "Okay. I'll only ask her about the Embassy's security posture then."

"It was a very gracious act from Ambassador Yao and the authorities back on Ryssa to allow Rhian to live with you." Very, very reasonably. As if the very thought of challenging such a reasonable assertion was unthinkable. "I do understand that the two of you have a very special relationship. I understand that her loyalties have become somewhat . . . conflicted. We do not begrudge her that. But please, do not make her situation any more difficult than it already is."

"Rhian's not having a difficult situation," Sandy told him. To her side, several aides had emerged from the Senator's doorway, and were awaiting the Vice-Ambassador. "She's having a ball. I've never seen her so happy and lively. And her social development's been amazing. I'm loving it, I've no intention of making her life difficult."

Ramoja's eyebrows were raised, and he rubbed at his clean-shaven jaw, thoughtfully. "She is becoming a remarkable young woman, I must admit. And we're all very grateful for everything you've done with her, and very pleased that she's been able to experience such personal growth. But she *is* under direct instruction to report if you ask her certain questions . . ."

"She's told me so," Sandy said frankly.

Ramoja nodded. "Then we're understood. It would be a great pity if certain authorities, above my head, began to get nervous, and decided that the present arrangements should cease." Now the Vice-Ambassador was emerging. Ramoja flashed her a truly dazzling smile. "It was a pleasure, Commander. Until next time."

And he swept off, to clear a path for his important charge. Sandy waited at the doorway as the Vice-Ambassador and his aides left, the two CSA agents close behind, no doubt transmitting furiously to others in the hallway outside. No damn way Ramoja was only here as a bodyguard, Sandy reflected darkly. It was an excuse to talk to people. To move in the corridors of power. Ramoja, like herself, was no ordinary GI. Exactly what that meant, for her old friend Rhian Chu, she'd yet to properly decide.

And she walked into the office, and closed the door behind her. The grey-haired Senator Lautrec was standing behind his desk, his walls adorned with books and flags, awaiting her with a broad smile.

"Cassandra! Do come in, do come in. And how are you feeling today?"

Sandy exhaled a long breath she hadn't realised she'd been holding. "Like I've just gone five rounds with a homicidal laser scalpel."

CHAPTER 2

"**H**e's getting worse," Vanessa muttered as they strode together beneath the covered walkway from the CSA HQ buildings to the flat rectangular sides of what had once been the SWAT Doghouse, and was now CDF headquarters. Further along loomed the cavernous new hangar bays, opening onto a vast courtyard crowded with military flyers. The space provided was, of course, far too small, but the CDF's new facilities on the periphery of the city were not yet completed, and so they were stuck with hasty renovations and add-on wings, for now.

"We'd be screwed without him," Sandy replied. General Krishnaswali had just finished chewing them out, with particular attention to Sandy's Parliament appearance. He had not, he'd stated, been at all impressed with such advocatory positions. The role of the CDF, he'd insisted, was to serve, not to champion. He'd been particularly unimpressed with Sandy's reminder that her role as CDF second-in-command was in conjunction with her role as a special security advisor to the President herself. She'd also considered pointing out that in her cybernetic-memory stored English dictionary, "advocatory" was not a word. But she hadn't reckoned it was the right time.

"He moves in bureaucratic and political circles that would drive either of us nuts," she continued as they strolled. "He gets our funding, he gets the bureaucratic and legal tangles ironed out, and he organises the broad framework like a dream. I couldn't do it."

A gust of wind scattered leaves across the grassy lawn, tossing the lush trees and garden plants. Thunder boomed and rumbled, echoing off surrounding buildings. A flash of white light lit the gardens, reflecting in windows.

"Even in SWAT he seemed more interested in organising than soldiering," Vanessa complained. Her nostrils stuffed full of cotton wool, her voice sounded somewhat nasal. "I wonder just how sharp the sharp end is ever going to get with him in charge."

Sandy shrugged. "The requirements of the job depend on the environment. A large part of our environment here is political and bureaucratic. If we didn't have someone in charge who knew how to do that, I doubt we could function at all."

Another boom of thunder split the air. The warm wind smelled of approaching rain, above the sweet scent of flower blossoms. The first heavy drops of rain spattered from a thunderous sky onto the transparent shield of ped-cover above the path.

"But then because the second-in-command is almost entirely in charge of strategic and combat considerations," Vanessa countered, "and her XO handles Personnel, it leaves the two of us with the most operational expertise having to answer to a technocrat who resents the fact that our real authority within the CDF is actually greater than his . . . only everyone's too polite to say so."

Sandy sighed, gazing out across the lawns as the rain really started to come down in a gathering rush. A frog hopped upon the grass, happily greeting the downpour.

"How the hell did us two idiots end up running an army?" she wondered aloud.

"We volunteered." Arriving at the door, security systems recognised them and slid apart immediately.

"Yeah, that'd be right."

Vanessa took another route through the corridors, headed for her next combat simulation drill in the training wing. Sandy headed straight for the maintenance bays. A brief uplink connection to her office schedules showed that she had the next two hours set aside for further work on the A-9 assault flyers, followed by the usual array of procedural reviews and strategy development sessions. Bureaucracy may have been Krishnaswali's speciality, and personnel management was Vanessa's obvious strength—her own was combat, pure and simple. New weapon systems, new unit organisation and coordination, a whole flock of new recruits, and someone had to put it all together and work out what it all did, in the event that something actually happened that required their services.

She entered the main maintenance hangar into the deafening racket of powerful engines, klaxons and maintenance equipment in a confined space, and took a moment to glance about and marvel at the progress that had been made over the last two years. All this used to be SWAT, attached to the Callayan Security Agency and vastly under-manned and underequipped to cope with the kinds of security threats currently facing Callay. Nine teams of fifteen "agents," it had then been, with some upgraded civilian flyers and armour suits.

Now, her gaze moved over rows of sleek, dangerous shapes about the hangar—assault flyers of several models, sinister in dark matte finish, weapon pods underslung with gun muzzles protruding like the stingers of dangerous insects. The CDF's airwing currently comprised four squadrons—troop-carrying slicks with assault-ship fire-support. Five hundred and twenty sharp-end soldiers—some from the old disbanded SWAT teams, the others recruited from police, public security, general volunteers and the occasional returning Fleet veteran. And they were still expanding, another two squadrons in the works and recruitment working overtime to find those rare candidates with sufficient physical and mental dexterity to handle the job—Vanessa's department. Five thousand people all told, when the office workers, technicians, planners and others were counted. A nine-to-one combat-to-support ratio was somewhat greater than she would have liked, but civilian-oriented organisations did things differently than the hard-edged military precision she was accustomed to. And besides, it wasn't her money to be worried about. So long as the sharp end was sufficiently sharp, it hardly mattered . . . and the CDF, she was increasingly proud to observe, were becoming very sharp indeed.

Captain Reichardt strode along the vast, echoing expanse of dock, eyeing the commotion that filled the upward-curling horizon. The scene was a confused jumble of loading flatbeds and personnel carriers amidst a small sea of people, many armed with placards, some merely with loud voices and bad language. About the berth entrance to the *Amazon*, armoured marines formed a protective cordon, weapons at the ready. Full battle dress, Reichardt saw, lips pressed to a thin, hard line as he strode. Duong was losing patience.

"Captain, what's the plan?" First Lieutenant Nadaja strode at his shoulder, in standard "away dress" for on-duty personnel—light armour hidden beneath combat greens, rank and *Mekong* patches prominent, as was the heavy pistol upon her right hip. About and behind, five marines under Nadaja's command were similarly dressed and armed. Reichardt could smell their tension as the echoing yells of the crowd grew louder. These were men and women who had seen combat against the League. High-powered weapons and armour, they knew how to handle. Unruly civilian mobs engaged in a peacetime protest was something else entirely.

"Neutrality," Reichardt said loudly enough for them all to hear.

"Remember, the Third Fleet remains neutral." It didn't sound right, even as the words left his lips. The Third being neutral implied that the Fifth was not. And the implications of a split between two integral parts of the Federation Fleet were frightening, to any true servant of the Federation. "We want confidence, not aggression. Aggression will provoke a hostile response. We are neutral mediators, you shall only strike to defend yourselves, no more."

He could feel the unhappiness radiating from Nadaja as they walked. She'd requested full battle dress, like the *Amazon* marines. Only it hadn't been the crowds that alarmed her. The situation between Third and Fifth Fleet representatives was becoming intolerable. It wasn't supposed to be like this. In all the military stories Reichardt had devoured as a boy, the various units of armies were invariably united, bonded together in the service of a great and powerful state representing great and powerful ideals. There had been competition between various units, and occasionally rivalry, but never outright hostility.

The Fleet, however, had grown into a strange beast indeed, during three decades of war against the League. Individual ship captains were often separated from their commanders for months on end. Command decisions were usually made in isolation. Captains interpreted orders, and followed personal hunches and biases. Alone and isolated in hostile space, ship loyalties became fierce, and loyalties to one's own captain above all others even fiercer.

Now, to make matters worse, the elements of the Fifth Fleet around Callay were ideologically extreme, due to some creative personnel distribution over the past few years. Internal divisions within the Grand Council and Fleet HQ had effectively rendered both institutions useless. At least during the war, captains had had the comfort of knowing that HQ did actually exist, however distantly removed. Now, with all command infrastructure gridlocked into a hopeless, ineffectual mess, where there should have been a single chain of command, there appeared only a yawning, empty void. No one, least of all a middle-seniority Third Fleet captain, had seen anything like it before—independent, strong-willed Fleet captains set free to deal with situations as they saw fit, while answerable to no immediately obvious higher authority. It wasn't supposed to be this way. This was worse than alarming. This was frightening.

The mob appeared to draw down to eye-level as they approached, no longer suspended on the angle of the station rim's upward slope. Dock-workers mostly—they looked more or less the same on every station Reichardt had ever visited, in worn, often grimy overalls or jumpsuits, and a taste for unruly hairstyles or personal adornments that contrasted sharply with familiar Fleet discipline. Along the station inner wall, less involved crowds had gathered at the fronts of stores, bars and hotels, watching the commotion with a mixture of enthusiasm, concern and worry. Fifty metres away Reichardt discerned a small delegation forming on the near side of the mob. They waited by a low, thick-wheeled dock runner, arms folded, watching the *Mekong* crew's approach.

"Captain," said a broad, Arabic-looking man in shoulderless over-alls, extending his hand. Reichardt took it as he arrived, his marines standing back, surveying the chanting, placard-waving crowd. The Arabic man's grip was powerful, his arms bulging with muscle. A small silver chain dangled from an earring, and curls hung at the back of his side-shaved scalp. His voice, when he spoke, was a deep Callayan-accented bass. "I'm Bhargouti, head machinist on station."

"Are you in charge of this demonstration?" Reichardt asked, voice raised above the echoing shouts.

"No one's really in charge, Captain," replied Bhargouti, with no small measure of defiance. "It's a spontaneous uprising." "And what," were the unspoken words that followed, "are you going to do about it, military man?"

"Okay then," said Reichardt, allowing his natural Texan drawl to reenter his voice, and displace the military formality. "What seems to be the problem?"

"The workers of Nehru Station refuse to service any Fleet vessel at dock until our list of demands are met." Behind Bhargouti, a large section of the crowd was now facing Reichardt's way, cheering loudly as that statement was made.

"We demand an immediate withdrawal of military customs posts and ID checks!" Bhargouti continued, raising his voice for all to hear. Another cheer echoed off the overhead, workers clustering closer for a view of the new confrontation. Lieutenant Nadaja's troops eyed the closing crowds with hard, wary stares. "We demand an immediate cessation of the intimidating presence and behaviour of Fleet marines and spacers on this station!" Another cheer. "And lastly, we demand that the Fleet immediately comply with the lawful commands of their democratic representatives in the Grand Council, and begin an immediate withdrawal of all Fleet vessels from station!"

A third cheer, raucously loud. Bhargouti looked around in satisfaction. Reichardt sized up the situation, gazing about with a level stare. When the noise died down somewhat, he spoke.

"I'm presently the senior captain of the Third Fleet in this system," he told them. "Now personally, I have no problem with your demands. Unfortunately, it ain't all up to me."

"And just who *is* it up to, Captain?" asked Bhargouti shrewdly above several shouted interjections yelled from nearby, quickly shushed by others. "Isn't your friend the Admiral taking orders any more? Or does he just make them up as he goes?"

"It's a fucking coup!" someone yelled. "That's what it is!" A chorus of supporting yells went up, echoing high and wide off the vast, cold metal walls of the station dock. Reichardt held up his hands, half-concedingly . . . and was a little surprised when the crowd quietened.

"I'm not going to get into a political debate here, sir," Reichardt told the burly dockworker. Despite his size, Bhargouti was clearly no muscle-head, his dark eyes gleaming with hard intelligence. "I'm a soldier. I take orders."

"You'd be the only one!" some wit cut in, to laughter and applause. Reichardt accepted it calmly.

"The point here, sir," Reichardt continued in much the same manner as he'd often heard his father discuss the price of cattle with neighbours back on the ranch near Amarillo, "is that *you* guys aren't exactly playing by the rules here either. Your stationmaster assures me this demonstration isn't authorised, and that you've all been instructed to return to work before this here station comes grinding to a halt. You've got ships backed up out there nose to tail waiting to get in, you've got no time for a protest strike now and you know it."

"Hey listen," Bhargouti said with firm resolve, playing to the crowd, "you worry about your employers, we'll worry about ours. We're not servicing Fifth Fleet ships, and that's final."

"Fine," Reichardt said immediately. Bhargouti frowned. "Don't service them. Frankly, I don't give a pinch of sour owl crap. The only thing that's concerning me right now is this." He pointed to the line of armoured soldiers positioned about downramps and the central stairway, surveying the crowd with expressionless, visored stares. "Fleet protocol don't allow the dock to be blockaded, sir, not in peacetime and not in war. Admiral Duong is obliged to clear this dock, one way or the other. Now first and foremost, I don't want anyone hurt here, and I don't want anything happening that leads to something else happening, and then before you know it, we're all neck deep in cow-shit, you got that?"

"Let 'em come!" someone shouted. "Let 'em try and move us, just come and try!" Some cheers went up, but the enthusiasm was by no means universal.

"Son," said Reichardt, turning in the direction of that outburst, "don't be a damn fool. You've made your point, you got the media their pretty pictures . . ." with a nod toward the small group of station media people, now manoeuvring for an angle on this new confrontation, but blocked by the surrounding wall of protesters, ". . . and staying here's only going to cost jobs, money, and a bunch of broken skulls. Don't service their damn ships if that makes you happy—they can do it themselves, they have the personnel if they have to. But let's not start something nasty here that we'll all regret later because we couldn't put common sense ahead of emotion."

"Five of our people were assaulted!" shouted a woman from Reichardt's left, elbowing her way to the front. "Three are still hospitalised! We're not the ones putting emotion ahead of common sense!"

"All the captains have spoken about that situation at length, I can assure you none of us are happy about it. But ma'am, when emotions run high like this, I can only suggest that dockworkers don't hurl insults at marines in bars—marines aren't known for walking away from fights, and they're not known for losing them, either . . ."

"One of those in hospital is a fourteen-year-old boy!" the woman retorted hotly. "The doctor says he was kicked at least ten times once he was down. Now what the hell could he have said to a group of Fleet marines to have deserved that treatment?"

Reichardt stared at her for a long moment, as the crowd rumbled and muttered, darkly. Then he turned his stare upon Bhargouti, questioningly. Bhargouti nodded.

"Rahul Bharti," he confirmed. "Green sector quartermasters's son. Real smartarse, sure. But just a kid, being stupid."

Reichardt felt a slow, burning anger building from somewhere deep in his gut. He didn't bother to hide it. "I'll find out who did it," he said. And turned a hard-eyed stare upon the woman who had spoken. She seemed somewhat surprised at his reaction. And, perhaps, a little intimidated. "They'll answer for it. I promise."

There was a low, murmuring silence. Bhargouti just looked at him, arms folded across a broad chest, eyes full of consideration.

"We'll talk about it," Bhargouti said then. "Give us a few minutes."

"Sure." Reichardt clapped his hands. "That'd be fine . . . ladies and gentlemen, thank you for listening, y'all just take all the time you need. Excuse me, please." He began moving through the crowd toward the cordon of soldiers, as senior dockworkers converged about Bhargouti. Third Fleet or not, he still received many dirty looks from the parting crowd as he passed. He did not, however, feel a need to glance around and check his blindspots. That was what Lieutenant Nadaja and her squad were for.

He arrived at the bottom of the ramp that led up to the massive, reinforced bulkhead between the FS *Amazon* and the station, the enormous mass of warship held suspended in one rotational gravity by several huge support gantries. At the top of the ramp, the main airlock was sealed shut, and further guarded by several more armoured marines.

"I'd like a word with Admiral Duong," Reichardt said to the foremost sergeant on guard at the bottom of the ramp, who saluted. Reichardt returned it.

"The Admiral is indisposed, Captain," said the sergeant, his voice muffled within the harsh, unwelcoming faceplate and breather. His eyes were barely visible behind the reinforced, graphically overlaid visor.

"We have civilian media at six o'clock, Sergeant," Reichardt returned. "A prolonged disagreement at your dock between me and you will surely make headlines. Is it your duty to create divisive headlines on Callay?"

"No, Captain."

"Please contact the Admiral." The sergeant retreated several steps up the ramp, turning his armoured back to further muffle any conversation that followed. Reichardt folded his hands to the small of his back, and waited. Lieutenant Nadaja and her marines continued to scan up and down the enormous, busy, curved expanse of dock, looking for vehicles, piles of cargo cans, dockfront doors or windows—anything that might give vantage to a hidden observer. Local security had issued a sniper alert for the docks nearly twenty-four hours ago, and while they seemed to be doing a good job of containing the problem, no one was taking any chances. Or rather, Nadaja had curtly observed in private just twenty minutes ago, no one except her stupid, stubborn Captain Reichardt was taking any chances, ordering an away mission without full armour, and wouldn't it just be *her* luck if some half-trained civvie terrorist managed to achieve what League marines, warships and GIs hadn't managed in ten years of war . . .

The *Amazon* lieutenant turned and beckoned to Reichardt, who followed him up the ramp, Nadaja's contingent behind. The heavy, double-sided airlock hummed open, revealing a harshly lit passage beyond. That passage in turn connected to a white, retractable passage with accordian walls and a narrow metal walkway along the middle. Breath frosted in minus twenty degrees celsius, the familiar chill pinching the cheeks, numbing the fingers. Then through the heavy, double-reinforced main hatch of the warship itself, and along narrow, familiar grey-metal passageways, ducking bulkheads and dodging saluting crew at regular intervals.

The Admiral's quarters were just off the bridge. Reichardt waited alone, Nadaja and her marines waiting in the mustering hall near the main airlock, as was customary for the escorts of Fleet captains. The *Amazon* marine knocked, his armour rattling. Passing crew gave wary, distrustful looks. The door hummed open. The lieutenant saluted, and departed with a thumping of armoured footsteps.

The Admiral's quarters were as sparse and cramped as any on board a warship. Admiral Duong rose from the chair at his narrow workdesk as Reichardt entered, plain and unadorned in a simple jumpsuit and jacket. They exchanged salutes. Reichardt's was calm and measured. Duong's, stiff and sharp. His angular, Asiatic features were drawn in an expression of hard displeasure.

"Captain. What brings you to my dock?"

"Sir," said Reichardt, carefully, "I thought I could be of assistance."

"I did not ask for your intervention, Captain."

"I thought it prudent." The look in Duong's eyes might have

reduced many other Fleet officers to nervous trembles. Reichardt felt only caution. And that too, he knew, was a reason he'd been chosen to play this most unwelcome of parts. "Have the protesters dispersed?"

"They are beginning to," Duong replied coldly, in a tone that suggested he hardly thought it mattered. "Your infamous *initiative* reaches new heights, Captain. I wonder what you shall try next, beyond your authority?"

"I have all the authority you do, Admiral."

"You are a captain," snapped Duong. "In this room, on this ship, you should know your place."

Reichardt held his tongue, lest he say some things he would doubtless come to regret. Besides, he was in no mood to start cursing Duong when the choicest of his curses were reserved for the spineless cowards back in HQ who hadn't had the guts to assign anyone above the rank of captain for these duties. Everyone knew that Supreme Admiral Bertali and his little gang of pro-Earth hardliners were behind the Fifth Fleet's move on Callay. Bertali's gang were a minority among senior officers, but still the rest of HQ were running scared, and no line admiral worth his or her salt had volunteered for the job of keeping an eye on Duong. And so it had fallen to the Callayan System resident, Captain Reichardt, whose notorious involvement in certain incidents two years before had kept him locked in local orbit, answering charges and political attacks from all sides.

The normal course of action would have been for the captain to be stood down, and answer the allegations in person while removed from duty. Instead, Fleet HQ had simply made FS *Mekong*'s Callayan posting permanent. Thus he had become something of a celebrity over the last two years, and gained a great deal of access to various Callayan leaders, including those in charge of establishing the new, controversial Callayan Defence Force. And seeing that he'd become something of a local expert on what was euphemistically known as the "Callayan problem," HQ had begun deferring to his expertise on the matter . . .

not that they'd ever have dared to actually *promote* him in accordance with his new importance. Thus, when the Fifth had arrived in system a little over a month ago, it had fallen to the reliable Captain Reichardt to figure out how to deal with the problem. Damn right HQ trusted him. They trusted him so much that all responsibility for decisions made were *his*, not theirs. He took the brunt of Duong's tempers. He would take the blame if Duong went too far. And he would be the most visible member of any opposition to the Supreme Admiral and his hardline cronies. The sheer cowardice took his breath away.

"Admiral," Reichardt said, "are you aware of the case regarding a fourteen-year-old boy named Rahul Bharti?"

"The matter is being looked at. Is that the only reason you're here?"

"This behaviour from Fifth Fleet personnel on station will not help your cause, Admiral . . ."

"Are you accusing me of direct responsibility?" Duong said angrily, his dark eyes flashing.

"What is an officer," Reichardt said coolly, "if not the defining example of 'direct responsibility'?"

Duong glared. "Captain, maybe you should take a look around. The current climate of Callay verges on sedition! This is not a world of strength and conviction, this is a world of decadence and privilege. While Earth was losing millions in the struggle, they danced and partied and got high on mind-bending stimulants . . . and now they want to control the Fleet? Where did they earn this right? And what on Earth could they have done to have earned the support of *any* Fleet officer? Particularly an Earth native like yourself, with a war record as esteemed as your own?"

"Democracy is democracy, Admiral," said Reichardt. "The Federation has voted . . . and wouldn't you know it, there's three times more Feddie citizens now who don't live on Earth than those who do. I'm a soldier of the Federation, I serve all Federation citizens, and quite frankly, Admiral, I don't see what my place of birth has to do with anything."

"You have no authority to obstruct me," Duong retorted sharply.

"You have no authority to even be here," Reichardt replied.

"My authority comes directly from Supreme Admiral Bertali, Captain Reichardt."

"And his comes from the Grand Council, who haven't said a word because they're deadlocked and pathetic, as usual. Yours is the authority of default, Admiral. It doesn't qualify."

Fifth Fleet Admiral and Third Fleet Captain locked stares for ten straight seconds. Duong then took a deep breath, and turned to his workdesk. There were photographs clipped into magnetic holders upon the wall above the desk. Faces of Fleet officers, some smiling but mostly not.

"I was in the war from the beginning," Duong said in a quiet, contemplative tone that did not quite disguise the steel beneath his words. "Thirty years and countless friends, it cost me. I remember what it was all for, Captain, even if others might have forgotten. The war was to save humanity from being warped by runaway technology into something unrecognisable. Now, people think that we have won, and that's that. They forget that the price of peace is constant vigilance, even in peacetime."

He swung back around to face Reichardt. "There is a GI, Captain, effectively running the Callayan Defence Force. An ex-League GI, from Dark Star itself. And would you believe it, she's becoming *popular*." He nearly spat out the word, as if it caused him pain. "As if it were a contest of celebrities. As if suddenly it does not matter what she is, and what she represents for the future of all humanity. This is the vector that the *new Federation* would take. As if the old ideals for which so many of us fought and died were all for nothing. Do you think they're all for nothing, Captain? Or does the concept not bother your moderate, liberal soul?"

"I've met the GI in question, Admiral," Reichardt replied calmly. "I find her to be a very decent person. The Federation I believe in is one where decent people are well done by. Whatever other baggage you choose to attach to it is your concern."

"Decency is no test," Duong said sombrely. "Most people are decent, whichever side they fight for. In our duties, Captain, we have caused the deaths of a great many decent League soldiers. It does not change the fact that the regime and ideologies that they served would have taken the human species in abominable directions. If the war taught me one lesson, it is that values must be fought for or surrendered. The defeat of the League does not make that adage any less true today."

"And if we cease to be soldiers, Admiral?" said Reichardt. "If we cease to serve the oath that we swore to? What shall become of our precious Federation then?"

Duong looked him straight in the eye, with utter conviction. "A Federation that works actively against the interests of the motherworld," he said firmly, "is not something that I would any longer wish to be a part of."

"Maybe I should move out," said Rhian, gazing inscrutably at her hand of cards. Anita sat opposite her at the living room coffee table, her own cards grasped between fingers adorned with rainbow-coloured nails, toying with the similarly colourful beads that sprouted from tufts of hair on an otherwise shorn scalp.

"Why?" asked Sandy with a frown, pausing midchew, her dinner plate on her lap. She sat upon one of the lounge chairs around the coffee table, in the centre of the main room of the house she called home. The floors were wood, the walls a stylish, rough-hewn red brick with mottled dark patches. To the front of the living room were broad windows opening onto a balcony, profuse foliage of the garden beyond, and all contained behind the high stone walls that typified the high-security suburb of Canas. Vanessa moved in the adjoining kitchen, mixing herself and Sandy drinks to go with their meal, which Anita had made for them the old-fashioned way—by hand, on the bare flame of the gas stove.

"I am a League GI," Rhian said matter-of-factly. "Unlike you, I am still in the service of the League. I am living in your house."

"It's your house too," Sandy objected.

"It's the government's house," Rhian corrected her. "You and Vanessa are here because you are important government officers. I am here because you are here. An afterthought."

"Chu, you're not a damn afterthought! I mean Rhian." Correcting herself with frustration—Chu hadn't gone by her old surname for two years now, preferring her given name in her new, civilian surroundings. She sat comfortably now on the living room rug by the coffee table, dressed in stylish black pants and a black silk shirt. A lean arm hooked over one upraised knee, holding her cards. Her beautiful, Chinese features were well suited to the fashionably short cut of her black hair, her expression as cool and untroubled as ever, eyes fixed upon her cards.

GIs had that look about them, even without the benefit of super-enhanced vision displaying the lower body temperature, and the lack of a jugular pulse. Just the way they sat, and moved, shifted their gaze from one object of consideration to the next. Sandy knew she looked like that herself, to another person's eyes. Anita shifted from time to time, moving her weight to prevent bad circulation, or muscle tiredness, or other aches and pains from developing. Rhian sat relatively motionless. Not like a statue. More like an effortlessly poised, presently dormant bundle of energy. Just waiting for a chance to explode.

Rhian's arrival on Callay had been the single most wonderful development of the last two years. Sandy had thought she'd lost everything from those years in the service of the League, all her old friends and comrades from Dark Star. She'd not come to know or like them all, not by any means. But with Rhian Chu, she'd had nearly three years of connection and slowly developing friendship . . . and three years in Dark Star had felt like twenty in most other places. While the rest of her team had been murdered by their own commanders, during those final, desperate days of the losing war, a small group, unbeknownst to her, had survived.

When the smoke cleared, Rhian had wound up under the ISO's wing. Once the ISO discovered her old commander had resurfaced, somewhat spectacularly, in the Callayan capital of Tanusha, they'd been only too quick to assign Rhian to the command of Major Ramoja, and reunite the old friends once more. Perhaps, Sandy reflected, they'd expected gratitude. Perhaps an opportunity to influence her opinions and actions, within her new role of authority on Callay. For her part, Sandy saw no reason to thank the murdering bastards who ruled over all matters of artificial humanity in the League for anything. They'd established a link between their own operative, in Rhian, and herself. It got them regular reports, and calmed the nerves of security operatives on all sides, who became very nervous in an information vacuum. That ought to be enough for them. She had her old friend Rhian back. That was certainly enough for her.

"Well, thank you for saying so," Rhian said, with a faint smile. Selected two cards from her hand, and placed them face down upon the table. "But the fact remains that if you were not my friend, then I would not be here. And if the politicians who are so scared about League influence on Callay learned that I was sharing your house, there could be further trouble. Couldn't there?"

As she resettled two new cards into her hand, and Anita unloaded two of her own, Anita met Sandy's gaze with a brief, intrigued smile. Far less concerned with politics, Sandy knew, than fascinated with Rhian's increasing self-confidence in her own powers of analysis where civilians were concerned. Her development, Sandy had to admit, had been remarkable. From a total novice in all civilian matters, in the space of two years Rhian had progressed to the point where local events no longer disturbed or puzzled her with the same regularity as before. Anita now teased Sandy, from time to time, that Rhian had now overtaken her ex-captain in some civilian matters—such as fashion sense. Looking at her friend's stylish black outfit, Sandy could only agree. But then, in some regards, that was Rhian—utterly meticulous and precise with the small details, yet often missing the broader picture.

"It's more my house than anyone else's anyway," Vanessa inter-jected, arriving back at her chair beside Sandy's with a drink in each hand. Sandy took hers, and Vanessa took her seat. "Me being the only one of us who's financially solvent and of reliable good character and long-term residence . . ."

"Oh, go on!" Anita protested good humouredly.

"It's true!" Vanessa curled into her chair, no difficult feat for her small frame, in tracksuit and socks following her shower. The skin beneath her eyes bore the faintest shade of dark, but otherwise there was only the cotton wool to show for the recently broken nose. It kept her breathing through her mouth, and allowed the injected microbials to do their work unhindered. "It's unheard of for anyone with less than five years' residence on Callay to qualify for a house in Canas. I'm here 'cause they wouldn't have let Sandy have it otherwise."

"And for the joyful pleasure of my company," Sandy remarked.

"Of course, baby." Vanessa extended a sock-clad foot, and gave Sandy's shoulder a reprimanding push. "And *you*," she continued, turning her lively gaze upon Rhian, "are here so we can keep an eye on you. Under the auspices of our new liaison relationship with the League Embassy, of course. But the main reason no one's leaked that information to Neiland's opponents is because the only thing those same opponents are more scared of than Sandy being best buddies with her old League mates, is the League's Embassy GIs running around without supervision."

"You keep me on a very short leash," Rhian said with a nod. "I'll remember to say that if someone asks." And raised Anita's five prayer-tokens by another five.

Sandy finished the last mouthful of her meal, and gave Vanessa an eyebrow-raised glance. Vanessa's return glance was highly amused. For the last two years, there had been an ongoing debate between them whether Rhian was an unintentional wit who said amusing things without meaning to, or was one of the best deadpan comics they'd ever seen. Not that she was ever genuinely hysterical. Just amusing. As always, with her old buddy Chu, everything was understated. But understated people everywhere, Sandy reckoned, were full of surprises.

Sandy sipped Vanessa's drink. It tasted of at least five local fruits, and several liqueurs . . . Vanessa had been introduced to the world of mixed beverages by one of Anita's friends a few months back, and now delighted in creating new concoctions. Rhian placed her hand of cards upon the table. Anita gave a "ha!" of delight, and laid down her own. Rhian raised both eyebrows.

"GIs aren't invulnerable after all," Vanessa remarked as Anita raked in the prayer tokens. Her pile was considerably larger than Rhian's.

"In a game of random chance," Rhian said mildly, "anyone can lose."

"Oh, it's not just random chance!" Anita scolded her. "You do a thing with your face every time you get a good or a bad hand."

"I'm a GI," said Rhian. "I don't do *anything* with my face."

"Yes, you do!" Anita sang playfully, handing the deck to Rhian for shuffling. Rhian gave Sandy a quizzical look, taking the cards to hand. They blurred between fingers with inhuman speed, as Vanessa and Anita watched in fascination. Sandy smiled.

"She's trying to get into your head, Rhi," she said. "She's psyching you out."

"How should I respond?" asked Rhian, in all honesty.

Sandy gave an exasperated shrug. "I don't know! Figure it out."

"You could stop doing that thing with your face, for one thing," Vanessa said mischievously.

"Don't listen to them," said Sandy. "Come on, Rhian, concentrate. We can't let any uppity organic humans start thinking they can actually beat us at anything. I mean, where would it end?"

"I don't mind getting beaten at things that don't matter," Rhian replied mildly, dealing the cards with a series of rapid wrist-flicks. Anita's cards skidded in perfect unison across the shiny coffee table, directly into her waiting hands.

"Have you spoken to Captain Reichardt yet?" Anita asked, fanning the cards in her hand.

"Might have," said Sandy, taking another sip of her drink. Anita removed a card and took another. Raised her bet.

"I'm glad he seems like such a reasonable guy," Anita continued. "I mean it can't be easy, can it? Standing up to your own people. Standing up to Earth, even?"

"He's American," said Vanessa. "That's different. Americans live on another planet entirely."

The USA's continued refusal to consider itself a part of any greater, global political entity known as Earth was the source of many old jokes. On Earth itself, such political isolationism was the subject of much ridicule. But for the many Federation worlds now opposed to the monolithic, conservative, xenophobic bloc that Earth was threatening to become, it provided a large opportunity. After all, the population of the USA had been one of the only significant voting blocs on Earth to actually vote in favour of the relocation. In the eyes of many Americans, the Grand Council had done enormous damage in centralising huge chunks of the planetary political system during the war, creating a morass of petty bureaucracy and unrepresentative officialdom. And US President Alvarez, alone of senior Earth leaders, had spoken out in favour of Callay's new role as the centre of the Federation. Although everyone knew the Americans could never miss a chance to get right up the collective noses of the Chinese and Indians, and no one on Callay was fool enough to assume American support went any further than that.

"You guys are doing the security for Secretary General Benale, right?" Anita had much practice trying to weed out as much information as possible from her less-than-informative friends. "How suspicious do you think it is that the sabotage happens just after he arrives on Callay? I mean, he's the closest thing Earth has to a global leader, even if the Americans don't recognise EarthGov. He's an old-Earth nationalist if ever there was one, he promises to come out here to try and calm things down, but no sooner does he arrive than someone sabotages the *Mekong*?"

"That's a conspiracy theory," said Vanessa. "Sandy doesn't like conspiracy theories."

"Ari calls them conspiracy facts," Rhian countered.

"Ari would," Sandy said shortly.

"You're not still mad at Ari?" Anita said in half-teasing disbelief.

Vanessa frowned, looking from Anita to Sandy. "Mad at him for what?"

Sandy sighed. "Oh, he's been babbling on about that damn tour Cognizant Systems is doing through the medical lobbies . . ."

"It's not just Cognizant Systems!" Anita retorted indignantly. "It's Renaldo Takawashi, Sandy. The man's a genius that comes along maybe once in ten generations . . ."

"Yeah, yeah, yeah," Sandy muttered, "I read the press release."

"Takawashi?" Vanessa made a face. "I read an Intel report on that . . . isn't he responsible for GI intelligence?"

"He's never been anything other than an independent researcher," Anita insisted, "but with the war on, the League government roped him into much of the foundational development for advanced synthetic neurology."

"Poor little man," said Sandy sarcastically, "he's been used and manipulated all along, never had anything to do with the League war machine *really* . . ."

"Sandy!" Anita looked genuinely indignant. "His work with neural regeneration using synthetic integration with organic tissue is just . . . it's amazing. For the first time we might be able to regrow destroyed brain tissue, cure what was previously irreparable structural damage, cure V-hooked burnouts, maybe even reverse criminal insanity! Imagine if they could reform murderers or rapists by rerouting the defective circuitry and then regrowing it."

"Wonderful, maybe they could cure subversive ideologies too,"

Sandy retorted. "League supporters, far right weirdos? You'd run out of friends real fast, 'Nita."

Anita was one of Ari's old friends—as underground as they came, and proud of it. It was hardly the most suitable company for two of Callay's seniormost civil servants . . . but then, Sandy's own knowledge of security and monitoring systems ensured that her various political masters had very little idea of who she entertained at home, something for which she was very grateful. She did not always get along with Ari's friends, with their progressive, League-sympathetic ideologies, and their love of all things hi-tech and subversive. Anita was different in that she was a business woman, despite appearances, and was at least relatively pragmatic in her approach to real world issues. She was also fun company, and was pleased to be Sandy's friend because she liked Sandy, not because Sandy was "that awesome, android superbabe" or whatever stupid crap the wide-eyed techno underground liked to say about her these days. She got nearly as sick of the worshipful adulation from that crowd as she did of the hate mail. More so, sometimes. At least the hate mailers didn't want anything from her (except perhaps death), and would never be disappointed that she'd failed to live up to their expectations.

"You're overreacting again," Anita scolded, "there's no reason to believe that . . ."

"Hang on," Vanessa interrupted. And turned a concerned frown on Sandy. "If this . . . Takawashi . . . is responsible for most of the League's advances in synthetic neurology . . ."

"He's not," said Sandy. "He was the head of a damn big team. It's a reputation mostly limited to the underground on Callay." With a dark look at Anita. "Who, for some reason, seem to have developed a fascination with such things."

Anita rolled her eyes. "It's still true, and you know it."

"But he's still technically responsible for . . ." and Vanessa paused, knowing from experience the value of being a little wary, bringing up such matters around Sandy, ". . . well, for you. And Rhi. Right?"

Sandy shrugged. "Sure. Technically."

"And that's where Ari is now, meeting Takawashi?" Vanessa, on emotional issues, had somewhere along the line acquired the disconcerting ability to read her like a book.

Sandy sighed. "He got an invite. He always gets an invite."

"And how is it," Vanessa wanted to know, "that I'm not hearing about the head of the League's advanced GI neurology research being in Callay all over the news networks?"

"Because the League generally says that *everyone* was involved in synthetic biology development. It's their way of challenging Federation ideology—if you want access to League technology and trade, you've gotta do business with people connected to GI development."

"Major Ramoja told me that the Callayan media have been saturated with those stories," Rhian added. "You know—League trade delegations arriving that include scientists or industrialists who were involved with the League war machine. There were a lot of protests at first, but now people are getting tired of it, and the media don't bother reporting it. He said."

"Damn," said Vanessa, looking thoughtful. Sipped on her drink, eyes momentarily distant. "I bet the Fleet noticed. Admiral Duong in particular."

"No question," said Sandy. "And I bet Cognizant Systems have some pretty senior arms to twist if they could get approval from the government right now, with everything else that's going on."

# CHAPTER 3

**S**andy awoke in her bed to find the house security network telling her that Ari was entering the side door. She uplinked to a camera, and a clear visual image of the lower corridor appeared upon her internal vision. It was definitely Ari, long black coat and all. Three in the morning—usual operating hours for Ari. She extended the uplinks further as she lay comfortably beneath the covers, and let the broad expanse of the Canas-network rush in upon her sleepy consciousness. Impenetrable multilayer barriers, constant monitoring . . . everything looked secure. In the Presidential hacienda not too far from here, President Neiland would be sleeping . . . or working late, or meeting with various other Federation world leaders. Asking for support. Begging for it.

Ari's footsteps ascended the stairs outside her door, then the door opened. Sandy bothered to open her eyes for the first time, and found his dark figure moving across the dimly lit room. Streetlight created a small patch upon the smooth floorboards. Brick walls and wooden bookshelves showed dimly in normal-vision. Pictures on shelves and the desk. Pictures of herself and Vanessa. Of Rhian, swimming with two of Vanessa's nephews. Of herself and Ari, at the surprise party his underground friends had thrown downstairs, many laughing faces. And one Rhian had found in a search through a League database, of Mahud, in uniform, looking cool and handsome. Her gaze lingered upon that frame for a moment, vision zooming and brightening to make the features come clear.

"Parliament went well?" Ari asked her as he took off his clothes. Not bothering to ask if she was awake.

"Like you didn't already know," she replied, in a sleepy murmur.

"Well, you're only number three on the news bulletins," said Ari. "You didn't cause another scandal and you saved that damn-fool President from getting herself blown up, so I'd say you had a pretty good day."

"I'll be the judge of that," Sandy said with a faint smile. "And what do you mean *another* scandal?"

Ari shrugged. "Habitual phrasing. I apologise."

"My very existence is one big scandal."

"Stop feeling sorry for yourself," said Ari, removing the last of his clothes and sliding under the covers. He moved immediately on top of her, a warm, welcome presence of bare skin and body weight.

"I'm not feeling sorry for myself, I'm just . . ." Ari silenced her with a kiss on the lips. Sandy returned it, passionately. And smiled at him as he pulled back enough to look her in the eyes, the tip of his nose barely brushing hers. His intelligent dark eyes were fixed upon her. His jaw, she noticed, was dark with stubble. She brushed at it with one hand, and found it unusually scratchy. So he'd been busy then. The Ari she knew was normally far more attentive to matters of personal grooming. "What did I do to deserve this treat?" she asked him.

"Being gorgeous, as usual. That's all." He kissed her again. They made love, lingeringly. Perhaps even more lingeringly than usual, Sandy managed to reckon, in the spare, fleeting moment of sanity that was all she could usually muster at such moments. There was an earnestness about Ari tonight that she found wonderful, and she was determined to enjoy it. She contented herself with letting him take charge for as long as possible, before finally the strain and tension became too much, and she had to lock her hands hard to the mattress, and brace her legs apart for fear of doing him damage. She alerted him, and he paused to let her roll over. They finished with him on her back, which was much safer, her face pressed gasping to the mattress as she unlocked her clenched fists one at a time, and hoped she hadn't torn the sheets again. Ari nuzzled at her ear, affectionately.

"The back of your head is really a . . . a lovely view," he offered in a low voice, with typical off-handed humour, "but your eyes are really much nicer . . ."

"We'll buy a mirror," Sandy offered, half-muffled against the mattress.

"Kinky, but inconvenient."

"Forget it, Ari," she told him, "I'm not going to risk it. This is the *one* moment I really do lose control. It's *dangerous*, do you understand me?"

"I trust you." He brushed hair away from her cheek, and kissed her there.

"Then you're a fool. *I* don't trust me, not then. You're just a thrill-seeker."

"I'm not a thrill-seeker, I'd just appreciate the pleasure of once being able to look my lover in the eyes when she comes."

"It could be the last thing you'll ever see."

"Sure, but how romantic is that?"

He ran a hand along her shoulder, feeling the receding tension in the muscle, a gathering, tingling softness. It genuinely didn't seem to bother him. Sleeping with a GI, one of her CDF comrades had less than charitably observed, was like sleeping with a hydraulic alloy press. A malfunctioning one, with a hair-trigger.

She rolled over, easing him off to one side. Ari surprised her by climbing straight back on, kissing her gently. But she was pleased, and more so when he entered her once more.

"Ari," she managed to gasp in his ear, "what's the matter?"

"What do you mean? You think because I happen to feel like making love to you that something's the matter?"

"You normally fall asleep or go straight out again," she replied, trying to think rationally. Something in her brain chemistry made that difficult, at such moments—although Vanessa professed that she was hardly a sim-tech scientist herself during sex. Ari's body moved wonderfully against her, and she gasped, wrapping her legs reflexively about him.

"Not tonight," he murmured, running a hand through her hair, then kissing down her neck. She tried to breathe evenly, thinking that it was probably nothing more than he was feeling horny . . . which suited her fine because so was she. But it had been so hectic lately, especially for someone in Ari's line of work.

"Ari." She took his head in both hands—gently, but in a way that gave him little choice but to pause, and look her in the eyes. She made her gaze as firm as possible. "You found something, didn't you? Something concerning me?"

Ari sighed. Cocked his head on one side to gaze at her, with reluctant admiration for her deduction. "I didn't want to tell you straight up," he conceded.

"You wanted to soften me up first?" With affectionate humour. "Well, it worked."

He kissed her again. Ari was a good kisser. Not a great kisser, perhaps, but what he lacked in sophisticated technique, he made up in honest appreciation. Then he rested his forehead against hers, and sighed.

"Sandy, someone's trying to kill you." She nearly laughed. Ari registered her mirthful restraint, and frowned. "Sandy, I'm serious, this is nothing to laugh about."

"Ari, someone's been trying to kill me from the moment I arrived on Callay."

"This is different!" His eyes were very earnest, and somewhat frustrated at her evident lack of common sense. Her humour faded somewhat. She cocked her head on one side, and gave him a reluctant *look*, daring him to alarm her. Ari's expression grew even more frustrated. "I don't know who it *is*! It's not that kind of information, it's —"

"Hearsay."

"No, it's not hearsay . . . or, okay yes, maybe it *is* hearsay, but it's damn good hearsay! Sandy, my source was very specific. The threat comes from inside the government, Sandy . . ." Sandy rolled her eyes with tired exasperation. "No, don't . . . don't do that thing with the eyes, you're not listening to me."

"Ari, how many times have you warned me that President Neiland wants to get rid of me?"

"I . . . I didn't say that at all! I said that you're fast becoming a political liability to her and she'll come under tremendous pressure to get rid of you one way or the other."

"It's the same thing, Ari." She took his face in her hands. "I appreciate the concern, seriously I do, but face facts—you just don't like Neiland. She's not going to get rid of me. She's my friend."

"Sandy." He removed her hands with determination, and fixed her with a very firm stare. "If your beloved President has to choose between forging a new alliance to complete the relocation, or saving your neck, which do you think she'll choose?"

Sandy gazed up at him defiantly. "What, you think my removal will be a precondition? Like the rest of the Federation doesn't have important things to worry about?"

"You're the public face, Sandy! It's . . . damn, it's never been about what you actually *are*, it's always been about what you *represent*!" Searching her eyes for some small sign that she'd understood, and was going to take his concerns seriously. "Look, at least tell me you'll be careful. All right?"

"I'm always careful."

"Sandy . . ."

"Okay, okay." She held up both hands in defeat, somewhat amused at his persistence. "I'll be careful. I'll be such a political cynic, I'll make you proud." And she rolled him over with an effortless twist, positioning herself comfortably on top. "You're adorable when you're worried about me," she told him. And kissed him on the lips. He didn't respond. Sandy sighed. "There's more, isn't there?"

"There's a killswitch."

Sandy frowned at him, not understanding. "A killswitch? What about a killswitch?"

Ari gazed up at her for a long moment. His expression was more than reluctant. As if this were something he'd seriously, seriously not wanted to have to tell her. Watching him, Sandy felt the first stirrings of genuine trepidation. Ari put both hands on her bare hips. Ran them over that pronounced curve to her waist, then up her sides and over her shoulders. The thumb of his right hand pressed firmly on the bone behind her left ear, fingers beneath her hair upon the very top of her upper vertebra, hard under the rear of her skull. Right where the insert implants were—small nodules of artificial resistance beneath his fingers. The fingers moved two centimetres to one side, and stopped.

"Right there," said Ari, quietly. "Fused to the brainstem. Triggered by some kind of attack code. Killswitch."

Sandy stared down at him, slowly growing cold all over. At first, she didn't believe it. But the look in Ari's eyes triggered doubts and suspicions of her own, long harboured but mostly ignored until now due to a lack of solid evidence. She didn't always trust Ari's political hunches, because she reckoned Ari's own obvious political biases usually got in the way. But where technology was concerned, he was deadly objective, every time. Particularly when that technology concerned her, and how she functioned.

"Oh no," she said, disbelievingly. Then, with a surging, profound frustration, "Oh no. How fucking *dare* they?"

"Sandy, come here." Ari put both hands on her shoulders and tried to pull her into a comforting embrace. Sandy resisted effortlessly, arms braced hard upon the mattress either side of him.

"Who told you?" she demanded, fixing him with a stare that would have turned most straights to jelly. Ari looked pained, but for an entirely different reason.

"Reliable sources," he said apologetically.

"It was someone at that fucking Cognizant Systems party, wasn't it? Who? A League engineer? Someone who worked on the advanced GI projects?"

"I'm sorry, Sandy, I really can't say. It's not in your operational brief as CDF second-in-command. I was actually working there, you know, it's not just a junket. I maintain sources and do research." Ari looked very concerned. Well, she supposed that was understandable. Given that the affectionate, beautiful, naked woman on top of him had suddenly transformed into an angry, eyes-blazing, steely limbed monster on his lap, arms braced like a cat ready to pounce.

"Shit," she said with that realisation, and sprang from the bed. She paced for a moment in the cool air, bare feet on the floorboards, hands on her hips and trying to get her head back into some kind of order. Ari sat upright in bed, pulling the bedcovers up to his waist, watching her with continuing concern. She pulled loose hair back from her face with both hands. "What else do you know about it?"

"Nothing," said Ari. "I've been trying to find out. But I don't know what codes you should watch for . . . I reckoned you'd know better than me anyhow."

"I don't suppose we can remove it?"

"No, it's . . . it's right in the spinal cord, Sandy. Inside the vertebrae. Maybe . . . maybe if some of the doctors took a look at it, they could find a way to neutralise it, or . . . or something, I don't know. But you know how good League tech is, that's why no one ever spotted it without knowing what to look for."

"It's not survivable?" Knowing better than to even ask. But she had to be sure.

"It'll fry the whole brainstem, Sandy." And then, somewhat cautiously, "You've never seen it used, then?"

"No." She stood still upon the floor, gazing through the gap between curtains and wall, where the street lighting fell upon the balcony beyond. Green tree-fronds swayed in a gentle night breeze, glistening with recent rain. The night air was cool upon her bare skin. She folded her arms. "No, not with us little obedient goody-two-shoes. Oh shit!" As another thought struck her, and she clutched both hands to her head, squeezing her eyes shut. "Now I know why they did that . . . shit, shit, shit!"

"Did what?"

"Oh . . . just a Dark Star file I broke into while I was there, warning of precautionary measures in case a GI commander went crazy. Shots to the head, that kind of thing. But nothing for me. No procedure. I guess the solution was too obvious." She looked sideways at Ari, sitting upright in bed. Watching her. "What about Rhian?"

"That's what I wanted to suggest," said Ari. "Get her in for a check-up. Because my contact wasn't sure, Sandy. Very sure about you, but not the others. You were always the greatest risk, though. They knew that. And you did defect, so really, they were right to worry."

"Oh, they were right about lots of things," Sandy muttered. "I hate those fucking bastards. I might be a soldier, but I'm a person too. They had no fucking right."

"Sandy." Ari climbed from the bed and came to her in the dim light. Took her hands in both of his, and gazed earnestly into her eyes. "Are you hearing me now? Be careful, it's not just physical threats I'm talking about. The network could get you too. Keep your barriers up."

Sandy frowned at him in suspicion. "How long have you been running around after this?"

"A while," said Ari. Sandy kept gazing at him, questioningly. Ari sighed in exasperation. "Sandy, don't you get it? I care about you. I care about you a lot."

"Once upon a time you thought I was a fascinating little project of yours," Sandy said reproachfully. Not really knowing why she said it, even as she spoke. But she was angry. And alarmed, and looking for a secure foundation.

"Sure, maybe I did think that once," Ari conceded with an off-handed shrug. "But I'm past that now. I mean seriously, you're not the only one who's grown up in the last two years. I like *you*. The rest of it just doesn't matter to me." And put a hand to her chin, tilting her gaze when she proved reluctant to meet his gaze. Raised his eyebrows at her, seeking her acknowledgement. Sandy sighed, and embraced him.

Sandy came downstairs at six thirty the next morning, a little late following her shower, and found that Jean-Pierre was dangling from the small chandelier above the open kitchen. Vanessa stood on the bench by the stove, her uniform unbuttoned in typical early morning disarray, and held her hands up to the chandelier, making appealing, chirping sounds. A big pair of round eyes peered anxiously over the rim, dexterous little feet clinging nimbly to the frame.

"Jean-Pierre! Come on, baby. Jump, Jean-Pierre, Mummy will catch you!" The bunbun turned back and forth with clever grips of its toes, seeking another option.

"How in the world did he get up there?" Sandy asked, straightening her shirt collar beneath the open jacket as she entered the kitchen and began arranging a meal of muesli and fruit around Vanessa's feet.

"It's what they do," Vanessa complained. "They climb trees and sleep in the high branches. Jean-Pierre! Look, it's not that far! I'll catch you!"

"Why is all Callayan wildlife so irredeemably stupid?" Ari asked, coming fast down the stairs in a descending rhythm of black boots.

"He's not stupid!" Vanessa protested. "He's just a little daft." And tried chirping at him again.

"He'll poop on your head," warned Anita from the lounge sofa, where she was jacked into her portable terminal, doubtless checking on her morning network scan. She'd slept in the guest room again—her job being what it was, she could pretty much work from anywhere. Sandy finished pouring muesli, and Ari anticipated her reach for the fruit bowl, grabbing a ripe majo off the top and tossing it hard at her. Sandy caught it with an effortless snap of the wrist, and began peeling it with a rapid motion of knife-blade against thumb.

"I mean seriously," said Ari, preparing his own bowl with curious glances upward at the stranded bunbun, "we could at least have a few genus of flesh-ripping carnivores . . . maybe a poisonous flying reptile or fire breathing fish or something."

"Yeah, that'd work," said Sandy with amusement, chopping the fruit with eye-blurring flashes of steel.

"Instead we get . . . that." Ari pointed disdainfully up at the chandelier. "Behold all you tiny humans, the pinnacle of the Callayan food chain. He is the bunbun, hear his mighty roar." Jean-Pierre fixed him with a golden-eyed, reproachful stare within an adorably cute, furry brown face.

"There's more worthwhile things in evolution than teeth and claws," Vanessa retorted.

"I mean we can't even eat them," Ari continued, "they're all fur and bones. I tell you, it's just as well humans arrived on this planet when we did, the local wildlife certainly wasn't going anywhere without us."

"How do you know?" Sandy replied. "Bunbuns have opposable thumbs, maybe there'd be a great bunbun civilisation here in another ten million years if we'd left them alone." Leaping to seat herself on the opposing bench, eating her muesli and watching as Jean-Pierre leaned precariously over the rim of the chandelier, nose twitching as he stretched toward Vanessa's outstretched hands. Then the chandelier shifted and swung, and Jean-Pierre scrambled back to a safer perch.

Vanessa clasped exasperated hands to her hips. "Maybe we could tempt him down with some honey?" Glancing at Sandy with great earnestness, seeking her opinion. Sandy shrugged as she chewed, struggling to hide her amusement. It seemed a curious predicament for two of Callay's most senior soldiers.

"I'll get him down for you," suggested Ari, reaching for the gun holster inside his jacket and withdrawing a black automatic pistol.

"Ari!" Sandy scolded. Over on the sofa, Anita fell over laughing. Vanessa glared. Ari shrugged offhandedly, and reholstered the pistol. Rhian came down the steps with a blur of rapid feet. Sandy did a fast double-take, as did Ari—Rhian wore tight denim jeans and a very fashionable cut-off shirt tied into a bow below the breastbone, leaving her tight stomach suggestively bare. She moved with a spring beyond her usual energy, positively cheerful with a broad smile for them all.

"Good morning!" And, with a glance up at Jean-Pierre's predicament, "Major Rice, if you don't mind me saying so, your animal appears to have a very small brain."

"He keeps his mouth shut," Vanessa retorted, "which is more than I can say for some."

Rhian moved swiftly over, and sprang effortlessly off the ground. In mid-air one hand grasped the chandelier, the other pried Jean-Pierre expertly from his perch, then landed with a gentle thump, the startled bunbun now clinging to her arms in bewilderment.

"Ari, handpass!" She moved to play on, football style, faking the handpass then spinning away, going for a pretend bounce behind the dining table, followed by a drop kick . . .

"Give!" called Vanessa sternly, jumping down from the bench and striding over, hands outstretched. Rhian grinned and placed Jean-Pierre onto the dining table. The bunbun ran nimbly on furry legs across the table and leaped into Vanessa's arms. Vanessa cuddled him and made cooing noises as Jean-Pierre tried to plaster her face with his little tongue.

"That animal's so cute it's sickening," Ari observed around a mouthful of breakfast. "You know, Ricey, if you'd treated your men that well you wouldn't be single."

"Sandy," Vanessa commanded, "silence the boyfriend." Sandy extended a foot from her seat upon the bench, and pushed Ari in the shoulder. "Men like you are the reason four legs and a tail suddenly became attractive." Ari clutched at his heart, dramatically.

"At least she didn't say men like you are the reason she started sleeping with women," Sandy offered.

"*You* haven't started sleeping with women," Ari retorted.

Sandy smiled. "Give it time." With a playful glance at Vanessa above her next mouthful of breakfast. Vanessa grinned back, trying to keep Jean-Pierre's searching tongue out of her ear.

Ari blinked. "Well I guess that won't bother me too much, provided I can watch."

"That's a nice outfit, Rhi," Anita called over from the sofa. "What's the occasion?"

"I have a day off today," said Rhian, beaming. "Major Ramoja has us all on duty rosters, and today's my free day."

"I haven't had a full day off in weeks," Vanessa sighed.

"I'm going to do some shopping," Rhian continued, "then I'm going to Denpasar to see the big wildlife enclosure, then to Patna to see that Festival of the Sun they keep showing on the news, that looks really nice . . . then I'm going to a football game in Santiello in the evening."

"You really like football, don't you?" Anita asked, resting chin upon her hand, elbow upon the sofa arm, gazing with obvious fascination. "Sandy's never gotten into sports, she says there's not a sport invented that's a technical challenge for a GI."

"She's right," Rhian agreed. "I just like being at the game. Everyone's so excited, and the crowd roars and waves banners, and the players all hug each other when they kick a goal. It's fun."

"I guess I just like my cultural events to mean something deeper," Sandy reflected around a mouthful. "Physical performance might be a big deal to a straight, but I just can't get excited about it. It's too easy."

"For *you*, maybe," said Rhian. "You have to learn to empathise better with straights."

And Sandy just stared at her, incredulously. Vanessa grinned, and Ari shook his head in smiling disbelief. Jean-Pierre struggled to be free of Vanessa's arms, bounding to the ground and trotting toward the familiar scent of Anita, who lowered a hand for him to sniff.

"It's strange," Rhian continued, apparently unaware of the minor commotion she'd caused, "I checked a database on the history of football, but when you go back far enough, most of the references are to a different sport entirely—one with a round ball and the players don't even use their hands."

"Oh that's soccer," Anita said, highly amused as Jean-Pierre tried to grasp her fingers with his tight little hands, and lick them. "Football began in India, and they got so huge they spread the sport around the world and it took over from soccer a few hundred years ago as the biggest football code."

Ari made a loud, quizz-show-buzzer noise to the negative. "Wrong," he said. "Football began in Australia, it was called Australian football. It was inspired partly by Gaelic football from Ireland, and partly by a game the Australian Aborigines played. India borrowed it from them sometime in the twenty-first century."

Rhian frowned. "I've never heard of Australia."

"Big, empty, boring place with lots of stupid furry animals," said Ari around another mouthful. "Lot like here."

"Rhi," said Sandy, fixing her friend with a solemn gaze. "Before you get going, could I ask you to do something for me?"

Ari also gazed at Rhian, the humour abruptly replaced by calculation. "Of course," said Rhian. "What would you like me to do?"

# CHAPTER 4

The ride over to HQ was not a pleasant one. Vanessa fumed all the way, although precisely what she was upset at, Sandy couldn't say.

Rhian simply sat in the backseat of the armoured government cruiser, and gazed out at the spectacular aerial view of passing towers on a carpet of green urbanity, gleaming bright in patches beneath the slanting rays of the morning sun. Here and there the sunlight flashed on the surface of one of the many tributaries of the Shoban Delta. The air seemed thick with morning haze, typical midsummer humidity rising off the wet trees and damp ground, darkening the sun to a deep, luxuriant orange in the eastern sky.

Sandy landed the cruiser on the exclusive pad atop the main CDF building of the broader CSA compound—facilities would be much better, they had been promised, when the CDF had its own compound, somewhere out in the brand new Herat district currently under construction beyond the outermost of the city's existing inhabited zones. Herat was also the location for the new Grand Council buildings, centred about an enormous structure whose size, when completed, would dwarf even the Callayan Parliament building. There was a Fleet Command building under construction somewhere out there too. No doubt certain indignant Fleet admirals thought that highly presumptuous.

She was walking across the rooftop pad with Vanessa and Rhian when she received a call.

"*Hello, Commander,*" came a youthful, enthusiastic voice in her inner ear. "*I've been arranging your itinerary for the day and prioritising departmental requests. Would you like an immediate rundown or would you prefer to wait until the office?*"

"I think that can wait, Private Zhang." Truthfully, she had her own automatic programs in place that sorted much of the scheduling and priorities for her. And she could access all of that remotely without any help. Her new secretary, however, was young, bright eyed and eager to be useful.

"*Yes, Commander. I've taken the liberty of redirecting your incoming calls and mail away from staff, which takes some load off them. I've also identified and return-contacted seventy per cent of those incoming calls and given them alternative channels to go through—most of them are interdepartmental, they've got no real business bothering you at all with their problems.*"

Sandy blinked in surprise, walking to the door of the rooftop foyer, flashing ID from her uniform pocket to the invisible scanners. She hadn't been aware she could tell half of her callers not to bother her. No doubt they hadn't wanted her to know, least it remove their access to her office. Maybe young Private Zhang would have his uses after all.

"*Thank you, Private, I appreciate that.*" The decorative foyer beyond the glass doors was a mass of interlocking security systems, mostly invisible to the unaugmented eye. She, Vanessa and Rhian headed for the stairs. Two suited men engaged in conversation turned to stare— partly in recognition of herself and Vanessa, Sandy reckoned, but also partly at the sight of three very attractive women, one of them wearing most un-martial attire, her stomach bare and slim curves exposed. Rhian flashed the two men a smile as they descended the stairs. Sandy repressed a smile of her own at the two men's expressions, wondering if *anyone*, on first acquaintance, would guess correctly which of the three was *not* a GI. "*Was there anything else?*"

"*Ah, yes, Commander, five minutes ago you received an urgent request from Sergeant Rajan for assistance with the new slash-four weapon pods in maintenance bay five. Apparently there's a problem only you can solve.*"

That didn't surprise her—until she'd placed the order for them, no one else in the CDF had even heard of the new slash-fours.

"*Tell him I'll be down immediately, put my paperwork on hold. First thing to know if you're going to be my assistant, Mr. Zhang—fieldwork comes first.*"

"*Yes, Commander.*" There was no mistaking the worship in the young man's voice. She disconnected the link, with a faint sigh of disbelief.

"Ricey," she said as they reached the bottom of the second flight of stairs, "could you take Rhi to medical and make sure she's introduced properly?"

Vanessa frowned at her, walking fast and tense. "You're not coming?"

"Raj wants some help in bay five, I'll be back before the scans are finished."

Vanessa looked less than impressed. "Sandy, you're going to get this checked out properly. I'm not going to let you just ignore it . . . they put a fucking kill mechanism in your head, Sandy, and you're acting like it's not a big problem."

"Vanessa, I'm not going to put my life and my job on hold every time some new panic arises."

"This isn't just any fucking panic, Sandy!"

"I said I'll be there." Very firmly. Vanessa looked exasperated. Rhian watched on, curiously. "I'm a GI, this kind of crap just goes with the territory."

"I'm warning you, Sandy, you're not half as invulnerable as you think you are."

Sandy held up her hands. "Not now, Vanessa. Take care of Rhi, I'll be there soon."

She took the next right-hand turn, striding fast. Telling herself that she really didn't need Vanessa's kind of well-meaning hysteria right now. Vanessa worried far too much. The last time she'd caught a cold, Vanessa had called around frantically to various biomedical specialists and branches, asking after various expert opinions on synthetic immunology until finally convinced that it wouldn't be fatal. Vanessa treated her artificial nature as if it was some kind of *condition*, one that needed to be fought and overcome at every opportunity. Sandy didn't want to be treated like a sick child every time some inevitable complication arose. And it troubled her that Vanessa didn't seem to understand that yet.

Bay five was dark and full of shadows. Sandy walked along a ferrocrete aisle, past tall, stacked crates and idle lifters, headed for the patch of bright fluorescence ahead. The din of activity faded behind her. To one side loomed the hulking shapes of combat landmates, humanoid arms hanging limply.

"Raj!" she called as she walked, looking for the sergeant's usual spot, wedged in between crates, up to his elbows in hi-tech innards beneath the sole ceiling light. There was no reply. She reflexively uplinked to the building network, and found nothing, just static. The network seemed to be down. Not surprising; all of these lower maintenance bays had until recently served other purposes, and the hardware had only been recently rewired to the secure, interactive standards required for military-scale weapons. There had been glitches galore. She kept walking . . . and saw the laser tripwire activate a split second before her shin passed through it.

She leaped as the explosion hit her, blasting her into the crates on her left in a spray of metal debris, the blurring crash of heavy impact, the rush of heat on skin. Through the swirl of flames, she sensed movement, and sprang into an explosive roll as high-velocity fire shredded the spot where she'd been, scrambling into an accelerating sprint as the fire tracked her from point-blank range. And saw, in that time-dilated rush of motion, a squat, menacing shape upon a pair of birdlike legs, twin rotary cannon for wings, each spinning with a roar of flames and fury. An AMAPS-12.

Sandy leaped to her right as fire clipped at the tail of her uniform, sailing upward over the row of crates and equipment . . . and felt/saw the second targeting system acquire her from the bay's far wall. She twisted in midair, a desperate contortion as a second burst of fire snarled, echoes yammering off ceiling and walls, fire ripping past . . . she reached and caught the trailing edge of a cargo crate as it sailed past below, snap-tumbling her trajectory downward just as the second burst thundered, and fire ripped the space where she would have been. Something hit her shin hard and she tumbled to the ferrocrete floor with a barely controlled crash. Flattened herself against the crate, pulling the automatic pistol from her thigh holster, for what little good it would do, and considered her options.

She was now crouched in the next aisle along the maintenance bay floor, between stacked rows of crates and equipment. From the aisle she'd just left, low-toned and dull in the lingering time-stretch of combat-sense, she could hear the first AMAPS stepping from its hiding place within an empty crate, with heavy, rhythmic thuds of metal-shod feet. From against the far wall to her left, similar sounds, as the second AMAPS stalked along the wall to a firing position down this aisle. Her pistol would cause little damage against an Auxillary Mobile Anti-Personnel System—that armour did not come with weak spots that a mere handweapon could exploit. Barehanded she was far more confident . . . but clearly the entire bay was rigged, even now she could hear the main entry doors grinding closed. Clearly the plan was to trap her in here, with these two mobile killing machines. Assuming there were only two. Likely there would be more smart-triggered explosives planted at strategic locations. Probably the maintenance bay's entire sensor grid was now tracking her . . . all of the receptors were down, and she received no feedback on her own uplinks. The implants in her skull were not powerful enough to penetrate the thick ferrocrete without a booster. It was a good plan all right. She was alone in here.

The footsteps to her far left came suddenly louder. The second AMAPS appeared with an elegant brace of weight-bearing leg-joints, and swivelled its smooth-nosed torso with alarming speed to point down the aisle. Sandy dashed through a gap between crates opposite as fire shrieked and clanged down the aisle, ripping a four-wheeled cargo loader to pieces, forklift, tires and leather driver's seat pinwheeling down the aisle like pebbles. At the end of the gap between the stacked crates, Sandy realised that there was no way out, and that whatever was in the crate stacked above, it was heavy enough that it didn't move when she pushed full-force.

Jump-jets roared over the advancing clang of the second AMAPS's footsteps, then a heavy thud—the first metal monster had landed on top of the row of crates over which she herself had jumped. Sandy sensed tightbeam communication, and knew the second machine was telling the first where she was.

Machine-gun fire tore into the crate above her head with an unholy racket, Sandy scrambling backward as the occasional round tore through the crate, and hit the underside above her head. She put both hands against the crate blocking the far end and pushed, artificial muscles straining at maximum intensity, her feet scrabbling for grip. The crate remained unmoved. Something exploded and crashed inside the crate above—if its contents were high explosive and detonated at this range, Sandy knew she was dead, GI or not.

She gave up trying to move the container, and instead holstered her pistol and sledgehammered a fist straight through the metal. She got her hands into the hole, and pulled with everything she had. Metal bent and tore with a rupturing shriek, as the skin of her hands also tore, painlessly . . . she kicked and made a lower foot-hole as well, which gave her more leverage. The hole became wide enough for her shoulders, and she got her arms through and pulled the rest of her body after with more brute power than acrobatic grace, and found herself wedged into a narrow space between the container wall and stacked boxes of ammunition. Heavy footsteps thudded closer. If the AMAPS fired into this crate, the explosion could take out half the bay.

She scrambled up, over the ammo boxes, wriggling through the cramped, blind space beneath the top of the storage crate, sending boxes crashing and clanging aside in her haste. Reached the far end of the container, slithered down into the narrow gap between ammo boxes and the crate side, and braced her feet and back as best she could. She pushed, maximum exertion, straining tension . . . the piled ammo boxes at her back could move no further, and the crate side was as hard and solid as one would expect of an interstellar shipping container.

Sandy's entire body contorted, legs forcing inexorably outward, muscles condensing to a consistency far beyond that of most combat alloys. The container side shrieked, then clanged loudly, as the entire top and left side welding burst free, and light poured in. She leaped for that gap, grabbed the jagged edge and threw herself out, falling to half-roll on the ferrocrete floor.

Heavy cannon fire tore into the container from the end she'd entered, a shrill roar of disintegrating metal. Sandy was up and running at full speed along the aisle, finding that it ended abruptly to the right where that row of CDF shipping containers suddenly ceased, and there were instead a number of newly acquired light armour vehicles awaiting integration into CDF ranks, and, oh holy shit, she hoped whoever was behind this mess hadn't rigged one of the tanks as they'd rigged the AMAPS . . .

A massive explosion shook the bay, Sandy riding the impact into a forward dive and roll as debris ricocheted at deadly velocity, followed by secondary explosions cracking like firecrackers at Chinese New Year . . . Sandy raised her head beside the last of the right-side storage crates, her brain in overdrive, and surveyed the row of light tanks on the open square of floor in the maintenance bay's far corner. The damn AMAPS were powerful enough for limited operations, but they weren't incredibly bright—Federation legislation prevented the installation of any sentient AI in a military unit's CPU, even the League hadn't been keen on the idea of city-levelling hovertanks with sentient free will. Like any non-sentient computer, the AMAPS were very bad at guessing. After all, the cargo crate *probably* contained ammunition, that would *possibly* explode if fired upon at close range . . . but then if there was also the very high possibility that the crate also contained the AMAPS' target, and the AMAPS' entire existence revolved around the elimination of that target, then surely the risk of an explosion was justified? League software programmers Sandy knew had been very impressed with their risk-analysis and awareness simulations, the usual set of amorphous calculations that she entirely failed to trust . . . how could one mathematically calculate "risk" as an objective concept, after all, in a mostly random universe? Her own brain, or that of any sentient, was vastly superior to any nonsentient computer at calculating such vague, abstract concepts, but still she struggled. The AMAPS, now no doubt flat on its back and badly singed in the continuing explosions, was now possibly reflecting (if AMAPS could reflect) that the bright-eyed little techno-geek who'd programmed its CPU hadn't known half as much about the universe as he'd thought he had.

All of this and more passed through Sandy's mind in the fraction of a second following her recovery from the explosion, which was fading now as the secondary explosions trailed away, and the crates stacked on top of the exploding one smothered the blasts. And in that continuing, drawn out time-dilation, Sandy found further time to be impressed with the design standards of that particular batch of ammunition, that only perhaps five percent had detonated, and a critical mass of explosive detonations had not led to a total chain reaction . . . which would not have taken out the entire bay, because any fool knew to disperse ammunition crates at even distances throughout any storage facility, but even so, she could well have been dodging large pieces of falling ceiling right about then. Ahead of her, her various sensory receptors registered one of the armoured vehicles activating full systems—engines, weapons and all. Please God, she thought, don't let it be one of the Ge-Vo hovertanks.

But of course it was.

With a throbbing din of repulsorlift engines, the Ge-Vo lifted slowly into a low hover. The turret made its characteristic vis-field acquisition wobble, protruding quadruple cannon levering up and down . . . Sandy had seen enough, rolled to her feet and ran back the way she'd come, through the choking smoke of the ammunition explosion. All her sending frequencies were tuned to full, but still she received nothing—the maintenance bay was too solid, and she was totally cut off from the outside network. The main doors had been secured. Doubtless those outside would break through in a few minutes, but those were minutes she did not have. The one saving grace, she reckoned, was that she was trapped in a warehouse stacked with weapons. Time to find one.

Sandy accelerated down the aisle between five-metre-high stacks of crates, hearing the Ge-Vo manoeuvring for a clear shot through smoke that would not bother its sensors. She leaped high and to the right where a gap between shipping crates presented itself, and smacked into the metal wall and clung. The gap between crates was narrow, and if she extended both arms out to the sides, she could hold her own weight with ease as her feet sought toe-holds on the rim of the lower crates . . . the slim gap descended four metres to the floor below and if she fell, she knew she could get wedged. She inched forward, awkwardly, hearing the Ge-Vo now accelerating cautiously down the aisle, sensors sweeping . . . but she knew the tank's own engines would interfere with its sensors' reception enough to hide any small noises or signatures she might make.

An automatic scan of her own memory files revealed that she did not possess an inventory list of the bay's current equipment. There could be anything in the crates around her, from armour suits to AP grenades to new uniforms. The odds of finding something useful by tearing crates open at random were not great, and the noise would draw fire.

A burst of fire ripped through the metal walls behind her and she simply dropped, catching her weight again two metres down the crevice as elecro-mag fire tore through crates and their contents. She wondered as she accelerated her awkward, spread-eagled progress, if the Ge-Vo pilot was also automated . . . or not. A rush of jump jets, and the second AMAPS landed with a heavy crash, legs straddling the divide, twin weapon pods angling downward at its trapped quarry. Sandy let go and fell to the floor, taking the impact, then exploding full-power off the floor. She shot five metres up and slammed into the AMAPS's underside just as the gun muzzles began to spin. The AMAPS staggered awkwardly, gyros readjusting for the new weight that clung to its belly. Sandy didn't waste time with a punch, but rather grabbed one weapon pod arm with both arms, got her feet against the AMAPS's leg, and twisted its torso sideways. The AMAPS's servos whined and cranked in protest, the machine's bird legs shuffling to retain balance as it lost its centre of gravity . . . one more shuffle and Sandy timed a hard kick at its leg, that landed with a crunch that might have broken heavy-duty hip suspension, and the metal foot came down on the gap rather than solid metal.

The AMAPS fell sideways, its right pod slamming into the lip of the gap as the right leg fought and kicked in empty air. Sandy maintained her steely grip despite the impact, and dangling from the

AMAPS's shoulder joint, got one hand onto the lip of the gap, and thrust hard upward with the other. Alloy-myomer muscles and perfect technique propelled all three tons of AMAPS up and backwards, then off the edge of the row of crates entirely. It fell, gracelessly, and Sandy propelled herself after it, catching the rim of the crate overlooking the open aisle as the AMAPS completed a three-quarter somersault and landed face first with a booming crash. Down the aisle, a visual adjustment allowed her to see the first AMAPS picking itself up from within the smoke from the ammunition explosion. Surely its sensors and CPU function had been jarred by the blasts.

Sandy swung from her perch and fell five metres to the ferrocrete floor, taking the impact with a comfortable jolt through her legs. The fallen AMAPS was kicking now, struggling to climb to its feet . . . and seemed, in that extended fraction of a second, to be somewhat confused between which action had priority—getting up, or acquiring its target, which was now standing an infuriating two metres to its side. It then appeared to realise that its weapon pods were not articulated enough to acquire its target from a prone position. The legs folded almost flat, seeking to get its broad, padded feet beneath it and rise. Further down the aisle, within clouds of drifting smoke, the second AMAPS was already upright, and turning to face its target. Sandy watched, calmly unmoving, and wondering if all the machines were quite as target-fixated as these two appeared to be.

The first AMAPS raised both weapon pods just as the second began to rise at Sandy's side. Sandy leaped for the top of the opposing wall of crates, as low and flat as she could calculate. The first AMAPS's fire tracked her up the wall of metal, but not before first riddling its companion with high-velocity fire. The second AMAPS, already bent and dented from its fall, staggered and wavered on unsteady legs, one weapon pod crashing to the ground trailing a long ammo-feed, thin trails of smoke rising from multiple precise holes drilled across its angular torso and limb assembly.

Sandy sailed over the rim and rolled comfortably . . . and was promptly fired on by a third AMAPS standing eighty metres away on an adjoining line of crates. Sandy rolled desperately as rounds whizzed and cracked around her, then fell into a narrow gap between crates, bracing her arms against the sides and nearly slipping as the left hand failed to brace properly . . . a glance showed her the reason—her left thumb was missing, and a further round had gone straight through her wrist, severing some of the nerves and tendons to her fingers. GIs were built tough, but not that tough. If she caught a burst from one of these things directly, or even took a freak round to the head, she was dead. Her limp, uncooperative hand left a smear of red plasma upon the metal wall as she pressed.

Jump jets roared as she reflexively tried to analyse the sound and figure which AMAPS was airborne, and where it was headed. Then a heavy burst of fire that could only have been from the tank . . . except that from the sound, they were not aimed anywhere near her vicinity. Even an automated gunner would not miss by so much, nor fire needlessly in an evidently dangerous environment. Surely someone else was . . .

"*Hi, Cap,*" came a familiar voice in her inner ear. "*Just like old times, huh?*"

There was a crash from nearby as an AMAPS landed with a roar of jets.

"*Hi, Rhi,*" she replied, experiencing a sensation that was difficult to identify past the combat-reflex, but she consciously reckoned must be relief. "*There's an AMAPS walking just about on top of me, could you please distract him?*"

She made a reflex transmission before she even realised she'd done it—a GI-specific tac-net that unfolded across her inner consciousness. The new, graphical vision of the maintenance bay flickered and buzzed as their antagonists tried to jam transmission between the two GIs, but GI frequencies operated on modulating sonic variations that were almost unjammable, at least with Federation technology. Rhian's presence interfaced with the tac-net, and suddenly Sandy knew everything

Rhian knew—saw with her vision, pinpointed her position, and registered her physical condition and armament (two electro-mag assault rifles, she was relieved to see).

Running down an adjoining aisle between crates, Rhian simply leaped, took a booted kick off one wall of crates three metres off the ground that corrected her trajectory so that she just cleared the upper rim, and fired a short burst in midair, which smacked cleanly into one of the AMAPS's weapon pods. She fell back to the ferrocrete, and continued to make up ground along what the tac-net visual now insisted was the left flank. The third AMAPS, across the bay, turned to fire at Rhian, but was too late. The second, finding its left-pod abruptly damaged, also turned, stupidly, to meet the new threat. Sandy leaped from her cover, got both feet planted and sprang for the adjoining aisle, flying low as the third AMAPS fired long range and again too late. Sandy hit the opposite metal wall, and fell gracelessly to thud onto her backside upon the ferrocrete. Then she was up and sprinting toward Rhian, who was likewise sprinting directly toward her. And, despite the deadening combat-reflex, she could have sworn she saw Rhian give her a brief grin as she came.

Rhian tossed the assault rifle in the air as they closed, and Sandy took it with a one-handed snap as they passed, neither decelerating, headed now in opposite directions. The Ge-Vo that had been chasing Rhian appeared directly in front of Sandy, its quad-barrelled turret swinging rapidly into line. Both GIs sprang abruptly into gaps in the metal wall on Sandy's left, and Rhian's right, and the hovertank's fire tore through empty air, ripping the jagged ends from transport crates, metallic debris scattering down the aisle with a thundering, echoing roar.

"*They all machines?*" Rhian asked as they ran, reflexively coordinating. The second AMAPS was between them on top of the stacked crates. It was next, Sandy didn't even need to transmit for Rhian to know it.

"*Yep,*" said Sandy. Rhian leaped straight up a vertical five-metre space between crates, caught the rim with one hand and fired a short burst into the second AMAPS's right-hand weapons pod . . . and Sandy saw the two-legged weapon platform stagger, trying to turn and meet the new threat, but Rhian dropped from sight immediately. Then Sandy stopped by the next aisle space, and also leaped vertically. She caught a grip on the rim with her left arm, not daring to trust the left hand for anything, and found the bewildered AMAPS's back turned directly to her. Her trigger finger vibrated—a burst of five into the right hip, another into the left and the same for each knee, all in less than a second. The AMAPS staggered—electro-mag fire was not a match for AMAPS main armour, but if you knew where to put it . . . Another staggered step and it fell. Sandy put another single-fire burst through the holes Rhian had made in the right weapon pod, her index finger blurring, then released and dropped to the ferrocrete fractionally before the third AMAPS shredded the spot where she'd been. The AMAPS crashed against metal as she fell, then something exploded (ammo, to Sandy's hearing) and blasted small pieces of AMAPS all over the maintenance bay, embedding many jagged shards in the ceiling and walls over a hundred metres away.

*"It's not fair, is it?"* said Rhian. And Sandy somehow found time to wonder at the irony of two artificially constructed humans, gloating at their superiority over inferior machine-intelligence. One GI, unarmed, had been in difficulty. Two GIs, sufficiently armed, was another story entirely.

The remaining AMAPS realised its predicament, perched on top of the cargo containers with no view of the ground and little support, and jump jetted down. The Ge-Vo continued its blind charge along the adjoining aisle, like a giant, lumbering predator enraged and frustrated by a pair of small, darting rodents. The machine's limited tactical coordination appeared to arrive at a basic plan—the tank would charge, and flush its prey into the AMAPS's field of fire. Except that Rhian and Sandy simply ran down the adjoining aisle, then darted once more into the gaps between cargo crates as the Ge-Vo reached the end wall and made a slow, idling turn in the cramped space. Rhian leaped high, and Sandy moved to the corner of a crate, back pressed to the metal.

Rhian aimed fast over her rim, put several holes in the AMAPS's forward sensory armourplate, ducking back as the AMAPS twisted back and sideways to fire upwards . . . and Sandy immediately ducked around, aiming with the weapon muzzle braced upon her left forearm, and put thirty rounds through the same two-centimetre space in the AMAPS's right weapon pod, directly above the ammunition feed. In a fractional second, the spinning machine-gun jammed, fragmented pieces of ammunition belt crushed inwards as the weapon's chain-feed drove them together, and one of the cartridges exploded. The rest followed, and the AMAPS disintegrated with a deafening roar of firecracker explosions that hurtled pieces of debris from one end of the cavernous bay to the other.

"*That's a weak spot,*" Rhian observed.

"*Once upon a time, people thought machines like that would take over the battlefield,*" Sandy replied, checking her weapon for heat stress. "*But now the most effective machines have ended up imitating people.*"

"*You're so philosophical, Cap.*"

"*And AMAPS aren't. That's why we win.*"

The Ge-Vo came shrilling back down the aisle the two GIs had come from. Sandy and Rhian leaped into the adjoining aisle and ran with it for a while, giving it enough signature of their running footsteps to draw it down to that end of the bay, and up against the wall where its options would be further limited. Plans changed, however, when the massive armoured entry door abruptly exploded inwards, showering torn fragments, and leaving behind the distinctive two-metre peeled hole of a shaped charge. Sandy and Rhian stopped and reversed, but the Ge-Vo continued to the end wall, decelerating to make the U-turn back up the next aisle.

No sooner had it exposed itself to the new hole in the entry door than a projectile-contrail whooshed across the end wall, staining the air across the end of Sandy and Rhian's aisle, followed by a loud metal crash and a deeper, echoing thud! The tank's shrilling engine whine slowly wound down from its high pitch, to a long, slow grating sound that seemed to Sandy's ears to be armourplate against a wall. She and Rhian exchanged glances. They jogged down their aisle, Rhian deferring to Sandy by long habit.

Sandy peered about the corner of the last crate in that row. The Ge-Vo was idling crookedly against the bay's end wall, smoke pouring from turret seams. A small, circular hole had been drilled just above the rotation ring of its turret armour, from which more smoke was pouring. Sandy turned around and looked at the hole in the entrance door. She was little surprised to see a small, female figure stepping through, hefting a massive electro-mag anti-armour launcher over one shoulder, eyes shielded behind a heavy, dark visor to guard against muzzle flash. Ge-Vo armour was damn tough, but as was always the way with military technology, the only technological field to have outpaced the tremendous advances in armour and protection was the physics of electromagnetic projection weaponry. If you fired a projectile at a high enough velocity, even the best military-grade armour was as useless as tissue paper.

Vanessa saw Sandy, and made a face.

"Well, what d'you know," she drawled, with a gesture of the heavy launcher, "the damn thing works. That's the lot?" Evidently knowing it was, for the lack of noise elsewhere in the bay.

"Seems to be," Sandy replied. "We'll do a sweep."

"I'll get it organised," said a wide-eyed lieutenant entering behind Vanessa. Beyond the hole in the entry door, Sandy sensed a mass of ready confusion, many soldiers poised with whatever weapons they could acquire. Shouts echoed behind as orders were given, scanning equipment organised . . . better to scan from range than sweep by hand, there was no need to risk lives unnecessarily.

"Oh," Sandy thought to add, "and while you're at it, could you get someone to look for my thumb?"

The med-bay was more spacious, clean and white than any Sandy could remember from her service League-side. It made her wonder if the CDF were truly a real army, and not the self-deluded, soft, undisciplined civilians most of the Fleet seemed to think they were. She sat by the side of an operating table, her left arm extended beneath an obscuring green curtain. On opposite sides of the table, two surgeons in full masks and gowns gathered over her arm. There were various implements in their hands, and various more on a side table—some that they used on normal human patients, and others utterly different. A multimode scanner suspended from the ceiling hovered above her hand.

On a screen to the surgeons' side, if she cared to look, was an intricate high definition image of her hand and forearm. A bio-alloy sheath now encased the bone of her lower thumb where it had been severed at midlength. That was the easy bit—GI bones regenerated just like regular human bones, with some encouragement from introduced nanotech solutions within the bio-sheath. More difficult was the hole through her wrist, which had severed the tendons to her index and middle fingers, as well as removing a piece of wrist bone and causing other structural misalignments. Full mobility could be limited for a while, the surgeons told her, and she wasn't going to be her usual ambidextrous self for at least a month. She'd also been clipped along the front of her shin, but that had done nothing but remove a centimetre of skin.

And she was alone, save the surgeons, who were utterly absorbed in this rare opportunity to study the inner workings of technology's most advanced synthetic human, and weren't much on idle chit-chat. Her solitude made her feel . . . well, glum, she supposed. Abandoned was too strong a word. But her troops were busy sweeping for further security breaches, the admin were busy cleaning up and counting the cost, and any spare friends she had in CSA Intel had now just found themselves with one more large issue dumped on their plate. The sudden storm of activity included Vanessa, of course, who on top of it all was now giving her the silent treatment, now that she'd gotten over the initial relief that her synthetic friend was still alive. Sandy couldn't see how she'd deserved *that*. Best friend or not, Vanessa's emotional swings remained a source of occasional confusion, and worse.

Movement down the corridor beyond the broad wall windows . . . Sandy recognised both Director Ibrahim and Ari easily, despite the sanitised gowns, hair nets and face masks. They took turns at moving through the airlock door, each subjected to a rush of further deconta- minating fumes, then the red light above the doors turned green, and first Ari was admitted, then Ibrahim. That much concession Ibrahim granted for their "relationship," Sandy pondered with a raised eyebrow, as Ari came cautiously across the shiny white floor, a relieved smile evi- dent beneath the mask.

"Hi," he said, a more subdued greeting than usual, and put a hand on her shoulder. And she was mildly surprised that he paid the sur- geons so little attention. All of his attention was instead focused upon her. "Are you okay?" Behind the concern, tension. Frustration, even. That wasn't good.

"I'm okay," she said, forcing a faint smile as she looked up at him. Ari brushed hair back from her forehead, gazing at her. Ibrahim came over, and Ari stood to Sandy's side, a hand still on her shoulder. Sandy rested her head gently against his arm, and smiled at the sight of Ibrahim in a spotless green gown. The mask did not fit him well. His large nose seemed to be protesting its imprisonment, struggling to make a break for freedom.

"Not a word," said Ibrahim. Sandy's smile grew broader.

"No, sir. This is going to blow out our budget."

"The budget, Commander, is the least of our worries. We have an infiltration."

"Obviously," said Sandy.

"Ari thinks it's rather a bad one."

"Just last night Ari was warning me that someone would try to go after me through this . . . damn killswitch thing. That didn't happen."

"It's not good, Sandy," Ari cut in. The frustration was plain in his voice now. His hand vanished from her shoulder to rub the front of the gown, seeking their usual deep pockets as he paced several steps, dark boots squeaking upon the shiny floor. "They got into the maintenance bays, for godsake. It had to be someone inside the CDF. But considering the security protocols we put in place, that shouldn't be possible."

"I wouldn't be rushing to conclusions," Ibrahim told Ari pointedly. Ari didn't look impressed. "Cassandra, I need you to be extra careful. We'll find who did this, but in the meantime, I want you to limit your movements and keep away from equipment bays, or any place where accidents or ambushes can be rigged in such a fashion."

"You want me to be a desk jockey?" Sandy asked, in mild disbelief.

"Sandy, your safety is important to the CDF. It's important to me. If you need to become a desk jockey to maintain your personal security, then that is what you'll do."

"What if I'm mortally wounded in a catastrophic chair-leg failure?"

"Sit on the floor."

Sandy sighed, and glanced up at Ari. Ari's expression was dark. And he was fidgeting absently, as if his attention were elsewhere. Which, given Ari's uplinks were nearly as advanced as hers, was definitely possible. That was definitely not good.

"Sandy," Ibrahim continued firmly, "we really can't begin to guess who might have done it. Certainly it *looks* like some pro-Earth conservative faction, but we should not assume anything . . . there are radical pro-League elements, after all, who see your presence as contributing to anti-League xenophobia and therefore an obstacle toward ultra-progressive politics on Callay. Or it could be a CDF soldier with a grudge from some history your checks did not detect . . . we don't know."

"What does Krishnaswali think?" Sandy asked.

"He's keeping an open mind," Ibrahim replied cautiously.

The senior CDF commander had not been to visit her, nor made direct contact of any kind since the ambush. She hadn't thought their relations had been *that* bad, personally. Maybe she'd been wrong.

She took a deep breath. "Sir," she began, and paused, annoyed at the plaintive note she heard in her voice. "I am second-in-command of the CDF. I have a job to do, and I take that very seriously. We have operational concerns that need to be ironed out, Vanessa's supervising the training of a whole new combat squad even now and if I don't have functioning vehicles and weaponry ready for them to use, there's not much point to anything."

"You'll have to try supervising from a greater distance," Ibrahim said firmly.

"Sir, I don't know if that's going to . . ."

"CSA Investigations will be assisting the inquiry," Ibrahim cut her off. "Krishnaswali wanted to keep it in-house, but the CDF simply does not have the manpower or skills for a major internal investigation at this point."

Sandy turned her gaze on Ari. Ari said nothing, standing dark and sombre at her side, fingernails drumming upon his chin as if he wanted to bite them, but was prevented by the surgical mask. Usually it was at this point in a discussion that he would jump in with some flippant, pointed observation or remark. Now, nothing.

"Surgeons," said Ibrahim, "what's your prognosis?"

"The hand will be fully functional in perhaps two weeks," came the reply. "The wrist won't have quite the same degree of articulation for months, though—we'll need to synthesise and graft some new bone, ferrous alloy of this kind doesn't regenerate fast or well enough to replace the piece of wrist bone that's missing. It might take a while to procure."

"I have a friend who might help," Sandy said. Ibrahim raised an eyebrow at her. Sandy saw the expression and shrugged.

"Quietly," Ibrahim warned her.

"Yes, sir."

Ari disappeared for a while, but returned just as she was exiting the sterile airlock and into the med-bay corridor. Striding briskly toward her, dark and handsome, hands thrust deeply into the pockets of a long-tailed black coat that swirled at his calves, having thrown the unfashionable lime green medical gear away as quickly as possible. His hand came out as he stopped before her, and placed it upon her chest, keeping her there. His voice, when he spoke, was low, his eyes sharp and earnest.

"Sandy, I've done some checks . . . Intel have nothing. No barriers violated, no traces left, nothing. Not even on the AMAPS' CPUs, nor the Ge-Vo. Whoever reprogrammed them wasn't just an insider with all the right codes, he had enough foresight to stall an investigation and cover his tracks. No outsider knows that software that well."

His dark eyes bore into hers, seeking her comprehension. Sandy thought about it for a moment. Then, "Ari. Why are you whispering? If you have something to tell me that you don't want anyone to hear, there are these things called uplinks . . ."

Ari rolled his eyes, but refocused quickly with tense frustration. "Because I want you to hear the tone of my voice, for one thing, because I damn well *knew* you wouldn't take this seriously."

"You've always had a very sexy tone of voice, Ari, but . . ."

"And also because I don't trust the networks here."

Sandy frowned at him. "This is the CDF, Ari . . . the Callayan Defence Force, not just anyone can hack into the networks and eavesdrop."

"And the Callayan Defence Force was established by the Neiland Administration to serve the Neiland Administration's own political goals . . ."

"Oh Jesus, not this again?" Staring up at him with genuine incredulity. "For the last time, Ari, Katia Neiland is . . ."

She broke off as the airlock hissed behind her, one of the surgeons exiting, pulling the surgical mask away from his face.

"I realise I may be talking to a bulkhead," the surgeon told her cheerfully, indicating the large, synthetic cast that moulded about her wrist, hand and thumb, "but please try not to move it very much." It felt warm. Sandy knew it maintained an ideal environment for the nano-solutions they'd injected into the wrist and bone-sheath to breed and repair, involving low doses of radiation that they fed off. Or so the doctors said. "Aside from that, if it gives you any trouble, please don't hesitate to call me personally. You have my details?"

"Cybernetic memory, Mr. Pan, I have everyone's details."

Mr. Pan smiled. "Of course. Well, take care and keep up the good work, Commander." He strolled off, looking very pleased indeed. All the medicos in med-bay seemed to enjoy themselves when she got injured a lot more than she did. Sandy turned her attention back to Ari.

"Katia Neiland is not trying to get me killed!" she said in a firm whisper.

Ari took a deep breath. And fixed her with a flat, wise gaze. "Sandy, do you trust me?"

"Trust you?" She gazed at him. Trying desperately to think how to answer.

"I mean . . ." and Ari took a deep breath. "I know I'm not always entirely . . . *there*, with the truth." Sandy refrained from comment with difficulty. "But you know I have my reasons. Don't you?"

"I trust who you are, Ari," she told him. "I trust that I know you . . . well, at least well enough. I trust that you'd never purposely do anything to hurt me. Is that enough?"

Ari shrugged, and glanced at the floor. Looking suddenly a little awkward. "I'd like it to be something more." And lifted his gaze, earnestly.

Sandy sighed. "Ari, why ask me now?"

"Because things are different now. Dangerous." With a glance at the cast on her left hand. "Because I think I sort of fell into the trap of thinking you were invincible, and . . . and that was pretty scary, just now. For me at least, I can't speak for supergirl . . ."

"I was scared," she told him. Not entirely certain that it was true, even as she said it. Not in the way he meant it. The implications scared her, after the fact. While it was happening . . . well, very few superfluous emotions survived past the combat-reflex.

"Not scared enough, I think," said Ari, pointedly. And he took a deep breath. "Sandy, this is just . . . so dangerous, this situation. The politics. Look, at least . . ."

"Ari, I'll be careful." Firmly. "But I don't believe in conspiracy theories. You know that."

"*Something* caused it, Sandy. Whatever you think just happened here, something caused it. Don't go about ignoring that because you're suddenly too scared to contemplate what happens if it turns out your nice, comfortable little life is suddenly . . ."

Sandy put her good hand hard against his chest, and shoved him backwards into a wall. Pinned him there, with a firm pressure to his chest, and a hard look in the eye. "Ari, I'm *really* tired of your constant psychoanalysing. You're not a shrink, in fact you could make a damn sight better use of one than I ever could."

Rather than resisting the hard pressure of her arm, Ari grabbed her by the collar and pulled. She could have resisted. But somehow, his lips had found hers before she could decide what to do, and her good arm braced her instead against the wall. His hands found her face, running through her hair, his lips warm, his closeness suddenly intoxicating. Someone could have come along the corridor at any moment, and senior officers were not supposed to indulge in such things upon the premises, particularly not where just anyone would see them.

His hands found the tight spots of her new uniform—the old one now largely in tatters—and she felt her temperature rise several more degrees. She kissed back even harder, struggling for air and getting her good hand behind his back, wanting to plunge it under his clothes and feel the warmth of his skin against her . . . and he pulled away, holding her in place with a physical confidence no other straight besides Vanessa ever dared. He knew how to hold her, and how to move her, if necessary. He knew when she wouldn't push back.

"I'm glad you're okay," he murmured, resting his forehead momentarily against hers. "Now stop ignoring me when I'm trying to tell you things that could save your life, or I'll get really mad with you." And he turned on his heel, and left her leaning against the wall, breathless and now slightly dishevelled.

"That's not fair," she complained. "You can't leave me like this."

"Promise me you'll listen," came the reply as he swept away down the corridor.

"Look, there's a bed just in there!" she suggested, trying to be reasonable about it. "We can polarise the windows, lock the door with a vacant sign, no one will know. Come back here and fuck me for a while, and I'll think about it."

"I'm not hearing the answer I want." He paused at the glass doors at the end, looking back at her, his expression glum. "No listening, no Mr. Pinky."

Sandy fought back a traitorous grin. "Please?" she said plaintively.

"First accept that my advice is sage and just."

"I'd rather just take the orgasm, thanks."

And Ari gave a tired shrug. "I tried." And continued looking at her, for a longer moment. Humour faded, as the implications slowly sank in. Suddenly, it wasn't very funny at all. And he shook his head in disbelief, opened the doors, and strode into the medical ward beyond. Sandy slumped her back against the wall, ran a hand through her hair, and sighed.

Rhian was standing by Doctor Obago's side in the private office at the far end of med-bay, gazing at a high definition display. She turned to look through the windows as Sandy approached between med-bay beds.

"Is Ari angry at you too?" Rhian asked as Sandy entered, and shut the glass door behind her.

"Ari and I have a difference of opinion about recent events." Rhian kept looking, a quizzical eyebrow raised. She had expressed curious scepticism ever since hearing of Sandy's new monogamous relationship. Not that she disapproved of Ari. On the contrary, she'd several times expressed irritation with civilian rules of sexual etiquette that prevented her from inviting Ari to bed herself. But she'd served with Sandy back in the League, in a small, separate, GI-dominated society where jealousy was alien and monogamy unheard of. And she'd seen Sandy's sexual appetite in action. Now, she wondered how Ari could find time to keep up.

"Ari and you seem to have different opinions about a lot of things," Rhian observed.

Sandy came over to stand by the monitor where it sat upon a side table—facing the glass wall that opened onto the med-bay. Medical privacy, another of those things she'd never had in the League. The back of the office was a minor lab, with glass dishes and various analyser equipment, and chairs where several junior medical personnel were working on various medical-type things . . . Sandy consciously limited her knowledge of medical procedures. Her experience of most such things in her life had not been pleasant. And she'd seen enough blood and human insides in her life to last her another five Hindu reincarnations, at least. Ten, maybe. The office smelt like antiseptic detergent, and she didn't like that either.

"Ari and I made a decision not to let our relationship cramp our professional style," Sandy replied, gazing at the display screen. It was clearly a three-dimensional, colour-coded map of a GI's skull. Rhian's, she reckoned, recognising the outlines and shapes of the implants about the ears and lower back of the skull. "What's the story, Doc?"

"There is no apparent mechanism," said Obago, hands folded in front of his white coat. He studied the graphic for a moment with pursed lips. "It should be here." He touched the screen at a point that Sandy reckoned would be about the hypothalamus. Obago pressed a button, and a new display appeared, this one of another GI's skull. Her own, Sandy recognised. "I obtained this from one of your earlier checkups," said Obago. "I apologise for not asking permission first, but time seemed of the essence."

"Of course," Sandy said blandly. The doctor's forefinger now rested upon precisely the same spot on the new display. Again his other hand manipulated a control, and the screen image zoomed in prodigiously, approaching microscopic detail without losing much apparent clarity or detail. Now the image appeared as a mass of cojoined, overgrown fibres, like a tangle of jungle vines.

"There," said Obago. "Can you see that?"

"I can see a lot of things," Sandy replied. "I just don't know what any of them are."

"Well, technically speaking, neither do I," said the doctor. "League synthetic technology is simply on another dimension from Federation capabilities. We don't even have the exact name for the microfilament substance from which both of your brains are grown. Except that it replicates human brain synapse activity almost precisely, as well as various chemical responses, and can integrate with synaptic implants almost seamlessly. Exactly how this particular implant works, I could not say . . . although maybe elsewhere on Callay or in the Federation there are experts who may know more, especially now that contacts between League and Federation are accelerating, at least a little. What it *does*, however, is clear enough."

He pressed another few buttons on the hand control, and suddenly one large, long filament among many turned red. It seemed almost organic, branching out at various points like a creeper sprouting leaves, integrating into the synaptic fibres around it. But now that Sandy looked at it, it seemed too big, too long and too thick compared to the other shorter, less organised strands.

"From what I can see from the readings," Obago continued, "it seems to be made from a material variant of something called ceta-velar-alloy, which is related to . . ."

"I don't need to know what it is, Doc, just what it does."

"Well, simply speaking, once activated by an external trigger, it turns white hot and explodes. There's a little organic battery charge up one end, enough for a boost that activates a chain reaction. It will kill you more or less immediately, give or take a few seconds."

"Can you remove it?" Sandy asked quietly.

"No." Obago shook his head, with absolute certainty. "I sincerely doubt even the best League people could remove it, it's too tightly embedded. Doing so would certainly cause irreversible brain damage. At the very least it would leave you paralysed."

Sandy took a deep breath. And looked at Rhian. Rhian looked back. And gave a small, wry twist of her lips.

"I guess they were more scared of you than me," Rhian offered.

"Can't imagine why," Sandy murmured. "I'm harmless."

# CHAPTER 5

She took the cruiser home at 5 PM that evening—very early by any senior official's standards. Stuck at her desk, all operational readiness procedures on hold due to the investigation and recovery, she'd come to feel like a spare wheel, fending off endless queries and expressions of relief from fellow soldiers that she was okay. Which was nice, on the one hand . . . especially the flowers, the box of chocolates, and the three bottles of wine and scotch various of her friends had found time to have sent to her office. It was nice to have people in the CDF who genuinely cared for her as a person, and to hell with her rank or other political circumstances. But sitting there all day while the CSA investigators insisted she couldn't continue her usual routine of field tests, training and integration exercises until they'd swept all the equipment bays for clues, and constantly bombarded by condolences for a tragedy that hadn't actually happened (hey guys, look, I'm actually still alive) had finally gotten to her. Well, she hadn't had an early working day for over a month now, so she figured she was due.

Canas was nearly ten minutes flight time from HQ. It presented her with her first truly free time to think, as the afternoon sun burned bright yellow in the west, and lit the glass sides of passing towers to blazing, vertical spires of light. She felt, Sandy decided, somewhat uneasy. Tense. Moody, even. The cast about her left wrist and thumb pressed hard upon the control wheel, her partially immobile fingers unable to manipulate the buttons. Bullets ripping past. The roaring thunder of high-velocity steel. It had been very close. She'd had innumerable close calls before, at various stages of her life. Most of those she'd written off as professional hazards, and simply dealt with. This one felt different. It wasn't what she'd been expecting from *this* life. Her new life. And they'd gone after *her*, specifically, because she was Sandy, and not simply another soldier in a war zone. This one was personal, and she found that profoundly unsettling.

And why the hell hadn't they used the killswitch? It didn't make sense, first Ari's warnings that someone was after her, and the related information about the killswitch . . . or she'd assumed it was related. Certainly Ari had. Maybe whoever had made this attempt hadn't known about the killswitch. Or hadn't had the capability to access it. Or maybe, crazy as the thought had seemed when she'd first had it, this was just a warning? It was poorly organised for one thing—her moment of greatest weakness had been directly after the first mineblast, when she'd been surprised, unbalanced and blown off her feet. But there'd been only one AMAPS in a position to directly benefit— it had missed, and from there she was always a good chance, being what she was, and having friends in close proximity. The rest had been strung out, like an obstacle course. Although a significant rearrangement of assets in the bay would have raised suspicions. Maybe there hadn't been a choice. So why take that option then, with those inadequacies? Surely they must have guessed that any ambush attempt on

Cassandra Kresnov had to be almost completely watertight to have a reasonable chance of success? Maybe this one hadn't been expected to succeed. After all, the slick nature of the infiltration, and the sloppy execution of the actual ambush, simply failed to mesh.

It would surely all make more sense if she had some idea who had tried to kill her. There were of course the usual stock of Tanushan religious radicals who had never ceased their strenuous objections to the presence of a murderous, soulless GI in *any* position within the CDF, let alone a senior commander. But clearly Ari was right in saying this attempt had taken a great degree of inside knowledge—knowledge such radicals were highly unlikely to possess.

More likely were the pro-Earth factions, either indigenous or imported, who saw her as the embodiment of all that was wrong with the direction Callay, and therefore the Federation, was now headed in. But then why remove her? Surely her presence actually *helped* such people, at some level, because it made their reformist, progressive enemies look bad. Kill the GI, and the pro-Earth conservatives would only make themselves look bad, and lend sympathy to their enemies. Something there didn't make sense.

Then there were two other, shadowy options—Federal Intelligence Agency operatives, or the League's ISO, the Internal Security Organisation. The FIA, of course, was undergoing a massive overhaul after the calamitous directorship split of the previous year. Half the senior directors still had not been found, mysteriously vanished into space, it seemed . . . or being sheltered by those with an equal interest in keeping certain skeletons firmly in their closets. The rest were in closed trial on Earth, much to the disgust of the collective Federation body politic, and even some on Earth in famously discontent nations like the USA, who demanded all trials be made public. Many of the FIA simply hated GIs. Many no doubt remained who suspected her of devious power trips, having gained the Neiland Administration's trust. Probably they'd reckon they were doing Callay and the Federation a favour in seeing her dead. But it seemed an awful lot of effort, considering the FIA's other problems.

Remnants of the old League government seemed a far more likely bet. Sandy knew where many of *their* skeletons were buried, and they doubtless knew that she knew. Probably they'd know she had a good friend who worked for the League Embassy in Tanusha, an Embassy that was, of course, run by the new, reformist League administration, with its comparatively cordial relations with the Federation. Probably the old guard suspected that she knew things that could damage them, if and when the new administration found out. But she'd already imparted many such secrets, and the new administration had been in power for nearly three years now . . . it only *seemed* new, given where the League had come from, politically speaking. Why wait this long to silence her, after the damage had surely already been done? Unless there were other political machinations in the offing, back League-side? Perhaps someone from the Embassy would soon come calling with some new questions for her consideration.

Sandy swore lightly to herself, steering gently to remain within the computer-generated skylane through the towers. Further ahead the afternoon thunderstorm was looming, massive thunderheads towering ten thousand metres tall, gleaming a bright shade of yellow in the afternoon sun and regularly flashing blue as lightning discharged in staccato succession, like gunfire on a colossal scale.

To make it all worse, she'd had no one to really talk to all day. Rhian had offered to stay around, but Sandy had insisted she make the most of her day off, and so Rhian had gone. Doubtless many had considered that strange, considering Rhian had also faced mortal threat . . . but Sandy knew her old comrade well, and knew it would take more than a little exchange of fire to dampen Rhian Chu's spirits. And of course as third-in-command, Vanessa's role was more concerned with personnel than Sandy's, and so she'd been very busy reorganising duty rosters and training schedules in the new chaos that had descended, and hadn't shown any sign of wanting to talk to her anyway, in their few brief contacts of the day. Sandy knew Vanessa was upset at something, but she still failed to understand the reaction. She was the one who'd nearly been killed, after all. And Ari, of course, had been out of contact all day.

Ari. The thought brought on a sigh. Sometimes it seemed that they just couldn't stop arguing. It was unexpected. She'd always assumed that a good, long-term, sexual relationship meant less arguments, not more. But then, as Vanessa had countered when they'd discussed it, who else was going to sustain her interest over the long term? Someone who agreed with her all the time? A "yes man"? She'd had enough of that back in the League, from soldiers under her command, or non-GI officers under instruction not to contradict her unless absolutely necessary. And she'd found that boring and disappointing in the extreme.

As Vanessa said, she loved a good argument. It was one of the major things she could get, here in her new civilian life, that her old League life had not provided. She found differences of opinion stimulating. She loved learning new things, even if they contradicted old understandings. And Ari's ability to surprise her, to make her challenge her previous assumptions, and to simply make her laugh, was probably the primary reason she found his company so stimulating. That, of course, and that devilishly sexy crooked grin that he used knowingly upon her to predictable effect. Yes, they clashed frequently on matters of ideology and style. It was sometimes frustrating. But then, she simply didn't see how it was possible to have all the good things, without also taking her fair share of the bad.

An absent-minded skip across her uplink monitors shot back a mass of highlighted points . . . there was a massive demonstration prepared for tonight in Velan district against the Fleet blockade, organisers were expecting at least half a million protesters. Secretary General Benale had held a major press conference on his tour of Tanusha, urging the Grand Council to reject the "undue influence and interference of the Neiland Administration." Fleet Admiral Duong had made a brief statement, rejecting calls from extremist Earth factions for the blockade to become official Earth policy until Callay and its supporters in the Federation abandoned their "ultra-progressive manipulations of the Grand Council apparatus."

"The Fleet is not blockading Callay," Duong now said as she opened that file, and watched his stern, shaven-headed visage upon her internal vision. The rank on the Fleet uniform collar was plainly evident, shiny badges gleaming against the stark metal backdrop of what Sandy guessed were his private quarters. The Fleet Admiral's eyes were the hard, calculating eyes of a man who had seen many battles, and lost many friends, yet had only had his convictions strengthened by his experiences. Sandy had met such people often, and distrusted them always. Her own wartime experiences, of course, had caused her precisely the opposite reaction. "This is a security operation, no more, no less. These are precarious times. The centre of power in the Federation is being relocated, and reconstructed. This is a time of great vulnerability for us all. The Federation constitution tasks the Fleet with the protection of the Federation and all its assets. That is what we shall do."

Sandy considered Duong's hard, unwavering eyes as the cruiser's navcomp took her into a gradual descent, and wondered at what thoughts might be passing through the mind behind them. A determination to uphold Earth's preeminence within the Federation, certainly. A distrust of the selfish, fractious colonies. But also, apparently, a sense of moderation, backed by the faultless discipline of a lifetime soldier. Surely he could not be enjoying his present role. He'd made himself into a politician, a lightning rod for the opinions of Earth-based extremists and colonial progressives alike. And the word was that he did not get along with Secretary General Benale at all, whatever their apparent political similarities.

She landed the cruiser on the yellow-striped transition zone inside the

tall, stone wall that marked the outer perimeter of the Canas high security zone. The cruiser came down in a gentle hover-and-bump of heavy
tires, Sandy largely ignoring the process to watch some children playing
football on the green field beside the high wall and transition zone.

Canas security was in the house when she made her way up from the
basement parking garage. She waited while they conducted their final
sweeps—uniformed men and women who specialised in network security, and were tasked with the upkeep of all security systems within the
Canas area. In the kitchen she discovered Jean-Pierre had wedged himself on top of the cupboards near where the stairs ascended to the upper
floor, gazing wide-eyed at all the strangers invading his house. He
recognised Sandy and began a relieved, plaintive chirping.

"Just wait," Sandy told him, pouring herself a makani juice first,
then climbing the stairs halfway to stand level with the kitchen cupboards. She leaned over the rails, extending her free left arm, disre-
garding the wrist cast. Jean-Pierre gathered his supple limbs, gave a
coiling wriggle, then leaped across the intervening space and onto the
extended arm, little hand/feet grasping as tightly as millions of years
of tree-climbing evolution had intended. Sandy held him comfortably
against her shoulder, heading back down the stairs and sipping the
drink from her other hand, wincing as Jean-Pierre tried to clean out
the inside of her left ear.

"I'm sorry," said a security tech at the bottom of the stairs, gear
packed in hand boxes, evidently headed for the door. "We didn't mean
to scare him, he just ran up there in a flash and wouldn't come down."

"He's not a very courageous animal," Sandy said with a smile.

"That was a pretty impressive leap," countered the tech, with a
glance up at the gap between cupboards and stairway.

"Oh, he's fine jumping sideways," said Sandy. "They do that all the
time in treetops. He just doesn't like jumping down. Falling's against
his instincts, I guess." As Jean-Pierre twisted about to fix the security

tech with a reproachful, golden-eyed gaze. "Say hello to the nice security man," Sandy instructed the bunbun. "I won't have xenophobic tree climbers in my house."

The tech extended a hand. Jean-Pierre grasped cautiously at a finger, and sniffed. The man smiled, looking slightly puzzled, and surprised, from the bunbun and back to Sandy. Sandy sipped her drink, and pretended not to notice. Nearly everyone who met her for the first time in a nonmilitary setting gave her that look. Particularly when she was holding and talking to a cute, furry household pet.

The security team departed and Sandy let Jean-Pierre out into the garden, where a number of tall trees soared from the lush undergrowth, and gave him plenty of exercise and freedom. She watched for a moment on the front decking as the nimble, furry shape clambered quickly up a tall trunk with precise holds and bounds. He could run away any time, certainly there were plenty of wild bunbuns of various species throughout Tanusha . . . no doubt Jean-Pierre met and associated with them often, particularly the lady bunbuns. But bunbuns were highly territorial creatures, and grew very attached to their place of birth and home. Like most well-treated, domesticated bunbuns, he came home every time.

Ironic, she reflected as she climbed the stairs to her room with her drink and a slice of fruitcake from the fridge, that it was easier to domesticate smarter animals as pets than stupid ones. Unless you counted livestock or fish as pets, which she didn't, personally. Livestock only licked your face if they found something edible on it. Real pets did it because they liked you. Poor bunbuns, though. Just smart enough to stay, but not smart enough to leave. Like GIs, she'd said to Rhian, once. But Rhian, of course, hadn't gotten the joke.

Consciousness was elusive. She drifted beneath the surface of lucidity, gazing at the ripples and roaring foam . . . like waves, viewed from below. Perhaps she was at the beach. At Rajadesh, or one of her other favourite surf spots. And if she reached with one foot, and found the sandy bottom firm against her toes, she could push off and break the surface into the sunlight and clean, fresh breeze above. And one of the regulars would be cruising past . . . maybe Peytr Lipinski, or maybe Tabo with his round, cheerful black face, and compliment her on a nice ride, and wonder if perhaps she'd come to drinks at the beach party they were having that weekend . . .

A high, cruising whine above the crashing surf. The sand felt unstable . . . a bump of turbulence. Memories triggered, reflexes . . . damn, she was dreaming. She wasn't on a beach at all. The realisation came as a mighty disappointment. Above her swam the lucid surface, a refraction of sunlight through a watery depth. The cruising whine remained steady. Then voices, and the noise of someone moving equipment. A rattle and bump of turbulence, disorienting. She knew that feeling well enough. She was airborne.

Finally her eyes flicked open. She was staring at a low ceiling. Her vision was clear enough, thankfully, and when she moved her eyes, she could see medical equipment to her side. There was someone over there, someone wearing a medico's white coat, adjusting equipment. Gravity tilted once more, g-forces pressing faintly against her back. So she was lying down. In an airborne vehicle. Surrounded by medical equipment. Aerial ambulance. Someone must have tried to kill her again. But the most disturbing part was that she couldn't remember a thing.

"What happened?" Her voice was small, yet clear enough. That was good, she knew from past experience that when the meds shot her too full of drugs, her voice was usually the first thing to go.

"Commander?" There was a woman leaning over her, in the white-coated uniform of a Tanushan ambulance officer. "Commander Kresnov, how do you feel?"

"I don't know yet. Tell me what happened." Jean-Pierre. Abruptly she felt worried for him, and was relieved to remember letting him run up the tree in the backyard—twenty metres over the house, he should be fine.

"We're not sure what happened, Commander. Canas security

alerted us after they responded to a personal alarm from your room. We got there within five minutes of their call, Canas security said they'd found you passed out on the floor. They said you'd been subjected to some kind of network attack, some foreign assault virus had penetrated your barrier networks and immobilised you. They physically disabled the house's network to disconnect it."

There had been Canas security personnel in her house, Sandy remembered. One had let Jean-Pierre sniff his fingers. She'd checked out the house's network herself many times, as had some of the brightest brains in the Tanushan techno underground, who knew where all the hidden pitfalls and shortcuts were located. So it stood to reason that whoever had tried to kill her had done so through the agency of Canas security . . . who guarded all the most important people in Tanusha, and were invulnerable to infiltration. Sandy moved her arm, and found that it was restrained.

"Why am I restrained?"

"I'm sorry, Commander, Canas security said you were thrashing around some when they found you. I didn't particularly want to share the back of an ambulance with a thrashing GI."

"Fair enough. I'm okay now, let me out."

"I'm really sorry but regulations won't let me. I've been instructed from the top, they say not to risk it."

Sandy wasn't sure of her own reaction. The calm felt decidedly like combat-reflex. The surreal dislocation was probably drugs. God knew what they'd shot her full of. All she knew for sure was that she didn't want to ask anything more that might alarm anyone. She had a mental checklist in her head, now, and she needed to check off some items. And she realised, in that slow, unaccustomed state, that she wasn't receiving any data through her uplinks. That was another question she didn't want to ask. Maybe they'd think she was getting upset.

"We're going to CDF compound, aren't we?" As calmly as she knew how to ask.

"Um, no . . ." the ambulance officer was now reaching for something, adjusting it out of her field of vision, ". . . we're headed to the Lloyd Hospital. They have the best biotech surgeons there, they'll know best how to make sure you're okay."

"I think it's a better idea to get back to Doctor Obago at the CDF. He's my regular physician. He's gotten to know my medical situation better than anyone else in the last two years."

"We'll definitely consult with Doctor Obago," the ambulance officer reassured her. And lifted into sight the implement she'd been adjusting—a hypospray, filled with fluid.

"I'm fine," Sandy said, her voice hardening. "I don't need another damn shot."

"No offence, Commander, but I'll be the judge of that."

"You're very self-assured for a simple ambulance tech." She tensed her arm, seeking critical muscle function, and felt only the faint twinge of reaction. The arm remained loose, the restraints hard and firm about her forearms, synthetic straps, far harder than steel. The ambulance officer smiled.

"Trust me, Commander, I'm uplinked to some very knowledgeable experts in the field of GI physiology. The shot is prescription."

Sandy focused inward, as hard as she could. Remembering what muscular tension felt like. The secret was not tension. It was to relax . . . relax . . . She breathed deeply, closing her eyes. The officer's hypospray was a small, low-powered pocket size. It gave her a little extra time.

The ambulance officer touched the hypospray to Sandy's bare arm, and Sandy felt the faint sting of pressure. Then a puzzled pause from the officer.

"Hmm, that's funny. It's not going in." Another faint pop against her skin. "It's leaving a mark on your skin, so the hypo's not broken. Very funny."

"Hysterical," Sandy agreed. Tension erupted in her right arm, and she unleashed it with a bang! that shook the stretcher as the arm restraint tore clear away. And caught the startled ambulance officer by the front of the white coat. "Stick me with that again and I'll impale you with it."

Bang! as she ripped her left arm free, releasing the stunned medico to reach for the cord at the back of her head and rip it clear . . . barrier restrictions evaporated, and suddenly the rush of network data flooded her mind in graphic, three-dimensional relief. A picture of their present location—they were almost precisely over central Tanusha, where Shinobu district blended into the broad Balikpapan Nature Park. Lloyd Hospital was in central-southern Tanusha, still five minutes' flight time away. Sandy sat up to undo the straps about her ankles.

"Commander, what the hell are you doing?" The medico had flattened herself warily to the side of the ambulance, eyes wide with alarm. Sandy ignored her, finished with the ankle straps and moved to the reinforced window at the front of the cabin, where the ambulance driver was staring back at them with some alarm, speaking rapidly into a headset microphone. Sandy hit the window with an open palm to disperse the impact of the strike, and it crashed explosively inwards as the driver ducked to his side. The resulting gap was large enough to crawl through, which she did, headfirst, and climbed into the empty passenger seat alongside the driver.

"Commander!" The driver was clearly alarmed. "We're just on our way to hospital, what do you think you're doing?" As Sandy stuffed the fractured dividing window back through the rear frame where it wouldn't get in the way. "There's no need for any alarm, Commander . . . I think that latest attack might have disoriented you in some way. Please try to think on what you're doing."

"Relinquish the controls," Sandy told him, uplinking to the ambulance's CPU and scanning its projected course ahead toward the hospital. The Tanushan central traffic network kept a careful eye on all emergency vehicles, had them priority-registered on the airborne net . . .

"I'm sorry, Commander, but I just can't do that."

Sandy hit him, the heel of her palm to the thick part of the skull above the ear. The driver lurched sideways against his belt, then slumped in his seat. Sandy felt for pulse and breathing as the medico in the back made a startled exclamation of shock and fear.

"Check on him," Sandy told the woman. "I didn't hit him hard, make sure he's not hurt." Her uplinks accessed the navcomp, overriding the old course and setting in a new one. Traffic Central tried to query, and she overrode it with a CSA priority code. The medico leaned through the open rear window frame, feeling at the driver's throat and skull, stopping his head from rolling about.

"Commander," she said, trying to keep her voice steady, "I think you're panicking. You should stop and think for just a moment. Whatever you think is going on here, I assure you, there's nothing . . ."

"Just shut up or I'll hit you too," Sandy told her. Truthfully she didn't like hitting straights if at all avoidable—the risk of a brain-splattered windshield was only theoretical, and in practice a hell of a lot less than that. But whatever the remote odds of a momentary loss of muscle control, she still didn't like doing it. The next fork in the new trajectory arrived, and Sandy steered the ambulance into a gentle left-hand bank with the passenger seat controls, following the string of aligned rectangles that projected up on the front windshield. The new course swung toward what the navcomp identified as Prasad Tower, a four hundred metre tall mega-high-rise that soared above the surrounding clutter of mid-sized towers in central Chattisgarh.

"*Hello 875,*" came the ambulance controller's voice over the cockpit speakers, "*we read that you have altered course, please explain.*"

Sandy ignored it, uplinking instead to the Prasad Tower's presence on the network, studying its layout, its security features, its occupation demographics. The tower's top levels were occupied by a VIP parking bay, beneath the rooftop landing pads for flyers and other larger airborne vehicles. A query light blinked upon the ambulance's com system. Another pressed upon her inner consciousness, her uplink software immediately tracing its origin back to somewhere within the CSA. She ignored that too. Lights blinked upon Prasad Tower's landing pads, the occasional vehicle arriving or leaving from the parking bay beneath . . . early evening traffic, late workers headed home. About half of the tower's massive glass sides were illuminated from within.

Her monitoring software informed her of nearby government vehicle trajectories altering toward her. She counted four. The nearest was less than a minute away. The tower's landing control had her slotted now, the windshield display rectangles stretching ahead to match up with the broad opening in the tower's side. Sandy began the landing cycle, automated systems deploying wheels, repulsor engines throbbing as their velocity slowed . . . and then the ambulance passed into a floodlit cavern of ferrocrete, the landing systems directing the vehicle to a yellow-striped temporary park beside the main conveyer belt park, as was procedure for emergency vehicles. Wheels touched and she shut down the engines, ducked under the unfolding side door, and out into the echoing, gusty bay. She realised she was still wearing her CDF uniform, and hastily unbuttoned the jacket, tossing it onto the passenger seat.

She ran swiftly toward the through-passage ahead as another cruiser came in for a landing behind, its lights blazing her running shadow large upon the opposing wall. Then into the broad ferrocrete passage, hearing the clank and hum of the parking bay mechanism echoing through the walls above the throbbing whine of aircars. Her uplinks informed her that the next cruiser approaching the entrance bay was an official, black-flagged government vehicle, the exact identity of which remained ominously blank despite her probes.

The passage opened onto the exit apron on the other side of the building. A number of people were waiting on the raised footpath alongside the vehicle conveyer belt, finding their transport waiting in line, nose to tail. A pedestrian crossing light blinked red, advising her not to cross the apron . . . Sandy ignored it, ducking and running past the departing end of a cruiser that lifted from the conveyer belt, hovering its way toward the exit. The repulsor field prickled her skin and made hair stand on end as she ran onto the pedestrian platform, and up the adjoining rampway that descended to the occupied, working floors below. It was a long platform, and she had barely started down it when a pair of dark-uniformed security guards appeared at the far end, stopped, and stared at her.

Sandy swore, reversed course and ran back up the ramp, shoving past several surprised suits as she did a U-turn and ran back along the line of office workers waiting for their cars. People stared at her as she passed, ducking several times as people moved to their vehicles on the conveyor belt, doors gull-winging upwards to let them in. The additional commotion in her wake told her that the two security guards were after her at speed. The waiting platform ended, and Sandy leaped down onto the conveyor belt, past the front of one emerging cruiser, then into the dark, mechanical cavern within. Above the entrance, clearly written in bright, red letters were the words: DANGER! MACHINERY IN OPERATION. DO NOT ENTER.

There was no room on the conveyor to squeeze past the next cruiser, so Sandy ran over the top of it, ducking beneath the low overhead as she did. Her vision spectrum-flashed on combat mode, making out the descending platforms ahead that loaded the cruisers onto the conveyor, and the various laser measurement beams that criss-crossed the passage, monitoring the position of all objects moving within. The next platform descended into the unloading mouth, a sleek, expensive cruiser resting within. The mechanism clanged to a stop as she approached, walking to hold a steady place upon the conveyor, and glancing back to see if the security guards were following. And restrained a faint smile to see the two guards waiting until the last cruiser had cleared the conveyor mouth before entering, so as not to stomp bootprints over its shiny windshield. But then, she pondered, private security were locally employed, and would have to answer to some stiff-necked suit in management for such infringements.

Another mechanism whined, and the cruiser on the lift platform rolled gently forward, comfortably matching velocity with the conveyor belt. Sandy walked up on the bonnet of that one too, rolling gently over the roof, then hurdling the rear field generators with one hand. Behind, the two security men edged past the tail of the previous cruiser and came running up the conveyor belt toward her. Sandy stepped onto the empty aircar cradle just as it thumped into motion once more, descending to allow the next cruiser above to slot into place. The two security guards arrived too late, and she spared them a sardonic wave. From the astonished looks on their faces, she reckoned they recognised her—no surprise that, there weren't many people in Tanusha who didn't these days.

"Ma'am?" one of them shouted to her above the whining mechanism. "Ma'am, what the hell's going on?" Then the platform descended into total blackness. Even past the deadening calm of combat-reflex, she was touched. "Ma'am," he'd called her—an anachronistic expression that had somehow lingered in Tanusha when it had long since died on other Federation worlds.

The platform then emerged into the main storage facility of the parking level, and moved sideways along its tracks. The tail ends of aircars were passing, each locked into a storage cradle. Sandy peered into the dull machine-light, eyes adjusting to the gloom of a totally automated environment where human sight was not required. The entire broad space, comprising perhaps three standard building storeys and all the space to the opposing wall, was storage racks for aircars. The huge space, echoing with shrill mechanical whines and clanks, was spanned by a series of vertical racks, like those slotted into an old-fashioned beehive. Along each of these racks were a series of vertical mechanisms—a chain of aircar cradles that rotated when one of its occupants was loaded or unloaded, cruisers descending on one side, and ascending on the other. At the very top, a cruiser would be deposited onto separate platforms that ran along the length of the racks.

Even as Sandy pondered the design, her own sideways-moving platform slowed to a halt, locking into place. There, a cruiser was waiting, its owner having called it up. The separate, twin conveyors upon which the cruiser's tyres rested began to move in unison with those on Sandy's platform. Sandy climbed onto the advancing bonnet of the aircar, rolled across its roof, and dropped onto the carrier platform atop the main storage rack. Its cruiser unloaded, the carrier platform took off along its railings, building shortly to a considerable velocity.

Ahead, Sandy saw several rotary chains in motion, and fell flat as the platform whizzed beneath several cruisers being rotated directly overhead, with a clearance of barely half a metre. It whined to a halt, in line with a new rotary chain that cranked empty cradles up one side, overhead, and then down the other . . . Sandy got up, crouching, and glanced around. Along this railing, her present platform only went halfway—at the other end another platform trundled away from her to the far wall, laden with another cruiser. She spared a glance down at the tracks themselves—they were just side rails housing magnetic runners. Directly beneath was empty space, a straight drop of three storeys.

Abruptly, the lights came on, a massive, staggered flickering of several hundred fluoros that darted randomly across the broad ceiling. The next cradle in her platform's chain was laden, the cradle's mechanical arms holding a cruiser in a careful grip, moving sideways now and threatening to push her off the platform. Sandy leaped, and grasped the empty cradle arms of the next chain along, swinging above empty space. Hearing at maximum enhancement, she could hear voices above the crashing, whining mechanical echoes. Location was difficult, but she figured they were looking for her. The floor would be an obvious location. And the walls. Which meant that the best way to stay out of sight . . .

She swung gently forward, and dropped between three sets of empty cradle arms to land on a cruiser's roof. From there, another cruiser was directly in line, and she leaped to that one, then through a gap between two more. The next chain along was moving down and so she waited until the next occupied cradle came level, and leaped gently onto that rooftop. A fast glance ahead at the approaching side wall showed a maintenance walkway halfway up, with a security guard moving slowly along, peering intently. At this angle, she was exposed, and flattened herself spread-eagled to the cruiser's smooth rooftop, unwilling to move as the rotary chain took her toward the ferrocrete floor. Her cradle reached the bottom of the rack, went sideways one car-width, and stopped.

Sandy nearly swore. To one side now, close enough to be heard above the echoing racket of machinery, came the sound of boots on ferrocrete. The cruiser she was lying on was now suspended barely a metre off the ground, which put her rooftop at barely two and a half. To her left, then, she could see the security guard's head, looking one way and then the other as he made careful progress up the aisle between racks, gazing up at the towering, tight-packed aircar berths above. Damn it, if he turned around at just the wrong moment, and looked at just the right place . . .

An overhead whine made her look up. Directly beneath the giant, three-storey rack, she could now stare straight up the inside, between ascending and descending walls of occupied and empty cradles. And directly overhead ran the central platform, headed now back to the wall with a newly loaded cruiser bound for downstairs. In three seconds it would pass directly overhead. Three storeys . . .

Swiftly and silently, she swung her feet beneath her, achieved firm purchase atop the cruiser's roof, and assumed a tight, bunching crouch. Leg muscles at optimum, Sandy fixed her eyes directly on the underside of the platform, and snapped her legs straight with a controlled release of accumulated tension. She shot straight upward between the two walls of aircars, and found she was approaching too fast. Twisted in mid-air to get a knee up as well, and hit the underside of the moving platform with a hard thud, hands grasping at the rim of an underside crossbeam, then swinging freely beneath as the platform continued upon its way toward the far wall. Leaping upwards was always an imprecise art, even for a GI. Particularly having been pumped full of drugs the names and effects of which she did not know . . . it was easy to miscalculate the degree of muscular tension required to rendezvous with a singular point in space precisely. Although she figured her limit to be about six storeys. Theoretically, she had enough power in her legs to leap high enough to catch low-flying aircraft, if she could hit them. Midaltitude flying aircraft, even—her own body weight was insignificant beside the potential energy in the quantity of synth-alloy-myomer she had in her thighs and calves. But the physics of leverage meant that whatever their power, her legs were simply too short to impart the required velocity on her body to clear higher than thirty or forty metres.

After all, she reckoned with a faint, ironic smile as she hung beneath the advancing platform, structurally, at least, she was only human.

The platform stopped at the wall where the adjoining platforms ran sideways, and began transferring that cruiser on board. To her left as she hung, Sandy could see directly along the midlevel engineering walkway, and several security guards gazing out over the cluttered scene. The nearest was not more than six metres away. She hand-over-handed her way to the side of the platform furthest from him, and quickly hauled herself up. She stayed flat, and rolled under the cruiser on its new platform, peering out between its wheels as the new platform took off sideways, then began descending again toward the ferrocrete floor. Again the descent took her within a few metres of another security guard at floor level, then blackness.

Finally the platform thumped to a halt, light now spilling in from the other end, and the cruiser moved forward onto the final conveyor belt, and its waiting owner in the parking bay beyond. Sandy simply crawled forward, keeping the cruiser above her, and lay flat upon the conveyor belt as it passed out of the ferrocrete passage and into the harsh-lit bay beyond. She could see no security guards or suspiciously waiting suits, just the usual row of commuters waiting on the platform beside the conveyor for their rides to arrive. A further uplink scan of the Prasad Tower vicinity showed her a state of yellow security alert, several orbiting aircars and some seriously encrypted transmission traffic from various unidentifiable sources.

The conveyor belt was segmented, of course, and her own segment cruised up behind two more aircars ahead into which passengers were currently climbing. Sandy performed a quick roll beneath the aircar ahead, hearing and feeling the throbbing whine overhead, and the prickling sensation through her hair . . . the repulsor field wasn't supposed to be dangerous, but then they'd said that often enough about a lot of supposedly safe, advanced technology over the centuries. She rolled to alongside the raised commuter platform, and ducked onward at a low run. Those waiting all appeared to be gazing in the other direction, waiting for their vehicles to emerge along the conveyor, and no one seemed to notice her sudden appearance.

Sandy ran straight for the exit . . . if she was lucky, one of the government suits would have left his cruiser at an emergency parking bay, all ready to be digitally hotwired. If she was really lucky, maybe a CSA cruiser—she still had plenty of CSA codes available, and knew numerous ways into that network undetected. A commuter cruiser took off past her with a throbbing, low pitched howl, headed for the broad, rectangular opening that led to open air, nearly half a kilometre straight up. On the painted stripes beneath one side wall, Sandy saw there was indeed a government cruiser sitting, and ran to its door.

"Commander!"

She spun, and found a man in a dark CSA suit just ten metres behind, pistol in hand. Anil Chandaram, a familiar enough face around Investigations. One of their seniors, in fact. He was frowning at her now, with no small degree of puzzlement, a gusting warm wind tossing at his hair, his suit jacket billowing out behind him. "Commander . . . what the hell are you doing? Who are you running from? I'm your friend!"

Past the deadening combat-reflex, Sandy found herself biting back a curse. Well, it had been a good try. And she had to try, if she wanted to live beyond the next couple of days. Something on the Tower schematic caught her mental eye. Multiple express elevator shafts, running straight up and down to one side of the opening outside. Another cruiser throbbed past, accelerating slowly toward the opening, running lights flashing off the walls.

"Anil!" she shouted above the noise. "Don't follow me! They'll say I've gone nuts! I haven't, I'm entirely sane and I know exactly what I'm doing! Tell them that! Look into my eyes now, and then you tell them that, when you see them."

Chandaram stared at her, orange running lights flashing across his handsome brown face, frowning disconcertedly.

"Commander, I don't . . ."

Sandy turned and ran, straight for the exit. For a brief moment, the vast expanse of nighttime Tanusha sprawled before her, a carpet of multicoloured lights and towers, the horizon stained a brilliant orange against the black of the sky, and below, the clustered surrounding towers that stretched up the flanks of the soaring Prasad Tower . . . the lip of the exit arrived, and she leaped, straight off the edge.

In that time-slowed moment, the first thought that came was how amazingly beautiful it was—the maze of streets between towers below, brilliantly lit with neon and traffic. Then the tower's side began rushing past, and the wind began tearing at her face and clothes, and she realised that even a GI, and particularly one with long-standing, deep-seated structural damage like her, was going to get hurt hitting the ground at terminal velocity. The express elevators ran down the side of the building to her left . . . she folded her arms back, and leaned toward that direction as the roaring wind grew to a deafening gale, and the tower side began rushing past at truly alarming velocity.

One elevator car was rushing by even now, too close, and she went hurtling past it, angling her trajectory to come in closer to the speeding tower wall. The second was descending below—they went from top storey to bottom at over a hundred kilometres per hour, she knew, and were something of an attraction for joyriders who enjoyed the half-gravity sensation on the way down. But now it was getting close alarmingly fast. As was the ground.

She spread-eagled, catching as much of the wind as she could with her arms and legs, trailing the fingertips of her left hand along the wall at over three hundred kilometres per hour and feeling the burning friction. An updraft almost threw her balance at the last moment, but she steadied with a plunging lurch like a falling leaf, and crashed onto the dome-top of the racing elevator with an almighty bang! as her hands caught hold and her skull smacked a melon-sized crater in the glass. Within the elevator, about twelve passengers yelped and leaped, staring upwards in fright. Her left, cast-bound hand slipped, and for a moment she dangled right-handed from her fingerhold on the upper frame. Still the wind roared, but without the previous intensity, as the descending capsule overtook several slower elevators on the parallel lanes. Sandy gave a calculated heave with her right arm, throwing herself upward and spinning about so as to seat herself atop the hurtling car, and gazed down at the broad, paved thoroughfare that led to the atrium entrance below. To her left, beyond the edge of that paving, were lush green gardens, split by footpaths and park benches.

The elevator began to slow, the wind gradually lessening as ground features became clear, people walking, shadows cast by a multitude of lights, groundcars passing on the near street, a queue outside a nearby nightclub. Sandy gathered her feet beneath her, calculated distances, and leaped hard outward. For a short distance, she soared, then crashed through thick tree-fern leaves, snapped a branch, then crashlanded in bushes, rolling as best she could in the entanglement. Struggled her way out to a lamp-lit footpath through the greenery and ran, dodging past a couple of startled pedestrians on the path, thankful that Tanushans, like city dwellers everywhere, almost never looked up.

# CHAPTER 6

Five minutes later she was in Balikpapan Nature Park, ignoring the wide avenues and narrower footpaths to trudge instead through the undergrowth, ducking through tangles of vines and ferns, boots sinking into the mud of recent rains. None of the aircars dispatched to Prasad Tower had followed. She could only assume that Chandaram had not reported her. The foliage obscured any view of the air traffic about the looming tower behind her, and she dared not uplink directly to the traffic net at this time, needless risk that it was.

Without the jacket, her uniform was not immediately recognisable as such, and the military green blended well with anything in the dark. Her blonde hair was more of a problem, but not enormously—she was dark blonde, not snow white. More problematic was that she possessed one of the most famous faces in Tanusha. The media, of course, had been intrigued by the image of Callay's very own pet GI, when the administration had begun to allow the free distribution of her face and name. Now, as she paralleled the diagonal avenue that cut from one corner of Balikpapan Park to the other, she began to regret that decision had ever been made. Anonymity, she reckoned, was one of those things you never realised you valued until you lost it. But to assume that the newly promoted second-in-command of the CDF could remain anonymous in a free and democratic society was ridiculous—and the public did, she grudgingly supposed, have a right to know.

Somehow they'd all managed to be shocked at how pretty she was. Never mind that among any people who knew anything about GIs, the fact that all GIs tended to be attractive in one form or another was common knowledge. Still the visual impact of her appearance had been profound. Vanessa reckoned that humans were simply geared that way—visually. So much of what everyone construed as reality was in fact subtle, subjective visual imagery that tricked people into value judgements they didn't realise they were making. That, Vanessa said, was how serial killers always blended into the crowd—they didn't *look* like serial killers. No one did. And pretty blonde girls with subtle expressions and an evidently agreeable personality (well she thought so, anyway) were rarely recognised as murderous walking killing machines. It had softened the public attitude toward her, no question about it. Which she still found amazing. But now, her fame kept her off the footpaths and away from casual glances.

The park was three kilometres across. Considering the shocked passengers in the elevator, no doubt someone had reported her plunge off the tower. No doubt also that Balikpapan Park was the obvious place for someone to lose her pursuers, particularly when that someone was an experienced combat soldier who knew how to hide. Equally doubtless her pursuers knew that it would take a massive sweep of the park, diverting all available manpower, to find her. Which would raise questions from media and others, questions she doubted those with the most immediate interest in finding her wanted asked. It was in their interests for all of this to be kept very silent. And in the interests of many more besides, she had no doubt. There was no one she could contact whose uplinks or other connections were definitely not being monitored, particularly if this whole thing went as far up the power structure as she suspected it did. For the moment, at least, she was on her own. At least until her closest friends realised what was up, and took steps to secure their connections.

The reply on the doorway intercom sounded distinctly unimpressed with the interruption . . . until the doorway camera lens swivelled into focus, and the tone changed in a hurry. Multiple heavy locks clacked and clanked, then the door opened enough to admit the face of a wide-eyed man with thick curly hair and a long, sharpened goatee. The man stared at Sandy, then stared left and right along the corridor, seeming somewhat surprised that she was alone. Then he stood aside, and ushered her quickly inside, shutting the door behind and reactivating the automatic locks.

"What the fuck are you doing here?" Gustavius Chan asked her with hushed incredulity. He wore a very loud floral shirt, only half-buttoned at the bottom where a glimpse of hairy navel was evident. Beneath the cuffs of his trousers, woollen slippers. The scruffy, unkempt appearance was offset by several gold rings and an expensive chain about his neck. "You're a CDF bigshot now, there's nothing here for you! I swear, I don't want you here, I don't want no more of Ari's damn trouble."

"You sure opened the door in a hurry."

"Yeah, because I didn't want to have to pay for a new one!"

"Relax, Gustavius, you're nowhere near important enough to interest a bigshot like me."

Gustavius frowned at her. Blinked several times, looking increasingly disappointed. "Really?"

"I needed to hide, you were closest."

Gustavius blinked again. "Closest? What, you mean like serious emergency 'closest'? Oh baby, what are you into? What the hell are you going to get me into?"

Gustavius had the shielded connections in his apartment that she needed to make a totally secure call—there was a time when she would have trusted the security of her own uplinks in any Federation city without question. Now, too many important people knew too much about her, and she wasn't prepared to take any chances regarding *how* much if she could possibly avoid it.

Gustavius then drove her to Ruiz district near Tanusha's easterly fringe, muttering and worrying most of the way. It took a conscious effort for Sandy to keep herself from uplinking, as the groundcar sped at nearly two hundred kilometres per hour in automated nose-to-tail slipstream formation along a major, east-bound freeway. Probably Vanessa would be going nuts by now, raising hell with an administration that had somehow managed to lose track of the second-in-command of the CDF, and didn't know how, or why. Sandy, of course, was not only not answering her incoming uplink calls, she'd completely disconnected them. She wanted the Tanushan network in total ignorance of her location.

Unable to uplink to even a basic street directory, Sandy was forced to find the address she'd gotten from her one brief call on the groundcar's own navcomp. Florence Tower, it turned out, was an A-grade tower in the central business district of Ruiz. The rest of the address was simply "Room 581," no floor numbers or other details given.

"What if it's a trap?" Gustavius asked as the groundcar broke ranks with the freeway slipstream and slid right. They passed over a broad river, one of the many Shoban tributaries across the broad forest delta, the car decelerating as it took the right-side exit to curl along the riverbank. Lightning flashed regularly now in several directions, illuminating entire cityscape horizons with brilliant, darting blue flashes. A few drops of rain spattered upon the windshield.

"A trap set by whom?" Sandy asked, gazing out at the blazing of reflections along the river where it wound through the approaching high-rise of downtown Ruiz.

"Jeez, baby, I don't know! Whoever you called!"

"They're among the most secretive people in Tanusha," Sandy replied. "Even you don't compare."

"Look, baby, I'm telling you . . . I'm not secretive! I got nothing to hide, I ain't been doing nothing wrong since you and Ari called in on me last year."

"I know," Sandy said mildly.

"You know?" The rain began pelting down, and the groundcar's speed slowed in accordance with all the surrounding traffic. Cruisecomp displays showed the car adjusting traction control and altering the canter of the rear fin and front airdam, creating greater downforce. "Then . . . then why the hell am I helping you? I mean, if I ain't done nothing wrong . . ."

"Of course, if your old League operative friends do come calling on another courier mission, you'll be sure to tell us, huh? Because then we can handle it quietly. Otherwise it'll have to go straight to CSA Investigations, and then it all becomes officially a part of the Callayan justice system, you understand."

"Sure, baby," Gustavius said reasonably. "Sure, I'll help. I don't mind helping, I never minded helping . . ."

The groundcar took another exit, powerful headlights barely penetrating the blinding deluge and the spray kicked up by other cars. But the car knew the way even if its driver did not, and steered them along the riverbank until the next exit, which took them under the freeway and among the narrow roads between residential high-rise by the river side. Then slowing for a right-hand turn across oncoming traffic in the pelting downpour, Sandy fighting hard to resist the temptation to uplink, just briefly, and check out the immediate neighbourhood. Just because Anita and Pushpa assured her no one could possibly know about this place didn't mean they were *right* . . .

The underground garage door opened on automatic as the car nosed down a steep driveway, then the thunder of rain upon the windshield ceased. Traffic Central handed control over to Gustavius, who guided the car between rows of expensive parked vehicles, including one entire row of aircars. Gustavius whistled as his gaze trailed across the accumulated transport . . . cruisers cost nearly ten times the price of groundcars. As a general rule of thumb, the more cruisers were parked beneath a residential complex, the more wealthy the occupants. Then the car's dash speakers clicked smoothly to life, the speakerphone activating apparently of its own accord.

*"Hello, Sandy,"* came Anita's voice. *"I don't recognise your friend, but I'll assume he's safe or you wouldn't have brought him, right?"*

"He's not staying," Sandy replied, mildly amused at Gustavius's wide-eyed expression. Doubtless he'd rigged his car's CPU himself, and thought its network barriers impenetrable to such easy infiltration. "He was just in the neighbourhood, owed me a favour or two. He's going to go home and forget he ever saw me, aren't you, Gustavius Chan?"

*"Oh now I know him, he's one of the old League network suckers Ari closed down in the last sweep. Considering he's not in prison, I can see why he might owe you a few."*

Sandy sighed, as Gustavius parked the car alongside the carpark elevators. "Maybe your security would be that much better if you didn't talk so much," she suggested.

*"Oh nonsense,"* said Anita, *"I don't care if he knows who we are. As it turns out, I'm checking files here, and we part-own his employer. So if he'd like to keep his job . . ."*

Gustavius's eyes widened further as the car's gull-doors hummed upward. "Oh shit, Raj-Bhaj Systems!" And accusingly to Sandy, "I didn't know you knew Anita Rajana and Pushpa Bhajan!"

"There's a lot of things you don't know, Gustavius. Keep it to yourself or they'll ruin your life."

"Oh baby, I know, I know!" He nodded vigorously. "Hey, my code's real good, ask anyone on the Basti-Net, I worked for them, did some Razz Barriers and got them out of about twenty-K in network tax . . ." Nervously avoiding Sandy's reprimanding gaze. "I mean, if you guys ever need a spare system-wrecker on the fringes, I'm your guy!"

"The deal was for transport, Gussi," Sandy told him, "not job opportunities."

"*We'll think about it*," said Anita. Which was enough, Sandy saw from the light in Chan's eyes, to make him think the evening hadn't turned out such a disaster after all.

"Oh great, thanks, thanks . . . hey, anything, anything at all, you won't be disappointed, trust me!"

Sandy got out, shaking her head. Waggled sardonic fingers at the enthusiastically waving Gustavius, and walked to the elevator as he drove off.

"*Was that smart?*" she said to Anita as the elevator doors sealed her in, formulating silently in her head on the local building network. It was bound to be secure, if Anita and Pushpa were using it.

"*What can it hurt, it never hurts to play a sucker, you never know what he'll cough up. Besides, we were moving the apartment in a few weeks anyway, no matter if something did leak. And it's not our only one.*"

No, Sandy thought drily, she didn't suppose it was.

"*You guys just like this cloak and dagger stuff far too much,*" she told Anita.

"*You can't talk, Ms. Please-help-me-I'm-in-trouble-again!*"

"*I get paid to be in trouble.*"

"*Semantic distinction, trouble means opportunity, opportunity means business, and I'm a business woman. So, what the hell happened to you this time?*"

The "apartment," Sandy saw as the doors opened to admit her, was actually an enormous penthouse suite that occupied the entire third-from-top floor. It was far less extravagant than some such places she'd seen, but well appointed all the same, with leather lounge suites, an enormous wall-TV, and modern art on the walls and counters. The entire far wall was in fact a window, beyond which the sheeting grey downpour gleamed multicoloured from the light of surrounding towers. The door automatically closed behind her, and Anita came in from one of the doorways on the right-hand wall. She wore loose, Indian-style salwar kameez pants and shirt, only these were threaded with luminescent stitching and colourful buttons, and a long, filmy sash about her shoulders that refracted shifting colour like gossamer thread. Even the fine hair of her shaven head seemed to gleam in the light, and the butterfly tattoos flapped their wings upon her eyelids when she blinked.

"Hello!" said Anita with characteristic brightness. "I'm so glad you're okay . . . would you like a drink? Something to eat? We've got food in the fridge if you haven't had dinner."

She gave Sandy a hug, then pulled back to look at her. Sandy's uniform shirt was torn on one sleeve and stained with dirt, grease from the parking-loader in the Prasad Tower, and several other things she couldn't identify herself. The boots were worse, though she had remembered to wipe her feet. Then Anita saw the cast on Sandy's left wrist and hand.

"That didn't happen on the way home," she remarked.

"No," said Sandy, "that was the first attempt on my life today. That was just guns and explosions, I can handle that. The second was the killswitch."

"I figured as much when you called," Anita said with concern. "What happened?"

Anita's friend Pushpa came out of the bedroom midway through the beginning of Sandy's explanation, then delayed them further by insisting on fetching Sandy a makani juice drink, and then both women sat and listened to the whole story.

"You're sure it was the killswitch?" Pushpa asked when she'd finished. "It knocked you unconscious, that sounds more like an infiltration key. Considering you're still here."

Her broad, brown face was creased with serious concern. Pushpa was the other half of the Raj-Bhaj partnership, both in business and life. Anita's friend since early school, Pushpa was slightly chubby, plain and understated. She now wore a dark blue salwar kameez, and her long, black hair was tied into a single plait down her back. Everything about Pushpa was sensible and practical. Between the two of them, they combined divergent personalities into a single, impressive operation that had made Raj-Bhaj Systems one of the most successful small-scale network operations in Tanusha.

"The infiltration key is a part of the system," Sandy said quietly. "Fast access, fast execution. Ari warned me about it last night. I downloaded a breaker circuit this morning just in case; it would disconnect that entire part of the network if I was infiltrated. Knocking me out in the process, but shutting down the network before the killswitch could activate."

"So you're saying that you owe your life to Ari," Pushpa said flatly.

"Yeah," Sandy sighed. "Bummer, huh?"

"Wouldn't wish it on my enemies," Pushpa replied. "He's on his way over, hope you don't mind."

"No avoiding it, I suppose." And she finally managed a faint smile at Pushpa past the deadpan. Pushpa smiled back that same faint smile reserved for private jokes. Many of which involved her old friend Ari.

"And you're certain it's someone in the government trying to kill you?" Anita pressed, far more wide-eyed about the situation than her partner.

Sandy sighed again. Ran her good hand through her dishevelled hair, and leaned back fully in her chair, stretching her stiffening spine. "I'm not certain about anything, 'Nita. Except that it's *very* hard to infiltrate Canas security. I can't do it, you guys can't do it . . ." Pushpa gave a faint, conceding shrug . . . which was a lot, coming from her. "And probably if we all pooled resources with a full dozen of Ari's old friends, we still couldn't do it. Which means it probably wasn't an infiltration."

"Someone was just following orders," Pushpa murmured, eyes

momentarily distant. Then snapped back onto Sandy with intent focus. "Then what about this big blowup in the maintenance bay?"

Sandy shook her head slowly. "I'm sure I have no idea. It was certainly pretty fucking ambitious, and required inside military knowledge and contacts. So I'm thinking the Fleet's gotta be in there somewhere. It was also pretty poorly executed . . . which could still be Fleet, they're into big-bang combat, none of this fancy sneaking around, it's beneath them. Mostly."

"Seems to me someone would have to be pretty angry to cause all that damage," Anita remarked. "Maybe it was more of a political statement. Maybe getting you was just a bonus for them."

"No shortage of people who hate the CDF," Pushpa agreed.

Sandy waved a dismissive hand. "So they blew my thumb off, big deal. I'm not as worried about that. It's the killswitch I can't defend myself against. If someone in the government wants me gone, and they've got *that* code . . . well."

Anita and Pushpa's stares were sombre. As CDF second-in-command, she was a government employee. A part of the system. If people higher up the system possessed the ability to erase her from the scene through the network alone, bypassing a GI's best natural defence—her combat skills . . . the silence said it all. Remaining anywhere within that system was a near-guaranteed death sentence. And until she knew which elements were trying to kill her, and why, it would be unwise in the extreme to let anyone within that system know where she was. Even loyal, trustworthy people might be monitored in ways they themselves didn't fully appreciate. Of all Sandy's inbuilt instincts, survival was foremost among them, and CDF/CSA protocols on such matters be damned.

"Buggered if I was going to let that ambulance fly me to a hospital of their choosing," she muttered then, reflecting for the first time. "Restrained and drugged. Fuck, *that's* what scares me—they should know me better, I *don't* like being restrained, least of all in a medical situation. It was like some total, outside ignoramus was giving the orders on where to take me and how to handle me . . . where the *fuck* was Ibrahim? Or Krishnaswali? Vanessa doesn't have command authorisation or capacity to intervene there even if she wanted to . . . but those two do. Couldn't they have figured what was happening, and how I'd react? The whole damn thing just feels like . . . like a *setup*."

Now she was scaring herself. She could see from Anita's expression that she wasn't alone in that. Pushpa just looked very, very serious.

"You . . ." Anita began breathlessly. "You don't think *Ibrahim* was involved?"

"No, I don't *think* that at all." She took a deep breath. Damn it, the combat-reflex wore off, and now the emotion came in a rush that threatened to reduce her to shakes. "It's just that the evidence tells me I sure as hell can't rule it out."

Ari was late, of course, arriving three hours later in a swirl of black coat and boots, darkened by brief exposure to the rain that was still falling gently outside. He strode across the wide penthouse floor toward where Sandy lay back on a reclining leather chair, hooked into various of Anita's processor systems by the slim connector cord in the back of her skull. Anita sat at her custom-designed, semicircular table, surrounded by monitor screens, a headset and goggles removing her from the immediate world.

"Hi, 'Nita!" Ari said loudly as he came over. "Don't startle, it's just me!"

"Ari," Anita replied just as loudly to hear herself above the plugs in her ears, "you could learn to be polite, you know, and *ask* to be admitted."

"No," said Ari, "you see, that's the first Tanushan rule of etiquette. Never ask for anything, just take it."

He bent over Sandy to kiss her on the cheek. The customary Ari Ruben worry, Sandy was surprised to see, was not evident. Just calm, businesslike concern. And he reached into his coat, pulled out an automatic pistol, and handed it to her. Sandy took it, checked the safety, dechambered a round and removed the magazine with rapid, reflex motion. It was nothing fancy—a Rohan-9, similar to what CSA Investigations used. Uplink targeting with armscomp interface and ID . . . though this one's ID was blank, ready for her to imprint her own signature. She checked it all with a brief uplink, sighted along the laser-targeting, found it millimetre precise against the penthouse's far wall.

"You realise that it's a violation for a CSA or CDF agent or officer to carry any weapon without formalised signature ID?" she remarked.

"That's . . . that's interesting." Ari scratched his head, a characteristic fidgety mannerism. "I actually realised, on the way over here, that all reality is the dreaming of a single subjective consciousness of which we are all a part in the broader cosmos."

"I like my realisation better," Sandy said flatly. "It's, like, relevant."

"Uninspired," Ari said with a distasteful shake of the head. "Unimaginative."

Sandy tucked the pistol into the pocket of the black jacket Anita had lent her. "Where'd you get it?"

"Why do you always want to talk shop?"

"Ari . . ." Warningly.

"Sandy." Firmly. "Don't worry about it, I've got it covered. The less you know the better."

"The better for who?" Sandy muttered, gazing out at the night-lit glow of misting rain above the broad, flat bend of river. Gentle currents stirred the mirror surface, and the drizzle brushed a faint layer of static across the perfect, multicoloured reflections. Above, the overcast sky glowed shades of red, orange and white that became increasingly difficult to separate as she shifted visual spectrums. A grey overcast night was rarely grey, over Tanusha. Just as brown river waters were rarely brown, and clear, starry skies were rarely full of stars.

"Better for whom, my petal," Ari corrected, moving to look over Anita's shoulder. "Speak like a civilised person, not like a grunt."

"I am a grunt."

"Only in bed." Beneath her headset goggles, Anita grinned. Ari gave her a gentle whack on the headset. "What happened, 'Nita?"

"Whatever it was," Anita replied, "it went through her defensive barriers like butter. See here . . ." she pointed to one of the display screens, ". . . that's all League network code. Even if you haven't upgraded for a couple of years, it's still a solid wall to any Federation infiltration basecode yet invented."

"I do upgrade," Sandy replied, gazing out at the vista of lights. "I've got my own evolution formulas, I play with things occasionally. Borrow stuff from here and there to keep it fresh, sometimes invent my own. I wasn't infiltrated because my barriers are obsolete or anything."

"And you borrow stuff from Rhian, don't you?" Ari added. Sandy knew him well enough to recognise the note of disapproval immediately.

"Rhi's fine, Ari. She gets the latest League codes, it's more compatible."

"For someone who defected from the League, you've become very unquestioning of League assistance lately."

"You're not the only suspicious person in the galaxy, Ari," Sandy replied. "I check everything."

"It had to be League code," said Anita, flipping up her goggles to gaze at the actual readout displays, abandoning the mobile viewpoint for a moment. "And it doesn't seem to have left any traces that I can see. Nothing we can give you that might give warning."

"Which means I'm vulnerable pretty much everywhere," Sandy confirmed. "If they know it's me, and can establish a two-way connection, I can get killed."

"Well . . ." Anita chewed on her lip, thinking it over. "Theoretically maybe. But a breaker code that powerful can't just operate off a mobile or independent source. And GI barriers are still incredible . . . I mean shit, I'm looking at your schematic here, Sandy, and considering that it's all League military-grade code supported by the most powerful neural interface known to biotech science, I'm totally screwed if I can see any way past it. Even independently designed *League* codework would struggle. No, in order to cut through these kind of defences so quickly, whatever that infiltration code was must have been designed on a parallel-track with your own network barriers, Sandy . . . and *those* had to be designed at the time *you* were being designed. Your brain, I mean . . . well, that is the only part of you that really counts. I mean, the one that makes you different from other GIs. Special. You know what I mean."

At another time, Sandy might have raised a semantic argument. "Sure," she said instead.

"You're saying," Ari said with a frown, "that she was initially designed, from conception, with a pathway integrated into the base-codes of her network defences that would allow for . . . for . . . instant infiltration?"

"Of a parallel-designed infiltrator, yes," Anita said with a short, certain nod.

"Don't make a poison without an antidote," Sandy said mildly. Ari and Anita just looked at her.

"Anyway," Anita resumed, "assassins can't just launch killer infiltrators blind down the network, unless they're very messy. And if these guys are political, then they can't afford to make too many mistakes, right? So they'll need to absolutely, clearly identify you. So the first thing we can do is confuse your ID signature, change your communication codes, that kind of thing. Make them wonder if it's really you, that should make them think twice.

"The other thing is that you shouldn't stay uplinked to the same connection for too long, that's just asking for them to find you. And be aware of the signatures around you—like I said, an infiltrator this powerful must operate off a powerful hardware system. Those big signatures are the ones you look out for, I doubt you'd be in danger from smaller systems. But if connecting to a smaller system, make sure it's not proxy-rigged or otherwise location-tracked to another, foreign system. That could just be bait, to lure you out."

"Or," said Ari, "you could hark back to the many, many centuries of human civilisation when people didn't have direct neural uplinks, and just not use them. People did manage it, I'm told, for entire lifetimes without going insane or withering mentally away . . ."

"They're lying," Anita retorted. "History's always written to make past ages look quaint and romantic. Life without neural uplinks must have sucked, Ari. You of *all* people should know that."

Pushpa emerged from the bedroom, pushing loose straggles of dark hair back into place. "Hi, Ari."

"Hi, Push. What's the neighbourhood look like?"

"No sign of it yet, news has yet to hit the media." She folded her arms, stopping at Ari's side to gaze at the hemispherical arrangement of screens. "I'd say you've got three hours, maybe four, tops. That long for the media to do their research, and then go basically nuts."

Ari looked concerned. "Why so soon? What's out there?"

"Independent reports of some commotion up the top of Prasad Tower," said Pushpa, with a critical eye at Sandy's reclining seat before the broad windows. "Some security guards chasing a blonde woman into the carpark mechanism."

All three of them raised their eyebrows at Sandy. Sandy gazed out the windows.

"Then someone several net-loggers presumed to be the same woman leaping from the top of the carpark exit," Pushpa continued. Eyebrows raised higher. "And then I did a broad sweep that found someone chatting about, like "holy shit, this person fell out of the sky and landed on our express elevator coming down the side of Prasad Tower this evening! Then jumped off and ran away as we reached the ground!" Several more clever people appeared to be putting two and two together. Straight humans don't jump out of towers very often. And live, anyway."

All three were now looking at Sandy with varying degrees of amazement, concern, or in Ari's case, mild exasperation.

"Poor Sandy," Ari remarked. "It's just no damn fun being a GI, is it, Sandy?"

"Shut up, Ari," Sandy sighed. "I was trying to get away clean, break from the network. I didn't see another way."

"Landing on an elevator full of people on the way down. Very inconspicuous."

"Damn it," Sandy retorted, "word would have got out about the attack in the maintenance bay anyway, I would have had to go underground at some point. This just accelerates the process a few days. I don't mind the media. I think it might help."

"The media? Help?" Ari looked incredulous, and walked around to the front of Sandy's reclining chair to look her in the face. Sandy looked up, reluctantly. "This is Tanusha, Sandy. The media don't help! Ever! You don't think maybe the hysteria of having some mad GI loose in the city will play right into the hands of all the conservative morons who said we should have locked you away and shipped you off to Earth when we had the chance?"

"They don't know for sure it's me," Sandy said calmly.

"There just aren't that many blonde, female GIs in League service in this city, Sandy . . ."

"Ari," she cut him off, "the population's gotten wiser than you think. Certainly the analysts have. There's old-guard League active too, we don't know if they have the odd GI about. Or it might have been new-guard League GIs behaving badly and running around outside the embassy. People will be concerned. They will contact the government, and the CDF, to check on my whereabouts and status. To which Krishnaswali and co. can either outright lie," she ticked off a finger on her good hand, "or they can obfuscate and mislead, thus creating even more confusion and questions of what they have to hide, or they can tell the truth—that they don't know, and that someone tried to kill me.

"There are people in the general public out there who actually like me, Ari. They'll question why the government can't protect me, why I felt I had to go totally underground . . ."

"They won't know that, Sandy, no one will know anything about where the hell you are."

"I'll make a statement." Flatly. Ari was frowning hard, arms folded. A dark, stylish figure, radiating disapproval. "To everyone—government, CSA and CDF. If they don't relay it, I'll tell it straight to the media."

"Damn it, Sandy . . . you'd . . . you'd break the chain of command?"

"When did Mr. Anti-Establishment get so damn conservative?" she asked him with a faint, creeping smile. Ari blinked in disconcertion . . . partly at her words, she guessed, but partly at the smile, too. She knew what that smile looked like, when she was in this mood. It was neither cuddly, nor amused. "The establishment is the problem, Ari, you said it yourself. As long as I played by their rules, I was a sitting duck and they'd have the upper hand. I'm going to let them know that the old rules no longer apply. Let them sweat. Maybe push them a little. Make them wonder just how far I'll go. Maybe they'll make a mistake."

"And how far will you go?"

Sandy reclined back into her seat, and let her gaze slide back over the broad stretch of river. "As far as I need to," she said.

Click, and the line opened. Connection established, with Anita's new ID signatures to confuse the receiver. Sandy waited, reclined on her chair by the penthouse windows, eyes fixed upon the flatscreen wall TV. Rami Rahim was doing his usual show, handsome and flamboyant, in cool clothes on a colourful set. The audience howled at a joke, beyond her immediate attention.

"*Hello.*" A cautious voice at the other end of the connection. A real voice, vocal cords and all, not a simulated formulation.

"Vanessa. It's me." She spoke aloud herself. Internal formulations could be simulated. Vocals could be too, of course, but good friends could tell the difference in the tones and inflections. Theoretically. Tojo's fingers massaged her wet hair, the towel about her neck keeping water from running down her spine.

*"Sure it's you. A little proof, please."*

"I still think you were wrong to dump Rudy. He had potential. You're just obsessive about small personal details."

*"Sure, I heard that once upon a time they believed in electro-shock therapy, maybe that'd cure a compulsive dullard. Do you need anything?"*

"I'm fine, thanks. How secure is this reception?"

*"It complies with Ari's specifications."* With dry irony. *"Sorry I took so long to set up, it's been a little crazy around here. Krishnaswali tried to keep me out of it, but Hitoru told me about the ambulance, and then your new secretary Private Zhang let me hook into his loop."* Sandy blinked in astonishment. Maybe the kid really *would* have his uses. Certainly he had guts, Krishnaswali could have busted him down to storeroom duty if he'd found out. *"Then Naidu let slip about the whole thing at Prasad Tower. Apparently his buddy Chandaram told him some interesting things about what you'd said before the skydiving act . . . I had a look at the map and guessed where you'd end up.*

*"Sandy, Krishnaswali dragged me into his office and chewed me out real good. He ordered me to tell you to return to duty at once, knew damn well you'd contact me. Wasn't stupid enough to ask me to turn you in if you refused, though."*

Vanessa's calm, rational tone filled Sandy with relief. She'd been half-expecting the occasionally irrational, emotional Vanessa Rice, filled with concern and worry. But Vanessa Rice, she sometimes forgot, was also the third-in-command of the CDF.

"What do you think about Krishnaswali?" she asked Vanessa.

*"Damn, I don't know. That's one of those nasty political questions, right?"*

"Isn't everything?"

*"Fucking nightmare,"* Vanessa muttered. On the TV screen, Rami Rahim was now doing his Fleet Admiral Duong impersonation . . . something about having had lunch with him just the other day, only to find he couldn't have any baartroot on his daal and rice, because the Fleet deemed baartroot too progressive. Most of Rahim's routines began with "I did lunch with such-and-such the other day." Tanushans always "did" lunch, even with family. The mostly young audience were

in stitches. *"Krishnaswali's so busy crawling up various politicians' arseholes it's difficult to tell what his actual opinion is."*

"We can't trust him?"

*"Silly question. Sandy, I got a call from your buddy Sudasarno, wanting to know what the hell's going on. Apparently your friendly President is very concerned. She has a meeting with Admiral Duong and Secretary General Benale in two days' time, and both of them are going to want to know what's going on with you. Ironic, I know, since those two bastards are among the prime suspects who'd want you dead, but I've yet to see a political operator in this city who couldn't talk bullshit with a straight face."*

"I don't know that they're the prime suspects, that list is too long to start picking favourites at this stage." Rahim was now in a pitched battle across the lunch table with the Admiral over the baartroot grinder. Admiral Duong pulled a gun and shot the baartroot stone dead. "Look, I've got a few of the usual suspects here helping check leads for me."

*"That's nice of them."* A little warily. Vanessa liked Ari, Anita and that particular crowd just as much as Sandy did. They'd certainly been frequent enough visitors at the house over the last two years. But, like Sandy, she had her own suspicions about motivations on matters like this.

"Yeah, well, you know this lot, they like their fun and games. Ricey, here's a couple of things. First, you take care. If people are after me, we can't assume they won't make the connection between me and you, which would make you target number two."

*"I know, I'm at Hitoru's apartment now. I've told everyone concerned about the Canas security . . . it's caused quite a stir, some VIPs are suddenly wondering if they should sleep in their own beds tonight."*

"I know, we're watching that too. Interesting to see which VIPs are concerned and which aren't. Those that aren't might know something."

*"Good thinking."*

"Ari's idea. So you haven't been home? What about Jean-Pierre?"

*"Oh no, I brought him too! You wouldn't think I'd abandon my baby,*

*would you?"* Sandy smiled. On the screen, Rami had launched into a frothing Fleet Admiral diatribe about the evils of baartroot, tight pants and VR pornography, the right hand occasionally snapping up in a Nazi salute, to be dragged hastily back down by the left hand, apparently without Rami's notice. Amazing how something as old as Nazism remained an historical reference point so many centuries later. Time faded some memories, and enhanced others, it seemed. His audience, having doubtless bottled up much fear and confusion in recent months about the Fleet presence in orbit, were letting all the tension out in a rush—some of them were nearly falling out of their chairs laughing. It was, Sandy observed, a curious civilian reaction to stress. And a much preferable one to some of the alternatives.

"The other thing is that you're now in charge of the CDF on the ground."

*"I know."* There was, for the first time, a brief pause. *"So what are you going to do?"*

"I've got some leads. Or I'm in the process of getting some, rather. Some things here don't make sense, and I think that if I can find out why, it'll tell me what the hell's going on."

*"Sandy?"* Another pause, waiting for a reply.

"Yes?"

A longer pause. Then *". . . Never mind. Take care of yourself. I've got some calls to make, all the senior officers need to be rebriefed."*

"Okay. Love you."

Again the pause. "Yeah, me too." Then a click as the line went dead. Sandy frowned. Two years she'd been acclimatising to civilian surroundings and civilian thinking, but still she often had that feeling she'd missed something. Something another natural-born civilian wouldn't have missed. Tojo had finished rinsing her hair into the bowl on the desk-edge behind her head, and now produced a hair drier.

"And how's the lovely Vanessa doing?" Tojo asked over the whistle of the drier, teasing out her wet hair with a brush.

"She's a lot like me—the more dangerous it gets, the calmer she becomes. She's fine with the bullets flying around, but if she burns her toast or stains a good blouse, it's best to just leave the vicinity for a while."

"You're too hard on her," Tojo retorted, in his characteristic deep singsong. That, plus his taste for personal decoration, had raised the hopes of many a single gay man before . . . but Tojo, to the great disappointment of many, was married (to a woman) with two children. Still, he was Anita's obvious first choice for Sandy's makeover—Tojo was a fashion designer with his own small, exclusive label. There were hundreds of such in Tanusha, Sandy had gathered. They had their own wild, underground scene, private fashion shows for the knowledgeable "in-crowd," decadent parties and plenty of designer VR or chemical stimulant. The dull, predictable, market-driven "mainstream" were definitely not invited. Although, of course, where the "underground" left off, and the "mainstream" began, was a matter for constant and acrimonious debate.

"She's my best friend, I'm allowed to be hard on her."

"No, you're not." Tojo gave her a gentle, backhanded whack on the shoulder. "You mean so much to her, Sandy, sometimes I just don't think you realise how much. I mean, just because she's so confident and gregarious in most things, it doesn't mean she's like that with everything. Underneath, she's really very soft and fragile."

Sandy tipped her head back to look up at him. "So am I."

Tojo rolled his eyes with a smile, and gave a shake of his head. The penthouse light caught the gleaming gold of an earring, brilliant against his black skin. There were likewise gleaming studs through lips and nose, and faint traces of lavender eyeshadow that shone with holographic depth, a curious effect against the reflective curve of his shaved scalp.

"That's a new earring," Sandy remarked. "That's a Catholic cross, right?"

"I don't suppose there are many other kinds," Tojo retorted.

"But you're not a Catholic."

"Nor even a Christian, I'm afraid."

"It doesn't bother you to be appropriating a symbol of deep spiritual meaning for billions throughout the Federation?"

"The most meaningful symbols are always the best to appropriate, that's how artistic statements are made."

"So you've taken the symbol of humankind's salvation at the hands of the Christian Messiah," Sandy continued implacably, "and turned it into a fashion statement."

"Of course." Tojo shrugged. "The spirit of artistic challenge to the powers of the day should know no fear, Cassandra, and no boundaries."

"And the fact that there's hardly any Catholics in Tanusha to get pissed at you is just coincidence, huh? When's one of your artistic buddies going to do a sculpture of some Hindu deity screwing a goat? In the true spirit of artistic subversiveness? I bet he'd make a pretty cool sculpture himself, hanging from a tree by his heels with his head shoved up his arse."

"You," Tojo said cheerfully, "are *such* a cynic."

"No, I just vote differently to you."

"An anti-League, cultural-conservative android," Tojo sighed. "You know, I think you're just trying to be complicated in order to impress me."

"Uh-uh, I've decided I find the term 'android' demeaning and insulting. I'm an artificial person, if you please, or a GI."

"You're a wonderful pain in the arse," Tojo retorted, teasing out her last wet piece of fringe.

"That sounds kinky," said Sandy.

"It is if you do it right." Tojo turned off the drier. "Come on, up." Sandy moved from her seat, following Tojo to a floor-to-ceiling mirror upon the penthouse wall near the entrance, where guests could check their appearance before heading out the door, Sandy guessed. "Well," said Tojo, with theatrical pleasure. "What do you think?"

Sandy looked herself over in the mirror. The first, pleasing thing to notice was that she hardly recognised herself. Her hair, for one thing, was now jet black. The obligatory dark coat came down to her knees—Tojo had suggested the longer, leather one was more stylish, but Sandy had insisted on the one that wouldn't entangle her legs, and had plenty of strategically located pockets. Beneath that, a thick, dark shirt tucked into comfortably soft, black, hard-wearing pants, made of some denim-like material she couldn't identify. And light ankle-boots of flexible fit . . . they were new, Tojo had warned her, and would chafe a new occupant. But Sandy had assured him it wasn't likely to be a problem for her.

"Hmm," was Sandy's only immediate comment.

She strolled closer to the mirror, pushing at her hair—she kept it midlength these days, which for her meant just above the collar at the back, but full enough to have body. The black fringe brushed above pale blue eyes that had never known another fringe but blonde . . . and Tojo, thorough professional that he was, had even done the eyebrows.

"I mean it's hardly glamorous," Tojo remarked, regretfully. "I wish you'd let me dress you up *properly* one of these days, Sandy. You're such a pretty girl, it's a shame to let it all go to waste in drab black and jungle green uniforms."

"I'm too broad," Sandy replied. "You're looking for a drag queen, all limbs and no hips. Boys make better drag queens than girls; that's what happens when you let homosexual men define feminine sexuality."

"Oh go on, you'd look *wonderful* in a side-cut hip skirt and a short top."

"Talk to Rhian, she's got the time and the inclination."

"Now, how on earth does that happen?" Tojo wondered, hands on hips, the fall of his sparkling satin-red shirt suggesting an all-too-masculine bulge of muscle within. "Two combat GIs from the League come to Tanusha, and it's the supposedly more advanced, adventurous, lateral-minded one who doesn't know a blouse from a T-shirt, while the supposedly less advanced, single-minded one becomes this wonderful, glamorous Chinese princess!"

"Easy," said Sandy. "Fashion is for narrow-minded people who think appearance is important."

"You'd have to be narrow-minded to think it wasn't! What do you think evolution's all about, sweetie, all those pretty birds flashing their mating feathers? Survival of the species, Sandy, we're designed for it!"

"You're designed for it. I was designed with other things in mind." She wrapped the coat about herself, and turned a calculating gaze on her tall, elegant friend. "Wars tend to change your perspective, Tojo. You see things that make you wonder what really matters."

"Rhian was a soldier too," Tojo objected.

"Sure. She was a damn good one too, but she *never* stopped to contemplate what it was all about. She never saw the big picture. She just did it and moved on."

"Well, I don't think of you as a soldier anyway, Sandy," said Tojo, placing a hand on each of her shoulders. "You're just a passionate, spirited, darling girl, and to me, that's all you'll ever be."

Sandy hugged him. It was, she reflected with her face against his chest, the nicest thing anyone had said to her for at least a month. Tojo hugged her back, then released her to hold her shoulders once more.

"So," he pressed, "what about the outfit? Do I pass the cloak and dagger subterfuge test?"

"With flying colours," Sandy told him with a smile. "I'll take it."

# CHAPTER 7

Ari sidestepped his way briskly through the crowd on Rue Bercy, headed from the metro station toward number 1489, which his observation of street numbers above building doorways told him should be several blocks up ahead. The crowds grew even thicker, a sea of humanity across a four-lane road that would normally be filled with evening traffic. The Rue Bercy cafe and restaurant staff manned the front of their premises, customary tables and chairs cleared well back from the moving throng lest they be overturned or swept away.

It was not a uniform protest by any means, Ari observed as he strode, hands thrust deeply into the pockets of his long coat. There was no single chant, no collective purpose nor apparent organisation, just a varied diffusion of different people in different kinds of clothes, some carrying placards, some shouting in accompaniment to a nearby audiophone, some singing, and some merely marching, simply to be there, and to take part. Rue Bercy was one of Tanusha's more popular nightlife streets, particularly here where it ran through the downtown mid-high-rise of Quezon district in northwestern Tanusha. The road ran long and mostly straight for several kilometres. As far as Ari could see, the entire length was now filled with a slow-moving river of people.

Ahead, a major intersection bore an enormous, ten-by-ten metre holographic display screen that appeared to project its brilliant image in three dimensions a full two metres out from the building wall. There was no sound, but the prominently displayed name of the electronics company beneath the screen also advised of quality uplink sound as well . . . Ari allowed his own uplink to browse the local advertising frequencies, and the screen freq was most obvious among them.

"*. . . and you can see when we zoom in here,*" a newsperson was saying, "*that this small dot coming down the side of the tower is actually a person.*" Ari frowned up at the enormous screen. As he reached a better viewing angle on the screen, the image began to make sense. A soaring, megarise tower in late evening, airtraffic passing in random flares of light, and a circular portion of the screen image graphically enlarged to track the progress of a small, fast-moving dot that hurtled down the tower's side. A dot with limbs. Limbs that were not flailing in frantic panic, as might be expected from someone falling off a tower. A large section of the crowd on the street were pausing to watch, blocking the path of those behind—luckily there were other screens, large and small, at various points ahead and behind, to prevent a major pileup.

"*Now whoever this person is,*" the newsperson continued, "*he or she seems to have had some skydiving experience before . . . see the way they're leaning to control the direction of descent? And now here . . . here comes the fun part. See this express elevator?*"

They'd been running this image for the last four hours, along with unconfirmed reports of Commander Kresnov's disappearance, but even so, Ari could feel the surrounding crowd take in a collective breath. The screen image looked like it might be some kind of security or airtraffic monitor, accidentally catching sight of something it wasn't designed for. The hurtling freefaller closed on the side of the tower, almost hitting it, then smacked onto the top of the racing elevator. Exclamations rose from the street, both alarmed and excited. A group of young people started chanting "Kresnov! Kresnov!" over and over, as if she were a star of the latest Bushido championships. Some others booed them.

"Pity she didn't kill herself!" someone shouted loudly, and was in turn greeted by a chorus of protests and cheers. Ari was marginally surprised that the protests were louder.

Animated debate erupted across sections of the crowd, then others marching from behind started to push through, breaking up the congestion and starting the procession flowing again.

"If it hadn't been for Kresnov," someone yelled a parting blow, "Earth would have torn us to pieces by now!" And that got more cheers than boos.

Such was the debate among the public, Ari reflected as he resumed walking. Earth versus Callay. Earth versus the Federation. And no wonder all the old anti-League people were increasingly worried that all the anti-homeworld feeling might translate into an increasingly pro-League sentiment . . . particularly when much of the anti-homeworld movement rallied so strongly around Callay's most prominent defender against the predations of the powerful, arrogant homeworld—Cassandra Kresnov, an ex-League GI. Earth was not yet a bogeyman to rival the scale of the League. "The enemy of my enemy is my friend?" Ari wondered. No. Not yet. But maybe soon, if things continued this way.

Number 1489 Rue Bercy was a midsized office tower. Ari walked along the broad, paved pathway between gardens, uplinks scanning the surrounding network. On a whim, he tried a broadscan, the kind of wide-ranging interface that Sandy performed so reflexively in this environment . . . the sheer scale was overwhelming, a profusion of fixed and mobile links, data-nodes and multidirectional traffic. On a purely visual level, it was a whole universe of gleaming, pulsing light. On a data-specific schematic, the sheer volume of information came crashing in like a wave, and even his automated processing software protested at the required parameters. He shook his head in disbelief, cancelling that scan and reverting to his more familiar, site-specific searches before he lost balance and started staggering. How Sandy did it, he had no idea. What must it look like to her? Psychologically, she was as human as anyone. How was that possible, given the mental complexity required to process such enormous data-flows? Surely there must be some overlap between the conscious self and the subconscious processes? And he recalled, momentarily, those times on peaceful evenings, when he could come home to find her reading in her comfortable chair with some music on the audio, and that distant look in her eyes, as if she were in some far removed mental dimension that he could never reach nor comprehend . . .

And then she would look up at him, with those calm blue eyes, and smile. There was something in that smile that still took his breath away and baffled his better judgement.

At the revolving door to 1489's foyer, where no one should be at this hour, stood a man in a suit, watching him. Ari kept walking, betraying no surprise, mentally rehearsing the tape-taught impulse to rip the pistol from its holster within his jacket and pull the trigger. From the man's posture, it took little guesswork to figure he was doing the same. But Ari had faith in his own tape-teach. He got his neural tech from a place most suit-wearing heavies in Tanusha couldn't access. Then the man seemed to recognise him.

"Ruben?" Ari's uplink registered an incoming ID signature, tentatively offered. He accessed . . . and damn it all, it was CSA Intel. It was the first time in nearly twelve months that Intel had beaten him to a site. Egotist that he was, Ari didn't like it. He offered his own ID back, pausing at a safe distance. And watched the Intel man's eyes widen at the signature.

"Curious coincidence to find Intel here," Ari remarked. "What's the occasion?"

The man shrugged. "No occasion. Did Ibrahim send you?"

Ari smiled, strolling closer. Regular CSA always asked that question. "No, no, I just have his authority. He's too busy, he doesn't direct me around." In other words, he could do what he liked, on his own initiative, with Ibrahim's personal blessing. Go places. Bend rules. The suit's eyes widened a little further.

"Why are *you* here?"

"You first."

An unconvincing shrug. "No reason. Just making sure the damn protesters don't leave the road."

Ari cocked his head on one side, and made a face. "Why don't you contact whoever your boss is, up on the seventeenth floor there, and ask if he'd be so kind as to let me in. Callsign Googly. I'm sure he'll make an exception."

The seventeenth floor was dark but for the blaze of night light through the broad windows overlooking the office space of desks, terminals and partitions. Ari strolled along an aisle between desks, moving aside for Intel personnel with projection cameras and spectrum analysers. There were at least twenty Intel present, he counted, sweeping exposed surfaces with pulsing blue light, treading carefully on the single lines of red tape along the aisles, denoting a "safe" surface, free from clues to be spoiled. Much of the activity was centred near the broad windows, where four scanner wands composed the corners of a rectangular space, four metres by two. A spectrum shift into ultraviolet showed the faintly pulsing, rotating waves of laser-light, scanning methodically over the intervening space. The result, in short order, would be a three-dimensional, multispectrum graphical picture. Hopefully it would reveal clues. To one side of the scanning rectangle, Ari recognised the chief investigator, in dark blue suit and tie, flanked by several others as he gazed upon the scene within the scanner parameters.

Ari walked over, and finally saw what lay within—two bodies, bloody and broken. Only then did he realise that the pale tinge to many surrounding faces was not just the absence of immediate light. He paused, forcing himself to peer more closely at the human carnage that lay between windows and desks. The pool of blood appeared a surreal, luminescent blue. Entrails . . . well, they all tended to look the same, in any light. And he was annoyed when he felt his own stomach begin to twist and complain. The chief investigator looked over at him.

"Mr. Ruben," said Anil Chandaram. "What brings you here?"

"I thought I had a lead on a contact," Ari replied. He strolled to Chandaram's side. The woman who presently occupied that space wisely vacated it. "Now I have the, um, nasty feeling one of those two . . ." he pointed to the mess, ". . . might have been it. There are two?"

"Yes." Chandaram nodded grimly. "Just two. I wasn't sure myself when I first saw it."

An impact stain showed briefly upon the window opposite the mess, illuminated by rotating laser-light. Ari frowned, peering closer . . . and saw blood on the corner of one partition. And gathered in small globules on the fronds of a leafy potplant by a workdesk. This work hadn't been dragged in from elsewhere. It had happened on the spot.

"GI, huh?" Ari observed with a very profound sinking feeling. Chandaram nodded.

"Couldn't be much else. This was done with just a couple of blows, but there's no collateral damage, nothing else broken, no sign of forced entry, no one lugging heavy equipment, no blood trails . . ." He shrugged. "Two people, standing close together, turned into that . . ." with a nod toward the gruesome object of attention, ". . . within the space of a second or two."

"Not even flung across the room," said the man on Chandaram's other side, who Ari did not recognise.

"If a GI hits you hard enough," Ari replied, "the fist goes straight through you." Both men looked at him. Ari decided against telling them that Sandy had informed him of that particular fact, in no uncertain terms, during one of their debates over sexual positions. He shoved both hands deep into his pockets, and glanced distractedly out the windows. On the street below, the vast river of protesters continued to march past, alive with banners, waving lights and occasional fireworks. A media cruiser hovered nearby, running lights flashing on special privilege from Traffic Central. Little wonder Chandaram hadn't turned the lights on at floor seventeen—no one wanted to draw attention to this crime scene just yet. Particularly not with the evidence lying in plain view of the windows, and media cruisers going up and down nearby, covering the march. "You have an ID?"

"We think the one on the bottom is Devon Mitchell." "Dewon," Chandaram pronounced it, with his Indian-Tanushan accent. Anglo names weren't the most common in Tanusha, where Europeans were barely twenty percent of the population, and Anglos only forty percent of those. "He's an employee here at Sigill Technologies, services division management. We got a call an hour ago, telling us to . . ." Across the office floor, someone finally lost control of their stomach, and vomited. "Look, for god's sake people," Chandaram said in loud exasperation, "the bathroom is just down there. We've got enough problems trying to manage the crime scene without you putting your dinner all over it! If you're going to lose it, go to the bathroom! Heroics just make you look more stupid, right?" With a hard glare at the shamefaced young Investigations woman who wiped her mouth and then ran fast for the bathroom . . . probably to throw up again and then get paper towels, Ari reckoned. Another man followed her. Then another.

Chandaram tucked his shirt in, mouth set with hard displeasure. "Anyway," he resumed, "we got a call an hour back from someone our voice analysis just matched to the same Devon Mitchell, telling us to meet him here, he had something very important to tell us. I got here forty-five minutes ago, and found this. The whole Sigill Technologies database has been fried by someone or something skilled and powerful.

We've got people looking, but it doesn't look like anything survived. I'm thinking that whoever Mr. Mitchell was about to expose could maybe have been employed here. Maybe a sleeper. Maybe that sleeper had the system bugged and monitored Mitchell's call, and got here before I did."

Ari hadn't had much experience working directly with Investigations—he was far more familiar with Chief Naidu's people in Intelligence. He only knew of Chandaram by reputation, as the guy most Intel people wanted to be working on their particular projects, when Investigations involvement was required. Sandy in particular had recommended him highly, having passed on much information on League network capabilities to Investigations, which Chandaram had used to unravel a large chunk of the old League regime's remaining underground network in Tanusha. Now, he was further impressed.

"Isn't that how Commander Kresnov first survived when she arrived in Tanusha?" Chandaram asked, appraising him with an offhanded look. "Taking a job in a technologies firm under false identification?"

Ari's return look was hard. Chandaram appeared not to notice. Loaded question, it was. Calling her "Commander Kresnov," knowing all too well the far less formal relationship between them. Not to mention the present situation. Ari knew exactly what he was being asked to do. And he didn't enjoy being used as a part of some other investigator's agenda. He wasn't sure Sandy would either.

"Sandy didn't come here looking for trouble," he replied in a low tone. "She was looking for peace and quiet. Whoever did this was differently motivated."

"I have nothing but respect for Commander Kresnov," Chandaram replied. "Not only is she a first-rate soldier and a patriotic Callayan, I also happen to think she's a very nice girl. I could use her help here."

"Secretary Grey's standing order is that she is absent without leave."

"Screw Secretary Grey," said Chandaram. Ari raised both eyebrows at the senior investigator. Chandaram's expression did nothing to indicate he was other than entirely serious. "The CSA's had to put up with that little shit for years as a sop to the hardliners on the left, since they're all so concerned that Ibrahim's a pro-League radical. He might dictate general policy, but I'll be fucked if I'm about to start taking direct orders from him. That's Ibrahim's job. If Grey doesn't like that, he can remove Ibrahim. But he doesn't have the balls."

Ari glanced about the office floor at that frank admission. Chandaram had spoken plenty loud enough for others to hear. All about, Investigations personnel continued about their business unfazed. Evidently they'd heard it all before, and were in total agreement. No question about it, he reflected silently, the pro-Earth, anti-League arseholes on the Left were right in one thing—the supposedly apolitical CSA was definitely *not* on their side. Figure that into any equation, when the shit really hit the fan.

Ari took a deep breath, and decided to divulge some information. "We're working on some leads. This was one—I got it from the maintenance bay ambush. There was a trace of code left over that matched some Sigill Technologies work when we ran a scan. I've been trying to find a certain sleeper for the last two months, haven't found a damn thing. This might be it . . . or maybe not. Maybe there's more than just this. I didn't even know it was a GI until now . . . so maybe this is something else entirely, I don't know."

"Old League?" Chandaram asked. "But how could it be?" he corrected himself. "Unless the old administration still has ties to the League's military apparatus?"

"That's Intel territory," said Ari, "not mine. Sandy thinks they'd like to, but the League military's going to be far too busy covering their arses for all the atrocities and other things that happened during the war. The investigations are still going on over there, plenty of heads have yet to roll. There're a lot of senior League officers too scared of their own government's review boards and investigations to be trying anything new against the Federation at this stage."

And he paused, chewing his lip to gaze distractedly out the windows once more. Chandaram waited with a frown.

"So what's the problem?" Chandaram finally asked.

"The sleeper I was looking for," said Ari, "was from Earth." Chandaram's frown grew deeper.

"Earth? That's like saying a fish is from somewhere in the ocean. Specifically?"

"I don't know. The FIA pretty much disintegrated last year with the Dali trials . . ." he shrugged, ". . . we'd be stupid to think that's all the old powers there ever had. They still haven't found half the old FIA leaders, after all. They're out there somewhere."

Chandaram blinked, eyes momentarily distracted, but not by the view. "And if this *is* the sleeper you're looking for?" Ari met his gaze, grimly. "A GI?"

"From Earth. Yes."

Chandaram pursed his lips with an inaudible whistle, and ran a hand through his black hair. "Have you told the Commander yet?"

"No." And forced a wry smile. "I'm about to."

"Good luck."

"No shit. And you guys thought I got all the best jobs, didn't you?"

"Major Ramoja says it's absolutely not one of ours." Rhian sat across the circular table from Sandy, back to the large potplant that spread its fronds above their heads. Multicoloured lights lit the dark, and wall-to-ceiling holographic displays shimmered with dancing shapes and figures about the dance floor. On the open floor itself, perhaps fifty young Tanushans were dancing (or thrashing, Sandy reckoned) to the thunderous, pounding beat.

"Not one of the reform government?" Sandy pressed. "What about the old Callahan administration?" She sat herself with her back to the wall, having selected the table in the furthest corner beside the rear staff door at the end of the bar. Tucked away amidst the confusion of light and bodies, the odds of being recognised seemed pleasingly slim. Except, of course, if one of the people who habitually tailed Rhian about the city saw them together. The dark shades felt slightly ridiculous upon her face either way, but it *was* a legitimate Tanushan "look," particularly for someone going for the head-to-toe "noir" she presently was. The dark tints were just another layer of distraction for her visual shifts to cut through, in this environment.

Rhian shrugged, lean and svelte in a tight leather jacket and stretch pants. "He says both. The ISO knows where all the League's GIs are. That's what he told me. And there's not one running wild in Tanusha at the moment." And she paused. Made eye contact past Sandy's shades, with a faint smile. "Or at least there's not *another* one."

"What do *you* think?" Sandy asked her pointedly. Rhian's mild expression never changed.

"I'm just a humble operative. I'm learning the rules of the Intelligence game, they're rather different from spec ops. I do what I'm told and try not to think too much."

"I don't believe that any more than I believe the ISO knows where all the League's GIs are." She took a small sip of her makani-and-vodka—it wouldn't do to be seen in such a club without drinks. Sobriety, in these surroundings, was always suspicious. "Have you heard anything about this Cognizant Systems?"

"Renaldo Takawashi?" Rhian said, surprised. "Sure, the Embassy's helping to organise the entire tour. It's been very popular among a lot of the Tanushan biotech companies. And a lot of the local health authorities, especially those in neurology. Do you think that's connected somehow?"

"I'm damn suspicious, that's what. Ari found out about the killswitch at that big function thrown by Cognizant Systems. His usual contacts among League-friendly techies, I don't doubt. Now there's talk of another GI loose in the city. One that Ari says he's been chasing for a long time

. . . or has suspected of existing, anyhow. One from Earth. How does any Earth-based organisation make an advanced GI? And why does *that* timing tie in so neatly with someone trying to use the killswitch to kill me? I'll bet anything there's a connection to Cognizant Systems in this, and Takawashi in particular. And I bet Ari knows it too."

"Ari hasn't told you?" Rhian sounded quite surprised.

Sandy repressed a tired, not-entirely-happy smile. "Rhi, there's a lot Ari doesn't tell me. I've learned the hard way not to bother asking."

"I would," said Rhian with certainty. "If I were him."

"You're not him," Sandy challenged. "How do you know what you'd do?"

"Priorities," said Rhian. Sandy gazed at her for a moment. And decided not to tackle *that* one right at this moment. Ari and Vanessa weren't the only two confusing people in her life.

"All right," she said instead, "what does Ramoja think about this rogue GI? Does he have any ideas?"

"None that he told me. Except to say that it's theoretically possible that the FIA were developing some kind of secret laboratory somewhere, there were rumours about it during the war. A laboratory experimenting with GI technology."

"The Federation doesn't *have* any damn GI technology, Rhi," Sandy said in frustration. "If the FIA had that kind of knowledge, they wouldn't have devoted so much effort during the war to finding new ways of killing GIs."

"Maybe they recovered a body," Rhian countered. "A corpse. Maybe they patched it together, found a way to make it work."

"Gee, the Frankenstein solution, what a comforting thought." Sandy was grateful the idea was such a long shot—it gave her the creeps. The kind of creeps that probably only a GI could get. Or one with her imagination, anyhow.

"Frankenstein?" Rhian was frowning.

"A very old book," Sandy explained. "A crazy doctor creates a living being by stitching together the body parts of dead people. It doesn't work out real well. Find it in a library one day when you've got time, it'll explain a lot about why people are scared of GIs. Gave me nightmares when I read it."

Rhian looked troubled by that. "A book gave you nightmares?"

"You get nightmares too, surely?"

"Sure." Still the troubled look, eyes fixed frankly upon hers. Honest and open, in a way she rarely found with straights. Except Vanessa, anyhow. "I had nightmares in the war. You know when." Sandy remembered an incident with dead civilians, and a little girl dying in Rhian's arms. And other incidents besides. "I still have night-mares, sometimes. About that time, and other things." A cloud then seemed to lift from her dark, oriental eyes. "There are children at the Embassy. I play with them sometimes. They like that. I don't think they've ever known a GI who plays with them."

No, Sandy didn't suppose they would have. Certainly she couldn't picture the trim, clipped and proper Major Mustafa Ramoja taking the time to play games with children, whatever his supposedly superior mental faculties.

"What do you play with them?" Sandy asked, gazing at her.

"There's a swimming pool," said Rhian with a glow of pleasure. "I like to swim. I give the children lessons, sometimes. And sometimes we have races, and sometimes we throw a ball around, or dive for things on the bottom." Sandy smiled, finding that strangely very easy to picture. And how ironic, that the very same patience, even temper and precise attention to detail that had made Rhian Chu such an effec-tive soldier, would also make her one of the galaxy's best childminders. "I really like children, Cap. Do you think they'd let me have one?"

Sandy nearly spat out her next mouthful of drink. And blinked at her old friend in astonishment. "Have one?"

"You know. A child." Rhian seemed perfectly serious. And Sandy found the time to wonder, briefly, how it was that every time she tried to talk immediate, serious business with Rhian, they ended up getting so utterly distracted.

"You don't think your total lack of a uterus or ovaries might mitigate against that?" she managed at last.

"I meant adoption," Rhian said patiently, as if she thought Sandy a little dense. "People at the Embassy tell me how good I am with children. They say their children talk about me, and say they like playing with me. I think I'd be a good mother."

"I think you'd be a great mother," Sandy agreed, wondering how the hell she was going to approach this one. It suddenly felt like she was back in the League once more, seated upon a bunk in quarters aboard a military station or warship, explaining to her troop of lower-designation GIs various things about the universe that she somehow understood, while they did not. She'd always been happy to oblige, then. And she was happy enough to advise her good friend. But now, something about it gnawed at her, frustratingly. "But you couldn't do it here. You'd have to go back to the League and ask for special consideration there. They don't let just anyone adopt, each case is judged on merits. And you'd be the first GI, if you asked."

Rhian thought about that for a moment. Then, "They won't let me, will they? I was designed to fight."

Sandy nodded, slowly. "That's right," she said, cautiously. "It's the kind of question the GI-advocates in the League never wanted asked. That's why they had most of our team killed. When there's no war, what are we for? It's okay with GI regs, they'd never want to do anything other than what they're told. But us higher-des GIs . . . we want to do other stuff. We want to make choices in life. Maybe we'll even want to adopt a child. So they're real scared of high-des GIs. Even Ramoja, I'm sure, despite all his denials. We could upset the entire League ideology—progress at no moral or ethical cost. They're chickenshit, Rhi, they think they can have it all without suffering the downside consequences. That's why there are so few of us."

Rhian frowned at the rim of her glass, tilting it about so that the liquid swirled just short of spilling. Flashing light caught the glass, made the bubbles gleam. The thumping beat made the surface jump and buzz. Without GI-standard hearing enhancement, the conversation would not be nearly so easy. But it was wonderful for covering their words against any potential spies, without forcing them to resort to uplinks . . . which for Sandy, given recent events, were at least hypothetically dangerous, even here. "What if I came here?" Rhian said then. "What if I joined the Federation? Became a citizen, like you?"

Sandy felt her breath catch in her throat. How many times had she suggested this to Rhian? Asked her flatly. Nearly demanded it, even. Her reasons then had been moral and political. But Rhian had been comfortable with what she knew best, where her life made the most sense. And it had been a comfortable arrangement. The best of both worlds, in fact—she could live with Sandy, and experience all the joys of the Federation, while still working for the League Embassy. Both sides got a vital conduit of intelligence and insight into the workings of the other, and the League government got Rhian out of their hair, away from where newly inquisitive League journalists and Parliamentary committees could ask her troubling questions about the fate of her teammates, and the reasons for her vaunted captain's defection. This sudden change of heart from Rhian was unexpected, to say the least.

Sandy took a deep breath. "You'd have a chance here," she said, nodding slowly. "In Tanusha, at least. The law here respects artificial sentience far more than the League. That's the irony, Rhi—this is exactly why the Federation opposes the creation of GIs. It wasn't right of the League to make you a soldier. They should have given you a choice to be whatever you wanted. By making you what they did, they violated your rights, do you understand that? My rights too. The creation of any GI, with a predetermined role in life, is an automatic violation of human rights."

"I like being a soldier." Rhian's gaze was utterly honest and calm amidst the blazing confusion of light and colour.

Sandy sighed. "Of course you do. You've never known anything else. But you've suffered for it. Haven't you?"

Rhian shrugged. "Major Ramoja says most civilians are unhappy because they don't know what their lives are for. So they come to places like this to dance and enjoy mind-altering substances . . ." with a nod toward the commotion on the dance floor, ". . . and then they go home at night, and have sex, and then go to work the next morning and repeat it all over again. After a while, they feel empty, like there's something missing. I don't have that. I know who I am. I know what I'm for. I don't have to wonder."

Sandy leaned forward on the table, tilting her head forward to fix Rhian with an intense gaze above the rim of her shades. "Then why do you want a child, Rhi? If you're so content?"

For the first time, Rhian blinked. And appeared, for a moment, slightly confused. "I'm good at it. Motherhood. Or I think I would be. Maybe it's like soldiering. Maybe it's just something I was meant to do. That's what it feels like."

Philosophy, from Rhian Chu. She never stopped surprising. Sandy knew that she ought to have been happy for her. This sudden desire for parenthood was unprecedented among GIs, as far as she knew. It marked a major milestone in her old friend's personal growth, and a groundbreaking one at that. But still something nagged, frustratingly. Something tense, and hard and urging to be let free.

"And what would you tell the child, Rhi?" she asked, leaning her chin upon a hard fist. "How would you explain what you are to an organic, un-synthetic child who has to live in a society very different to anything you've known?"

"I'd tell her the truth." With frowning earnestness. "Her," Sandy noted. So Rhian wanted a daughter. Somehow that didn't surprise her. "She'd accept that. Children accept anything. And she'd love me, and look up to me."

Sandy nodded slowly, her stare holding firm. "And when she looks up to you, how will you explain that she can't hope to measure up to your standards? That she'll never be so strong, or so capable? That if she tries the things you do, she'll only get hurt? What if she comes to fear that she'll never be able to truly make you proud?"

"She would." Rhian was slightly indignant now, the unflappable calm beginning to slip. "I wouldn't want her to be a soldier, she wouldn't be designed for it. She could do anything. I wouldn't care. So long as she was happy, I'd be happy."

"And what about when she gets teased, Rhi? When the kids say she's Frankenstein's daughter? When children she'd like to have as friends get told by their parents after school that her mother is a murderous killing machine with the blood of hundreds on her hands?"

"They wouldn't say that!" In a raised voice, now, a look that was not quite anger, not quite fear in her eyes. Dawning desperation. "They're not all like that. And those that are . . . I wouldn't let them say it!"

"How would you stop them? The whole planet's saying it, Rhian."

"I'd get her educated privately," Rhian said stubbornly. "She wouldn't need to get teased."

"And so she'd become isolated from other kids. Alone. The media would call her a freak. She'd hate them for saying bad things about her mother. She'd hate herself for causing you so much trouble. And you'd have to deal with your love for her being the thing that slowly tears her apart."

Rhian stared away at the dance floor, swallowing hard to restrain obvious emotion. If she weren't synthetic, Sandy reckoned her face might have flushed red. Her dark eyes shimmered with moisture, the upset of frustration. Or fear. Rhian Chu was fearful of little. Sandy leaned further forward across the table, her fist clenched tightly beneath her jaw.

"It's unfair what they did to us, Rhi," she said in a low, harsh voice. "We can't ever be entirely at home. We can't ever be entirely happy.

We serve society, but we can't ever entirely participate in it. We protect its benefits, but can't ever be allowed to entirely enjoy them. It's time you realised that. Realise what you are, and where you are, and stop assuming that everything will just be all right. D'you hear?"

Rhian looked back at her. Upset. Affected by her words, and her opinions, in a way that no straight ever would be. Sandy realised her fist was clenched painfully tight, and slowly relaxed it open, leaning back from the table. Rhian continued to stare at her, in helpless pain. Sandy took a deep breath, and found she was tight all over. Her gut hurt, and her shoulders were stiff and painful. The look on Rhian's face slowly began to dawn on her, with creeping horror. Damn it all, where the fuck had that come from? She took another deep breath and stared down at the tabletop, regaining wits and composure that had somehow fled in that last, harsh outburst.

"Rhi," she managed again, in a low, soft voice that barely carried above the thundering rhythm. "I'm sorry. I didn't mean to upset you. It's just . . . I get scared sometimes. And I just don't want to see you . . ."

"You don't think I should have a child?" asked Rhian, as clear and plain as ever, fighting the emotion down with great determination. Sandy could only admire her bravery. Rhian did not run away from unpleasant possibilities. She confronted them directly, as was her nature.

"Rhian, I'd love to see you adopt a child." And Rhian looked as puzzled at that as she'd ever looked in all the time Sandy had known her, some of the emotion slowly draining away. Sandy sighed. "It's not about what I want, Rhi. I'm trying to make you think. I'm scared you don't see all the possibilities. I don't claim to be brilliant at everything, but you know I'm good at seeing possibilities."

"Sure. You're the best tactician in the universe."

Sandy restrained a small, modest smile. "Maybe. Rhi, let's be sure we understand each other. I don't trust Ramoja. I think he's a decent man with an impeccable value system. Unfortunately, that value system allows him to do *anything* in the name of the greater good, do you get that?"

"He'd sacrifice minor assets to achieve the final objective," Rhian confirmed.

"Exactly."

"Wouldn't you?"

"With you guys back in Dark Star?" With a faint, sad smile. "My combat record was hardly perfect, Rhi. A few big objectives, I just failed."

"Andres Junction," Rhian volunteered, thoughtfully.

"Exactly. I could have taken the whole facility. We could have, rather. If I'd been prepared to lose half my unit. There were other Dark Star commanders who were, their strike records were better than mine and HQ knew it."

"Captain Zhou."

Sandy nodded. "He's one."

"He was an arsehole."

Sandy smiled. "He's also dead, as were most of his unit before HQ could even bother making a decision to get the rest of them killed. Zhou saved them the trouble. And that makes me a much better commander than him, because it's an awful waste of training and experience for senior combat officers to get themselves and their people killed after just a few missions. Survival is my highest function, Rhi. It's also my highest priority when it comes to my friends, whether it's you, or Vanessa, or Ari, or Anita, or whoever. But you have to think, Rhi. You have to consider worst case scenarios. You have this infallible knack for just ignoring bad things, and getting on with your life no matter what gets thrown at you. That's something wonderful about you. But it's also a blindness.

"I think you *could* have a child. I think she, or he . . ." with suggestive, raised eyebrows at Rhian, who shrugged, ". . . could grow up to be a wonderfully well-adjusted young man or woman, and actually benefit from such an unusual upbringing. No question it would broaden her mind, and make her look at things differently from other children. That could be a big advantage for her. But to avoid the traps, you first have to know where they are. Right?"

Rhian nodded, slowly. Then, "It's not easy for me, Cap, I'm not as smart as . . ."

"And that's bullshit, right there," Sandy cut her off, levelling a forceful finger at Rhian's nose. "There's no such thing as 'smart.' The difference between our psychologies is structural; raw intellect has nothing to do with it. You can structure your thoughts similarly to mine if you try. If you learn. Can you do that?"

"You want me to be careful of Ramoja?"

"Always."

Rhian bit the inside of her lip, thinking hard. "And I also have to be careful of everyone in Tanusha? The CSA?"

"Definitely."

"Then who do I trust?"

"Me," said Sandy firmly. "And Vanessa and Ari and the others. Your friends."

"I have friends in the Embassy, too."

Sandy shrugged. "Then trust them also. The trick is to be aware of where everyone's real loyalties lie. When the bullets start flying, and they have to choose between you, or their other loyalties, which way will they go? Even friends can have conflicting loyalties."

Rhian nodded, thinking that over. "I think Major Ramoja might know more about this new GI than he's saying," she said then. "He has contacts around. He doesn't tell me some things because he knows I'm your friend. Some things, I don't think he wants you to know."

Truly, Sandy nearly said, but didn't. Sarcasm directed at Rhian, even the good humoured kind, was simply not fair. She'd meant exactly what she'd said about Rhian not lacking intelligence. She just spoke, and thought, the way that she did. It was that most treasured of GI traits—character. Confusing it with stupidity was stupidity itself.

"If I can find out," Rhian continued with great seriousness, "I'll tell you."

Sandy paused for a moment. "You'd do that?"

"It's your city, not Ramoja's," Rhian said reasonably. "If there's something the League knows that can stop this GI, then Tanusha deserves to know about it."

Sandy nodded. "I agree." Sandy reached with her good hand, and grasped Rhian's upon the table. Squeezed it, and felt the steely, crushing tension in return. "So you're serious? You'd like to become a Federation citizen?"

Rhian made a thoughtful face. "Maybe. There are all kinds of hidden traps. Bad possibilities on all sides. I'll have to think about it."

Sandy smiled broadly, with great affection. "You do that. And whatever you decide, I'll always be here if you need me."

"I know," Rhian said mildly. As if anything otherwise had never occurred to her.

Rhian left by the front exit, blending perfectly as she moved through the crowd of partygoers. Sandy waited several minutes, then got up and went through the staff access door. Down a corridor, she found two Arabic men seated at a small table, guarding the rear door while playing backgammon.

"Tashiq, Mohammed." She thanked them, clasping hands with each in turn. "Thank you, guys. I owe you one."

"Hey, hey . . ." Mohammed waved her off, theatrically. "No problem. Come back any time. Maybe when things get quiet you and Ari can bring some friends, we have a party, yes?"

Sandy returned his smile, gave further thanks and retreated into the narrow laneway at the club's rear. Her boots splashed in puddles as she made her way along the lane, sidestepping a utility sweeper that trundled past on thick tires, a yellow warning light strobing along the alley's length. The alley adjoined a narrow side road, where council bins lined the sides, carefully colour-coded for the automated pickup trucks. Sandy paused in the shadow of one bin, scanning toward the busy road at the far end, alive with road traffic and passing late-night pedestrians.

A large, sleek groundcar sat in the middle of the lane, its windows blank. Sandy pressed her shoulder against the bin, and pulled the pistol from within her jacket, scanning up and about her. Without her uplinks, she felt vaguely blind . . . but she could not rule out the possibility of any ambusher having tripwired the local network receptors in anticipation of precisely her usual, network-scanning reaction. On the dark walls above, her sharpened vision could distinguish several small windows and a couple of fire escapes. None appeared to be occupied.

She recalled the memory of the vehicle's licence number . . . found it, shifted it to an internal data implant, and ran a quick search against all those she had on storage. It took only a split second to find a match, with names, photographs and detailed files to follow, most of which she recognised immediately.

"Damn it," she muttered softly to herself. There was no chance that it was a coincidence, to be finding *this* particular car parked in the lane beside the club she'd been visiting. As to who had tipped him off . . . well, she'd have to have a word with the cousins Tashiq and Mohammed later. It would be easy enough to walk in another direction. But most people in these circles knew better than to threaten her. If he'd made the effort to get here, it could be important.

She stepped around the side of the bin and walked calmly toward the car, pistol held comfortably to one side in her good hand. A series of multispectrum vision shifts determined that there appeared to be four people inside, though the complete tint-out made it difficult to be sure. The car remained silent as she approached. When she reached the driver's side window, it hummed downward. An Indian man with rough features and heavy brows gazed at her from within, head resting lazily on the headrest, chewing on something that Sandy suspected would be considerably stronger than traditional pan. He grinned at her, lazily between chews, revealing perfect, off-white teeth. Doubtless they wouldn't have looked so good if it weren't for the various available treatments that covered for the full range of chewing addictions.

Sandy scanned about the lane, equally unhurried, then looked down at him.

"What's up, Paras?" she asked him. Paraswamy grinned more broadly, evidently finding something amusing.

"You're always so cool, Sandy," he said admiringly. "You're just the coolest, most gorgeous babe on the delta, you know that?"

"What do you want?" Flatly. Paraswamy grinned again. Jerked a thumb over his shoulder.

"Guy in the back wants to see you." Sandy raised an eyebrow. Paraswamy was running a taxi service? In person? The person in the back seat must have had some serious clout. The rear window hummed down also, Sandy's vision comfortably accounting for the gloom to make out Ali Sudasarno, looking nervous, uncomfortable, and totally out of place in his formal dark suit and tie. Sandy bit back a very bad word. Sudasarno opened the door and moved over on the seat. Sandy spared the alley one last look around, then got in.

The groundcar was certainly big, with seats facing each other limousine-style, and a dividing window separating the front seats from the rear. Also prominent were a display screen . . . no, *two* display screens, a small refrigerated bar built into the dark leather side panelling, an uplink terminal, and numerous control buttons along the sides that no doubt did all kinds of decadent and useless things. Sandy took the rear-facing seat opposite the Presidential advisor as the door locked automatically behind her . . . that didn't bother her, it wasn't like they could lock her in if she wanted out.

"Close the divider please," said Sudasarno to the front seats, where another man sat at Paraswamy's side, watching in the rear-view mirror

. . . which was probably there specifically for viewing the rear compartment, Sandy reckoned, given that all rear-view assistance to the driver came in the form of wide-view vid displays. "We had a deal," Sudasarno said more firmly, when the divider did not close immediately. A humming sound, and then it did.

"We're still being bugged," Sandy remarked as the divider slotted firmly into place in the ceiling. Sudasarno rummaged in a coat pocket, and removed a small, black, disk-shaped device. Pressed a few buttons, flipped a switch, and Sandy instantly registered a frequency-surge that jammed much of her own, subconscious reception. Those weren't uplinks, but rather simple, integrated implants that could register the operation of electronic or magnetic devices in various proximities depending on their output. The smothering sensation emitted by the little electronic jammer was not pleasant.

"Now we're not," said Sudasarno. And turned his anxious, concerned gaze upon Sandy, loosening his tie with his free hand. His eyes did a fast double-take at the new look, dark hair, shades and all. "How are you, Sandy?"

"I'm busy," she replied pointedly, removing her shades and folding them into the pocket of her jacket. "What's so important to Neiland that she has you employing notorious underworld figures to track me down?"

"You're not answering your uplinks and we didn't know who else to call . . ."

"You can leave me a message with Ibrahim or Vanessa," she told him, knowing well in advance what the answer would be.

"The President wanted me to talk to you directly." Meaning that neither Neiland, nor anyone within her immediate circle, trusted either of those two people to pass on a message precisely as delivered. Nor within the timeframe required. "She's not happy, Sandy." With a pained look that made it clear that if Neiland was not happy, sure as hell no one else was allowed to be. "Sandy, if there was a security threat within the system, why the hell didn't you just stay put and let us fix it?"

"Let *you* fix it? You mean the Neiland Administration can fix something that no security expert I've yet spoken to knows how to fix?"

"Sandy, you've caused a mess!" Sudasarno burst out, with building exasperation. "We'd just gotten you to a point of political neutrality, and now you've gone and made media headlines all through the Federation . . . or at least they *will* be headlines, when they reach the other worlds. Now you've split everyone into people who think either that you've finally lost the plot and gone nuts, thus implying that Neiland was crazy to let you come as far as you have, or those who think the entire government system is now suspect because it can't even keep the second-in-command of the CDF safe! The media are openly speculating that there's some kind of plot to kill you within the President's own staff . . . I mean, damn it, we're only trying to negotiate the future of the entire Federation here, Sandy, you don't think a little advance warning would be out of the question?"

Sandy watched him for a long moment. She really didn't like being lectured by any young, know-all political whizz kid . . . and never mind that Sudasarno was actually far older than she was, in simple years lived. Often necessity demanded that she grit her teeth, and bear it. Now, however, was not one of those times.

"Sudie." Firmly, making sure that his entire attention was upon her. "First of all, there is someone within your government trying to kill me. In all likelihood, it's someone allied with the pro-Earth hardliners—your enemies, Sudie. Katia's enemies. I don't see how that hurts you—find the bastard, or bastards, show them to the press, it only makes your enemies look bad."

"You ran away, Sandy! Without Neiland's knowledge, without your immediate superior's knowledge . . ."

"What's Krishnaswali been saying about me?" Sandy cut in, suddenly suspicious of exactly what the President might have been hearing.

Sudasarno looked away through the side window, holding something back. "Look, I'm not at liberty to discuss anything like . . ."

"That's okay," said Sandy, "I'll find out another way." Sudasarno stared at her. It was a direct threat to the administration's power base, and they both knew it. "There are people in high places who are more committed to me and my goals than to you and your President," she was telling him. And the President could fight it, for sure . . . but in the glare of the media spotlight, replacing senior CDF and CSA personnel would have caused a huge row, not to mention the damage to planetary security in such a sensitive period. Sudasarno held up both hands, taking a deep breath.

"I don't want to fight with you, Sandy. That wasn't my intention in coming here. I wanted to warn you."

"Of what, specifically?"

"Fleet Admiral Duong has expressed grave concern at your unexpected "AWOL status" . . . his words. So has Secretary General Benale. We think it's going to be brought up at the meeting tomorrow. A lot of very influential people back on Earth are demanding your removal as the barest precondition to any kinds of talks . . ."

"The Fleet don't want their HQ based on Callay," Sandy countered, her eyes narrowing at him with what she hoped was intimidating effect. "They want to remain an Earth Fleet, not a Federation Fleet. That's big stuff, Sudie. Do you really think it'll matter two tiny turds to that agenda whether I'm in the CDF or not? What's the CDF to the Fleet, anyway? Just a goddamn planetary militia rabble. We only interest them on ideological grounds, they think they should have all the military power in the Federation bar none. They're bullshitting you, Sudie, they're just looking for a political agenda with which to scare people into thinking the same way they do. "Oh look, that dangerously progressive Neiland character lets a GI into her precious CDF and now she's run amok." It's a headline grabber. You can't ask me to make strategic decisions based upon simple political grandstanding that won't make any difference to the Fleet's true agenda in the long run anyway."

"And since when were you the one in politics?" Sudasarno was actually getting angry now, his dark eyes flashing. "Your job is to take orders within the system, Sandy . . ."

"My job description has contained an *enormous* amount of latitude ever since I first signed on," Sandy shot back, "simply because no one else knew what the fuck they were doing!"

"We signed on an expert advisor, Sandy, not a goddamn loose cannon!"

"We can't just let them kick us around, Sudie," Sandy replied calmly. "The worst security scenario we face is them thinking that we can't and won't fight back."

"This is politics, Sandy," Sudasarno said firmly, leaning forcefully forward in a way that very few work acquaintances would dare with her. "Your analogies are all military. They're two different worlds, and they don't often translate."

"On the contrary," Sandy replied, just as firmly. "*Everything's* a conflict, Sudie. The very laws of the universe themselves. The collision of hydrogen atoms in every sun to make the fusion that makes all life possible. Every part of the universe is constantly in conflict with every other part. The reason I'll never be a pacifist is because it's not always all bad."

And Sudasarno could think of nothing to say to that at all.

Paraswamy opened his driver's side door as Sandy climbed out of the rear, and walked with her to the garbage bins at the end of the lane, where the shadows would hide them from a casual glance from the far end.

"I can't remember the last time you did anything *for* the government, Para," said Sandy, with great irony.

Paraswamy grinned toothily, still chewing. "It's the government, girl—they pay good money."

"I'll bet they did. All cash."

Paraswamy shrugged, still grinning. Looked her up and down, rubbing his bristly chin with a gold-ringed hand. "Nice look. You going to Ari's tailor now?"

"If you want some chitchat, why don't you try me again in about a year? I might have a spare minute or two then."

"City might not be here in another year," Paraswamy countered cheerfully. Sandy just looked at him. Paraswamy's look turned shrewd. "I have a friend in customs," he said then. No great news there, from a master of the Tanushan blackmarket. "She says she found an irregularity just a few days ago. A consignment somehow made it through the security screens without a proper inspection seal. She halted it and called a superior to deal with it, but word came down not to worry with it. The next day, the consignment had disappeared."

Sandy's eyes narrowed slightly—it was as much of a curious frown as she was prepared to allow herself, in this company. Never a good idea to let on how much you were interested, Ari had told her often enough. "Happens often enough, I gather," she said. It didn't, actually—Callayan customs were generally excellent, by high Federation standards. But the volume of intersystem trade was such that the inevitable few consignments here and there would not be missed . . .

"This consignment was addressed to a government department."

Which *did* get Sandy's attention. "Which one?" she asked.

"Silent address," said Paraswamy. Meaning that for security reasons, the precise identity of the intended recipient was not publicly listed. Such deliveries would be taken by general government mail, then sorted in-system, where there was no chance of anything unpleasant being planted on the delivery in-transit, nor any chance of outsiders keeping notes on which department or government employee had received what deliveries.

"Well, that's very interesting," Sandy remarked, "but not in itself alarming."

"You check it up," said Paraswamy, knowingly. Spat out his pan on the rain-wet lane. The red colour stained a puddle. Paraswamy reached into a pocket of his jacket, rummaged in a plastic packet for another, and popped it into his mouth. "I think you'll find it very interesting."

"What else do you know?" Paraswamy shrugged. Sandy grabbed him by the front of the shirt, in no mood for games. "Don't tempt me."

"Tempt you to do what?" Again the toothy smile. Infuriatingly unworried. "I know you too well, Cassandra Kresnov. Some people are still scared of you, huh? I think you're just a pussycat. What are you going to do, hurt me?"

It was tempting. But not tempting enough. Sandy let him go with a push. "If this delays me, or costs anything, I'll get back to you." Pointing warningly at his chest. Paraswamy shrugged, adjusting his shirt and jacket.

"You just can't get enough of me, can you, baby?" And he cackled, toothily.

# CHAPTER 8

"I don't know what to tell you, Ari." Vanessa stood atop the best vantage spot on the Herat Complex grounds, fully armoured and sweating in the mid-morning sun. The visor display told her, among a multitude of other things, that there was a cool breeze blowing from the south east, but it did her precious little good beneath layers of micro-compressor and myomer-powered ceramic. "I'm on the highest alert we've got, it doesn't go any higher."

"*Look . . .*" Ari's voice sounded agitated in her earphones. Lately, that was as usual. "*Just keep an eye out, will you?*"

"Oh, well, that's real fucking useful advice, that is," Vanessa snapped, hefting her assault rifle with power-assisted ease. The laser-target assist flickered across her visor as the muzzle moved, highlighting fire-trajectories in her field of view. "Where would a CDF officer be without such sage advice? Anything else?"

*"Vanessa, I'm not trying to tell you how to do your job, I'm just saying that there's something here that looks very suspicious . . ."*

"There always is. No interruptions for the next hour please, I'm going to be busy."

She disconnected, and scanned once more across the broad, open space before her. From atop the Central Chambers of the new Federation Grand Council building, she had a mostly uninterrupted view across one hundred and eighty degrees. At her back, the enormous curving ribs of what would soon become the Chambers' central dome soared another ten storeys high. Two construction cranes loomed upon either side of the nascent dome, silent and idle at the moment, their crews sent home with the rest of the Herat construction teams for today.

To her left and right were other buildings, the beginnings of stately grandeur emerging from within the mass of construction gantries, cranes and obscuring canvas sheeting. Between the flanking buildings the main access road curved in from the heavily fenced perimeter in a giant U shape. Within the U, an enormous court of pavings and gardens was emerging from the chaos of digging and earth moving equipment.

This, the new district of Herat, was to be the new centre of the Federation. The imposing scale of it all drove home the stakes involved in recent happenings like nothing else could. Not merely the size of the grounds under construction, but the style. It was the architecture of power, all grand domes and pillars, beautiful yet authoritative, with influences borrowed from several of the greatest empires of human civilisation—Indian, Arabic, and European in particular.

Beyond the tall, wrought-iron fence around the grounds' perimeter, the road was clear of traffic save the usual police patrols. At either end, large roadblocks manned by thick lines of police in armoured riot gear held back enormous crowds of protesters. The chanting reached Vanessa's ears clearly enough through her helmet's audio receptors, and if she blinked the right icons, inbuilt software could sift the mass of

noise for anything potentially alarming. According to software parameters, anyway, which she didn't trust a millimetre. Besides, she had
more important things to bother herself with.

"*The Maharaja is at ETA one minute,*" announced a controller on tac-
net. "Maharaja" was Secretary General Benale. President Neiland, as
befitted a good host, was already here. "Dacoit"—meaning Admiral
Duong—the tac-net further advised her, was five minutes' flight time
away, having come down by his own shuttle to Gordon Spaceport. If
Vanessa wasn't so certain the CDF's tac-nets were so secure, she
wouldn't have risked allowing her underlings to brand Duong with the
Hindi term for "bandit." "Maharaja," of course, was pure irony.

Vanessa peered over the rim of her rooftop vantage point. Far
below, a grand flight of steps led up to a broad marble floor, decorated
now with guards, functionaries and leafy tree ferns in pots beneath
enormous stone pillars. There was commotion there now, official media
and documentors scurrying upon the stairs for positions, some arguments with local security, a groundcar pulled up too close on the road
and being asked to shift quickly before the procession arrived.

Vanessa scanned the tower-studded horizon, and spotted a row of
incoming vehicles, breaking into local airspace where civilian traffic
was not allowed. Tac-net eliminated the need for mundane communications—Vanessa could see the graphical display of all Herat district,
including the immediate status of all her units and others. She
switched to a broadscan display of the immediate foreground as the
convoy of vehicles approached, and saw a multispectrum view of all
neighbouring buildings, parks and available spaces, computer-sifted
for hostile activity, meaning anyone looking to shoot at the Secretary
General as he passed overhead. Nothing registered.

"*We look clear,*" came Rassmusen's voice on the tac-net. Meaning that
no one had tried to shoot down the convoy yet. Vanessa switched to rear-
view perspectives where several units were guarding the rear of the
Chambers—more half-completed gardens, and more buildings under

construction. Beyond those, the unspoiled wilderness of the Shoban Delta, a horizon of unbroken trees and rivers, lifting into the southern reaches of the Tuez Mountains in the distance. It was the obvious direction from which threat would come, or could come, with everyone facing the other way. Except that the immediate forest behind the grounds was strewn with enough covert, buried and implanted sensory equipment to track individual insects in their flight, and watch the mating rituals of local frogs and bunbuns.

Directly ahead, the first of the vehicle convoy was now coming in to land, midway up the approach driveway. Underside wheels unfolded, and the black, armoured cruiser touched with a bump of heavy suspension, then drove the rest of the way on four wheels, idling to allow the next vehicle down to catch up. Vanessa raised her rifle in the direction of the leftwards group of protesters beyond the fence, magnifying the visor display to get a good look through the sight. Fists were raised as each convoy vehicle whined overhead, placards waved as jeering yells pursued each arrival. Someone lit off some small fireworks, little incendiary rockets soaring skyward to detonate near a cruiser's underside with remarkable accuracy. The crowd cheered. The riot police on the barricades looked agitated, and the tac-net registered a sudden upsurge in police communications.

*"Major Rice,"* came a voice in her ear, tac-net identifying it as belonging to Chief Malakian, the head of Parliamentary Security, or S-4. *"Threat assessment and response has been called for."*

"From a couple of firecrackers?" Vanessa replied. "Zero and zero. Let 'em shoot." Damn security squibs, she thought darkly to herself, flicking to other monitors and tac-net locations, determined not to be fixated on the colour and movement, and thus miss the real threat. The next convoy vehicle came under fire from two rockets, one of which burst immediately before the windshield in a puff of white smoke. More cheers from the crowd, and the clearly audible chant of "Fuck the Fifth! Fuck the Fifth!" So they thought they were shooting at Admiral

Duong. But then again, she reckoned Benale, or any senior Earth politician, would have suited them well enough.

"*Major Rice,*" Malakian's voice reappeared in her ear, "*the organisers are demanding an immediate threat assessment and action. The security guide-lines clearly stipulate that aerial hazards must be dealt with immediately in proximity to any red-zone airspace . . .*"

"What d'you want me to do?" Vanessa snarled. "Open fire on a bunch of civilians because they've got a couple of illegal party pops? I don't care how bad it looks on the news feeds, those cruisers can take direct hits from far worse than fireworks and I've got more important things to worry about! If you're that concerned, get the cops onto it. Now stop clogging the audio."

She disconnected, refraining from uttering a few more choice phrases for all to hear. She did *not* like giving the local security access to tac-net, they weren't familiar enough with CDF operating protocols to be much more than a nuisance. If Sandy were in command of this operation, she doubted it would have happened. But because it was being commanded by a mere major, Krishnaswali had seen fit to over-ride her recommendation. Just as he'd seen fit to allow Duong and Benale's security teams their own bandwidth for independent tac-nets on the local network, forcing a certain CDF major to stay up half of last night in conversation with those security team leaders to coordinate the protocols so they didn't trip over each other's feet.

It was one more hassle on top of every other recent disaster, and Vanessa was *not* in the best mood of her life this fine Tanushan morning. Particularly when she had to put up with the renegade, tag-team duo themselves interrupting her with VIPs on approach to give warning of some new plot they'd uncovered to source illegal weapons through some obscure branch of the Foreign Office . . . she hadn't made sense of all the details, but Ari had sounded alarmed. That Sandy had let him contact her suggested she was too. But damn it, Sandy of all people should have known that the one thing a commander on active duty *didn't* need was too much peripheral information. But of course, for Sandy's augmented brain, there was no such thing as too much information. Well, some of us are only human, she'd considered snapping more than once of late, despite knowing it was unfair. Deal with it.

Upon the approach driveway, the convoy formed up as the final vehicles touched down, and began rolling toward the broad main stairs. One convoy down, and the second on approach, tac-net switched to phase-two, focus-scanning along a new set of parameters. Amongst Vanessa's team not a word was spoken. They knew their jobs too well for that. Ten storeys below Vanessa's vantage point, Secretary General Benale emerged from a cruiser in the centre of the convoy. He took his time getting up the stairs, between handshakes, pleasantries, and much smiling and waving to the small media contingent and stage managed well-wishers. And she did a fast double-take at one low-angle feed on tac-net—several Tanushan school children, no more than six years old, presenting the Secretary General of the United World Council with native flowers.

Children? It was all she could do to remain focused on her job, and not blow her top completely. They'd *assured* her there would be no children. It wasn't *safe*, she'd told them, reviewing the original plans presented to her. The bureaucrats in question had complained that it was only a *couple* of children, and they wanted a softer image of Callayan greetings to Earth's senior politician than the usual suits and ties. No, she'd said. And now, they'd ignored her. It *wouldn't* have happened to Sandy—they'd never have dared. With or without Krishnaswali's approval, she was going to kick some heads in when this was over.

At the top of the stairs, Vanessa saw on her visor tac-net display, President Neiland greeted Benale with a smile and a handshake. It all looked pathetically, fraudulently civil. God, she hated politics. And switched her fullest attention back to the landing vehicles in Duong's convoy, who were coming in from the north rather than the east, and were thus avoiding any colourful groundfire. Admiral Duong's arrival didn't help Vanessa's mood any, given that she'd personally have bet several limbs that he was in some way responsible for the attempts on Sandy's life. She was in *such* a bad mood, with the cumulation of recent events, that it truly didn't surprise her at all when the first missile contrails erupted a little over sixteen hundred metres away.

"Live fire!" she yelled on tac-net at the same time as twelve other voices, and tac-net switched fast to combat mode with a flurry of new electronic linkages. "Live fire! Everybody move move move!"

Tac-net showed an eruption of activity below her position, security swooping on Benale, Neiland and others, hurtling them in through the main doors at speed with weapons drawn as the rest of the entourage scrambled madly in panic. The two missiles were at one thousand metres and closing fast, tac-net back-tracking their point of origin, highlighting a residential block on the Herat perimeter. The grounds' defensive firegrid sprang to life, multiple emplacements within the half-finished gardens springing from the ground, zeroing upon the racing threat. Vanessa knelt behind the low wall rimming the Chambers' edge, and saw only too well that both missiles were headed straight for the convoy parked beneath her position.

"Red squad!" she snapped, even as the firegrid erupted in multiple streams of fire. "Get mobile, target tac-net HT5 . . ." a location square upon tac-net's regional map illuminated in illustration, ". . . get me those launchers at the source."

A minor storm of exploding projectiles erupted across the incoming missiles' course with a deafening roar . . . one missile vanished amidst the explosions, the other emerged nearside, tumbling, then ploughed into the gardens and exploded in flying clods of earth. To Vanessa's left, several of her soldiers were scrambling from their positions as a Trishul flyer howled hovering into position upon the rooftop edge. Armoured soldiers leaped onto the rear hold ramp, which sealed behind them as the Trishul's engine nacelles angled and the flyer tipped dramatically nose-down, accelerating at maximum toward the source of the missiles.

"*Was that both?*" she heard someone from security yelling on tac-net. "*That's it? We got 'em both?*"

"We are condition red!" Vanessa announced sharply. "No relaxing!"

The words were barely out of her mouth when tac-net registered multiple new contrails, four more from the original position, and another four . . . no *six* . . . coming from a new site to the north. No, eight . . . *ten.*

"Green squad, get mobile, target tac-net GT3!" There were fourteen now, another four soaring skyward from the original location. Six were coming in flat like the last two, the other eight arcing straight up into the clear blue sky. It took military weaponry to fire so many high-V missiles so close together. And there was nothing she could do, because sweeping surrounding tower blocks had not been her responsibility any more than was making sure those weapons hadn't fallen into the wrong hands in the first place. In that brief, time-frozen moment, as the missile contrails arced high, long and white, she recalled the two little children upon the broad verandah below. And now, here came the rest of Admiral Duong's convoy, having abandoned landing upon the approach road to skim airborne toward the steps at head height, scattering people in all directions.

The firegrid opened up on the low-flying missiles; again the roar of detonating projectiles ripped the air just shortly above the heads of the fireworks-firing protesters, whose mass disintegrated into a running, falling, screaming panic. Several warheads exploded in a fiery rush—the first two had been low-yield practice shots, Vanessa realised. Another broke apart, then fire tracked the last three at blinding speed across the near sky, erupting explosions streaking straight toward the chamber's grounds . . . one exploded, and the previous broken warhead blew the approach drive to hell as it fell. A fifth ran wide and slammed a high stone wall with a building-shaking boom! The sixth performed a final evasive twist, then slammed into one of Duong's convoy of cruisers, which exploded even as passengers attempted to jump down to the stairs, bodies and debris scything across running, scattering personnel.

Then the high-trajectory missiles were falling, firegrid emplacements making fast, swivelling adjustments, weapon muzzles blazing skyward in a protective shield. Fully the first half were struck on the way down, eliciting a split-second rush of hope. But then the reasoning behind the high-low fire-spread became clear, as rushed emplacements lost their fire sequence in the hurry to adjust to new targets on totally opposing trajectories. One whizzed down past Vanessa's nose and blew much of the broad stairway to burning shards. Another ploughed into the parked cruiser convoy, blasting one into a flaming somersault amidst the smoke and debris. More vanished in midair explosions, Vanessa crouching with squinting determination not to leave her position as metallic fragments rained down, and firegrid detonations tore a ceiling of fire just armspans above her head. One last explosion shook the foregrounds, and Vanessa allowed herself to believe she might live through it after all . . . and the last, spinning missile ploughed into the chambers' roof ten metres to her right. Directly on top of where Hydek and Gavaskar had been crouched, awaiting further orders.

"Airborne squads!" Vanessa announced as visibility vanished amidst the cloud of roiling debris. "You have local command, those are residential locations so maintain a midintensity assault pattern and watch for local network infiltration."

And was amazed at how steady her voice remained amidst the chaos. To her right, tac-net informed her, several more soldiers were running to the aid of Hydek and Gavaskar.

"*Red Leader copies*," came back one reply. "*Green Leader copies*." Four armoured assault flyers went fast and low toward the origins of the missile attacks.

"First and fourth squads, maintain that perimeter! Third squad, close cover for the VIPs, maintain an outer perimeter around their security." Tac-net showed those eight soldiers on ground level rushing to comply, their positions moving through the Chambers' graphic to shadow the cluster of dots that marked Neiland, Benale, Duong and their security . . . so Duong was still alive. She hadn't noticed either way until then.

Ambulance sirens howled, several were rushing up the approach drive, taking a bumpy detour around the crater there. From below, at the foot of the broad stairs, flames crackled and wounded screamed, as others shouted desperately for help. To her right, soldiers had reached Hydek and Gavaskar . . . Gavaskar was alive, there were shouts for a medic, and more instructions to remove armour. Vanessa remained crouched, jaw tight, eyes fixed only on the tac-net display. She knew she had frozen. Maybe that was okay, there was nothing more she could do but watch. Vid-displays from red and green squads' approaches lit her visor . . . a green squad flyer came under fire from a missile, took evasive action amidst a cloud of countermeasures. The missile missed. The second flyer let fly several volleys of machine-guns and rockets, clearing the rooftop in seconds.

Red squad met with small arms fire, rapidly ended with two bursts of high velocity fire. Through the drifting smoke of pulverised ferro-crete, she made out a quad-barrelled, personnel-mounted missile launcher, lying on two rooftop deckchairs beside a row of potplants. A second later, tac-net identified it for her further benefit—a Kawamatsu AT-3, Federation model. The assault rifle by the dismembered corpse that had fired upon the flyer was also Kawamatsu-made. For some reason, beyond the immediate concerns of tactics and survival, that rang alarm bells.

Tac-net showed the two of her four aerial units still on the grounds, their transport hovering nearby in lethal anticipation. Another unit was now inside the Chambers, providing close quarters support to VIP security that included the elite Alpha Team of Presidential guards. Her perimeter was now thin, but ample enough. And she dimly realised, then, that someone in security was shouting at her on tac-net, demanding to know more, as flyers now poured armoured troops onto the rooftops of the two residential blocks from which the fire had come, while others established defensive positions upon the streets around the base, halting traffic and yelling at gawking pedestrians.

"That's it?" was all Vanessa could think. Long range bombardment with military-standard weaponry . . . a hell of a lot of effort to acquire the weapons and plan the assault without detection, but for very little strategic result, save a lot of smoke and noise. Just like the first attack upon Sandy. Click! went her brain, in that dazed, hyper-sensed slow motion. That first attack had been little more than distracting. The second, more lethal attack had come shortly after. Probably not by the same people who carried out this one. Damn, green and red squads were probably wasting their time, better to leave these shooters to the cops.

"It's not over!" she announced onto tac-net. "All units, listen close—we're going to treat this one as a decoy!"

"*A decoy!*" spluttered the same unidentified security man.

"Stay sharp and watch yourselves, don't rely too much on procedure, we're going to assume there's been a breach! Don't trust anything, I don't like the smell of this one at all."

"*Major Rice,*" the security man cut back in, "*on behalf of the Secretary General, I demand to know what is . . .*"

"If you don't get the fuck off the tac-net," Vanessa snarled, "I'm going to have you declared a security threat and shot! SHUT UP!" Then to the troops on her right, "Hussein, Silchenko, Yadav, with me!"

She unhooked the rapelling cord on the front of her armour, placed it upon the lip of the wall and activated the fuse—a flash of smoke and it sealed tight to the stone. She grabbed the slim wire in one armoured hand and leaped from the edge, even as the other three ran to follow her. The winch howled as it unwound, and then she was falling past enormous stone columns, through rising smoke and clouds of debris, flames and running people below. On the tac-net, the terse, fast commands of red and green squads sweeping the buildings. Below that, the brief commands of other unit leaders on the ground, closing up the gaps left by red and green's departures.

Ten storeys straight down, then the stairs were rushing up, littered with debris. She hit, cut the wire, ran up the remaining half-flight and toward the broad main doors. The Grand Chambers' central hall was colossal, its broad floor gleaming, its high walls covered with scaffolding for work on statues and decoration. Vanessa's armoured footsteps echoed as she ran across the front domed atrium, toward the long hallway beyond, noting the wounded lying against the walls, tended by small clusters of terrified people. Blood spilled on the beautiful floor-tile patterns.

The run down the central hall was long, and gave her further time to assess the situation. Neiland and Benale, the tac-net showed her, were two levels down in the prearranged secure zone—the kitchens, which were themselves halfway to the bomb shelters . . . but those had not yet been fully completed. Duong was separate from the others, with his own small team of Fleet security—marines, no doubt, good close quarter fighters but perhaps not so adept at assassination techniques.

She stared at the visor display while running, allowing the suit's powered myomer musculature to do most of the work, and saving her energy. The assault *was* well organised, she wasn't about to let its lack of success blind her to that. Ari and Sandy had just found evidence of higher-level complicity in the supply of arms where they shouldn't have gone. People up that high had a lot to lose. They didn't take such huge risks without good reason. And so a long-range bombardment was all they had? Not damn likely. On the first page of every assassin's guidebook was the simple rule—first, get close. Long-range bombardments were an iffy proposition. No, what they wanted was a single shot to the head at close range . . .

Tac-net detected gunshots from the kitchen, and her heart missed a beat. A graphical leap and zoom, and she heard it clearly, many urgent voices, the crash of what might be stainless steel benches, and a distant, muffled shooting . . . too far away to be immediate, she realised with a rush of relief.

"*This is Alpha Leader,*" came Chief Mitchel's voice then, cool and professional. "*We have gunfire nearby, I estimate it might be coming from Admiral Duong's position.*"

Vanessa flipped channels at speed. "Hello, Amazon One? Amazon One, do you copy?" And cursed that the one group of people she might have welcomed on the tac-net had turned down her request in the planning phase. "Can anyone contact Amazon Team? Is Dacoit in contact?"

She took a hard right into a smaller corridor, aware of her three soldiers closing behind with their longer strides, then arrived at a stairwell and rattled down it at speed. All she had on the tac-net was the dot representing Duong's position—those trackers were mandatory, com frequencies weren't. More muffled gunfire.

"*. . . I'll take four and check it out,*" one of the Alphas was saying.

"*Negative, if the Admiral's in trouble he'll ask for help.*"

The shooting seemed to grow louder. Vanessa left the stairwell in a lower corridor, unadorned walls, exposed, dangling electrics and unfinished construction, her three fellow troopers almost at her heel.

"*. . . big fucking trouble!*" suddenly came a panicked burst of transmission that tac-net identified as Fleet marine. "*It just fucking came outta nowhere . . . I can't contact the others, we've got localised jamming, I don't even know where the fuck I am . . . !*"

Vanessa arrived at the big doors that led to the kitchen, braced open now with two Alpha Team men in dark suits covering their approach, lean black weapons in hand.

"Marine, calm down and tell me your situation!" Vanessa snapped, halting at the junction before the kitchen doors. Her troops rattled and crashed hard into position along the corners, covering each direction.

"*I . . . I dunno . . .*" a pause for hard breathing. "*I dunno how many, it all happened too fast, we lost the LT and then . . .*" Static, as the line went abruptly dead. Vanessa swore under her breath, taking in this lower-level schematic upon her visor, trying to figure the situation. Beyond the kitchen, the main passage to the underground bunker. In the intervening rooms, storage, temporary quarters for Chambers staff, a veritable maze of half-completed, half-constructed passages and rooms.

"*Major Rice,*" came Mitchel's voice, "*we are in position to deploy five men to assist.*"

"Negative," Vanessa commanded. "Alpha Team will hold its defensive position and maintain highest alert." There was a brief silence.

"*Copy, Major.*" And Vanessa got the distinct feeling that Mitchel and she were thinking exactly the same thing. Past the thumping heartbeat and quickening adrenaline, she felt the first real stab of fear.

"Alpha One," she continued, holding her voice steady with an effort. "I want you ready to get everyone up to the surface real damn fast, you got me? I can't draw more people down here without stretching the perimeter—we already have emergency evac on its way, I want all VIPs in those evacs and away from here as fast as possible."

"*Return to the surface?*" asked Benale's security, breathlessly. "*What about those missiles?*"

"*I copy that,*" said Mitchel, ignoring the interruption. "*What about the Dacoit?*"

"I'll get him. When I give the signal, get the hell out, no detours."

She gave fast hand signals to her troops, and rushed down the left-hand passage, assault rifle poised and ready to move at the slightest motion. Tac-net showed a right-hand corner leading past the kitchen—Vanessa flattened her back to the right wall, covering leftwards while the helmet eyepiece unsealed and swung out into the corridor, to show her a clear view of empty passage. She spun and ducked low, Sergeant Yadav closest behind—he was seniormost, a former SWAT private rapidly promoted to cover the influx of raw recruits. Private Silchenko was youngest and greenest, but talented. Private Hussein scored well in skills, but less so in tactics. A picture formed in her mind—an instinct—of what she could count on, and who, and when. And immediately she heard Sandy's voice in her memory: "don't predict anything, just react."

She moved fast and light down the passage, Hussein remaining to cover the last cross-junction. Paused again at the next corner, then raced across. Two more like it and she'd be at Duong's position—a storage room with multiple exits, doubtless his marines had liked it better than the kitchen, and they hadn't been real thrilled about working in conjunction with Alpha Team and the Secretary General's security. Vanessa couldn't really blame them.

There was construction equipment at the next cross-junction, scaffolding blocking half the way and newly installed electrics dangling. Vanessa scanned first, then spun about the corridor edge . . . there was an armoured marine lying face up on the hard floor. Only the basic armour for away missions, not the full combat kit that she wore herself. She took in the marine's injuries without dropping her eyes from the corridor ahead—one shot to the forehead. At the doorway to Duong's storage room, another assault rifle lay upon the ground, scarred where two precise shots had torn it from its owner's hands, presumably while holding it blindly around the doorway and firing.

"Okay, people," Vanessa announced, trying to keep her voice calm while feeling something cold and fearful attempting to creep up her spine. "We've got ourselves a GI down here. Maybe more than one." Waving Yadav past as she spoke, to cover the next junction down. Silchenko followed, moving swiftly backward, covering her back.

"*Copy, Major*," said Mitchel. "*Are you certain?*" And not just panicking at the first sign of blood, he meant.

"Among non-GIs, I'm one of the best shots I know," Vanessa replied. "But I'm not this good, no damn way." No light came through the slight gap in the doorway. Vanessa reached into a leg-pouch, and withdrew a miniscan. Activated the button, and rolled the small, armoured sphere in through the gap . . . a flash of multispectrum activity from the sphere, and a patchy, 3-D graphic swept across her visor, angles changing as the ball continued to roll. No activity. It looked clear. Vanessa took a deep breath, and slammed an armoured foot into the door, slamming it open . . . it crashed upon an obstruction inside and she stepped forward to brace with her shoulder so it didn't rebound, rifle scanning the darkness with feverish intensity.

Her heat-scan showed many blotches upon the floor. Human sized, and larger. Tac-net found a local electrical circuit attached to the network—she let it access, and the power came on in a flickering buzz of fluoro. The storage room looked only mildly untidy, the odd box knocked from a pile against a wall, some construction sheeting fallen from otherwise empty shelves. Only that between the rows of shelves lay the lightly armoured bodies of Fleet marines. Vanessa walked cautiously to one wall, then along. Many of the fatal wounds were head-shots. Those that were chest-shots were actually several holes so close together that the light armour had ruptured. There had been ten marines in Duong's entourage. In the storeroom, she counted seven . . . and Admiral Duong.

She stared at him for a moment, lying crumpled behind a row of large crates against the wall, two of his marines fallen on either side, almost on top of him in their futile efforts at protection. Duong's lifeless hand still gripped a pistol, heat-scan showed the muzzle still warm. His stern, hard features were frozen in a sightless grimace. Most dead people Vanessa had seen appeared astonished at their own demise. The Admiral looked affronted, as if scandalised that death should dare such an improper advance.

"We lost the Admiral," she heard herself say. "I count eight dead marines, mostly head-shots." Her soldier's mind had little difficulty reconstructing the final moments—the panic, the wild shots in the dark, the fast, lethal shape that moved and fought with inhuman speed and precision. She'd seen it herself. Had faced it, in combat drills against Sandy, when she had volunteered to demonstrate the difficulties of facing GIs at close quarters. She'd often been cautious with Sandy, knowing what she was, but never, ever genuinely afraid. Until now.

"*Major*," came Lieutenant Hiraki's hard voice over tac-net, "*I have movement at CT2*." The graphic flashed up on Vanessa's visor . . . the Chambers' north wing, one level above ground floor. And suddenly she could see what Hiraki saw—a motion sensor graphic that told of a single figure moving fast through deserted passages and rooms.

"Shut him off!" Vanessa snapped, hurdling the bodies of dead marines as she rushed back the way she'd come. "Be highly visible, let him see you! Flush him toward our best firezones!"

"*Copy that*," came Hiraki's terse reply, and tac-net showed gold squad moving rapidly to comply. Vanessa crashed out into the corridor, gathering her troops as she went. Tac-net highlighted a possible route from the target to the gardens outside . . . Vanessa blinked it away with irritation, there was no way this GI was headed outside where his advantages would be neutralised. No, there had to be another way.

"Alpha One, stay put . . ." as she darted a quick glance at the next cross-junction, then rushed onward, ". . . this could be a ploy to get you out of the kitchen. Command, tac-net's telling me all underground access is secured but won't say how—can you confirm?"

There was a pause as someone back at HQ rushed to check that request. Vanessa headed for the nearest small, service staircase, bashing a door off its hinges and rushing upward. One of the Trishuls was requesting permission to fire, hovering in low besides the Chambers' north wing.

"Permission granted," Vanessa replied, breathing hard as she raced into the empty upper corridor, noting that Hiraki's unit had now left its perimeter position and was entering the north wing on the ground floor. Abruptly the target vanished, as the motion-sensor lost acquisition.

"*He's descending*," Hiraki announced. "*Give me a full defensive spread, he's not getting out this way.*"

"*Major*," came HQ's delayed reply in her ear. "*We read all underground transit access as blocked by security measures . . .*"

"Yeah, but how?" Vanessa retorted, panting. "Welded plates, ferrocrete blocks, what?"

*"The records don't specify."*

"Then get onto whoever wrote the fucking records and ask them! Fast!"

It was yet another of those things that weren't within her purview of responsibility. A mere CDF major didn't have the time or resources to triple check every entry into the database—she was forced to *assume* the people who'd done so were competent, and go from there.

Fire erupted on tac-net audio, armour-readings showed several members of gold squad firing, tac-net flashed their visuals up on Vanessa's visor, and for a brief moment she saw a lower corridor erupting with assault-rifle fire, but no sign of a target.

*"I think I got him!"* That was Private Zainuddin, harsh and breathless.

*"Gold four, target 360, brace!"* That was Hiraki, cover screening fast west behind his line . . . he must have seen something. Another burst of fire, then . . .

*"Fuck, I'm hit!"*

*"Stay down, four . . . three and six, pincer flank, lay it down!"* More dots moved to comply on tac-net, a coordinated formation switching to cover a moving target, laying down fire as they went. Vanessa raced into the north wing main hall, across a broad floor of patterned tiles and chairs for waiting, large wall display screens blank in the deserted silence . . .

"Alpha Leader," she announced, "this one's not staying to fight, he's buggin' out! Get to the surface now, move move move!" And saw a sudden rush of activity from the lower kitchen as Alpha Team sprang into action, rushing all VIPs out of the kitchen. Vanessa raced across a broad food court behind huge stone pillars, dodging past chairs and tables and sprinting up the main north wing passage, hearing gunfire directly ahead now over the thudding of her team's footsteps. Explosions, as Hiraki let loose grenades at a speculated target . . . and

Vanessa saw a sharp flash of movement upon Private Leung's transmission, then static.

*"Leung's down,"* Hiraki announced. *"The target's headed for the CT4 stairwell."*

"Got that," said Vanessa, and turned to leap down the next broad stairway, newly installed signs upon the walls indicating the underground transit down this way . . . a quick glance at Leung's vitals showed that he was dead. "Secure the stairwell, watch for booby traps, he might have had plenty of time to set up. I'll take the station's south end."

The corridors opened into what would become a mass transit entry when the Chambers opened, designed for the thousands of commuting staff who would work in the Grand Council Chambers. The ramp walkway sloped steadily downward. Vanessa switched her helmet's optics to tripwire scan, but saw nothing. Yadav on her left side, Silchenko on her right, Hussein guarding their rear, they hurdled the ticket scanners, past broad display screens of the underground network and train timetables. Vanessa skidded low to the corner of the first of multiple descending stairways on the right, Yadav and Silchenko racing across to take up covering positions. From the position of the stairwell Hiraki's target had gone down, Vanessa reckoned even a GI would take a full minute longer to get to the platform . . . but would be much closer to the north-end tunnel, and escape, when he came down.

She plunged around the corner and down the stairs, well aware that against a GI, the first indication that they were under fire would come when the point man took a bullet through an eye socket . . . but she was senior, and if she didn't set the example, lesser ranks could be forgiven for never advancing at all against GIs. Down the steps alongside silent, stationary escalators and blank panels where advertisements would soon garishly adorn the walls.

Then she hit the bottom, and found herself on a broad, empty central platform between two half-completed magnetised rail lines. Yadav, Silchenko and Hussein came down behind, and she gestured them to spread out, Yadav with her, the other two on the other side. Yadav leaped down onto the tracks, to cover that low angle, while Vanessa crept with slow, careful steps along the platform, weapon and helmet vision scanning, trying to keep every heavy footstep, every rattle and creak of armour, to an absolute minimum. She could see the left-side tunnel entrance ahead—the right was blocked by the central shop cubicles and central elevators, but she had a clear feed from Hussein and Silchenko. Nothing. The silence was eerie, broken only by the soft background chatter on tac-net—red and green squads cleaning up some final resistance out at the residential blocks, Alpha Team leading VIPs to safety and evacuation on ground level, perimeter units rearranging positions to maintain full coverage . . . tac-net muted it all, aware that none of it was directed at her, nor required her immediate attention.

A minute flicked past. He should have been down by now. Vanessa scanned quickly over the regional schematic once more, wondering if maybe he'd backtracked on a lower level and would come down behind them . . . the schematic showed it wasn't possible, the traffic-flow management design had ensured that all passages up from the station went directly to the Chambers' ground floor with no intersecting. But then, if the schematics were untrustworthy . . .

"*No booby traps on the stairwell,*" came Hiraki's voice, "*I'm approaching ticket level, no sign of target.*" The vitals of his remaining squad members were all displayed green—tac-net immediately informed the direct commander if they ceased, a precaution that was especially necessary when facing GIs. Often opposing soldiers didn't have enough time for a syllable's warning.

"Nothing here yet," Vanessa replied, trying to keep her voice level, for the sake of her guys. It was difficult, her breathing coming in sharp, rapid gasps, and only partly from the long run. Sensors did not indicate so much as a breath of air moving through the tunnels. Maybe they *were* sealed further down. "I don't trust these schematics entirely, stay alert. He might be hiding somewhere between us, or waiting for . . ."

A single shot cracked off the high walls and ceiling, and Silchenko's vitals leaped, then flatlined. "Down!" yelled Vanessa, and hit the platform on braced elbows, then sprayed fire across her most likely guess. Glass panels on intervening platform structures exploded, Yadav's fire joining hers from above the platform rim. Vanessa pumped a grenade into an elevator for luck, the explosion ripping debris across the platform and rails.

A grenade shot hit the wall opposite Hussein's position, crouched low on the right-side rails, the blast knocking him over, showering him with debris. Tac-net attempted to trace the grenade trajectory from the angle of the explosion . . . Vanessa reached a half-crazed decision and shoved herself up into a low run, crossed between two intervening platform structures, and went into a sliding crouch across the tiles to open up an angle on the right-side rails. Something moved lightning quick across the platform ahead, and Vanessa flung herself back, shots cracking millimetres from her nose to shatter glass behind her. She rolled up with her back to the store cubicle before her, surrounded by shattered glass, and heard the next grenade shot a split second later . . .

"Down!" she yelled, and saw the platform just in front of where Yadav was peering over the rim explode in flames and shattered tiles. She sprang up and fired through shattered glass, pumping her own grenades in quick succession, and saw a lean, dark figure somehow, inhumanly leaping and rolling across the platform a few centimetres ahead of her bullet strikes . . . grenades hit the platform, and blew that view to hell. Vanessa stared through the erupting debris, weapon ready with trembling intensity, waiting for the dark figure to reappear above the rim of the left-side platform where it'd gone . . . and recalled, in a fractional second's memory, Sandy's calm analysis of GI reaction times versus those of even the best humans. She dropped quickly behind cover, just as the next shot nearly clipped the top of her helmet.

"*Major!*" shouted Hussein.

"No!" Vanessa shouted as he leaped from the rails onto the platform rim, and ran low and crouched to her position, laying down expert cover fire as he came. "Get d—"

Another shot, Hussein's head snapped back, and the armoured suit crashed to the platform like a stringless marionette. Vanessa held back a scream, biting down hard to keep the tears from her eyes. Yadav's vitals were still active, but brainwave activity showed him unconscious. She was dimly aware of Hiraki's voice, harsh with anxiety.

*"Major, do you require assistance! Should I continue to hold this position!"* Usual strategy was that he would hold that position for her group to flush the target in his direction. He did not have command authority on the tac-net, he didn't have access to everyone's vitals as she did.

"No," Vanessa found herself answering. "Don't come down. Stay where you are." It was just murder. She knew what would happen next. She couldn't bear to see her old friend Hitoru Hiraki add his own corpse to the pile. She levered herself up to peer through the shattered glass, rifle ready. She had no vision below the lip of the platform, now. Asking for help to acquire that vision was impossible—anyone who came within line-of-sight of this GI was dead.

She was only a little surprised when she heard the crunch of a footstep directly behind her. She spun, knowing it would be the last thing she ever did . . . her weapon hit something immovable—a hand, she registered, clamped around the muzzle of her rifle. Another hand smashed her armour in the chest, and she was flying backwards into the wreckage of the platform cubicle, minus her weapon. The remains of the glass wall collapsed on her. And then she was staring up at the dark, leather and synthetic-clad figure before her, clutching her own weapon by the muzzle in one hand, another pointed directly at her face.

Several seconds passed, and Vanessa realised she was still alive. Perhaps there was some use to paying further attention, if just for a few more seconds enlightenment. The GI, she noticed with no real surprise, was female. Broadly built, but of only moderate height. Famil-

iarly broad, in fact, with shortish blonde hair. So familiar, in fact, that
. . . but a direct gaze at the face dispelled that sudden horror as fast as
it arrived—it was a stranger's face that gazed down upon her, cool and
emotionless. A leaner face than Sandy's. Not as attractive. There was
no light in her eye, no familiar, subtle expression. Vanessa sensed
nothing of warmth or humanity from her. It was as if the space before
her was just void, occupied by a lethal, human shell.

"Helmet," said the GI. The voice was as flat and emotionless as the
face. The weapon in one hand gestured at her helmet, wanting it to
come off. Vanessa's hands reached for the seal beneath the chin, moving
dazedly, as if on automatic. Snap, and the chinstrap came away, then
the breather mask and visor unsealed with a release of pressure. Vanessa
pulled the helmet off, feeling her short hair plastered and sticky
beneath, cold with sweat in the open air. She disconnected the insert
from the back of her head, and felt the flow of tac-net information
abruptly cease, all additional visions and patterns vanishing from her
mind's eye. The GI just looked at her. If she was curious or surprised,
amused or angry, she gave no sign.

"Vanessa Rice," said the GI. "You're Cassandra Kresnov's friend."
Somehow, that didn't surprise her much either. It wasn't exactly clas-
sified knowledge.

"I am," Vanessa replied, her voice hoarse with defiance. "You
remember that, just before she kills you." For the first time, there was
a glimmer of reaction in the GI's eyes. Perhaps amusement. Perhaps
anticipation.

"I expect she'll try," was the reply. The voice remained as flat as
before. "You nearly managed today. You're an excellent soldier, for a
straight." Somehow it didn't sound like much of a compliment. The
GI walked across crunching glass, and put a foot on Vanessa's
armoured chest, the rifle muzzle held unwaveringly to her forehead. In
the armour suit, she might have tried to trip the GI, and wrestle.
Except that she'd tried that before with Sandy, in power armour, as had

several others who'd dared. None of the fights had lasted more than a few seconds, except when Sandy prolonged them by not trying as hard, for demonstrative purposes.

"I want you to tell her something," the GI continued. "Tell her that if she wants to disable the killswitch, she'll have to contact me. Otherwise it will kill her. It's just a matter of time."

"Not before she gets you, you mechanical piece of shit."

The GI nearly smiled. Nearly. "Her time is shorter than she thinks. I know. Tell her to contact me, or she'll die."

The dropping knee-smash, like all the GI's other moves, came out of nowhere.

# CHAPTER 9

**S**andy strode fast along the corridor, Hiraki leading the way, rifle to his shoulder and a mean swagger to his step. Soldiers moved aside in passing. Many recognised her, despite the dark hair, and saluted. Some stopped in their tracks, and snapped off salutes so crisp they sizzled, defiance in every postured muscle.

When they reached the entrance to the med-bay, Hiraki took up guard, rifle at cross-arms. "I'll be okay," Sandy told him.

"Even so," said Hiraki, scanning one way, then the other, with slanted, dangerous eyes. He was, Sandy had gathered, in an exceptionally bad mood. First, Vanessa had held gold squad back from the airborne assault on the residential buildings the missiles had come from. Then she'd held him in place while the GI had killed two of Vanessa's squad and then escaped. In Sandy's estimation, Vanessa had been right on both calls—the first because the threat assessment against an offensive assault at the buildings was low, and she'd wanted her best squad leader in reserve for something more serious; and the second because if Hiraki had gone into the Chambers' station, he and most of his squad would also have been dead. Lieutenant Hiraki, of course, didn't see it that way.

"You've got duties," Sandy reprimanded him. "I don't need an armed guard in my own building."

"It's not your building, it's the government's." Hiraki didn't even look at her. "You need a ranking officer here in case of wandering bureaucrats."

"I won't get reported." A pair of CDF soldiers passed, recognised her and snapped salutes. Everyone knew she wasn't allowed to be here. The expressions on passing faces was enough to suggest that even General Krishnaswali might not discover her presence until she was gone. And if he ordered her detained, it was unlikely to be obeyed. "Get back to your unit, that's an order."

"You're out of uniform," Hiraki said pointedly. "I'm not." Sandy half-rolled her eyes in exasperation.

"Fine, have it your way." She walked into the med-bay, and found seven of the twenty main beds were occupied. Vanessa was up at the end, propped on her pillows with her head bandaged, reading over various comp-slates, a half-eaten sandwich and a steaming cup on the bed tray to her side. She met Sandy's gaze immediately. Sandy felt her heart leap, with an unexpected shock of relief and fear . . . it could so easily have been different, and now it really hit her. Vanessa returned a faint smile. Sandy responded, then stopped by the first bed, where a private named Rafale—one of Hiraki's—was lying.

She made her way along the line, talking briefly to each of the four who were awake, reliving the scenario and voicing her strong approval of their efforts—she'd uplinked the full tac-net record upon arrival, and knew exactly what had happened. Then she reached Vanessa's bed, and pulled up a chair.

"Hi, gorgeous." Leaned to kiss her on the cheek, not wishing to make too much of a fuss in front of the troops. Vanessa caught at her hand as she sat back—a light, grateful grasp. She wore her ops jacket over the dressing gown, stitched with many patches on the arms and shoulders. SWAT Four, Sandy recognised one. And the main CSA patch. Her college coat-of-arms patch too, though that had nothing to do with military service—Ramprakash University, she'd done an MBA there, of all things. It had been Vanessa's habit, back in SWAT, to adorn her jacket with all the units she'd served in, and all the places she'd once belonged. Somewhere along the line, other CDF officers had started copying that habit, and then the enlisted troops too. Although less than two years old, the CDF was already beginning to accumulate peculiar traditions.

"Cold?" Sandy asked, with a glance at the jacket, knowing full well that wasn't why Vanessa was wearing it.

"Feel stupid sitting in this damn polka dot gown." Vanessa glanced down, distastefully. "I mean seriously, polka dots? Which idiot in procurement ordered these horrible things?"

"Not my department." Sandy gave the standard reply.

"We're soldiers, not nursery rhyme characters."

"Let me make a note of that."

Vanessa snorted, giving her a wry sideways look. Sandy was relieved to see that she didn't look too bad. The bandages were wrapped diagonally, covering most of her right eye, cheek and ear. There was a cheek fracture, she'd already been told, and a corresponding one on the back of her skull where it had been slammed on the platform. Otherwise it was just concussion, which healed nearly as fast as fractures with microsynth treatments. Bits of wild dark hair stuck up through the swathed bandages, defiantly. Under the eyes, the last traces of blackness from the previously broken nose were still faintly visible.

"Been getting beaten up a lot, lately?" Sandy suggested.

"So what else is new? Does Krishnaswali know you're here?" With a sombrely measuring look from her good left eye. Sandy shook her head. "Great, so either he finds out and orders you detained, or he doesn't find out, and gets furious because no one told him."

"Fuck him," said Sandy. Vanessa considered that for a moment, offhandedly.

Then, "Yeah, I guess so," she decided. And gazed blankly across the ward for a moment. Sandy followed her gaze, turning in her seat. And saw young Private Moutada, unconscious in his bed, right arm swathed in bandages over bio-casts within a mass of fluid-tubes. The microsolutions healed the burns, encouraged the growth of new, unscarred skin, and formed new nerve pathways where the old ones were destroyed.

"He'll be okay," Sandy said quietly. "They can reconstruct the hand and wrist, it'll be just like new. Maybe better."

"Doesn't help the others much, does it?" Vanessa met Sandy's gaze once more as she turned back around. "Nor all Duong's marines." Pause. "Nor Duong."

"It wasn't your fault."

"Damn it," said Vanessa, with a sudden flash of dark irritation, "I don't need a lecture. I *know* it wasn't my fault. The whole fucking system was compromised from the beginning. They snuck a GI right into the damn Chambers through the underground. The missile attack drives everyone right into the exact place they wanted them. We were set up from the start. I'm *not* blaming myself, I can do my own damn shrink-work."

Sandy gazed at her for a moment. "Well, good," she said, injecting just enough of an edge into her tone, "I'm real pleased to see you don't have a problem."

"I'm angry," said Vanessa, a little more calmly. "And I'm not going to deal with all this emotional shit now. I have things to do."

Sandy took a deep breath. If that was the way Vanessa wanted to play it, she would oblige. "Are you going to be okay with the rosters?" she said instead.

"Sure, I've got Rupa doing revision plans on her spare time, even Arvid was surprised to learn he does know one end of a comp-slate from another. It's not so hard when suddenly no one's going home to sleep. We'll cover for you. Though it might be nice to know how long for?" With a questioning look.

"That's why I'm here." There was no point keeping her voice down —the soldiers in nearby beds could no doubt hear, with their enhanced hearing. But amongst CDF soldiers, she didn't mind the knowledge spreading. "That last lead we were on. Went back to the *Senate*."

Vanessa frowned. "That stray arms shipment?" Sandy nodded. "Where in the Senate?"

"Don't know. It gets kind of lost after that, even Ari can't get access to Senate files real easy. But he did find out what was in the shipments. Hi-Star multifire-type twos, plus ammunition."

"So somehow," Vanessa said slowly, "a couple of military grade, multifire rocket launchers get through customs en route to a Senate address, then wind up in the hands of a Tanushan radical nationalist movement. Ari should have fun trying to join those dots."

"Well, he's hardly bothering with the Senate," Sandy replied, "that's just banging your head against a bureaucratic wall. But he *was* talking to some contacts who know the Callay Rashtra. It looks like this was coming for a while."

"I bet Ari's real pissed he didn't notice."

"Well, that's the thing," Sandy countered, "Callay Rashtra were such patsies, they had everything fed to them on a spoon, and they bought it. Someone in the government gave them the equipment, gave them the intel, set them up for the whole thing. Ari reckons they were lured to make the rocket attack, and think it was their own idea. He *doesn't* think they knew about the GI."

"So the home grown Callayan loonies take the blame," Vanessa concluded, "while the real masterminds stay hidden."

"Giant fucking setup," Sandy confirmed. "And it worked."

"Yeah," Vanessa murmured. Her gaze slid to the small display screen upon the opposite wall, angled so the rest of the ward could view it. It was a local news channel, of course. The broadcast had slipped into what was being called by some the "holy shit" mode, where the screen was filled with blurred, uneven live images of explosions and flaming wreckage. Glimpses of weapon fire and confused carnage were interspersed with experts, espousing their very well-paid opinions. Several, to Sandy's small surprise, had books to sell, or analysis-services to promote. A few had once been CSA. And, worse, Special Investigations Bureau.

"Been following this?" Vanessa asked, sombrely.

"My seekers buzz me whenever something interesting comes up," Sandy replied. "Lots of buzzes lately."

"Saw Benale's speech?"

"Uh-huh."

There wasn't much more to say. The Secretary General had been furious. The kind of shaking, head-sweating fury that usually followed a close brush with death, in Sandy's experience—particularly when the person in question was utterly unaccustomed to such things, and was inclined toward mortal offence at the smallest inconvenience to his person. Or, rather, his Very Important Person.

There had been a huge barrage directed at the CSA and the CDF, for their "utter and inexcusable failure to provide even the smallest modicum of basic security." And another barrage for the Neiland Administration, and President Neiland herself, for "direct responsibility in stirring up some of the basest emotions at work within the Callayan political spectrum." Such an incident, he had stated, with beads of sweat gleaming in the lights on his shaved scalp, was "a grave provocation to the forces of Federal unity that Earth and its institutions represents."

"That last line was certainly a killer," Vanessa completed their mutual train of thought. "'If the government of Callay cannot even provide the basic security required for a simple summit meeting, how in the galaxy can they possibly be trusted to hold and protect the very seat of all Federation authority?'"

"Subtle little fuck, isn't he?" Sandy murmured.

"What's the Fleet doing?"

"They're in conference," Sandy said with a sigh. And hung her head, elbows forward on knees. Her neck was stiff, and she had the beginnings of a most rare condition—a headache. "Official next in command of the Fifth is Captain Rusdihardjo. Makes Duong look like a moderate. It's not going to be pretty."

"Convenient," said Vanessa. Flatly, her good eye dark with sombre meaning. "For people who'd like that promotion." Sandy nodded, wearily. "We're going to lose the stations, aren't we?"

Sandy nodded again. "They'll interpret their security prerogative independently, as is their right. Earth's a long way away, they're authorised to take whatever action they require. Intel thinks it'll be a full blown blockade. Maybe worse."

"That's not good." There was a brief silence, but for faint footsteps in the corridor beyond, and a muffled conversation between doctors. "A blockade is already a violation of Callayan sovereignty within the Federation charter. Anything more is . . . well, war."

"What really shits me," Sandy said with eyes narrowing, "is that for someone out there, this is turning out exactly the way they'd planned. I have to find that GI. She's the link between us and whoever's planning this whole mess. And if she's leaving you cryptic messages to pass on to me, maybe she'll talk rather than shoot."

"Track record there doesn't seem great," Vanessa murmured.

"GIs," Sandy said firmly, "are unpredictable. They're not machines. Higher-designation minds can't be programmed like regs. I think the message was a sign of that."

"Or maybe it's exactly what she was told to say," Vanessa replied blandly. "Maybe it's a part of a plot to get your hopes up and your guard down."

Sandy shrugged, concedingly. "Either way, I have to try. It's so much easier when they talk without shooting."

"All the same to me," Vanessa muttered. Sandy gazed at her, worriedly. Vanessa turned her single-eyed stare upon her, with dark emotion. "If she won't play civilised, promise me you won't go all soft and mushy, huh? You can't play a gentleman's game with a chimpanzee, Sandy. If she so much as blinks, you fuckin' waste her, you got me?"

It was fury, pure and simple. Worse than fury. Hatred. Sandy gazed at her friend for a long moment, and felt a slow, creeping dread moving in the pit of her stomach.

"Sure," she said finally. "Sure I will." And glanced down, for the first time, at the comp-slate resting on Vanessa's lap. Zoomed on the writing there. It was a letter. To Mr. and Mrs. Hussein, parents of young Private Omar Hussein. And she recalled in a flash a cocky, confident young man with an easy grin. A little arrogant, in the way of so many young Tanushan men, but full of spirit and life . . . "esprit," Vanessa had termed it before, in her fluent French. A word larger than itself, and much to be admired. She'd never had to write a letter like that herself, Sandy realised. All the soldiers she'd lost directly under her command had been GIs. And GIs had no one waiting at home to grieve when the letter arrived.

"It's not fair what GIs can do, Sandy," Vanessa said quietly. "It's real convenient when they're friendly and on your side. But on the receiving end . . . it's just not fucking fair. They were good kids. Good soldiers, too. They didn't stand a chance."

"Ricey." Sandy reached for Vanessa's hand upon the covers. Clasped it gently, and gave a light squeeze. "She's her. I'm me."

William Reichardt sat in *Mekong*'s captain's chair, and listened to the procession of bad news over station com. About him, the cramped metal spaces of the warship's bridge glowed the dull red of full alert, all posts occupied, terminals and operators interfacing in a familiar embrace.

"Captain," called the com officer, "we've reports of shooting in green sector, as many as seven casualties. Dockworkers, I think."

Reichardt set his jaw hard, and did not answer. Station feed was still broadcasting full schematics on Fleet encryption, and on his chair's primary display screens he could see the small blue dots of Fifth Fleet personnel spread throughout the station's circumference. It still ached—the stationmaster's final pleas for intervention clear in his memory, the thumping crashes in the background as *Amazon*'s marines had battered through the last barriers of the desperate bridge crew. There were few things William Reichardt enjoyed less than sitting helpless and watching while bad things were done. He was not, at this moment, feeling at all pleased or proud of himself. From the expressions on the faces surrounding him, he knew he wasn't the only one.

"Sir," said Cho from armscomp into that pause, "shouldn't we at least talk to Rusdi?"

"That's Captain Rusdihardjo on this bridge, shipmate," Reichardt replied, eyes not leaving the displays. "And we've got nothing to talk about."

"Captain . . ." Cho persisted, ". . . couldn't we at least try and get the stationmaster out of detention? That's just *nowhere* in the procotols, it's just plain illegal . . ."

"And shooting recalcitrant dockworkers with Fleet marines is?" Reichardt glared across the tight, display-lit space at his first mate. Cho looked exasperated, tense with anger and concern. "The Fifth just lost its admiral, Cho. This isn't a rational military procedure. This is revenge. Talking won't help."

"Captain," came first com again, "I have a secure transmission from *Pearl River*."

"Captain's chair," said Reichardt.

"*Billy*," said Captain Marakova in his ear the second his connection established, "*I've given you an hour to think it over, and now I want an answer. What's your next move?*"

"Lidya, I have no authorisation to deal with this situation." It took several seconds for the signal to reach *Pearl River* and return, from mid-orbit to high geostationary and back. Reichardt's display counted the seconds for him.

"*Utter nonsense, those gutless fools left you in charge, they're in no position to complain if they don't like your actions. Rusdi's always been half-crazy, you know what I think happened here.*"

"Yeah," Reichardt replied, not bothering to keep the frustration out of his voice, "I'm not real interested in political conspiracy theories right now, Lidya. Neither am I in any frame of mind to initiate hostilities with the Fifth Fleet."

His eye strayed over the nav display as he spoke. Four major stations servicing the world of Callay. The Third Fleet, under his unofficial command, had one warship docked at each, and three more in geostationary "watch." *Mekong* was the only carrier. *Pearl River* was an intercept cruiser, as were three others of similar class—plenty fast for deep space engagements, but equipped with only small marine complements, and not designed for boarding and occupying. The other two were rim hunters, midsized and equipped for outer-system sweeps, where pirates and raiders liked to hide. Lots of sensory gear, plenty of mobility, but not much firepower.

In situations short of a shooting war, carriers were most useful, and most provocative. *Amazon*'s complement of three hundred marines, plus another three hundred from the *Yangtze*, now held Nehru Station, and its entire thirty-thousand-strong resident population, completely under Fifth Fleet control. Carriers on two of the other three stations had done likewise—Ryan Station was oldest and smallest, and only required several cruisers' complements to secure. Four carriers . . . one hell of a provocation. One didn't send four carriers to a supposedly friendly system unless there was a great suspicion that they'd be required. Damn right his old friend Lidya Marakova was suspicious.

"Hell, Lidy," he muttered into his headset mike, "thirty years.

Thirty years we've been doing it this way—a planet here, a few stations there. Thirty years out in the cold, away from civilisation, making our own rules against opponents who didn't always believe in them. Now we're back in civilisation, and it doesn't recognise us . . . or we don't recognise it. What the hell's happened here?"

"*Someone should explain to Rusdi that she was never betrayed.*" Marakova's voice was filled with contempt. "*The Federation didn't abandon her or her values. Rather it had never accepted her damn values in the first place. Somewhere out there in the cold, she forgot. That is all that's happened here.*"

"She thinks she came home from the war to find her husband in bed with another woman," Reichardt countered. "*That's* what we're dealing with here. She's real pissed, and I'm not going to start playing chicken with someone who doesn't know how to flinch." His screen illuminated briefly, indicating another incoming call. "Hold on, Lidya, I've got Verjee on the line." He switched to the local, station line. "Hello, Captain Verjee, what can I do for you?"

"*Captain Reichardt,*" came the new voice, with none of Marakova's easy informality. "*Due to recent events, the station is now facing crew shortages in cargo and docking departments. This is an official request from acting-Admiral Rusdihardjo that you deploy a complement of your troops to help fill this vacancy.*"

From the neighbouring seat, Cho stared at him in disbelief, sharing the higher officers' linkage to all operational com. Reichardt took a deep breath.

"I'm not deploying anyone from *Mekong* into an unworkable environment," he replied, with what he thought was commendable calm. "You reinstate the stationmaster to his rightful post and release all the dockworkers you've detained, and I might reconsider your proposal."

A pause at the other end. "Is he fucking kidding?" Cho mouthed to him, silently. Reichardt just shook his head.

"*You misunderstand the nature of this communication, Captain. This is not a request, it is an order from a senior officer.*"

"I do not accept Captain Rusdihardjo's new promotion," Reichardt replied with a hardening tone.

*"We are a long way from any committee to decide the issue, Captain. As I understand the order, you shall either comply with this instruction, or you shall be found to be in defiance, and removed hencewith."*

"Like fuck you will," growled someone from the other side of the bridge. "You can try," Reichardt said simply. There was no immediate reply from the other end. Anxious faces around the bridge turned Reichardt's way. Familiar faces. Close friends, many of them. People who'd been there when Kresnov had ordered the orbital strike upon Tanusha's Gordon Spaceport, and gotten them embroiled in this two-year-long mess. Some who'd been there far longer than that, through combat against the League, through horrors and terrors he'd never have wished on anyone, least of all his friends.

The Fifth Fleet had gone through those horrors too. Only it hadn't been the same Fifth Fleet, then. When it had all ended three years ago, lots of ships were decommissioned, lots of crews stood down and eager to return home. Somehow, the hardliners had all stayed. Many of those from broken squadrons in the other Fleets had also, somehow, gotten transferred sideways into the Fifth. Reichardt had always known these people existed. But he'd never seen so many of them all crammed into the one space at the same time. In command of so much firepower, in orbit around the world that was to become, God willing, the new centre of the Federation. Something had gone very badly wrong with the whole process for things to end up like this. It made him wonder, for the thousandth time in recent days, if that alone didn't prove what the likes of President Neiland had been saying all along, about the bureaucratic despotism and corruption that had grown into the old, Earth-centric Grand Council over thirty years of war, unlimited budgets, military secrecy and centralised power.

What would these people give to hold onto their preciously acquired authority? What would they do? What had they done already? And how in the name of all the hells of all humanity's many religions had *he* managed to end up holding the can?

"*Captain*," Verjee said at last, "*we are the Fleet. We cannot be so divided. You have no authority to reject acting-Admiral Rusdihardjo's demands.*"

"Fine, you tell her to start abiding by Federation law, and I'll place myself entirely within her service."

"*That is not your call to decide, Captain.*"

"Nor hers to blockade what is effectively the capital world of the Federation."

"*Not yet it's not.*"

Reichardt nearly smiled. There it was, right there. Four little words, one enormous problem. "But it is, I'm afraid, Captain Verjee. Little thing called democracy. The people of the Federation have spoken. I serve their wishes. You only serve Earth's wishes. Until your attitude changes, you have no authority, by Federation law, over me, or over any vessel of the Third Fleet. If you attempt to assert such authority, the Third Fleet within Callayan space shall be left with no other choice than to resist by any means necessary, in accordance with our oath to serve the people of the Federation. Do you understand that, Captain Verjee?"

Another link established itself to *Mekong*'s com. This one came directly from *Amazon*.

"*Captain Reichardt,*" came Rusdihardjo's cool, mild voice. "*Your position is very clear. At least, now, we all know where everyone stands.*"

"Indeed, Captain," Reichardt replied. "Indeed we do."


"I'm not listening to you," Sandy told Ari, gazing out at the blazing carpet of light that was nighttime Tanusha. A gentle breeze, smelling of rain and recent thunderstorms, tossed at her hair. Beyond the rooftop security railing, fifty storeys below, lay Chatterjee Park, dark and crisscrossed with lighted paths.

"Wh . . . why aren't you listening to me?" Ari gave her a sideways, concerned glance, gloved hands upon the railing. He'd had false retinal overlays done long ago, but he still worried about fingerprints. Sandy had assured him often that no Tanushan organisation she knew of, legitimate or otherwise, concerned themselves with fingerprints. But, well . . . some people called Ari paranoid.

"I'm not sure," said Sandy. "Perhaps it's the two years of lies and secrecy in all the time I've known you."

"Oh, right . . ." Ari nodded. "I guess that could be it, huh."

The target of their attentions, the Golden Welcome Hotel, stood upon the northern end of Chatterjee Park. Perhaps fifty storeys tall, it was shaped like a giant, four-sided pyramid. Fancy lighting flashed along its angled corners, and at some points decorative lasers strobed the overcast sky.

"He's bound to be very well guarded," Ari attempted again, in a mild, matter-of-fact tone.

"I know," said Sandy. "That's why you're going to help me."

"Um . . . when I said very well guarded, Sandy, I kind of meant the network barriers as much as the physical ones."

"Enough with the false modesty. I know you can get me in."

Ari coughed self-consciously. "What if I don't want to?"

"Then I'll probably get caught, and it'll be very embarrassing for the CDF, CSA, President Neiland and Callay in general."

"Sandy . . . look, I do a lot of things in the service of this wonderful planet and its . . . its charming, worthy inhabitants," Sandy rolled her eyes, "but I never just outright go and break the law." Sandy looked at him. "Well okay . . . I *do* fiddle a bit at the edges, but I'm allowed to, that's the wonder of the new security legislation."

"You're telling me that you're a *professional* law breaker? Oh, that's all right then."

"I'm trying to tell you," Ari said with the beginnings of impatience, "that just breaking into a private company's data files is illegal."

"This isn't a big enough crisis for your security legislation to cover?"

"You're a soldier, Sandy. Special circumstances cover Intel operators only."

"So help me, Mr. Bigshot Intel Operator, and I'll be a part of your operation."

Ari sighed, knowing a losing situation when he saw one. Lightning leaped upon the distant horizon, outlining a forest silhouette of towers between, stretching away into the distance. On streets below, people flowed like a river, alive with lights and the occasional, airborne streak of amateur pyrotechnics.

"They're rioting over at EarthGov Embassy," Ari commented. "My friend Sanjay was there, he said the marines guarding the place looked nervous." There was a note of disbelief in his voice. Ari criticised Tanusha often, but it was his home. He'd lived here all his life, and had no intention of leaving. Sandy wondered what it was like, to be that attached to a place, and see it all turned upside down so quickly.

"Cops must have done a good job though," she said. "Considering no one's dead yet."

"Give it time," Ari murmured. "I've never seen people so angry. I mean, a *blockade*. They're blockading *commerce*. That's like banning a musician from playing music, or . . . or a net addict from diving."

"Or a nymphomaniac from screwing," Sandy offered.

"This friend of mine, Sanjay . . . did you ever meet Sanjay?"

"Not yet."

"He was a key organiser in a group called 'Callayans Against the War,' one of the pacifist groups protesting the League-Federation war. He said nothing could ever justify violence. Now he's throwing stones at the EarthGov Embassy." Ari shook his head in amazement.

"Only people who've never suffered," Sandy murmured, "and never known what it's like to lose everything at the point of a gun, could ever think there was nothing in the world worth fighting for."

An hour later, Sandy walked along the central path of Chatterjee Park, gazing up at the enormous, sloping side of dark glass, tapering toward its pyramidal apex far above.

"*What a horrible design*," Sandy formulated upon Ari's tailor-encrypted tac-net. It linked, he said, into particular subroutes within the local Tanushan network, and built those narrow-access protections into its tight encryption base. She couldn't uplink into the network herself, nor download vast quantities of data other than what Ari fed to her via relay, but it did allow verbal communication between them without (Ari insisted) leaving her vulnerable to the killswitch codes. "*Mathematicians and geometricians should leave architecture to real architects.*"

"*I like it*," came Ari's predictable reply in her ear.

"*Looks like something out of Orwell*," Sandy retorted.

"*Who?*"

"*Never mind*," Sandy replied, with as close as uplink formulation allowed her to come to a sigh. Sometimes she couldn't help but think that multicultural, vibrant, artistic Tanusha was somewhat wasted on Ari.

Sandy entered through the main lobby—an enormous, high-ceilinged space with cutaway hotel levels ahead, and a broad, sunken lounge-restaurant to the left. Sandy panned her vision across the broad reception desk to the right as she walked, letting Ari see the security guard at the far end, scanning the lobby.

"*Ari, I'm going to take off my sunglasses, this guy's going to ping me.*"

"*Yeah, okay . . . I'm into it, you're clear.*" "It," of course, was the security system monitoring the lobby by remote, which included facial recognition. It would also tend to register anyone wearing sunglasses inside as worthy of double-checking, as would the guard by reception. Exactly how Ari managed to fool a high-grade visual security system into not recognising her, Sandy didn't know—her own uplinks (when she could use them) were superior where simple hack-and-disable routines were concerned, but those kinds of sledgehammer routines were of little use to a covert operator like Ari. This kind of thing required subtlety . . . something an alarming number of her friends had accused her of lacking, at one time or another.

She removed the shades and pocketed them, her gaze wandering disinterestedly as she walked. Hotel guests wandered the lobby, heading in from a meal, or heading out for late-night drinks or shows. None of their outfits appeared to cost less than a CDF officer's monthly salary. Or yearly salary, she reflected with a glance at several outrageous gowns with enough jewellery to fill a small store at the Rawalpindi gold souk. Callayan tourism had fallen during the initial troubles two years ago, and then soared once the relocation was announced. Now, Sandy thought sourly, the continuing troubles appeared almost a part of the package—come visit Callay for the wide spaces of the outback, for the unrivalled nightlife of Tanusha, and for the thrills and excitement of a genuine political crisis, complete with assassinations, intrigue, and more tension than ten holovid dramas.

She made it across the lobby without the guard or anyone else recognising her, and slipped the sunglasses back on as one of numerous elevators opened to admit a new group directly before her. One of those, she noted with relief, was a similarly dressed underground-noir type, with a long black coat, boots and a tall, spiky mohawk. So at least she wasn't going to look totally out of place. She ducked into the empty elevator and pressed the door-close before the next group of guests could arrive.

"*The central elevator would have taken you up further,*" Ari said reprovingly in her ear.

"*And more people use it. I don't want to be recognised.*"

"*Hold on . . . no, okay, I see another way. Take it to the top and turn left.*"

The elevator made it to the thirtieth floor without interruption, and Sandy exited to find that left was the only way she could go—to the right, the hall ended with the angled glass of the hotel's exterior, beyond which the city lights shone blurrily through the falling rain. Sandy passed a well-dressed couple too engaged in hilarious conversation in the hall to notice her, and glanced at the holographic wall displays at the next T-junction. A display of the entire pyramid structure stood on a low podium cut into the intersecting corner, shimmering with light, its main thoroughfares and attractions highlighted in red, blue or gold.

"*Ignore that,*" Ari told her, seeing what she saw through their encrypted link. "*That doesn't tell the half of it.*"

She walked to the end of the hall, hearing strained on maximum trying to filter echoing conversation and footsteps from the throbbing hum of the aircon vents.

"*Stairwell on the left,*" said Ari. "*Down two flights.*" Sandy entered, and rattled down at speed. And paused at the level twenty-eight door as Ari said, "*Wait. Two security passing near, they're fully integrated.*" And gave a faint whistle. "*Very fully integrated. I could get you their Acred-file numbers if you wanted.*"

"*Just try sticking to the job, Ari.*"

"*Sorry. Old habits. You're clear, they went past.*" Sandy entered the hall, and went left. "*Now, you've got a maintenance door coming up on your left. I can get you a . . . three-second window to open that door and close it again before the sweepers reconfigure my integration module and notice the hack.*"

"Got it." She saw the door, on the left, clearly marked NO UNAUTHORISED ADMITTANCE. Ari's signal counted toward the three-second window as she approached. And she saw the guest room door click open just ten metres further on. The departing man—African, in a loose, flashy blue outfit—was still chatting loudly with someone inside the room as he backed out. Sandy grasped the door handle, opened as Ari's signal hit zero, and slipped inside without the distracted guest appearing to notice. Closed the door behind her, well inside Ari's parameters, and continued within.

Inside was a dark maintenance passageway. A large bundle of pipes and wires ran across the ceiling ahead, and built-in ladders climbed the walls into crawlways along the sides. She ducked under the pipes, not hearing any other activity beyond the relative din of aircon and pumping machinery, here away from the soundproofed guest areas. The lighted doorway beyond stood open to what looked like empty air.

Sandy arrived, and found that she stood on a metal grille footway, twenty-eight storeys above the open hotel floor. From far below, music blared, and lights flashed. The floor was huge, one entire side of the pyramid structure devoted to entertainment and, by the looks of at least half of it, gambling. Casino tables sprawled, surrounded by milling crowds of the well dressed and affluent, and several hundred bodies danced on a nightclub floor beneath the soaring, sloping glass ceiling. To the right, along the vertical inner wall, the footway led to a crossbridge, where angled wall met the vertical. Intervening, how-ever, was a metal grille security door.

"*That's not on the graphic,*" said Ari.

Sandy sighed. "*I could climb around.*"

"*Um . . . no, that's all tripwired, you'll set it off. Just wait, I'll find it.*"

Sandy crouched in the shadow of the doorway and waited, watching multiple directions at once in case of wandering maintenance staff. From the audible deep rush of ventilation systems, it seemed to her that the building was massively overpowered. Being an assault commander made her something of an expert on modern architecture, if from a slightly different perspective than the average citizen. Most Tanushan buildings of this scale possessed remarkably low energy requirements, thanks again to strict central regulations encouraging "environmental sensibilities." Not, of course, that Tanusha's twenty-five underground and peripheral fusion reactors meant that the city could ever be short of cheap, zero-polluting energy. But "environ-mental sensibilities" was one of those codewords for that peculiarly Tanushan aestheticism that one found everywhere, meaning natural sunlight, convection-assisted ventilation, and the absolute minimum of what the planners liked to call "structural imposition" . . . meaning, at its most simplistic, anything that got in the way of a view. "Organic building," was the other codeword. Buildings that breathed, and dispersed heat and energy, and people, like a natural, living organism.

This damn pyramid only seemed to live on life support, as evidenced by the noisy machinery pumping air, water and heat through its unstreamlined bowels. Sandy wondered how the hell anyone had gotten this design past the planners. Unless "variety," that other much-loved concept of the planners, dictated that there should be at least one ugly, inefficient, League-style monstrosity in the city. A landmark. Architects, Sandy thought, like artists, seemed to suffer from the illusion that uniqueness was a value in itself. As far as she could see, a unique piece of shit was still a piece of shit, by any other name.

"*I still don't like this damn building,*" she muttered.

"*Oh, come on,*" Ari said mildly. The distraction would not bother him, she knew—he liked to talk while he worked. It was something they had in common—multiple-track brains. "*Look at that enormous, sloping sheet of glass, cascading with rain and all lit up with internal lights and external lightning and the city lights outside . . .*" Showing off, to demonstrate exactly how good his visual feed was. "*Isn't that an amazing sight?*"

"*It's amazingly inefficient. Spectacle is the shield behind which insubstantial people hide.*"

"*Oh, so this is an* ideological *objection. Nice to have some company in my irrational, ideological frenzies . . .*"

Sandy snorted, and gazed over at the crossbridge. It disappeared into what looked like another open doorway like the one she was presently in. She could jump the distance comfortably, but someone might see it. Given Ari's network capabilities, it seemed a pointless risk to take.

"*At least we know why they wanted you dead,*" Ari said after a moment.

"*We do?*"

"*To kill Duong. It wasn't ideological at all. They just wanted you out of the way so they could kill him.*"

*"Vanessa did a great job,"* Sandy said firmly.

*"Sure. Sure she did."* A little anxiously. *"But you're the only one who could have stopped that GI."*

*"Maybe. So Callay Rashtra were set up to take the blame?"* Callay Rashtra were the latest local extremist group to be splashed all over the news. Several senior CSA people had immediately issued gloating "told you so"s, having trumpeted warnings about Callay Rashtra for the last several years. Ari, who of course had met several members personally, didn't believe a word of it. They were not, he'd insisted, anywhere near organised enough to pull off operations of such complexity as a rocket attack upon a major summit. Where such judgements were concerned, Sandy took Ari's opinions over all others as a matter of policy.

Of course, not even the Fifth Fleet, led by the particularly incensed Captain Rusdihardjo, and cheered on from the sidelines by Secretary General Benale, had been able to link Callay Rashtra's attack with the GI who had killed Admiral Duong. Instead, they questioned whether there had been a GI at all, implying that it was all a fabricated plot by shadowy Callayan authorities to deny complicity. Given how little information regarding internal security workings anyone in power was actually allowed to reveal to the public, it was a difficult charge to counter. Not that it would have made any difference, Sandy reckoned.

*"And invite everyone to blame it on Callayan extremists, sure,"* said Ari. *"And affirm to right-minded people everywhere that the Fleet is only here for our own protection . . . I mean clearly, Callayans just can't be trusted with their own affairs."*

*"Let alone control of the Fleet."*

*"Exactly. Try that."*

Sandy grasped the handle on the security gate, and multiple locks clicked open. She ducked through quickly, closed it behind her, and walked along the footway and across the crossbridge. Below, the band were playing something hyper-techno, with lots of electronic harmonics and a skitting, unpredictable rhythm. Damn, this really was

Ari's kind of place. No one seemed to notice the dark shape upon the overhead walkways, and she ducked through the end doorway . . . and into what appeared to be a maintenance room for the automated window cleaners. Several of the insectoid, sucker-footed robots awaited in maintenance cradles.

Sandy flitted from shadow to shadow, pressing herself to one corner wall and listening hard . . . heard the faint, electronic manipulation of controls further along the passage beneath the sloping glass, and the weight of a body shifting in a control chair.

*"Ladder ten metres to your front,"* said Ari. A maintenance worker emerged from a doorway, turning unawares to resume work on one of the glass cleaners. Sandy darted silently across to the ladder, and rapidly climbed several levels. From there it was a relatively simple matter for Ari to override the controls for the maintenance elevator, into which she climbed. The maintenance elevator rode up the side of the pyramid at a forty-five-degree angle, suspended by overhead rails and passing through maintenance levels along the way. Sandy sat upon the lowest row of seats provided, the elevator floor sloping before her at that same forty-five degrees, and saw through the porthole the face of one worker who was waiting for the elevator, and was evidently surprised when it didn't stop.

At level forty-nine, at the top of its rails, the elevator did stop. The doors unfolded outward, and Sandy jumped lightly from her seat to the ground, and headed along the short, dimly lit passage toward where the pyramid's central elevator shaft would be. Part way along, the end security door opened with Sandy not five metres away.

*"Oh, shit,"* said Ari. *"Hide."* The corridor here was straight, and the nearest doorway was five metres behind her. Even with her speed, Sandy knew it was impossible.

*"Can't,"* she said. The maintenance worker—a round-faced man of Chinese appearance with a thin beard—stopped and frowned at her.

*"Damn,"* said Ari. *"Do something."*

*"Like what?"*

"Who are you?" the worker demanded, suspiciously. Sandy supposed it wouldn't help much to put her hands in her pockets and whistle nonchalantly. "What are you doing in here?"

*"I dunno!"* Ari retorted. *"Punch his lights out!"*

*"Ari,"* Sandy formulated, somewhat testily, *"I'm not about to go around putting civilians in hospital. Jam his uplinks, if he's got them."*

And the maintenance worker's suspicion turned to frowning puzzlement, indeed as if he'd just attempted to raise the alarm, and found his uplinks strangely nonfunctional. On a flash of inspiration, Sandy whipped off her sunglasses, and strode forward. The worker took a pose that suggested he did know how to fight (fight-tape was a popular expense among many blue-collar Tanushan workers), and Sandy ran a purposeful hand through her hair, brushing back the wet fringe to give him a good look at her face. He froze, eyes widening.

"C—Com—Commander Kresnov?" Incredulously.

"That's right," she told him. "You surprised me. I'm here on a mission. It's very important that no one knows I'm here."

"You . . . you . . ." The man seemed to be having difficulty getting his head around it, for which she supposed she could hardly blame him. "You broke in?"

"Yes. I need to speak to someone here privately."

*"Sandy,"* Ari said plaintively in her ear, *"this is not a good idea . . . he . . . he could freak out, he could tell everyone and then they'll sweep their systems and find me, and then . . ."*

"You're here to see Takawashi?" the maintenance worker exclaimed as it occurred to him, his eyes widening. "Or, no . . . hold on, you don't like Takawashi, do you? You ran away from people like him in the League?"

"That's right." How much he knew would determine how she ended up playing this, she reckoned. Let him keep talking.

"My . . . my buddies and me were talking about it . . . you know, having Takawashi here and all that, we wondered if you'd met him yet. I reckoned you'd hate his guts." Gazing at her, with wondering excitement.

"*Pay attention, Ari,*" she formulated silently, "*see here the knowledge and wisdom of the ordinary Tanushans you're always disparaging.*" And to the maintenance worker, quite bluntly, she said, "I'm not here to talk to him. I'm here to steal something from him." And she could all but hear Ari's exasperated sigh from the other end of his uplink. The worker blinked, rapidly. Then thrust a hand into his jumpsuit pocket, and withdrew a small, round security insert-key.

"I'll probably lose my job for this, but . . ." and he thrust the key into her hand. "Take it. I'll say I lost it. He's got his own security systems rigged through the penthouse, this'll get you access past the initial barriers, you can disable whatever you like from there."

Sandy smiled at him. "Thank you," she said, and meant it.

The worker shrugged. "We're practically at war, and you're the boss. As far as I'm concerned, you were never here."

Sandy clasped his arm. "If you do lose your job, contact me through the CSA. I have a few friends who could find you another one."

She slipped past him toward the security door. "*Gee, I wonder who's going to be doing the job hunting for your new friend?*"

"*Stop complaining. Sometimes it takes a bit of feminine subtlety, Ari.*"

"*Let me make a note of that.*"

The lift door opened a silent fraction. Sandy hung within the elevator shaft, suspended by the steely fingers of her right hand from a structural beam just below the doors. No light came through the narrow gap. Behind, in the shaft, the elevator cables began whirring once more. The car itself remained a good forty storeys below, shuttling mostly between the ground floor, and the bottom twenty storeys that held the majority of the hotel's guest rooms—logically, within a pyramidal structure. But surely even the soft whistle of high-tension cables would penetrate the room within, as perhaps would some breeze.

"*Clear*," murmured Ari's voice in her ear. Not that he needed to murmur, really. But the lower his voice, the more hearing she'd have to devote to her surroundings. "*Sorry for the delay . . . he's got it rigged like a maze, mostly League-codings, too. But it looks okay now.*"

Sandy gave a couple of experimental pulls with her right arm, testing the grip and the leverage. Then she tensed, and gave a sharp yank. Flew briefly upward, thrust her casted arm between the doors with her left leg, and slid quickly through, her right hand retrieving the pistol from inside her jacket even before she'd cleared the doors. Then, in a low crouch with pistol ready, she surveyed the room.

As expected for something named the "Presidential Suite," it was enormous. A broad, dark polished floor was softened by an expensive rug, before descending several steps to a sunken lounge in front of the angled windows that formed one corner of the square floorplan. The four-sided, glass pyramid met its apex directly overhead, structural supports ending in an overhead square frame, leaving the actual tip entirely transparent. Laser lights blazed skywards from their overhead mounts, sweeping the rainswept heavens with choreographed patterns. The elevator shaft, before which Sandy now crouched, was located in one corner of the suite, leaving the rest of the floor bare, but for the luxuriant, modern furnishings. In another corner was a grand, wide bed, surrounded on all sides by the soaring, electric view of nighttime Tanusha, spectacular even dimmed behind the steady fall of rain.

"*Not bad for a studio apartment,*" Ari couldn't help commenting. "*Where's the bathroom?*"

"*Just beside me, there's a curtain adjoining this elevator,*" Sandy formulated a reply. "*Just as well it's one-way glass, though—not much privacy, otherwise.*"

"*No. Considering all the depraved things Mr. Takawashi is reputed to do in his lofty towers.*"

Sandy moved silently across the floor, careful to skirt the carpet in case of hidden pressure sensors. She certainly didn't feel very hidden, considering the three-sixty degree views of cityscape. Lightning flashed in the middle-distance, throwing her shadow dancingly across the sofa and vid-screen arrangement to one side of the floor centre. A large fish tank, used cleverly to divide the open space, added gliding, bubbling colour to the darkened space.

Sandy paused beside the vid-screen, unspooling a cord from her pocket, inserting one end into the back of her skull, and the other into the socket provided beneath the screen. It was a familiar data-rush, a sudden graphical illustration of so many old patterns. League patterns, and a whole different philosophy of base code and interweaving textual design . . .

"*There's the private database,*" she said as she found it, "*I knew he'd need a booster to access . . . are you reading this?*"

"*Yeah, I'm getting flashes . . . damn it, Sandy, slow down a bit, that's too fucking fast for anyone's mental health.*"

"*No time,*" she said. "*He's not going to store much here in the apartment, but if we could just find an itinerary, or some proof of business dealings, we might get some idea of why he's here in Tanusha at all . . .*"

The flow of data stopped, as if a cord had been snipped by a pair of scissors. Light flickered to life through the apartment, a dim, atmospheric glow of soft insets about the floor and angled ceiling structure. Damn it. Sandy knew better than to go fully into combat mode, or scan furiously about with her weapon levelled. The only GI-trap that could have worked in these surroundings, with so little cover, was the entire floor rigged to blow. Which would not have been preceded by the lights turning on.

"Okay, where are you?" she announced resignedly, disconnecting her cord and standing up. Ari registered no surprise or protest in her ear, having established very conclusively that Mr. Takawashi and entourage were presently at a large function on the other side of Tanusha. Ari, in fact, said nothing at all. No doubt the security systems had cut off their communication channel when activated.

There came a faint, rustling motion from the bed in the far corner.

Then a slim, long-fingered hand grasped the covers, and pulled the man himself upright in a slow, unfolding movement. He was thin, elegantly dressed in a silver kimono with pink petals. He held a slim black cane in one hand, and seemed uncertain of his balance without it. And his shoulders were shaking, faintly, as if he were . . . laughing. A soft, hissing chuckle, with evident, unexpected merriment.

"Cassandra Kresnov," announced a soft, faintly wheezing voice. He moved forward, steady enough with the aid of his cane, in a slow glide of silver robes across the polished floor. The smooth yet gaunt face remained in shadow, the suite's illumination being little more than mood lighting, on their present setting. "The great strategist, outwitted by an old man. I am amazed, truly amazed."

"If I'd come here to kill you, pal, I wouldn't have bothered with all this sneaking around." Adjusting her vision to penetrate the gloom. Takawashi's dark, half-oriental eyes were fixed upon her with unerring fascination. Something about them made her uncomfortable. Cold, even. He seemed so . . . sure of himself. Few people did, upon first meeting her.

"But you, Cassandra Kresnov, would never have come here to kill me," said Takawashi, the faintest traces of a smile curling at his thin, taut lips. The cane tapped upon the hard floor as he glided closer, then stopped, just five metres away, beyond the furthest of the leather chairs that surrounded the vid-screen.

"You don't know me," Sandy said coldly. "I'm far more than the sum total of all your psych-simulation experiments."

"Oh, Ms. Kresnov," Takawashi sighed, shaking his head with tired humour. "If only it were true." And the smile grew a little broader, with genuine, devilish amusement. "But here's the little secret," he said, leaning forward on his cane, conspiratorially. "None of us are."

He beamed at her for a moment. And for one brief, startling moment, Sandy found herself reminded of her old friend, the Callayan senator, Swami Ananda Ghosh. Another old man, leaning upon his cane, face lined with age and beady eyes brimming with wisdom. One derived his wisdom through science, the other through faith. Was one wiser than the other? Was science wiser, for always providing answers where faith so frequently failed? Or was faith the wiser, for always asking the questions that science could not answer? And she blinked herself back to the moment, but Takawashi was already gliding away, down the steps of the sunken lounge, headed for the small drinks bar.

"The maintenance worker in the corridor," Sandy said, watching his descent, curiously. "He's one of yours?"

"Maintenance worker?" Takawashi paused upon the lower step, swivelling part way to regard her. "I have made no use of any maintenance worker." And he smiled, knowingly, like a kindly uncle teasing his niece about a new boyfriend. "I do understand, Cassandra, that you have numerous admirers, here on Callay. Unsurprising. Your social skills were always amongst your most surprising developments."

"How did you know I was coming?" Sandy pressed, determined not to be swayed by Takawashi's tantalising bait, so artfully dangled before her.

"Ever the pragmatist, even so," Takawashi sighed. He sipped at his drink. From the involuntary pursing of his lips, she guessed the clear substance was not water. "A man in my position has the luxury of keeping the audience waiting. Tonight's engagement has been temporarily postponed. Even a master of bio-science suffers the odd cold every now and then. Particularly at my age."

Another sip. Sandy merely watched, and waited for him to answer the question. Takawashi smiled, indulgently. "Dear girl, I knew you were coming. Of course, you have the pretext of wanting to find out about this rogue GI running about the city, killing senior Fleet admirals on a whim. But mostly, you could not pass up an opportunity to meet with me."

"Don't flatter yourself. If I knew you were here, I wouldn't have broken in."

Takawashi laughed, the smooth, drawn face abruptly stretching into deep, aged creases, that vanished as his expression regained his previous, calm amusement. "Come, Cassandra, you have not touched your drink. I assure you I have not spiked it with GI-specific chemicals, you know full well that there are none that could harm you from just a small taste."

Sandy took a small, almost negligible sip, her eyes not leaving his. A cocktail, with an alcoholic base and . . . makani fruit juice. Her favourite. Something must have registered in her eyes, for Takawashi smiled.

"Wonderful, is it not?" he said. "Taste. Smell." Lightning flashed nearby, briefly obliterating the suite's broad shadows. "Sight, and . . ." he waited, and then came the booming rumble of thunder, ". . . sound. Wonderful that we should take such pleasure in such simple things. Some people most admire the human species for intelligence. Others for courage, or spirit, or imagination. I most admire the human species for pleasure. Imagine the selfless wonder of a species whose neurological reaction to the universe's stimuli is . . . pleasure." He beamed at her. "I understand that you yourself are well versed in the art of pleasure. I wonder if your present environment continues to provide you with such avenues as you had become accustomed, when you were a soldier."

"I'm still a soldier," Sandy said flatly. "And quite frankly, Mr. Takawashi, that's not a question for polite company, in this city."

"Old men become coarse and mannerless with age." With a gleaming smile. "There was a time, I understand, when you seemed to accumulate bed partners like an entomologist accumulates beetles. Perhaps the Federation has civilised you? Transformed you into a model of 'polite company'?"

There was knowledge behind his question. A depth of insight that turned her stomach cold, and raised the hairs on the back of her neck. Surely he couldn't know her personal details from direct sources. He must be guessing. But they did not feel like guesses. They felt like . . . probing. Seeking long-suspected answers to questions he'd long wanted to ask. Oh, so much he must have known about her, in those early years of her life. How he must have watched. Her instinct was to shove his curiosity back in his face. But that would only demonstrate the power he held over her, with that knowledge. If he wanted to know, fine. Give him a taste. Make him want more. Give her power over *him*.

"In truth, Mr. Takawashi, I find my sexual urges have become more controllable." Meeting his gaze calmly. There was no doubting the intrigue in his eyes. "Not receded, as such, not in intensity." Ari could attest to that, she thought . . . but kept to herself. "But they do not distract my thoughts as they once did, during idle periods." And once begun, now she could stop. Once, that had been a problem. "I think now that they were a way for my brain to seek an outlet. An escape of pent-up energy, if you like. Now, here in Tanusha, I have so many other things to occupy my attention. Whole parts of my consciousness and my personality have been unlocked that previously lay dormant. I believe I have found an equilibrium that I did not possess in the League . . . and in fact that the League was incapable of delivering me. I owe the Federation. In many ways, I feel I owe them my life . . . for my life without the things I have found here, I now find impossible to imagine."

Takawashi's expression unsettled her. There was more than fascination, and more than excitement. It was a look of deep, deep affection. "I had suspected, I had suspected!" He clicked his fingers repeatedly, as if in some kind of triumph. "And tell me, which aspects of mundane, civilian life do you most enjoy? Surely you haven't lost your taste for reading and music . . . but tell me, have you attempted an instrument yourself? Do you cook?" And paused as something most especially fascinating occurred to him. "Or have you found yourself taking particular interest in a *religion*?"

Sandy smiled, sipping at her makani and spirits once more. "In time, Mr. Takawashi, in time. First, tell me about this GI."

Takawashi laughed, with a rasping rattle in his throat not present when he spoke. "Very well, Ms. Kresnov. Very well played. Come, sit with me." He waved a silver-robed arm down the stairs, at the sunken lounge. Sandy nodded, and Takawashi began a slow descent. Sandy detoured to the fish tank at the top of the stairs, wanting Takawashi to take a chair first, and give her the choice of seats. "This is a painful business for me, Cassandra. My fascination in the field was not intended to produce soldiers."

"So you've said on many occasions," Sandy replied, pausing before the fish tank. Callayan reef fish, multicoloured and lovely on the eye. Evolution followed the same paths in similar environments. An astonishing discovery, it had been for Earth's first explorer-starfarers. Water was water. Gills, fins and a streamlined shape were highly efficient. Nature loved efficiency, and punished the inefficient with ruthless consistency. Only where worlds offered environments radically different from Earth-like, prime worlds like Callay, did evolutionary patterns significantly alter . . . and faster-than-light technology gave humanity a vast enough range that the habitation of such worlds, although possible, was hardly necessary. Prime worlds were roughly one in ten thousand. A G-Class freighter, with a single-jump range of a hundred light years, and capable of dual or even triple-jump routes, was within theoretical range of many times ten thousand systems. Less hospitable worlds than Callay were typically bypassed, along with the vast majority of systems possessing nothing even vaguely habitable to oxygen breathers of any species.

"We limit ourselves with our choices," she abruptly recalled Takawashi as saying once. It had been in an interview she'd seen . . . on Callayan television, wonder of wonders. Callay had been taking a greater interest in such people of late, and in relations with the League in general . . . for which Sandy supposed she could take at least partial credit. Or blame. The interview with the great man of synthetic neuroscience had been quite a coup. "The spread of spacefaring humanity was supposed to be the great, species-shaping challenge that would mold us into a better, more diverse, more capable people. But for all our wondrous accomplishment, our greatest promise remains unfulfilled. We bypassed the difficult worlds, we ignored the most challenging environments . . . we found at least one intelligent species upon the furthest reaches of our space, and we retreated in fear and caution.

"The League was founded by people who believe humanity's greatest promise is yet to be fulfilled. Synthetic, biological replication technology is merely a logical extension of this philosophical tenet. It is the constant yearning for self-improvement, for discovery, expansion and renewal, that makes us truly human. Evolution made us who we are, but evolution lost its grip upon our destiny from the first moment an ape brandished a tool and used it to manipulate his environment. *We* now have control of our destiny. And we must evolve ourselves, for our own reasons, and our own purposes."

A prospect, of course, that terrified much of the Federation, given that the League's stated reasons and purposes seemed mostly about commerce, power and ideological supremecy. Terrified them so much, in fact, that they were prepared to fight a war to stop it all from happening . . . and thus ensured that synthetic biotech would develop in precisely the direction whose possibility had so frightened them all in the first place. Developments like GIs. Like Cassandra Kresnov.

Sandy wondered what the fish would make of it all. Stabiliser fins, a sleek tail and gleaming, flashing scales . . . they seemed perfectly happy. Or would do, if happiness were a part of any fish's repertoire. She didn't want new limbs, or new capabilities. Being a GI had its benefits . . . but if she had to choose between her superhuman physiology and uplink capabilities on the one hand, or the simple joys of music, food and sex on the other . . . well, the choice was really no choice at all.

Of course, it *was* kind of nice to have both. Maybe Ari was right, maybe her rejection of League philosophy was really just the luxury of the insanely wealthy to spout wise pronouncements about how money wasn't everything. And she sighed, straightening to make her way down the steps. Takawashi, gentleman that he clearly fancied himself to be, waited for her to seat herself first.

"I have information," he said, easing himself into the black leather sofa with the help of his cane. He sat with his back to one angled wall of glass, Sandy with her back to the other. Seated, she could not see the elevator doors across the room, but fancied she could hear anything that attempted to enter. "I fear I know exactly what and who this GI may be. Of all the unlikely possibilities, it seems the most logical option."

"Tell me." She sipped her drink. Tested her uplinks once more, failing to find any trace of Ari's signal. She did not dare probe with her own, whatever Takawashi's apparently friendly demeanour. Probably Ari would not be panicking. Yet.

Takawashi took a deep breath, gazing up the short steps to the fish tank. A large transport glided low overhead, multiple running lights flashing, clear beyond the transparent ceiling. "Several years ago," he began, "before the Federal Intelligence Agency effectively collapsed, their operatives struck at a secret facility of ours. A deep space research facility. Numerous experimental specimens were stolen . . . for research, we presumed. Several of those specimens were of the very highest designation."

"Alive?" Sandy asked, eyes narrowed upon Takawashi's face.

"No. Inert. But fully assembled. Brains included, but not integrated."

"And you think the FIA has managed to activate one of these specimens?" Dubiously. Whatever his protestations, Takawashi was still effectively a leading figure of the League military-industrial complex. The possibility remained distinct that he was simply lying through his teeth. "Neurology is the most difficult part. How would they have the knowledge to achieve that?"

"They stole it," said Takawashi, his gaze sombre. "But not from us. From you." Sandy's gaze never altered. She was too good at hiding her emotions among people she didn't trust. But for Takawashi, no doubt, her utter, still silence spoke volumes. He sighed. "It is my belief, Cassandra, that the knowledge that the FIA acquired from studying you, during that . . . terrible episode two years ago, was enough to allow them to understand particularly how an advanced mind of your capabilities functions, in technical terms, and integrates with the entirety of your physical structure. Understand that they already had the hardware, so to speak. They merely required the knowledge to install it."

"Many of my systems are specific," Sandy said quietly. "Even from the other high-des GIs in my team . . . they had personality and depth rivalling anything I have, but my scores across all performance fields were routinely higher. Not just in creativity and tactics, but reflexes and coordination too. What are the odds that anything they learned from me could be applied to a . . . a body they stole?"

"Because that was the prototype they stole from us," Takawashi said flatly. "Based on your design, and integrating the same advanced neurological pathway breakthroughs. The technology has been stewing for some time, Cassandra. It never went into mass production, partly upon my own recommendation. I did warn them that your path would be unpredictable. As it turned out, I was right.

"Wrong, however, in my more dire predictions regarding possible hostile outcomes . . . and happily wrong, I readily concede. But the neurological development models at that time were open ended. There was no choice but to allow a personality to evolve. Your neurological design required a long development period—far longer than any of your team mates in Dark Star. The end result, I see here before me, and find extremely pleasing. You have become an admirable young woman, Cassandra. I am so very pleased to see that you have expanded so far beyond your initial, foundational psych-tape. The military, however, were somewhat less pleased."

"It's been two years," said Sandy, her stare fixed unblinkingly upon the slim, gaunt man in the chair opposite. A flash of lightning illuminated his face into peaks and hollows, tight and almost fleshless. "I plateaued mentally when I was about seven. If this GI is based upon my design . . . how is that possible? She should be barely self-aware."

Takawashi leaned forward slightly in his chair, glass held suspended between slim, brown fingers. "Tell me, Cassandra. What was the last book that you read?"

"I'm not going to play games with you, Mr. Takawashi," Sandy said firmly. "This is not quid pro quo. This is the security of my planet."

"No games, Ms. Kresnov, I assure you," Takawashi said mildly, with a faint wave of his unoccupied hand. "What was the last book that you read?"

"*A Nairobi Christmas*," said Sandy. "By a Kenyan author, J. C. Odube, written two hundred years ago."

"I'm not familiar with it. What was it about?"

"In the late twenty-first century, a Kenyan-English journalist searches for his sister-in-law in Kenya, who has vanished. He discovers she had become involved in a conspiracy between competing superpower interests, involving Indian technology companies and Chinese defence contracts. It juxtaposes those trials of the late twenty-first century against the main character's own colonial heritage, and asks whether a people or a nation's future is really ever their own to decide. It won something called the Nobel Prize for Literature in its day."

"A fitting choice of topic, under today's circumstances," remarked Takawashi, with obvious intrigue . . . and continued briskly before Sandy could protest as to relevance. "Do you think you would have enjoyed this book . . . say, fifteen years ago? When you were but two years old?"

"No," said Sandy.

"Why not?"

"I'm not sure I was even reading at that age."

"You were," Takawashi assured her.

Sandy stared at him for a long, suspicious moment. Takawashi smiled benignly. "It's complicated," Sandy said at last. "It assumes a lot of basic knowledge on the reader's part. From twenty-first-century Earth political demographics to simple things, what it's like to live on a planet. I understand I was raised on a research station?"

Takawashi nodded confirmation. "Mostly, yes. And you lacked such knowledge, at that age. The acquisition of knowledge is vital, is it not? Particularly in combat? For example, how would you feel if your formative learning tapes had simply told you the entire A, B and C of advanced special operations combat tactics, and injected it directly into your brain?"

"Preformed knowledge presupposes the infallibility of the programmer," Sandy replied with certainty. "It's not something anyone should enter into with any assumptions. Particularly as my capabilities were higher than anyone preceding me. No one knew what I was capable of, and thus no one could truly tell me how I ought to operate. I had to find all that out for myself, and I rewrote most of the Dark Star operating manuals in the process."

"And here lies the conundrum of the field," said Takawashi, holding up a bony forefinger for emphasis. "The acquisition of knowledge is time consuming. Military planners in the League have long wished to slash the lead time between GI production and mobilisation . . . but whenever attempts were made to simply force the required knowledge in a preconstructed manner down their throats, entire units were invariably lost.

"To lock in preconstructed knowledge at an early stage is to inhibit the psychological development of the subject. Learning is curtailed, and personality growth stunted. Yet the theoretical value of such an approach to the military continues to exist, not merely because of logistical considerations, but because of loyalty. Imagine, if you will, an army of Cassandra Kresnovs." With an amused smile. "Liking sex better than weapons drill, reading books by long-dead Earth authors with little regard for the League's attempts to indoctrinate you with progressive League philosophy. Getting into philosophical arguments with ship captains and other, less amused superiors."

"A disaster," Sandy said drily.

"One creative, dissenting mind can be contained . . . for a time, at least. But imagine if numerous such minds got together. Commingled. Cross-pollinated, if you will. I daresay you would have left the League far earlier than you eventually did, had you gained such exposure to like minds, with whom to further shape your subversive ideas. Or foment a rebellion."

"You could have warned them more strongly," Sandy suggested.

"I've already told you I did." And he gave a mild shrug of thin, silver-robed shoulders. "But they ignored me, and then I settled in with curiosity to watch the outcome, knowing that it was their own stupid fault if it all went wrong. And hoping against hope that you would survive, and grow, and perhaps one day even blossom. It was a happy, happy day when I learned you had disappeared. I thought I knew where you would go. But even I could not have predicted what an impact you would make when you got there.

"Of this rogue GI, however, I know several things. If she is what I think she is, then you are right—she is less than two years old. She did an awful lot of damage to Admiral Duong's very-well-trained marines, and showed enough creativity and desire for self-preservation to live to fight another day. And, she would appear to be the most likely source of the killswitch codes that nearly claimed your life, and forced you underground . . . thus depriving the CDF of its most prized asset.

"I fear that this GI, Cassandra, is not only devilishly clever, but highly knowledgeable. For this to be so, at her present age, she must have been subjected to an awful lot of preconstructed psych tape, to accelerate her mental development. As such, her development pathways are fixed and rigid, rather than unformed and alive with possibilities, as were your own at a similar age.

"This is not a being that reads books, Cassandra. This is not a being that appreciates art, or admires the sunset on a glorious evening, or possesses any of those higher, more abstract functions outside of her primary, psychological focus. Far more than you yourself ever were, or were capable of becoming, this is a being that exists solely to fight, and to kill, for a predetermined purpose. And I am afraid that it will be for you, and you alone, to discover whether this makes her a more effective soldier than yourself, or less so."

"But she's like me." Frowning as she spoke, trying to get her head around the conundrum that Takawashi described. "Based upon my design."

"Yes."

"To what extent?"

"Are you certain you really want to know?" Sandy just looked at him, unimpressed with the evasion. Takawashi repressed a small smile. "Of course. Psychologically, I'm sure, the two of you would be chalk and cheese. Physiologically . . ." and he gave a small shrug. "Well. You may as well be sisters."

"'Am I certain I really want to know,'" Sandy muttered, waiting for the cruiser's painfully slow communication link to kick in. From the driver's seat, Ari wisely refrained from comment. Or unnecessary motion. "Didn't think I'd like the implications, did he?"

Well, she didn't. She didn't want to know that an exact copy of herself, with her own enhanced neurological systems, could turn out to be a murdering psychopath. A *sister*, the man said? That was a provocation, right there. Takawashi knew such terms meant nothing to any synthetic being. He was trying to get at her somehow, trying to exploit his hidden agenda where she was concerned . . . most likely the same hidden agenda every senior League official of late seemed to have with her, trying to recruit her back into the fold of an organisation that murdered her friends and left her for dead . . . click, the connection opened up.

"Hey, Sandy," said Vanessa, rumpled hair sticking out in patches beneath her bandages. Her face was sideways on the screen—she was lying down, head on the pillow, activating the vidphone on her hospital bedside table. "*'Bout time you called, I was getting so tired of sleeping.*"

"Goddamn it, Ricey," Sandy snapped at the cruiser's dash, "what did you mean 'a bit like me'?"

Vanessa blinked. *"Beg yours?"* she said.

"You said in your report . . . which I'm just rereading here . . . that the GI looked 'a bit like Commander Kresnov, in general build.'"

On the display screen, Vanessa shrugged against the pillows. The half of her face that was visible beneath the bandage looked decidedly reluctant. *"She looked a bit like you. She had a longer face. Leaner. Not as cute."*

"Yeah, thanks, that's a real comfort."

*"But physically, sure. About the same height, broad shoulders, strong hips. Blonde. Nice breasts."* Trying vainly to placate her with humour. Which was good, because it showed the budget Sandy had insisted be allocated to the CDF's medical wing, for equipment and to capture staff the quality of Dr. Obago and his crew, had been well spent. Injury recovery times were down sharply on what even the most advanced Callayan hospitals could achieve. Vanessa even looked better, her fully visible eye bright and alert, her cheek healthy with colour as the micro-synthetic and harmonic accelerator treatments reknitted and regrew over the fractures, and encouraged tissue repair, at a rate that would have been startling just thirty years ago. *"Why? What's going on?"*

Ari made himself useful by filling Vanessa in, while Sandy gazed out at the gleaming, rain-wet suburbs of Tanusha, and fumed. Vanessa's face grew steadily more sombre. But hardly surprised. Nothing bad about Sandy's artificial nature seemed to surprise Vanessa any longer.

"You should have told me," she said to the dash-screen, as soon as Ari had finished. In the driver's seat, Ari resumed his former, studious silence.

*"Told you what? That the GI that nearly killed me just happened to look a little bit like you? I try hard to be relevant, Sandy, it's one of my happier traits."*

"How many goddamn high-des GIs are there who look like me? What are the odds? You should have told me."

On the screen, Vanessa shrugged, exasperatedly. *"Okay, so I should have told you. Forgive me for somehow remembering to worry about your own emotional state after I've nearly been killed."*

Sandy exhaled hard, and stared off across the gliding, banking spectacle of midnight Tanusha. "Fine," she said shortly. "I'm sorry. How're you feeling?"

*"Better. Might get the bandages off in another day."*

"Good." A short pause, filled only by the muffled whine of the cruiser's engines.

*"So you reckon you might have a sister, huh? You want me to bake a cake?"*

Sandy shook her head in faint disbelief. "Have a good night, Ricey, sorry to bother you."

*"Love you,"* Vanessa volunteered before the line disconnected.

"Yeah, me too." And touched the disconnect, manually sending the screen blank. Another moment of silence, as they cruised toward north-central Tanusha. Sandy rolled her head against the chair back, and looked at Ari.

"No opinion to volunteer?" she asked.

Ari shook his head, glumly, bottom lip protruding. "Nope."

"That'd be a first."

"Let me rephrase that—I'd rather asphyxiate myself with soiled underwear than offer an opinion."

Sandy snorted, and stared once more out of her window.

"So," Ari ventured after another moment's silence. "What's up with you and Ricey?"

Sandy frowned. "What's up?"

"You've been snapping at each other the past few days."

"I haven't been snapping at her." Ari raised his eyebrows, eyes flicking meaningfully back to the dash monitor. "Okay, that was my first snap. Mostly she's been snapping at me." And it suddenly worried her that Ari had noticed. Maybe she'd been right to worry about it before, and it hadn't just been another attack of social insecurity.

Maybe she should call Vanessa back, and apologise? "Why do *you* think?"

"Ah . . . I'm not answering that." Decisively.

"Worse than soiled underwear?"

"Much worse," said Ari.

Sandy sighed.

# CHAPTER 10

Ari's idea of low visibility, secure accommodation for the night turned out to be a mega-rise fly-in hotel. They left the cruiser for the automated parking to handle, got a booking at the upper lobby with one of Ari's many IDs, and took a room just one floor down from the parking bay.

Ari made calls and net-scanned while Sandy showered, then took his own shower, leaving her free to sit on the bed in a moment of solitude, and gaze out through broad, five-star windows and the brilliant city beyond. She wished she could talk to Vanessa, but dared not use the uplink. Besides, Vanessa would most likely be sleeping. And things were a little more complicated there than she was used to. It frustrated her, that complication, right now when she most needed Vanessa's insight. And she wished she possessed the insight herself to know what the problem was. But she didn't . . . and never really had.

It would have been easy to become frustrated with Vanessa, for dumping it on her right now . . . but Vanessa was lucky to be alive, and understandably upset at recent events. But Sandy couldn't believe it was that simple . . . could Vanessa now feel truly uncomfortable with her simply for being a GI? Not after all they'd been through.

She was very lucky, she told herself instead, that Vanessa were alive at all. It terrified her, that close call. Somehow, despite the dangers, she'd never truly felt that Vanessa was at risk. She was so cool, so professional . . . almost a GI, in fact, in the degree of confidence Sandy had become accustomed to placing with her in all things operational. But that was stupid too. GIs could survive things that straight humans couldn't. On top of all their skills, GIs had a margin for error. Vanessa did not.

And fuck it, when was she going to finally get wise, and stop making stupid assumptions about her environment and her life? Every time she thought she'd finally gotten on top of this new life of hers, something else happened that shattered all her carefully constructed truths. It was becoming alarming—not just the inevitability of the events, but the depths of her own naivety.

Ari emerged from the bathroom in his white hotel robe, dark hair damp and scruffy, and sat down at her side. Copied her pose, gazing out at the vast expanse of light and colour.

"What are you thinking?" he asked.

"That Takawashi's not telling all he knows." Ari nodded, but said nothing. "I mean, what the fuck's he doing here anyway? I think Ramoja's trying to find this GI as much as we are. Maybe he wants to cover the League's arse on something. Takawashi got sent to help."

"Wouldn't help the League much if it turns out a GI they had some hand in murdered Admiral Duong," Ari pointed out. "It wouldn't quite re-start the war, but it wouldn't help."

"Maybe." Ari slid across to kneel upon the bed behind her, and began massaging her shoulders. They were tight, as always at this hour, and his fingers moved with the assuredness of two years familiarity. Or less than two years, she thought vaguely. She and Ari hadn't started sleeping together immediately after their first meeting. Despite their continuing, deepening friendship and mutual curiosity (or in Ari's case, fascination), it had taken three months for her to finally lose her natural suspicion of his motives, and invite him to bed. Ari had been pleased, but no more than that. Partly, he was just too confident a young man to start turning cartwheels at any female invitation, having had plenty of previous experience. And partly, his interest in her truly *hadn't* been that kind of sexual obsession. Or not mostly, anyhow.

It didn't bother her. They were comfortable together, and it was convenient. Had been convenient then, too, for them both—for her, because there were very few men who considered themselves her equal who weren't terrified of her, or otherwise unattracted to her . . . and for him because he was always busy, always preoccupied by other matters, and simply lacked the time or inclination to spend the attention on a woman that most women demanded. She sometimes wondered if that was all it was—convenience. At times, it felt a hell of a lot more than that. At others . . . well, for all their closeness, Ari remained secretive, and occasionally distant.

"Don't try to change him," Vanessa had warned her, when they'd first started sleeping together. "That's the most basic rule of civilian relationships, Sandy—we learn it real early, but you might not have heard it yet. Don't think he'll change as soon as he's with you. He won't." And she'd been right, again.

"I keep trying to think of this GI," said Sandy, feeling her shoulders slowly relaxing into his firm, squeezing grasp. "It doesn't make sense. First she tries to kill me with the killswitch, then she spares Vanessa and leaves a message for me to contact her."

"So now you *don't* think she was just bullshitting?"

"Oh hell, I don't know." Air traffic hummed by on a near skylane, running lights flashing. Nearly soundless past the windows. "Maybe she knows. Maybe she knows her . . . relationship, to me. Maybe she's curious."

Ari massaged for a while in silence, working his way carefully down her spine to the small of her back. "Can a high-designation GI kill civilians and feel no remorse?" he said then.

"I don't know," Sandy murmured. "I couldn't. If what Takawashi says about her age is true . . . well." She didn't need to finish the sentence. Ari knew only too well the implications of a preformed mind, as opposed to a randomly evolved one.

"Ramoja's got reports of your early years of service," he said instead. "He liberated them from Dark Star files. They said you showed remarkable care to distinguish between combatants and non-combatants even then."

"I know," Sandy said mildly. "I broke into all those files while I was still there. It scared me, when I was older, that I couldn't remember much of my life in my earlier years. I had to know what I'd done. It was a relief to read that."

"I bet." Ari's thumbs probed where buttock and hip joined, a point of frequent discomfort for her. Sandy repressed a wince. "What about tearing a couple of civilians apart with bare hands? Workmates that she might have gotten to know over a couple of weeks, at least, when she was working undercover?"

"That's what I was thinking," Sandy said quietly. "I don't know how it's possible for her to be stable. She's executed her gameplan pretty well so far, infiltrated a civilian tech company for cover and probably code-access, then helped set up a bunch of extremist patsies to take the blame for Duong. That's an awful lot of lateral thinking, even if she was just following instructions from higher up. She still had to pass the interviews at Sigill Technologies, for one thing. It doesn't make sense—she's too damn smart to be a drone, and too fucking murderous to be that smart."

"An employee Intel interviewed said she was calm and pleasant," said Ari. "No apparent sense of humour, no personality quirks . . . just mild, understated and professional."

"I've been described that way."

Ari planted a kiss on top of her head. "Not by anyone who knows you."

"I'm calm," Sandy replied. "Most of the time. Control comes with the psychology, I'm sure. I'm goal-oriented, but only when I want to be. Maybe . . . hell, I don't know. Maybe we're not that different."

"Oh, shut the fuck up," Ari rebuked, and gave her a sharp cuff across the top of the head. "Please, bring back the calm, logical Sandy—this one's suddenly gone all morose and pitiful."

Sandy didn't reply. And found a moment to hope that Ari wasn't cheating on her with other women—if he was getting accustomed to whacking his girlfriends about the head, some without ferro-enamelous skulls were liable to hit him back.

"You've never been the places I've been," she replied. "Nor done the things I've done. That's not yours to judge."

"Sandy." Ari rested both hands upon her shoulders. "I've killed people too. Two years ago, with the shit going down, several times I found myself the only thing standing between terrorists and the people I was supposed to protect. It . . ." and he took a deep breath. "It's horrible. And I'm . . . I mean, the CSA instructors told me I had natural aptitude and everything, and even in the circles I moved in before the CSA, it's not like I'd never seen blood before . . . but I had a hard time coping with that, for a while.

"But people die, Sandy. People die all the time, the universe is this . . . this enormous *process*, and we're just wheels in the machine. At first, I found that just . . . so fucking depressing. But, you know, the more I thought about it, the more it made a comforting kind of sense. I mean, I'm a part of something bigger. The process, you know? I chose the side of order, and those damn lunatics . . . well, they chose anarchy, or . . . or ballroom dancing, or some other horrible, violent extreme."

Sandy repressed a smile. "And . . . and d'you see?" Ari continued, with building force, hands tightening upon her shoulders. "It's not just me that killed them, all this . . . this stuff about personal responsibility . . . well sure, I mean, personal responsibility's important, modern civilisation would disintegrate without it, to say nothing of . . ."

"Ari," Sandy interrupted gently, "you're wandering."

"Sure. Sure." With a flustered attempt to refocus his typically undisciplined thoughts. "Where was I?"

"Personal responsibility. Wheels in the machine."

"Oh, right. I mean, am I making sense?" Sandy flash-zoomed in on his reflection in the windows, gazing over her shoulder. It was a face that seemed made for intensity, with the dark brows and deep, dark eyes. An intensity forever undercut with unpredictable, irreverent humour. "Personal responsibility is a selfish, self-centred notion. We . . . we feel guilty because we always think everything's about *us*. When in fact it's not, none of us are in control of those circumstances, we're all a part of something so much larger, and . . . and just like when any two forces of nature collide, there's damage, and suffering. But no one ever blamed an earthquake for being immoral, or a meteor shower, or some flesh-tearing reptile on a planet with interesting wildlife. Yet that's what we are. Just another part of the natural order."

"That sounds dangerously like a belief system," Sandy murmured, as his hands resumed massaging her shoulders and neck. "Whatever would all your underground friends think?"

"Well hey, you know, I'm working toward mysticism, slowly . . . I read in a magazine there's nothing quite so impressive to Tanushan women as a man whose mind is as expansive as his penis."

"I've yet to see evidence of that."

A brief pause. "No, actually, now that you mention it, me neither."

"So you killed four people, Ari. They were in the process of trying to kill other people at the time, and probably would have died some other way if you hadn't been there, but even so, that's terrible. I wish you'd never had to do it. But it doesn't bear any moral comparison with what I'm responsible for."

"Responsible?" Ari's voice was disbelieving. "How can you be responsible when you weren't given any choice in any . . ."

"Phrasing," Sandy said quietly. "Simple rule of civilisation—you do something, you're responsible for it. No, it's not fair. But that's the whole point. Do you know how many people I've killed?"

A silence from Ari. He brushed loose hair back from her ear. "I never thought to ask," he said at last. "I didn't think you were counting."

"I don't know the real figure because I didn't see the final results of all the rounds I fired," Sandy replied, distantly. "But I know it's more than five hundred. Straight humans. Mostly young, I think. Almost entirely combatants, at least in direct combat. Indirectly, who can say?"

Ari had nothing to say to that. She turned to face him, and knelt opposite on the bed. His eyes were concerned. Worried, even.

"I agree with you," she told him. "I had no choice. Until I was about eleven, I wasn't aware there even was a choice. That's the League's fault for making me what they did, and I've never forgiven them for it. I never even signed up. I was just born into it, and that life was the only thing I'd ever known.

"But it doesn't change the fact that I did it. Not someone else. Me." She searched his eyes, seeking . . . something, she didn't know what. Understanding, perhaps. But how was that possible, when she did not entirely understand herself? "I'm past crying about it. I've done that. And I think a part of me never stopped crying, and never will. So many people died in that war, and I can't see that tears will bring any of them back.

"But I have to find this GI, Ari. I have to find her, and stop her. Maybe she's not as bad as Takawashi says. Maybe she's just like I was—young, brainwashed, and not knowing any better. Maybe . . . I don't know, maybe I can salvage something of myself from all this, something of that time in my life. Know where I come from, maybe. Make sense of it all."

Her eyes hurt. That was unexpected. She glanced aside, trying to control it, and mostly succeeding. When she looked back to Ari, her eyes were damp.

"But one thing's for sure, Ari. I swore to myself a long time ago— all those lives I took, however innocent I was in the taking, they can't all be for nothing. All those young men and women, who should still be alive today." A tear slipped down her cheek. "I owe them that. I owe them to try. Even if it takes a lifetime."

Ari left shortly before dawn, reassuring her that it was nothing serious, just another one of his numerous Tanushan contacts on his uplink. Sandy's uplinks remained disconnected, and she had to take Ari's word for it. She lay in bed for a while after Ari had dressed and departed, pondering the curiously empty sensation within her mind. Like a missing limb, she reckoned. And she recalled reading of a time before synthetic replacements when those who had lost limbs, and lived out their lives as such, had told of a "phantom limb syndrome," where they could still feel basic sensation, and even pain, from nonexistent nerve fibres. Data-withdrawal did something similar, and at times her stream of consciousness would abruptly break, darting off to access some piece of information that turned out not to exist.

She slept for another hour, rose to order breakfast on the hotel intercom, then showered once more to get her hair back into place—at its present length, if she slept directly after a shower, it stuck out like a bunbun nest the following morning. Then she sat on her bed, cross-legged before her breakfast tray, and watched the latest news on the TV . . . which was also a strange experience, as her lack of uplinks compelled her to simply sit and watch, with no data-adjuncts pulled off the broadcast data stream, no clarifying tidbits, no graphical illustrations, no random searches for associated information. Up until now, she hadn't even realised how much she did such things, without noticing.

Secretary General Benale, the newscast said, had departed Tanusha for Nehru Station. Apparently, to no one's great surprise, he felt safer there. Probably the fact that numerous previously moderate Callayan politicians had referred to him as "colonial scum," in front of reporters, had reinforced this perception

*"Given that the Secretary General has repeatedly failed to condemn the Fifth Fleet's imposition of a full blockade,"* the TV reporter said to screen, *"and has in fact appeared to almost condone it in some references, there can be little doubt now as to the sympathies of Earth's political leaders at this time . . ."*

She flicked channels—manually, another strange inconvenience—and found a panel debate of academics and others seated around a table.

*". . . no doubt at all in my mind,"* a white-bearded man in Arabic robes was saying, *"or indeed in the mind of any impartial observer, that the murder of Admiral Duong was nothing more than a pretext staged by certain pro-Earth forces, for the Fleet to impose a full blockade upon our world, and therefore upon the hopes and aspirations of the two-thirds of all the Federation's people who do not presently reside upon Earth itself . . ."*

*"No, I'm not challenging that assessment, Mr. Rahmin,"* the moderator cut in, *"I merely ask what the purpose is? I mean, if the motivations are that transparent, what long-term advantage is there to Earth? This whole episode will only increase anti-Earth sentiments throughout the rest of the Federation, surely . . . or even the anti-centralisation sentiment on Earth itself, such as in the USA?"*

Mr. Rahmin and the other panellists were unable, in Sandy's opinion, to provide a satisfactory answer to that one. They were too rational, she reflected as she munched on a fresh piece of fruit. They based their assertions upon the assumption of a rational universe. But war, Sandy knew from experience, and the concepts of loyalty and belonging that drove it, were certainly not that. They were gut instincts, primordial as the urge for sex, or the roar from a football crowd when someone was spectacularly injured upon the field.

And perhaps, she thought further, that was where the problem lay. The conflict between the League and the Federation had begun as a contest of ideas—ideas of progress, morality, and conflicting visions for the future of the human species. But it had degenerated from that relative high ground into a conflict of baser instincts, us-versus-them, the enlightened against the morally challenged.

Which worked for a little while, of course, while the war was on. But now, the organs that ran the Federation had begun to define themselves by war and conflict. War had given them meaning and purpose. War had brought them together, and made them strong. And now, what would the Federation become, without conflict? They needed it. Not technically, and certainly not economically, although there were elements of both. But emotionally, as surely as the netwave addict needed his daily shot of hallucinatory code. Admit it or not, they were hooked, and they'd do almost anything to avoid losing control of their precious Fleet.

It would be two weeks before the people of Earth even heard about the actions of the Fifth. Another two weeks for comment or orders to return. Maybe the Grand Council would give the order to stand down . . . or as seemed more likely in these days of political gridlock at the highest level, maybe not. In the meantime, the Fleet could strangle the Callayan economy all they pleased. It wasn't a state of affairs that any presidential administration should be prepared to tolerate. Sure as hell the CDF wouldn't, if she had anything to do with it.

The doorbell rang. Sandy frowned, pausing in midbite. With no uplinks, she had no way of knowing who was on the other side. Perhaps it was room service again—Ari had said he was going to leave her something at the service desk. But yelling out a question would not do—the person on the other side might only be attempting to discern whether she was actually in the room. If he was going to find out, she'd rather he did so in person.

She slid off the bed, tightened her robe and pulled the pistol Ari had given her from its holster on the bedside table. Considered peering through the eye hole, as she approached the door, but decided against it. GI eyesockets were reinforced at the back with light myomer, but if an attacker knew GIs well enough to know the required calibre . . . She tucked the pistol into the pocket of her robe, grasped the handle lock firmly, then thumb-pressed the release and opened a fraction in one fast move.

It was Ali Sudasarno, frozen in midfidget with his neck tie.

"Cassandra?" His eyes flicked down. "Is that a gun in your pocket?"

"That's supposed to be my line," Sandy quipped. Sudasarno looked puzzled. Sandy took that response as a fair sign that he was not being coerced by armed persons behind the doorframe (very few inexperienced civilians gave any response to anything superfluous, with a gun pointed at their head) and she reached out and yanked him quickly inside the door. Closed it, locked it, and dragged him further into the room.

"What the hell are you doing here?" she asked, eyes hard with mild alarm. "How did you know where I was?"

"I have, um, sources." Sudasarno readjusted his suit lapels from where she'd pulled them out of alignment. And glanced at the half-eaten breakfast upon the bed. "I'm sorry, did I catch you at breakfast?"

"Tell me how, or I'll hurt you."

Sudasarno gave an exasperated, youthful smile. "Look, Sandy . . . I'm really sorry I snapped at you the last time we talked, I'm not normally like that, I assure you . . ."

Sandy grabbed him once more, one hand upon the belt, the other by the shirt, in a flash lifted and thumped him back against the wall beside the TV. His head hit the decorative wall painting, pain adding itself to stunned disbelief upon his youthful face.

"Sudie," she told him, gazing upward as she held him effortlessly suspended, "you've just put both of our lives in danger. Tell me how you found me, or I swear I'll be forced to start breaking bones until you do." His eyes fixed on hers with disbelief. "I swear it."

"Your . . . your car's bugged . . . I mean Ari's car. The cruiser."

"Who bugged it?"

"I . . . someone who works for Secretary Grey, I'm not sure . . ." and saw the narrowing of her eyes, ". . . look honestly, I don't fucking know! Sandy, you're hurting me! My belt . . ."

"Who monitors the bug?"

"Kalaji . . . he . . . he works for the Secretary." Desperately. "Sandy, I needed to know where you were! I was instructed to keep in contact with you and now you won't answer your uplinks . . ."

"Your calls least of all, I don't want to get fried." She dumped him back down. Sudasarno gasped, grabbing his belt and loosening. Sandy turned to where she'd left her clothes last night, neatly stacked for easy dressing, placed the pistol upon the bed and untied her robe.

"What do you mean 'my calls least of all'?" Sudasarno protested. "Sandy, I work for the President, I'm no threat to . . ." And stopped with a gulp as Sandy dropped the robe before him and began dressing quickly.

"There's been a lot of things happening in this city lately that couldn't have happened without some real senior help," Sandy said darkly as she pulled on underwear and pants—the same clothes as yesterday, unwashed, and too bad if they smelled. "My bet is Secretary Grey's department's involved; as Secretary of State he's certainly got all the resources and talents at his disposal."

Sudasarno looked incredulous. "You're accusing Secretary Grey of . . . ?"

"I'm not accusing him of anything," Sandy snapped, pulling on her shirt and jacket. "I'm saying there's a better than even chance that his department's been infiltrated. Which means that you're not the only person who could have found out where I am."

She tucked the pistol and holster into the pocket of her jacket, and grabbed a last handful of fruit from the breakfast tray, stuffing it into her mouth and chewing powerfully. Grabbed a bewildered Sudasarno by the arm and hauled him to the door.

"Ever done a basic combat course?" Sandy asked around her

mouthful as she grasped the latch, releasing Sudasarno's arm to hold the pistol within her pocket. "Escape and evasion?"

"Sure." He nodded. Past the light brown skin, he looked a little pale. "After the Parliament Massacre they were compulsory."

Sandy swallowed her fruit. "Then you'll know the basics. If I say 'down,' you get down. If I say 'run,' you run. Don't crowd me, don't grab me, don't obstruct my field of fire. Got it?"

He nodded, very nervously. "Got it. Sandy, who do you think . . . ?"

"And save the questions." With a firm stare. Sudasarno shut up, swallowing hard. Sandy yanked the door and slid through, just enough to double-check both ways along the hall. Then gestured quickly to Sudasarno, who followed, shutting the door behind him. A man appeared down the end of the long, door-lined hall. Sandy remembered the shades in her pocket, and put them on . . . it looked suspicious to be wearing them indoors, of course, but not extravagantly so in fashion-obsessed Tanusha. And dark hair or not, she didn't want to risk being recognised just now.

The man approaching was wearing a business suit and carrying a briefcase. Of Indian appearance, plus athletic build and stride. Shorter than the average, as with most GIs . . . Sandy flashed her vision to infra-red, and registered the heat shades of his body . . . and found them normal for a straight human.

"He's okay," she murmured to the nervous Sudasarno. Of course, it didn't guarantee he wasn't a hostile, it just meant she could handle him in a split second without having to pay him too much attention in the meantime . . . They walked past, barely making eye contact. Natural enough in any big city, Sandy had long ago gathered.

"I have a cruiser," Sudasarno said in a low voice as they approached the end of the corridor.

"Not safe," Sandy replied in a similar tone. Snapped a quick look both ways at the T-junction, then led him right, toward the elevators. "Might explode the moment you start it up."

Sudasarno stared at her. "Hold on . . . why am I suddenly a target? Hell, why am I even coming with you . . . no one's after me, just you!"

"And if they make an attempt on me now, and you survive, you'll be able to join the dots right back to whoever planted that bug."

"Well, hey, I can do that right now . . ." From his suddenly distant gaze, Sandy guessed he was connecting an uplink, probably to call for help. She grabbed his arm as they walked, warningly.

"Don't," she told him. "A GI can monitor the entire hotel network. If you make any kind of call, she might assume help's on the way and attack immediately."

They arrived at the elevators, and Sandy pressed the upward call button. The corridor in both directions remained empty, as her hand remained fixed about the pistol grip in her pocket. Unable to access the network, she felt blind. She wasn't going to have any advance warning if attacked this time. The temptation to just briefly access an uplink was extreme, to catch a glimpse of what lay beyond. But it was a glimpse that could cost her her life.

The elevator arrived, and they rode it up two floors to the hotel main lobby. There were people around, patrons and bellhops, and automated luggage trolleys that trundled cautiously across the carpet as new arrivals came in. Sandy surveyed the surroundings coolly as she and Sudasarno walked toward the service desk at one end of reception . . . "Don't gawk around," she told him, "you'll draw fire." And to the lady at the service desk, "Hello, I'm Asma Goldstein, I believe my husband left me something?"

"And what was his name?"

"Dori Goldstein." And handed the lady a credit card . . . with Tanushan registration, it passed for multipurpose ID. And she found time to reflect that it wouldn't have been so easy if Parliament had managed to pass the Citizens' Card bill, but even after recent horrors, the Callayan public weren't quite ready for mandatory, all-purpose ID cards. Evidently quite a few of them *had* read Orwell. Or maybe they just knew what Ari always told her—that hackers and forgers were so competent these days, a comprehensive ID system would only work against petty violators, while the big players continued to go where they liked throughout Callay in total anonymity. After a moment of searching beneath the desk, the hotel lady found a small handset and placed it on the counter.

"There you are, compliments of Mr. Goldstein."

"Thank you." It was a mobile phone, Sandy reckoned from the look of it—they weren't very common in Tanusha, filling just a niche in the electronic gadget market. She departed, pulling Sudasarno after her. "Don't stare around!" she told him in a low voice. "This is a terrible ambush spot, even this GI seems to have some idea of covert activities. The target environment's not primed, she'll have no advance plan or surveillance. Very tricky if she wants to get away."

They headed past the broad stairway leading to the upper carpark, headed instead for the outer wall express elevators. There were glass doors and polished surfaces ahead, and at extreme, motion-sensitive visual enhancement, Sandy could see just about everything in the lobby that she needed to see. Or nearly.

"You're posing as Ari's wife now?" asked Sudasarno, as if trying to distract himself from the situation.

"One of many conveniences. You don't think I look Jewish?"

"Not enough for the Tanushan Jewish community." Glancing about once more, anxiously. "They're pretty conservative in a lot of places, don't intermarry much, try to keep the bloodlines intact. The scourge of genetic dispersal, and all that." As a political advisor to the President who tracked voting trends would surely know. And he spared her a glance, taking in the dark hair and shades, the dark jacket, and the effortless poise of her stride. "Frankly, Sandy, I think you're a Jewish mother's worst nightmare."

"And how do you figure that?"

"Because you're an Indonesian Muslim mother's worst nightmare too. If I took you home to meet my mother, I'd be disowned."

Sandy managed a faint shrug past the deadening calm of combat-reflex. "Sure, but it'd be worth it for all the great sex, huh?"

"Spoken like someone who doesn't have a mother."

"Don't rub it in."

None of the four express elevators were presently docked. Sandy and Sudasarno waited to one side of the gathering crowd before the elevator doors, confronted by a vast panorama of Tanushan morning cityscape beyond the glass walls.

"Shit," Sudasarno muttered under his breath as the tension began to get the better of him, "I can't believe this is . . . are you sure?"

"Sudie," Sandy said calmly, gazing straight ahead and covering both ends of the hallway with her peripheral vision, "in my business, there's no such thing as "sure". If you don't play the odds, you'll die. You'll notice I'm still alive, and I plan to stay that way."

"Why the express elevator? Couldn't we have taken the smaller . . ."

"We'd have to change halfway, and if a GI's locked into the local network, she might be able to hack that elevator car, make it stop where she wants it. Express elevators are pretty much unhackable."

"We're not endangering these people?"

"It's a civilian environment," said Sandy. "Everyone's endangered no matter what we do. That's the bitch of these FIA arseholes." One trusted that even an FIA-raised and bred GI had enough civility not to fire into a car full of civilians. One trusted any hostile act would wait for a better opportunity, to ensure she got away. But if the mind in question was as cold as Takawashi had suggested . . . Well, in that case, who was safe anywhere?

The car arrived. Sandy waited until the last of the small waiting crowd were in, and then followed with Sudasarno. It deprived them of a view, standing by the doors as the group of perhaps thirty people jostled to grasp the side railings, and gaze out at the breathtaking vista of morning cityscape beyond the transparent shell of the elevator car.

Sandy took a casual hold of one of the leather straps upon the ceiling-to-floor synthetic ropes that were arranged in a circle within the car. Sudasarno did likewise, as the doors closed with a final, warning bell, and a friendly voice announced on the intercom (in English and then Mandarin—the most common tongue of non-English-speaking tourists) that the express elevator would fly down the side of the tower at a hundred kilometres an hour, and internal gravity would be reduced effectively by a third. Some children clutching to the outer railing, and staring half a kilometre straight down, squealed in delighted anticipation. Another little boy howled in distress, clawing at his mother's leg. Sandy thought briefly of Rhian, and smiled, faintly.

"I hope no one lands on top of us when we're halfway down," a nearby tourist with some unidentifiable off-world accent remarked. People laughed. Sudasarno gave Sandy a wary sideways glance, which Sandy chose to ignore. The car began to descend, with a gathering rush of muffled sound. As gravity grew steadily lighter, and the tower wall began to rush by at blurring speed, Sandy felt the strange, surreal sensation of time appearing to slow. The natural-light colour and texture of the surrounding people, their clothes and hair and skin tones, vanished into a blur of bodytones, temperatures and flash-registered motion as an eyelid blinked, or a parent grasped a child's hand more tightly.

And she turned her head, sharply, to find one humanoid shape amidst the crowd that was not moving, nor grasping tightly upon a rail or strap, nor even admiring the view. Female, about her own height, and gazing straight at her. Of a cooler, nonbiological body temperature. No visible pulse at the jugular.

Sound ceased to register. All extraneous information flows stopped. There was just her, and the other GI, standing perhaps three metres apart with stares locked. No move was made. Slowly, Sandy phased her vision back to regular light, overlaying that imagery on top of the hair-triggered, combat hues. The other GI's eyes were pale blue, her shortish hair a light, straw-blonde, protruding beneath a baseball cap.

She wore comfortable cargo pants with thigh pockets, and a light, waterproof jacket over a T-shirt. The collar on the jacket was raised. From behind, that plus the cap would block any clear perception of body temperature. At least one pocket of jacket and pants appeared to bulge with weight, the exact nature of which was difficult to tell—you could do so with straight humans, because weapons were heavy, and posture altered just minutely to compensate. A GI's posture was rarely so affected.

There was a child, clasping his father's hand, directly alongside the GI. Gazing outward and down, in the opposite direction. Sandy realised she couldn't move. A GI on hair-trigger reflexes might have weapon in hand and be pulling the trigger, before a conscious decision to change her mind could register. Two GIs, facing each other, suffered from a mutually reinforcing "no return scenario" . . . as they'd called it, studying such phenomena in Dark Star. It had been a purely hypothetical scenario, then. Two GIs, facing each other . . . impossible, since the League was the only side to produce or deploy GIs. But the scenario was a constant in training, where the first move, once made, was far too fast for the conscious mind to easily halt . . . and when reinforced by the reflexive response of the opponent, the momentum toward the kill-shot became unstoppable. The other GI might be merely shifting weight, or turning her head to look another way . . . if it triggered a draw, the other GI had to retaliate. *Had* to. And a firefight in a crowded elevator car would be a disaster. Unarmed combat would be even worse.

She was dimly aware, then, that Sudasarno had asked her a question. She moved the tip of her little finger, just a fraction. The GI's gaze did not alter. Nothing did. Sandy accelerated the motion, moving the entire little finger, then ever so slowly allowing all the fingers on her left hand, grasping the leather strap, to join in. She had no other notion of what to do if the GI drew, or otherwise attacked, than to attempt to grab and restrain her from lashing around, hopefully saving thirty innocent tourists from being smeared all over the car's interior. Perhaps she could smash a hole in the transparent wall, and leap out, thus depriving the GI of a motivation for violent action. Somewhere in the distant background of her hearing, a child squealed laughter . . . the tops of smaller towers were passing now, gravity was low, and it was doubtless very exciting.

Slowly, her entire hand moved, a part of that gradual, flowing motion. Then, without any sudden movements, or rapid extensions, she extended the arm, and grasped Sudasarno's suit lapel as best she could, with the thumb still immobile and bound. Still it was steely strong.

"Don't move," she said calmly, just loudly enough to be heard above the hum of descent, and the babble of excited children. No one was paying them any attention. "Don't say a word, don't move, and don't panic. If you can do that, we'll be just fine."

Sudasarno neither moved nor spoke. Sandy guessed he was summing up the situation, although she could not turn her head to see. She could imagine well enough his eyes following the rigid line of her stare, and realising who the object of attention must be. And the terror that would follow. Dimly, past the combat-focus, she realised she was mad at herself. Should have taken the stairs. Should have called for an air-taxi. Should have done anything other than lead to this standoff, in a crowded elevator, where the very people she'd sworn an oath to protect were going to be the first to die, if something went wrong. But the first step to lessen risk was to remove yourself from the situation. And she'd done that, the fastest way she'd had available. It had been the right thing to do. Hadn't it?

The hum of descent began to ease as the ground neared. A passing elevator flashed by, on its way back up. The GI simply stood, backside leaned gently against the handrail behind, utterly unconcerned with the expansive view to her back. Just gazing, with pale blue eyes within a face that was somewhat attractive, but less so than Sandy might have expected, of a GI. In fact, it occurred to her, this was quite possibly the ugliest GI she'd ever seen. Which wasn't saying much, against the uniform beauty of League GIs. It was a face that could still attract male attention, in passing. But would tend to get overlooked beside herself, or Rhian, or most other female GIs she'd known. Somehow, that rang alarm bells. Hadn't her creators wanted her to be pretty? League philosophy held that uniform good looks would help with socialisation and self-confidence, and thus inspire a counterreaction of good feelings toward those around him or her. A virtuous circle, they'd called it. Had the FIA altered her original, League-designed appearance? To what ends? What, in their eyes and plans, was this GI *for?*"

The ground approached, and the elevator slowed. A standoff in an emptying elevator, with its short turnaround time for new passengers to crowd on board, could create even more unwelcome attention. Possibly even the intervention of security officials. Sandy decided she had to take a risk.

"Are you getting off here?" she asked the GI. "Or are you just joyriding?"

The GI raised an eyebrow, as if curious at this approach. Sandy's heart sank. She'd known lower-designation GIs to sometimes raise both eyebrows. Rarely one. It was an expression that, in most cultures, seemed to imply a degree of subtlety, or irony, that lower-des GIs usually failed to grasp. But given what she already knew about this GI, it was hardly a surprise.

"I heard it was a fun ride," said the GI. Her voice was very ordinary. Female, mild, and clearly spoken. Her enunciation was perfect, down to the syllable. "Though I've heard that some people like to come down faster."

Oblique, ironic reference. Damn. Even Rhian didn't do that. Although her old League buddy Tran might have. Tran had been about Rhian's designation—damn clever, with loads of personality, but not the creative, lateral thought process of herself . . . or maybe Ramoja.

Although Ramoja hadn't entirely convinced her yet. Quoting Shakespeare was one thing. Understanding it was another. Being able to quote it, understand it, and still find it tedious, as Sandy did herself, was to her mind the greatest sign of intellectual depth yet found. In a GI, anyhow.

The hyper-analytical time dilation of combat-reflex created such tangential lines of thought. When operating at such furious speeds, her brain was very bad at just doing nothing.

"If you want to talk to me," Sandy said, "that's fine. I'd like to talk. I just think we should leave these other people out of it, and go somewhere private."

"I think that would be fine," the GI replied agreeably. For the first time, her eyes flicked away from Sandy, to fix on Sudasarno. Even through the lapel of his suit, Sandy could feel him tremble. "Friend of yours?"

"Maybe," said Sandy.

"He's a liability to you," the GI continued. The elevator slowed steadily, the ground coming nearer, walkways about the tower's base, and people moving by. "He led me straight to you. You should get rid of him."

Sudasarno's eyes were wide. The GI's tone remained mild. Sandy saw nothing on her face to suggest she was joking.

"No one's getting rid of anyone right now," Sandy replied, her gaze fixed with unblinking determination. The GI just considered her. The elevator arrived. The crowd's excited babble continued about them, unaware. A child said loudly that she felt so heavy now. They turned from the glass, and clustered back toward the door. Sandy remained unmoved, her left hand clasped upon Sudasarno's shoulder as people milled and pushed past, and the door opened. She was between the GI and the door, but she couldn't turn her back. Didn't dare.

The GI pushed gently off the rail, and strolled calmly past, dawdling as the crowd slowly cleared. Gazed Sandy directly in the eyes, from point-blank range, hands innocently in pockets. It was so tempting—a quick strike with the right fist, a snatch for the gun, something to end it right then and there . . . but she dared not, considering all those still in the crossfire. And more than that. She wanted to know.

The GI moved on as the crowd cleared, Sandy walking after with a hand upon Sudasarno's shoulder, past the new crowd gathered behind the entry barrier in the waiting hall. As soon as they were clear, the GI fell back to walk at Sudasarno's other side, keeping him between them as they strolled across the broad, high foyer floor toward the mega-rise tower's looming, revolving doors.

"Sudie," Sandy said without looking at him, as they emerged into the early morning sunshine. "Go home. Whatever you wanted to tell me can wait."

"I'd rather he stayed," the GI said calmly, as they strolled together. Outside, a security guard paced, unaware that anything was wrong. "He might call for help."

"He won't," said Sandy. "Where do you want to talk?"

"Just up here will be fine." Another fifteen strides and the GI stopped. Sandy stopped and Sudasarno too, thin, quiet and very pale. Sandy strolled a couple of paces, to make certain the frightened young advisor was not in the line of sight. On the broad, paved space before the enormous glass foyer wall, people stood and conversed, or awaited those they'd arranged to meet. Stairs led down across a broad, quarter-circle curve, interspersed with pockets of urban greenery. At the bottom, between two flights of stairs near an artificial waterfall, business people and tourists clustered at cafe tables for breakfast. Beyond, a cross-road met a major Tanushan highway, six lanes filled with zooming traffic, tightly packed and interlocking with the ease of collective automation. The sidewalks were busy with morning traffic, a seething mass of people.

It all seemed eerily calm and orderly, despite all the world's events.

People went about their lives, on streets that had just recently been jammed with protesters, and lined with armoured cordons of riot police. Perhaps, the thought flashed across Sandy's hyper-speed mind, some of these folk had been at the protests themselves. One uniform by night, another by day—such was the Tanushan way, in good times and bad. The mega-rise tower soared high overhead, reaching for a clear, unattainable blue sky. The morning air was crisp and fresh in a way that off-world visitors from cities with less than Tanusha's zero-emission controls always remarked on. People passed on all sides, oblivious to the identities of those among them.

"Strange, isn't it?" said the GI, with a faintly curious glance about. "Hiding here is so easy. The best way to hide is don't. Trying to hide will only attract attention. You hide in plain sight. Like everyone else does. All these people, hurrying about their busy little lives, not knowing shit from gold. Just stand in their midst, as plain as you can. It makes you invisible."

"You're wrong," said Sandy. "Two things Tanushans always differentiate between—shit and gold."

The GI might have smiled, but faintly. A stray gust of breeze caught her hair, lifting loose strands. To an untrained, unaugmented eye, she might have looked average, plain and human. And without Sandy's need for disguise, she dressed less self-consciously too. She looked like she fit in, Sandy realised. Like she could blend effortlessly into a crowd. The perfect covert operative. And exceptional good looks would only attract attention. Only custom-design combat ops could afford to be distractingly pretty—a small pleasure to counter an alarmingly short life expectancy during the war. It didn't necessarily make this GI any less dangerous, however.

"Do you have a name?" Sandy asked.

"Do I have a name?" the GI replied, with slow, sceptical contemplation. And glanced slightly away to one side, eyes narrowed in thought. "There's a philosophical question. What constitutes a name?

We're not born with them—they're imposed upon us. Like everything else."

"As GIs, that's something we're stuck with," said Sandy. "It doesn't make names any less significant for us than straights. All identity is self-constructed, ours and theirs."

"I'm not self-constructed," the GI replied easily. "I was born this way."

Sandy's eyes narrowed. "What way?"

The GI smiled. "You of all people should know, Cassandra Kresnov." With a mild irony, voicing that name. "You trained the CDF at the Parliament, didn't you? They're very good, for straights. Not that it made any difference . . . but you had to know that too. If you need a name, call me Jane. It's plain and simple. Like me."

Sandy was glad for the combat-reflex. Its deadening calm hid the growing, cold dread in her gut.

"The FIA activated you?" Sandy asked.

"Sure did." With cool, utter nonchalance.

"And how do you feel about that?"

"About existing? I'm grateful, naturally." She shrugged. "It's good to be alive, wouldn't you say?"

"That depends on what you do with the experience," Sandy replied.

"I think I make pretty good use of the time," said Jane.

"I think you could do better."

Again the faint, narrow-eyed smile. "You think you're better than me, is that it?"

"It's not a contest."

Jane shook her head faintly, in mild disbelief. Gazed about at the sunny urban sprawl about them. A police car cruised by on the side street, and stopped at the lights, to Jane's utter unconcern.

"You're kidding yourself," she said finally. And looked back at her, coolly. "You know that, don't you?"

"Enlighten me."

"This place. All these people. This system. It sucked you right in, didn't it? You think you're one of them now. But you're not."

"You went to all this trouble just to tell me that?" Sandy didn't bother to disguise the rising disgust in her voice. "I'd rather you just ambushed me in my sleep. It would have saved me the trouble of pretending to be interested."

"I was instructed to kill you," Jane replied with an utter lack of emotion. "If I got the chance. But I'm learning. I've this profession, do you see? I was born to it. I'm not all that old yet, and you know how GIs mature. If I'm going to improve, and expand my horizons, I need to study others. That's why you're not dead." And nodded to Sudasarno. "Him too. But I'm told you're rather like me. I was based upon your design, they said. And so I wanted to know. To see the older me, as it were."

"And what do you think?"

"I'm disappointed." Very calmly. Sandy could not remember ever having felt so pleased to be insulted. "You don't know who you are. You're delusional. Happiness is accepting your true nature. It's not here, in this city, not for you. Certainly not for me."

"Listen, junior," Sandy told her, not bothering to restrain the rising edge to her voice, "I'm just a kid myself compared to a lot of these people you look down your nose at, but compared to you, I'm ancient. Let me fill you in about a thing or two that might have escaped your vast perception.

"You're very young, less than two years old, if what you say about being based on my design is right. I'm seventeen, and I can't remember a thing from when I was that age. These are your formative years, do you understand that? When you reach my age, if you do," (heaven forbid, she barely managed to avoid saying) "you won't remember anything about this. Not this meeting, not this operation, not Tanusha or Callay itself, get it? Your mind is immature. Undeveloped, no matter what your intellect.

"You've been tape-taught. Stored knowledge, pre-constructed and formulated for someone else's purposes. It's not reliable because it's not yours. The Federal Intelligence Agency made you what you are. They hate GIs. You're an experiment to them. Your whole psychology is an experiment. You speak as if you're making a free choice of lifestyle. Your body is not your own, your future is not your own, your life is not your own and your mind is *definitely* not your own. You're not a free person. Your opinions aren't worth a thumbnail full of earwax to anyone. You're not a person. You're just an empty, walking, talking shell. And the saddest thing of all is you don't even realise it."

"I kill because it's my nature," Jane replied in a low, harsh voice. Her unblinking stare was intense. Somehow, Sandy hadn't expected a reaction. It surprised her. "You think you're civilised, but you're still a soldier. You're still looking for your next fight. Anticipating it. You couldn't function any other way. And yet you reject your true self, and live your life as a lie."

"You kill," Sandy retorted, "because you're programmed for it. The FIA don't believe GIs *have* any other purpose, they wouldn't have given you any other kinds of tape because they wouldn't have believed you capable of anything more anyway. You think that pseudo-philosophical crap you're feeding me represents intellect on your part? It's a manipulative rationalisation designed to stop you from questioning. All intelligent beings question, unless given believable rationalisations within which to construct the parameters of their personal reality. Everything you think you know has been predetermined by the people who made you, *including* your rationalisations. And you think you can lecture me on life? You pathetic little moron, you don't know what life is."

"And yet I have the codes to the killswitch," said Jane, with quiet menace. "It's hard to be right when you're dead."

Sandy nearly laughed, contemptuously. "You idiot, most of humanity's most correct and righteous people have been dead for centuries. You think you can make me less right by killing me? You'd only prove my point."

"Why do you think . . . ?"

"Excuse me," someone interrupted to one side. Sandy, Jane and Sudasarno all turned to look at the new arrival—a tourist, presumably, to judge from the large photo-map he held in both hands, the back-pack over his shoulders, and four people who seemed to be a wife and three children waiting behind. All appeared Chinese. The man smiled as he approached. "Hello, sorry to bother you . . . could any of you please direct me to the Vandaram ferry service? My wife and I . . . we wanted to take a river cruise, the rivers here are so pretty."

Looking askance at Jane, much to Sandy's alarm. But perhaps given the choice between a dark "noir-chick," a starch-collared young suit, and a mild, ordinary-looking young woman, the choice wasn't so strange after all.

"I'm sorry," Jane said mildly, "I'm a tourist too. These two are locals." The man looked at Sudasarno and Sandy, expectantly. Sandy wondered once more at her shades, and if tourists were as familiar with her face as local Callayans had become.

"Oh, right . . ." said Sudasarno, with forced congeniality. Sandy's enhanced hearing heard the strain in his throat. "That's the Vandaram River down there, yes? I don't know this area well, but I remember clearly the ferry terminal is just ten minutes' walk from here. If you just head down this road until you hit the river, and then turn left, it's a pleasant walk along the bank."

"Wonderful," said the man, in one of the Federation's several distinct Chinese accents, "thank you very much."

He beamed a smile and departed, as Sudasarno and Sandy wished him a happy holiday.

Jane gave her a sardonic look. "You would give your life for people like him?"

"If it came to that."

"What a waste," Jane said softly. "There's so many of them. And so few of us. We're special."

"Everyone's special."

The other GI shook her head. "I'd rather not have to kill you." The Chinese tourist and his family went past, waving thanks as they headed off toward the river. Sandy and Sudasarno waved back. "We could come to an understanding."

"There's no deals here," said Sandy. "You oppose everything I believe in." Her stare fixed upon Jane's face. "And you're right enough about my nature in one thing—you threaten me, you threaten the things and people I love, and I'll kill you."

Jane gave a faint, dangerous smile. "You try that here, in public, and I'll unload a clip into this crowd. You know I don't miss. How many lives is it worth to you, to stop me?"

"I don't plan on making a trade," Sandy said coldly. "You can go. I won't follow you. Not here. But know this . . . if you don't behave yourself, I'll catch you. I'm original League technology. You're a cheap copy. I'll kill you, and I'll make it slow, and painful. That's a fact, not a threat."

Jane considered her for a moment longer. Her pale blue eyes were unreadable. Perhaps she regretted. Perhaps she hated. Or maybe she merely considered, adding equations of probability and strategy in her doubtless capable mind. It was too much to hope that she actually considered the content of her words. She wondered if Jane actually heard her words at all, or if she was as blind to the underlying moral arguments as deep-sea creatures were to colour. One image, two realities. One sentence, two understandings. With such a person, reason became impossible. The software that processed the words was so utterly different, they may as well have been speaking different languages. She watched the GI named Jane turn on her heel, and stride coolly from the scene, with a dread that numbed her to her soul.

"Oh dear lord," she murmured beneath her breath, watching that departing back mingle and fade into the flow of streetside pedestrians. "What in the hell have they gone and done now?"

"You're just going to let her go?" asked Sudasarno then, recovering his voice with an abrupt, startled terror. "You're just going to let her walk off like that?"

"I can't track her covertly without uplinks," Sandy said quietly. "She's not making idle threats, Sudie. She'll kill civilians just to warn me off. No way I call anyone else onto her tail. They don't know what she's capable of. It might trigger a massacre."

"Then how the hell else are you going to catch up with her again?" Sudasarno's voice was high with barely restrained panic, hands waving. "After what she's already done? By the Prophet himself, Sandy, you can't just let her walk away!"

"I can't take the risk, Sudie." She fixed him with a very direct gaze. "You know the stuff the xenophobes all said about me, when they first found out about me? All the fear, all the hatred? I never deserved it. I think she might."

anessa left gold six last, holding her beret in place as the flyer departed in a roar of hyper-fans. She made no attempt to run with the others, but instead walked as steadily as she could in the declining gale, and paused a moment upon the rim of the rooftop pad to observe the scene. Gold two and three roared up and past from their perimeter LZs below, troops jogging quickly along garden paths and up the outer stairways, spreading out to cover all the ground level exits. As she unfocused her vision, she could see a visual outline of the State Department Wing, its security codes acquired only with the authority of the Supreme Court itself, so closely were such access codes guarded these days—in metal vaults unconnected to any network, like bullion or gemstones.

On pathways through lush Parliament grounds gardens, people in suits stopped and stared at the commotion, or stood up from outdoor cafe tables, where some were eating late breakfast, or conducting early business. S-2

Security, a separate branch of government security specialising in State Department and diplomatic matters, conferred bewilderedly in small groups about the perimeter. Further back along the State Department wing, where the building adjoined the main Parliament building, she could see other security personnel—S-3, meaning Parliament Security—standing and watching with evident concern. On the local network, her visual graphic showed encrypted transmissions spiking dramatically. And she winced—processing two visual fields simultaneously did nothing good at all for her headache, and she damped it down accordingly. Beyond the beautiful, arching dome of the Parliament building, several CDF flyers were making their final approach.

She turned and walked about the pad perimeter, headed for the rooftop entrance where her troops had disappeared. A pair of S-2s climbed the stairs and emerged from the glass doorway, staring up at the approaching CDF flyers. Then both looked at her, and her uniform rank.

"Major," said one, with astonished concern. "What's this about?"

"This is a security lockdown," she told them, raising her voice over the approaching howl of engines. "By order of Director Ibrahim, all State Department facilities are now under a minimum twenty-four-hour quarantine." The younger S-2 looked more than just astonished, as if he hadn't seen anything quite this exciting in the short time since he'd joined. "Cool, huh?" Vanessa added, and pushed through the doors before the approaching flyers made her headache even worse.

She ignored the lift and took the stairs—carefully—and then entered into a broad, shiny hallway with large portraits on the walls, and photos of the capitals of various Federation worlds.

"Great," she remarked to Private Ijaz, who was standing guard at the bottom of the stairs, "no more bright light. Stupid invention anyway, sunlight." She removed the sunglasses with painful blinking, and stowed them in a pocket. "This'll be a real tough assignment, Private, guarding a staircase from undersecretaries and speech writers. Think you're up to it?"

Private Ijaz grinned, his rifle still shouldered, as instructed. "Major, can I get you a painkiller or something? Someone's bound to have one in an office around here . . ."

"Kid, I'm pumped so full of painkiller I could have flown here myself." A dark figure was approaching down the hall, avoiding confused, milling office personnel with casual ease. "You have my permission to hit on passing secretaries, but only if they're *really* cute."

"Yes, sir," said Ijaz, with a delighted salute as she turned to leave. Vanessa returned it, and noticed a woman nearby raising an eyebrow . . . presumably at the "sir," Vanessa reckoned, but damned if she was going to allow "ma'am" to breed in the CDF, as if an officer's gender was an issue of the *slightest* significance for privates to worry about . . . and she realised that there were quite a few milling suits in the hallway, most of them breaking off their bewildered conversations to stare at her. She ignored them and walked to meet the approaching dark figure halfway.

Ari reversed direction, slowing his lengthier stride to match hers.

"Hi, Ari."

"Hi, Ricey. You look like shit."

"Yeah, well I feel like I've been defecated from some orifice or other. How's Sandy?"

"She's fine. Your, um, beret's not on . . . quite the right angle."

"Oh fuck it, I think either I wasn't standing up straight, or the mirror was crooked, or the ground was sloping on some strange angle when I put it on . . ." Ari gave one corner a decisive tug as they walked. "You're sure it's not just my head that's crooked?"

Ahead, the hall opened into a broad, circular atrium with a domed skylight overhead. There was an important-looking eight-pointed star on the floor, and two soldiers presenting a calm front to a pair of frustrated suits who wanted to use the elevator. Several S-2s stood and watched, halfway between concern and bemusement.

"You spoke to Krishnaswali?" Vanessa asked as they entered the atrium and turned left. Corporal Chang gave her a mildly aggrieved look over the heads of the troublesome suits. Vanessa spared an ironic smile, and gave a thumbs up. Chang repressed a smile of his own.

"Um, yeah, he wiped me off his shoe as he came past," Ari said mildly. "Didn't even offer a handkerchief." Ari, Vanessa reflected, was even more obtuse than she was. She could definitely see why Sandy liked him so much, whatever the downside of his ideology and profession . . . and, more to the point, found him so attractive. She shared the sentiment herself . . . or mostly. Except that somehow, with Ari, she found herself bantering in a comfort zone that felt much like the now regrettably-rare lunches with cousins Pierre and Margarite—the French side of her family, the side she clicked with. The men she liked to sleep with she preferred big, strong and conveniently silent. No, the only smart, bewildering, intriguing people she generally wanted to sleep with were women . . .

"Yeah, well," she sighed, "you'll have to excuse him, you're not catching him on his best day."

"Oh right, it's a weekday, I forgot. He's pleased you came along?"

"Oh, ecstatic," Vanessa said drily. "Your idea?"

"Why do you always assume that I'm the sole source of your daily misery?"

"Experience."

"Funny, that's what Sandy says."

They turned right at the corridor that ran along the building side, sunny windows overlooking lush garden grounds along the left wall, office doors to the right. A pair of larger, more important doors at the far end, guarded by Privates Mohammed (that was Mohammed number four, on Vanessa's mental list—the one whose mother was a concert-level tabla player) and Kravchenko. Both saluted as she approached.

"Oh, knock off the salutes, guys," Vanessa told them as she returned it, "it's too much effort."

"But the General's inside and he'd kill us, Major," Kravchenko replied, keeping her face straight with difficulty. Inside, a waiting room was lined with pictures of important people around the walls. A frustrated-looking secretary sat in his chair by the next main door, terminal headset hung upon the dead monitor—in total lockdown, nothing worked.

"What?" Vanessa asked indignantly as she caught Ari giving her one of his very curious, sideways looks. They paused before the main doors to Secretary Grey's office.

"Sandy says how popular you are with your guys," said Ari. "I think I can see why."

Vanessa made a face. "They don't love me on the training track, I'll tell you that."

She pushed the doors open, and they stepped into a broad room with an oval meeting table, surrounded by chairs. Before the broad windows, Secretary of State Grey and General Krishnaswali were exchanging pleasantries . . . unpleasantly, Vanessa noted with little surprise. She stopped behind a chair, both hands upon its back to stop the room from spinning. Damn Ibrahim. Why couldn't he have let her stay in bed?

Secretary Grey's head snapped across to stare at them as they entered. Krishnaswali stood poker-straight before him, immaculate in his dark green uniform. Like Vanessa, he wore only a sidearm at the hip. Unlike Vanessa, his uniform collar and shoulders were decorated with the additional gold pins of rank.

"Oh, wonderful," Secretary Grey snarled upon sighting Ari, "Director Ibrahim's personal attack dog. At least now I have no illusions about what this whole thing's about. You tell the Director that he'd damn well better get used to having his authority challenged, and just because he resorts to these kinds of dictatorial pressure tactics, I'm fucked if I'm about to stop it just for him!"

"Well . . ." Ari raised his eyebrows in mild bewilderment, and scratched at his thick hair. Vanessa thought she must have worn much the same expression last Christmas, when her six-year-old nephew Yves had accused her of treachery for misleading him all those years about Santa Claus. In her light headed state, she found herself suddenly struggling to repress a grin. "If you feel that way, Mr. Secretary," Ari continued, "maybe you'd better tell him yourself."

Not surprisingly, Grey seemed infuriated by Ari's manner. He was a tall man, with a curiously unformed face that seemed to lack either sharp edges or soft curves. His eyes were dark and deep, almost puppy-ish, and his ears stood out sharply from beneath dark, wavy hair. A devotee of the Union Party's conservative left wing, he'd long been regarded by many as the weakest link in President Neiland's Administration . . . but political logic meant she couldn't ditch him without a leftist revolt. Vanessa hated political logic. And recalled Sandy's favourite Tanushan comic/commentator, Rami Rahim, saying in a recent spiel how he'd gone to have lunch with Secretary Benjamin Grey, and "then an empty limousine pulled up, and Secretary Grey got out."

"I've had it," Grey exclaimed, with the air of a man who'd reached his limit. He strode forward several steps to confront Ari directly. Ari's gaze was distinctly dubious. "I'm all out of being polite with you people. The CDF and CSA are supposed to be assets of the State Department, and I get nothing from you but obstruction and suspicion. Especially from you . . . Jesus Christ, what the hell was Ibrahim thinking even admitting the likes of you into the CSA? Let alone making you his personal right hand . . . you've planned this all along, haven't you? Concocted some evidence to give Ibrahim an excuse to crack down on the *one* department in this entire Administration whose services Callay can least afford to be without at this moment!"

"Well, then," Ari said offhandedly, "maybe if you'd kept better tabs on the activities of your people, you wouldn't have let, um, Junior Assistant Director Samarang source a bunch of illegal weaponry through customs using official authorisations." Grey stared, blinking rapidly. "He's in custody now," Ari explained. "He confessed to the shipments but claims he didn't know they'd be used to assault the summit.

"Now . . ." he raised a finger, ". . . maybe it's just me, but I think it's, um, rather curious that Samarang's assistant, Enrico Kalaji, tried to disappear yesterday when I paid him a visit . . . ran real fast down the corridor and jumped from a low balcony, actually. And it's a shame that I lost him, because it would have been, um, pretty interesting to hear him explain exactly who in the State Department gave him the order to bug Ali Sudasarno's cruiser, and how it was that the crazed GI who killed Admiral Duong somehow had access to that bug, and used it to find Commander Kresnov . . . who, incidentally, was trying to hide from exactly that GI. And those she suspected were helping her."

Secretary Grey just stared at him, blankly. Ari looked more closely, as if peering through a window to check if the lights were on inside.

"I could go over it more slowly if you didn't follow," he offered.

"The bottom line, Mr. Secretary," Krishnaswali cut in sombrely, "is that we need to comprehensively search the entire State Department database so that we can trace the leads, and hopefully find out if this GI is receiving inside help. Agent Chandaram will be here shortly, he can explain the procedures to you better than I can. But it's imperative that we have your utmost cooperation on this matter. Will you give it?"

Sandy leaped from the flyer's rear ramp the moment the landing gear touched the pads, and jogged quickly across the wet pad with a borrowed raincoat held above her head, boots splashing on rapidly accumulating puddles in the downpour. The raincoat also had the benefit of blocking all possible view from the snooping super-lense imagers the media liked to use around an action scene—it would be better for all concerned, she knew, if the fewest necessary people knew she was here. Inside the rooftop doors, she took a moment to shake off the raincoat, and hand it to Private Ijaz, as the other two CDF soldiers she'd shared the ride with did the same. Ijaz added them to his pile beside the rain-streaked glass doors, to be dispensed among the next departing group.

"This one came in damn fast, huh?" Sandy commented, shades pocketed as she gazed out at the sheeting rain across the Parliament complex. Beyond the majestic central dome, lightning forked and slashed across the black sky.

"Sure did, sir," said Ijaz, who was plainly far more interested to see her than the newly arrived storm. "And it's barely even midday, usually in summer they don't arrive until at least midafternoon."

"Yeah, well, everything's been pretty crazy lately. Why should the weather be different?" She brushed off her jacket and pants, and tried on her shades once more. "What d'you think? On or off?"

"Don't know who you'd be fooling in this building, Commander."

Sandy considered that, then nodded agreement and tucked the sunglasses into a pocket. "True enough. Much traffic inside? I still can't use uplinks."

"The President's here," Ijaz offered. "I'm not sure where though . . . somewhere on the north side, I think, she wasn't allowed full access and wasn't very pleased about it."

"I'll find her," said Sandy. "I'll just follow the loudest screams."

Ijaz grinned. And said, as she made to descend the stairs, "Commander, it's real good to see you again."

Which pleased her enormously. "It's real good to see you too, Private." And departed before she could succumb to the temptation for sexual innuendo that even in the CDF, she wasn't supposed to make with enlisted personnel . . .

She strode along the broad lower hall, brushing at rain-wet hair and noting that most offices were empty as she passed . . . probably most State Department staff had gathered elsewhere to pass the time. At the circular atrium, Corporal Chang directed her northward, and found a spare headset so that she could listen in to operational chatter. She continued on, past busy CSA agents in suits who mostly didn't notice her identity as they exchanged notes and compared comp-slate codes and building schematics as they swept the entire State Department wing, floor by floor, room by room.

She found Vanessa in an open, north side meeting room that looked more like an exclusive VIP's club than anything else—a series of booth-style tables and comfortable leather bench seats, all of decoratively carved wood with trimmings and wall paintings that looked distinctly South Asian and Arabic by inspiration. The tall north wall windows overlooked green lawns and gardens. Vanessa stood before the glass-walled booths on the east side, firmly confronting a very important looking suit who loomed over her in evident displeasure.

". . . I'm afraid you're going to have to call and say you'll be late," Vanessa was telling him as Sandy approached.

"I am not making a call that gets filtered through your monitoring system," the man insisted loudly. Sandy recognised the face—the Foreign Minister of Arkasoy, no less, several hundred light years from home and not at all happy that his schedule had been interrupted. "My world's security will not allow me to make any official transmission through the filtering software of any foreign security agency."

"I'm sorry, Mr. Atkins, but a lockdown is a lockdown. I believe we'll be finished in a few hours, maybe less."

"I'm not a part of your damned security crisis," Foreign Minister Atkins snapped. Vanessa had to tilt her head well back to look him in the eye, coming barely up to his armpit as she did. "I'm a visiting foreign dignitary on official business with a diplomatic visa, I've nothing to do with your internal security matters!"

"I'm sorry, sir," Vanessa said flatly, "but if you're in this building, you do." Atkins' own security agents were waiting patiently nearby, seeming quite unsurprised at Vanessa's stubbornness. Doubtless they'd explained it to their VIP several times. Equally doubtless their VIP hadn't cared to listen. Sandy waited between table booths, casting a glance around. She recognised several more important faces amongst bored, frustrated guests, plus personal security and various assistants. Waiters in spotless white tunics hurried to and from the kitchen, bringing drinks and snacks, valiantly attempting to keep irritated guests from exploding by placating them with sustenance. Through the old-fashioned blinds across the windowed booth behind Vanessa, Sandy saw President Neiland herself, seated at a table, chin glumly on fist as Agent Chandaram from Investigations attempted to explain the situation to her. Nearby, several dark-suited Alpha Team agents kept careful watch over the proceedings.

God help them if there was a security emergency here, Sandy thought. So many overlapping security operatives, it would be a wonder if they didn't all kill each other in the crossfire.

"I'm sorry, sir," Vanessa answered Minister Atkins' latest complaint, "but Callayan security procedures take precedence on Callay. There's nothing I can do."

Atkins swore beneath his breath, and swung about to storm back to his booth seat. And paused, frowning hard at Sandy, with evident recognition. And swung back around to stare at Vanessa, as if wondering if she'd seen. As if thinking a dangerous escapee was about to be arrested. Sandy wondered who he'd been talking to.

Vanessa met Sandy's gaze, and smiled, tiredly. "Hey-ya." Sandy smiled back, walked up and gave her friend a warm hug, because who really gave a flying fuck about all the people watching, anyway?

Vanessa returned it. "You know," she said against Sandy's shoulder, "I could get used to you as a brunette. In fact, I've been kinda wondering if I should go blonde myself . . ."

"No, no, no," Sandy said adamantly. "It's not you."

"Says your personal committee of one."

"So I'm getting conservative in my old age. Come, sit." She took Vanessa's arm, and guided her gently to the nearest booth, pointing to Lieutenant Sharma to take charge of any future VIP tantrums. Sharma nodded an acknowledgement with a smile, and Vanessa took a seat gratefully, Sandy sliding in beside her with most of the room's eyes fixed firmly upon the backs of their heads.

"How's the head?" Sandy murmured, leaning close so that the many pairs of enhanced eardrums behind them would be most unlikely to hear.

"S'fine," Vanessa murmured back. "This latest generation of neuro-peps are just wonderful . . . you know, they respond to enhanced brain-wave activity? The more you think, the better you feel. It's actually good to be active, 'cause I don't feel so bad, now."

She sounded, Sandy reckoned, slightly dreamy. Which struck her as funny, somehow, and she resisted the temptation to hug her again. It was just so nice to see her and to have her to talk to once more.

Vanessa frowned slightly, gazing at her from barely a hand's breadth away. "What about you? That damn GI could have had you, from what I heard."

"Worse—Sudasarno and an elevator full of civilians." She sighed, and hung her head. Vanessa's frown grew deeper.

"Bothered you, did she?" she asked. Vanessa's ability to read her emotions always amazed her. It was a totally different relationship from hers with Ari. Ari always seemed surprised and amazed at her thoughts, an amazement tinged with fascination. Vanessa was rarely amazed. She empathised.

"I don't know," Sandy murmured. And shook her head, faintly. "I'd always thought complexity led to intelligence. I mean, that's why humans are humans and bunbuns are bunbuns."

"You leave Jean-Pierre alone."

Sandy smiled. "But logically—our brains are more complex, thus we have morality, right? I mean, morality is a higher intellectual func-tion, surely—that's why the old fear of a humanity overrun and enslaved by machine intelligence hasn't happened, right? Humans have created machines significantly smarter than themselves . . ."

"If you do say so yourself," Vanessa interjected.

". . . but humans haven't been enslaved," Sandy continued, "because the intellect required to do the enslaving also entails a sufficiently advanced consciousness to be subject to moral doubts and questions. And enslaving humans is unconscionable."

Vanessa made a face. "Sandy . . . I've been a corporate number cruncher, and I've been a head-kicking grunt. Neither profession is exactly philosophical, my tiny little mind is *way* beneath this at the moment . . ."

"I'm saying that I'd always thought GIs were capable of more," Sandy explained, her gaze earnest. Vanessa looked tired. But she tried, if just to please her. "I'd always insisted that even the lower-des GIs could be so much more than just soldiers if they tried. If they were given the opportunity, and a reason to care. I mean, look at Rhian— just two years here and suddenly she's become all chic and sophisticated. Just the other day she was telling me she wanted to adopt a child someday . . ."

"Really?" Vanessa perked up immediately. And smiled, picturing that. "Wow. That's fantastic, what did you tell her?"

"Vanessa, please, I need you to listen to this. I want to know if I'm nuts or what." Vanessa sighed, and raised a conciliatory hand. "So more complexity means more morality, right? And, I mean, the thing that makes me really different from Rhian is the brain structure, on a neurological level . . . I don't understand most of it, I'm not a technician. There're people who speculate that the technology is so fucking advanced it probably isn't even *human* . . ."

"Talee?" Vanessa questioned. The Talee were a question that always got Vanessa's attention. And a lot of other people.

"Sure," said Sandy. It was common enough speculation that the Talee had provided League scientists with the first synthetic neurology tech. Yet another reason for Federation citizens to be terrified of the possible directions the League might take the human species in— without the majority, Federation consent. "But mine's different even from Rhian's. More advanced . . . I don't know how, it just is. More complicated pathways, able to process more information simultaneously without going crazy like Ari says would happen to any straight who tried to download uplinks at my speeds. Segmented consciousness. Rhian sees everything simultaneously. I compartmentalise."

"It's a wonder you're not schizophrenic," Vanessa remarked, with more concern than fascination.

"And now this GI. Jane."

"She calls herself Jane?"

"Maybe the FIA gave her the name . . ." Sandy shrugged, ". . . I don't know. But she's smart. To have done what she's done so far . . . real fucking smart. And I met her, Ricey. I spoke with her, face to face. I looked her in the eyes, and I saw just . . . nothing."

Now Vanessa was really paying attention. Sandy thought she looked a little spooked. "Nothing at all?" she said.

"She reacts," Sandy explained. "She smiles a little, now and then. And I think I made her a little angry, telling her she didn't know shit."

"Well, there, surely that's something?"

Sandy shook her head. "It was almost like a mechanical response. Or not mechanical, as such, just . . ." and she took a deep breath, trying to find the words. "Facial expressions are like symptoms, right? Symptoms of an underlying cause."

"Emotions."

"Well yeah . . . but emotions are structured within a broader psychology." She shook her head. "Damn, I never had much use for psychs, but I could use one now."

"They exist within a context," Vanessa ventured calmly. "The context of that person's personality."

"Yes. Exactly. This Jane . . . the emotions might be there, and the facial muscles might move, but the context . . . the broader personality . . . I don't know." She searched Vanessa's face for understanding. "I didn't *feel* anything. Does that make sense?"

"Sure. One morning two years ago, I rolled over in bed and looked at Sav. Same feeling."

"No way. Sav was a confident, exuberant, funny guy who also happened to be an egocentric arsehole. Hell, he had enough going for him to make you want to marry him . . ."

"Yeah," Vanessa muttered, "big fucking recommendation."

"But you felt *something*, for good or bad."

Vanessa put her right elbow up on the seat back, and leaned her head against that hand for support. Fixed Sandy with a slightly glazed look, head tilted, one quizzical eyebrow raised in question. A waiter deposited drinks at a nearby table booth with a clink of glasses. Vanessa waited until he had passed out of earshot before resuming in a low voice, weary yet focused.

"Sandy, I used to be a suit myself, for one brief, bleak, lonely period in my life. I know a bit about the interstellar corporate bigwig circuit. I checked up on Takawashi, lying in my hospital bed in my awful polka dot pyjamas. These functions he's attending every second night . . . just amazing. Every big name from the top end of town is there . . . of course, in Tanusha, it takes a few weeks to fit them all in, but still. Even some Progress Party reps."

"Federation biotech hasn't seen anything like what his technology can do," Sandy replied cautiously. "If there were some relaxation in trade, in a few areas, the money to be made here is enormous."

"In this political climate? The last thing Neiland needs is more speculation that she's dragging the Federation toward League progressivism." Sandy nodded, biting her lip. That bit didn't make sense. "Mostly the media's been too busy with explosions and gunfire to notice much, but there were a few stories. The Administration immediately released a statement saying that Takawashi was on Callay on a 'personal visit,' and had not been invited. And the Neiland Administration continued to oppose any and all attempts to relax controls on all advanced biotech . . . blah, blah, blah.

"But I checked further, and here's the thing. He *was* invited. The State Department has an invitation on record." Sandy frowned at her. "That's how he got the diplomatic visa. But no one I talked to seemed to know who exactly made the invitation. Or they wouldn't tell me. This is a very wealthy, very powerful man, Sandy. He doesn't take a month out of his busy schedule for no good reason. And he just happens to be here at the same time as our friend Jane runs amok . . . with help from the State Department."

"Damn," Sandy murmured. "You think Takawashi has some kind of personal interest in Jane?"

"And in you. He's responsible for much of what you are, right? So he's also responsible for much of what Jane is. Only he says this theft took place several years ago, very conveniently about the same time the FIA grabbed you here, and about the same time as the old League administration was getting real nervous that they were losing the war, and what would happen when people found out how far beyond the legal limits they'd gone in creating advanced GIs, and taking steps to get rid of the evidence."

Sandy blinked at her, as that possibility unfolded with a rush. "Oh, shit."

Vanessa nodded, with that same weary purpose. "I bet you Jane wasn't stolen. I bet she was offloaded to the highest bidder. Or maybe even for free. I mean, Takawashi loves his GIs far more than he loves the League, right? Especially the military."

"He'd do it just to spite them," Sandy muttered. "And he'd tell them the evidence is destroyed. And Jane gets sent to the FIA. Who operate in such a total information blackout that they can do all kinds of illegal stuff with her that they can make her into whatever they want."

"So the question is," Vanessa continued, "why the big deal about Jane? Takawashi's a neurol . . . a neurologist." Managing to bite out the word through uncooperative lips. "I mean, what makes her special? She's gotta be different from you, or he'd have just dumped her. Maybe he'd been working on something special with her, something he didn't want to see destroyed."

Sandy gave no response. Vanessa waited for a moment. Then lifted the supporting hand from her face, and poked Sandy in the arm. Sandy's distant gaze shifted onto her friend.

"I was a failure," she murmured. "I was a great success while I lasted, but a long-term failure. Loyalty was a part of the test parameter. I failed."

"And a wonderful, glorious failure it was too."

"Jane won't fail. She might die, but she won't fail. She won't defect. That's why she's so smart at such an early age. That's what Takawashi was working on."

"What was?" said Vanessa, struggling for focus.

"A loyal GI. One whose personality could be predetermined. One who wouldn't slowly evolve over seventeen years. Who wouldn't change her mind. All the combat effectiveness of a Cassandra Kresnov, without the downside risk." She stared away at a far wall, beyond the booths and patrons' heads. "I didn't want to believe that was possible."

"It might not be," Vanessa replied. "Jane's still young."

"If I get my way, she's not going to get much older."

Vanessa half shrugged. "Them's the breaks, I guess."

Within the office behind the glass opposite their booth, Sandy saw that Neiland was staring at the pair of them, darkly. There was an indication to an aide, then, and the aide opened the door. Pointed two fingers at Sandy and Vanessa, then pointed "inside." Sandy sighed.

"Now the fun starts," she murmured, sliding out of the booth seat, and waiting to give Vanessa a hand in case her head started spinning again. "Where's Ari?" she thought to ask as Vanessa carefully stood up.

"I sent him away," Vanessa said drily. "Before he started a fight he wasn't going to win." With Neiland, Vanessa meant. The President, and Commander-in-Chief of CDF and CSA. Ari's ultimate boss. Not that that would stop Ari, once paranoid certainty had set in.

"Good move," Sandy murmured, and they walked together to the door.

The President sat on the far side of the room's table, gazing at the inbuilt display screen and chewing at the inside of her lip. To one side sat Agent Chandaram, to the other, Ali Sudasarno. The aide who'd opened the door, Sandy didn't recognise. Sandy and Vanessa took old fashioned, leather seats with their backs to the glass . . . Sudasarno pressed a button on his table console, and the glass polarised to deep black. Neiland gazed at them both, and then at Sandy in particular, with hard green eyes. She wore her red hair loose today, in counterpoint to a pink blouse beneath the dark, formal suit. Somehow, it didn't soften her expression much at all.

"Your timing stinks," she said flatly, looking straight at Sandy. "I need the State Department, Commander. I need credibility. I need Callay to look like a world that can handle the task of hosting the Grand Council in a year's time. Right now, we're a laughing stock. If all our newfound allies among friendly Federation worlds pack up and go home, and strike their own separate deals with Earth and the Fleet, no one will be less surprised than I."

"It's not us, Ms. President," said Sandy. "We've been interfered with again—as long as Earth remains the central power in the Federation, they'll retain the means to infiltrate our security and organisations, and screw us any time they like. If anything, it strengthens your arguments, and it gives Federation worlds even more reason to be scared of Earth-centralised power and the Fleet."

"Commander." Neiland leaned forward, elbows on the table. Her green eyes flashed. "Perhaps you didn't notice, but we're under blockade. When news reaches Earth of the reasons why, they'll think it's justified. Their admiral was assassinated, on an official visit, with us providing the security—apparently by a pro-Callayan extremist group. You tell me a rogue GI did it, but there's no proof . . . except for Major Rice's combat records from the scene, which provide far too much sensitive material about CDF operations to unfriendly interests than we can afford, and that are so complicated no major news organisation would understand it even if we did release it.

"And now you're trying to find proof, and you've shut down the State Department to do it . . . damn it, Cassandra, what kind of victory will it be for Callayan competence if our own State Department turns out to be the source of our problems? I mean, this . . ." and she waved a hand at the display screen, ". . . all this stuff Agent Chandaram's been showing me, all these infiltration codes and suspicious mail transfers, this isn't evidence! This is a pile of naughts and zeros! Earth factions believe Callay is spiralling into out-of-control sedition and rebellion, and are determined to retain control over the Fleet to protect themselves from the chaotic horror that the Federation will *surely* become with us at the centre of it, and this bunch of technical rubbish is your only answer? I need clear, unassailable evidence! Nothing else is going to get it done!"

The President, Sandy noted, was fairly angry. About as angry, in fact, as she'd ever seen her. Sandy took a deep breath.

"Have you been talking with Captain Reichardt?" she asked. Neiland stared at her, incredulously.

"That's your answer? I'm talking about losing the one thing we've been fighting for these last years—losing the new Grand Council's sovereign and total control of the Fleet—and you want to start a fucking war?!"

"Ma'am," said Sandy, with great deliberation, "I can get you those stations back." Neiland's green eyes locked with her own, pale blue ones. For a moment, no one in the room appeared to breathe. "But I'll need Reichardt. It can't be done without him."

Neiland broke eye contact first, looking aside at the flat, smooth wood of the table. Closed her eyes, briefly, and massaged her head with one hand. "So you get the stations," she said. "What then? What's to stop Captain Rusdihardjo from backing off and blasting the whole facility?"

"War crimes," Sandy said simply. "It didn't even happen in the war, much. Combatants are supposed to take and hold civilian stations, not destroy them. To do it in peacetime, against an ally, would destroy their credibility."

"That's a hell of a gamble," Neiland said sombrely. "You say it didn't happen much . . . I recall that about half of the war's casualties were civilians living or working on orbital or deep space facilities. So it happened a *lot*, didn't it?"

"Depends how you measure it," Sandy said calmly. "Lots of desperate situations in the war."

"Damn it, Cassandra, you think this isn't desperate?"

Sandy waited until she was sure the President was calm enough to offer her full attention. Then, "It's your choice, Ms. President. I can get you the stations. If it happens with Reichardt's help, it can't be called sedition, and they can't just blame it all on us. Then it's up to them how hard they want to push back. Either way, we've only acted in self-defence. And we'll look strong in doing so. Strength with which to reassure our nervous friends."

Neiland stared at her for a moment longer. Then the stare flicked to Vanessa. "You've seen Cassandra's plans, Major?"

"Yes, ma'am," said Vanessa.

"What do you think?"

"It'll work," said Vanessa.

The President scowled. "You've never done off-world ops before."

"Then why ask me?" Vanessa replied with a smile. Another world leader, full of power and not knowing Vanessa, might have exploded at the scandalous informality. Neiland only looked exasperated.

"You're no help," she said.

"Thank you, ma'am."

They'd barely stepped outside the office when Sandy and Vanessa were confronted by a young man in an awkwardly ill-fitting suit. He seemed barely able to contain his excitement.

"Sandy, I've found . . . oh, I mean Commander Kresnov, I've . . . I've found it! I've found the parallel subsystem matrix that . . . that . . ."

"Agent Yoong," Sandy said patiently, "why don't you take a deep breath, and come with me out into the hall."

Yoong looked a little flustered. "Yes, ma'am . . . I mean, Commander." Sandy put an unhurried hand on his back, guiding him toward the doors and away from curious eyes. And studiously ignored Vanessa's silent mirth as they went. Vanessa found the breathless young men of Intel just hysterical where Sandy was concerned, and teased her about it often.

"Now," said Sandy as they reached a relatively deserted stretch of hallway, "what have you found?"

"Ma'am . . . I mean Commander . . ." Yoong paused, and took a deep breath. "I think it'd just be simpler if you uplinked to the network and let me show you."

"I can't uplink to anything right now," Sandy said patiently, "there's bad people with mysterious access to my whereabouts who have a certain code that could kill me."

"Yes, I know, ma . . . Commander, that's what I'm saying! I've found it, I've found the sleeper system someone put on the State Department network that locked into CSA and CDF systems and let them trace your location!"

"Show me," Sandy demanded.

Yoong blinked at her. "Well, if you'd just uplink . . ."

"On your comp-slate." She pointed to the little unit in Yoong's suit pocket. Yoong blinked at that too, as if only just remembering he had it.

"Oh . . . right, of course." He took it out, flipped it open and began rapidly downloading material from a personal database. "Here, you see, Commander, this is a triple slash version of the vega series of trace rerouters . . ."

"Yeah, yeah, yeah," said Sandy, snatching the slate from his hands. The 3-D graphical sequence on the screen looked familiar, she recognised the shapes and formations with that portion of her brain that registered facial or speech recognition—reflexively and without quite knowing how—but that didn't mean she knew all the Feddie-Tanushan techie jargon they liked to throw around at Intel. Just because she knew what it was didn't mean she always knew what it was *called* . . . and she scrawled rapidly through multiple facets and angle-shifts upon the screen with a tracing forefinger, frowning as she tried to figure exactly what it did on a network the size and scale of the State Department's. "You found this where?"

"It was a subfile of a worker named, um . . ." and he snapped his fingers, trying to remember. And Sandy's multitrack brain somehow found time to marvel at how such a genius with codes and numbers could still have difficulty recalling simple names. People's brains stored information in funny ways. "Damn it, I was just looking in his file . . ."

"Kalaji?" Vanessa suggested. Yoong stared at her, eyes brightening.

"Yes! Kalaji . . . Enrico Kalaji!"

Sandy frowned at Vanessa. "One of Ari's geese?" she asked.

"One of Junior Assistant Director Samarang's," Vanessa agreed. "Or so he said."

"Oh yeah," said Yoong, "he's one of Samarang's closest . . ." and he frowned at Sandy. "Ari's geese?"

"For his wild goose chases," Sandy explained, scrawling rapidly through the screen graphics. "Damn, I can't make this out, it's been too long since I actually *looked* at any code. Anyone have a cord?"

"Oh, yes," said Yoong, fumbling in a suit pocket. "Um . . . just . . . right here." He pulled out the connector lead. Sandy took it, slotted one end into the comp-slate and the other into the slim insert socket beneath the hair at the back of her skull. The data-wall didn't hit very hard, with just the little comp-slate. In no time she'd found the file and opened the program . . . it unfurled before her in multilevel complexity, but nothing as advanced or complicated as the League-level tac-nets and security formulations she was familiar with. Here was the branch that connected to CDF central, and from there the links into main schedules and protocols, and over there the bypass subroutine that allowed what was supposed to be secure, encrypted information to be passed on to a third party along undesignated channels on the outside . . .

Samarang worked for Secretary Grey. He'd been ordered to track her, including having her and Ari's vehicles bugged . . . damn good work if you could bug anything Ari operated. But then, she recalled, the cruiser was on loan at short notice. Very sloppy, Ari. Kalaji was in direct control of the surveillance, and was apparently feeding it to friendly Ms. Jane. Why . . . well, if she found him, she'd ask him. She only hoped she found him before Jane did . . . as no doubt did CSA Investigations, who were becoming very sick of cleaning up Jane's mess after her.

But now, the monitoring software was secured, the leak in the State Department closed down, and no one was going to know with any degree of reliability where she was at any given moment. Jane still had codes that could trigger the killswitch, but wouldn't know where to search on the network at any given time to use them, making any remote attack attempt akin to the proverbial needle in the haystack, on a network the scale of Tanusha's. Caution was still required. But suddenly, she could use her uplinks again.

Sandy disconnected the cord from the insert, grabbed the startled Agent Yoong by the suit lapels, and planted a firm kiss on his lips.

"Thank you!" she told him delightedly, handed him back the comp-slate, grabbed Vanessa by the arm and hauled her briskly down the hallway. The astonished young agent stood in her wake, clutching his comp-slate, his light brown skin slowly turning a bright shade of pink.

"And you complained before Ari you couldn't find a man," Vanessa remarked scornfully as Sandy remembered the state of her head, and walked more slowly. "Intel's just teeming with all these nice, well-groomed boys . . ."

"Child abuse," Sandy retorted.

"He's at least thirty!"

"Still child abuse. I wanted a lover, not a pet. Vanessa, I need you to set things up. Can you do that?"

For a moment, there was no reply. "What's the time frame?" Vanessa said sombrely, after that moment had passed.

"Two rotations minimum."

Vanessa made a short, hissing sound through her teeth. "Sandy . . . the President's right, you know. I haven't done orbital ops before."

"I have. I know what it takes. You'll be fine, I promise."

"Why ask me anyway?" Vanessa asked with mounting exasperation. "Why not Krishnaswali? He's in charge, it's going to be his decision anyway."

"Because he's the administrative, political and strategic commander, and he knows it," Sandy replied, taking a left, headed for the main flyer pad. "He was the safe political choice, not the practical operational one. Why do you think Ibrahim insisted you come along?"

"Sandy, I . . ." Vanessa took a deep breath, ". . . I can't do this. I can't be constantly fighting with my superior! It's not how units are supposed to operate! Damn it, I even felt *sorry* for him this morning, having to tell him I'd been ordered along against his wishes . . . he *knows* he's not in full operational command and I just don't know how long he's prepared to tolerate that!"

"He's never made any secret of his political connections, that's the way he's chosen to operate. They happened to include Secretary Grey . . . I mean hell, Ricey, I'm not even sure how much to trust him in light of all this. Ibrahim evidently felt the same."

"Well, that's just fucking great," Vanessa retorted in rising temper, "Ibrahim needs a proxy, you go running off on one of Ari's goose chases, and I get left holding the detonator! You know, you always leave me stuck with this kind of shit, and I get sick of it!"

Sandy stared at her, incredulously. "Always?"

"Always!" Vanessa glared angrily at a passing Intel. The Intel looked hurriedly elsewhere, and quickened her pace.

"Name another time."

"I'm not making a fucking list, okay?! I feel like shit, I don't want to do this now!"

Sandy stared ahead down the hall, her jaw hardening. Vanessa fumed. A restroom door approached on their left. In a moment of firm resolve, Sandy made up her mind, grabbed Vanessa by the arm, and hauled her toward the door. Vanessa protested, but Sandy's grip was steely tight. The ladies room was a sparkling, tiled and gold-fixtures affair with broad mirrors and soft, inset lighting. And empty, Sandy discovered with a quick check beneath the stall doors as she released Vanessa's arm—there were very few people left on this level save CSA and CDF personnel. She turned back to Vanessa, who stood in the centre of the tiled floor and stared at her with no small displeasure.

"Vanessa." Firmly, folding her arms at two metres' distance, so she could take in all her body language at a glance. For this one, she felt she might require every clue she could get. "You've been snapping at me for the last few months. I want to know why."

"Snapping?" Incredulously. "What, you think you're so infallible, and I'm so even-tempered, that me snapping warrants some kind of emergency? You bruised my arm, damn it!"

"I'm sorry," said Sandy, attempting an even tone. A part of her was damn worried. Frightened, even. Vanessa was the best friend she'd ever had. Doing anything that might jeopardise that friendship was scary on a level that bullets and grenades had never truly reached. That part of her wanted to beg, to plead, to placate or admit to any perceived wrongdoing, just to make things right again. But somehow, with Vanessa, she didn't think that was going to do it.

"I didn't want to say anything before," she continued, "because you know I worry that sometimes I don't understand. I thought I might have misinterpreted . . . but then Ari remarked on it himself . . ."

Vanessa opened her mouth to interrupt, but Sandy overrode her, ". . . and there's just so much going on, Vanessa, I can't afford to have this hanging over us when things really get serious."

"You can't afford?" with raised-brows irony. "Oh, that's nice to know, I'm pleased you've got our relationship into the right operational perspective."

For the first time, Sandy felt her cool slipping. "Damn it, Ricey . . ." She looked aside, running a frustrated hand through her hair. "Okay, I used the wrong word! I said 'afford,' as if it were an operational matter, when it's supposed to be emotional . . . I do that! It's my upbringing, it's my nature, call it what you will—sometimes I say the wrong fucking thing, and I'd expected better understanding from you than to jump on my head! You know what I meant!"

Vanessa put hands on her hips, and looked down. Scuffed at the spotless tiles with a heavy boot. "Look, what do you want me to say?"

"I don't want you to *say* anything. I want to know why you've been getting pissed at me." She couldn't help the pleading, imploring note from creeping into her voice. "I mean, I do the wrong thing sometimes. I know I do. If I do something wrong, or if I upset you somehow, I want you to tell me about it. You're the best friend I've ever had, Vanessa, and I . . ."

"Look, I . . ." Vanessa raised both hands, in extreme frustration, ". . . I can't tell you now! It's not a good time! In fact, it's the worst possible fucking time I can think of."

"I can't deal with this here, and that out there, at the same time! I'm not good at this kind of thing, I don't want to have to try because I don't know how I'll respond! Now you're not leaving this bathroom until you tell me!"

Vanessa put a hand to her forehead and massaged, as if the pain had become abruptly worse. "Oh God," she muttered, "and I'm full of drugs too . . . no, look . . ." as she came to a decision, ". . . I can't do this now, Sandy, or I'll say something that'll really fuck things up properly."

She turned to leave. Sandy crossed the space between them in a flash and grabbed her shoulder. Vanessa flashed a blow at that arm, which Sandy caught and immobilised in an unbreakable grip. Vanessa's expression, immediately before her, was desperate.

"Sandy, please! I'm sorry I snapped at you . . . my head's screwed up, I'm full of painkillers and I wasn't thinking straight. Just let me go, huh?"

"No."

"Sandy, look, I'm in no state for this . . ."

"Just tell me!" With no small degree of desperation herself.

"I can't!"

"Why the fuck not?!"

"Because I'm in love with you, you moron!"

Sandy stared. Opened her mouth to speak, but nothing came out. Her grip on Vanessa's arm dissolved. Vanessa pulled her arm free, in agonised exasperation. Turned to go, took one step toward the door, and stopped. Sandy tried desperately to think of something to say. Only one thing came to mind—why does everything always have to be so hard? But somehow, she didn't think that would help very much.

"When you say *love* . . ." she finally managed to venture, ". . . what . . . do you mean, like . . ."

"Oh shit, what, you want me to repeat myself?" Vanessa made for the door.

"Wait! Wait, wait, wait . . ." Sandy hurried after her, grasping Vanessa's uniformed shoulder—Vanessa swung at her arm, Sandy allowing the hard contact if it meant Vanessa was facing her once more . . .

"Stop grabbing me!" Vanessa's large, dark eyes were intense with emotion. "Damn it, Sandy, you're such a . . . such a . . . goddamn stupid meathead sometimes!" I guess I must be, was all Sandy could think in reply. "I mean look at you, all broad shouldered, bulletproof and beautiful . . . you know the guys all call you Supergirl? When there's no officers around, it's all 'Supergirl says this,' or 'Supergirl would have done it that way.' But you really don't have a clue, do you?"

Sandy stared at her in growing desperation. She didn't know what to say. Felt uncertain, suddenly, of the tiled floor beneath her black boots. She glanced frantically about the bathroom in search of some inspiration, something that could assist her. A crutch to lean upon. There was nothing. Vanessa's dark, pain-filled eyes bore into her, shimmering with tears and more frustrated by the second.

"I mean look at you," she continued. "You didn't suspect a thing, did you? Do you see now why I didn't want to say anything? Why I haven't wanted to say anything? Why the hell didn't you listen to me? I'm the one who knows what I'm talking about here!"

She broke off, with a wave of final defeat, and turned once more for the door. Sandy grabbed her, bodily from behind, and restrained her in a tight embrace.

"Oh God, Sandy, stop it!" Vanessa tried to fight, then gave up as she realised the futility. Sandy just held her, not knowing what else to do. If she let go, Vanessa would leave. Somehow, she couldn't let it happen. Vanessa tried reasoning. "Sandy. Sandy? Come on Sandy, let go. I'm a busy girl."

"No."

"No?"

"No. Never."

Vanessa dropped her head with a shuddering sigh. "Look . . . Sandy, we can talk about this later, now isn't a good . . ."

"Why does . . ." and Sandy broke off in distress, unable to find the words. "Why does it have to matter? I mean fuck . . . I love you too, Ricey, I love you so . . ."

"It's not the same thing!"

"Isn't it?" Desperately. "We love each other, we're together all the time . . ."

"Jesus Christ, Sandy, to you of all people I shouldn't have to explain about the birds and the bees!"

"What, it's just sex? Fuck it, Vanessa . . . it's just sex! It doesn't mean anything—it's fun, it's great to share with someone you love, or even like, but why the hell does it matter if we don't have sex?"

"It just does, okay! Look, for fuck's sake, let go!"

"No!"

"I won't run away! I promise, I'm not Cinderella and it's nowhere near my bedtime, now let go!" Sandy released her, and Vanessa turned on her, fuming. "It's . . . look, just listen very carefully, you poor, backward little army bumpkin, because I'm only going to explain this once. I'm bisexual. That doesn't just mean tits-and-arse gets me wet, you understand? It's a genetic, psychological disposition, Sandy. It means falling in love, and that's something . . . *far* beyond a little recreational screwing. Am I making sense to you here?"

"What, you're saying you think you have a monopoly on love in this relationship?" Sandy retorted indignantly. She jabbed a finger at Vanessa's chest. "I will challenge you on that! How the hell would you know if you love me more than I love you? You're not me, you can't know how I feel!"

"Oh, no." Vanessa almost laughed in despair, putting both hands over her face. "I just died and woke up in a bad science fiction movie. I can't believe I'm trying to explain to an android what love is. You don't even understand the distinction."

"An android?" Now she was upset. Vanessa never called her that. "Is that how you think of me?"

"Have you ever been in love, Sandy?" Vanessa challenged, ignoring that question. "Think really, really hard." Sandy just stared at her. "All the men you've slept with, and God knows it's a lot . . . did one of them ever leap out at you as special? Did you ever find yourself obsessing about him? Wanting to be near him, for no particular reason?"

"I was never around men like that, Ricey! They were either fellow GIs, all of whom were lower designation and didn't think like I did, or they were straights—usually officers—who always kept me at arm's length. I never had the chance, I never met the right kind of guy . . . and besides, it's all a goddamned conditioned social response anyway!"

"Oh bullshit . . ."

"It is too! I swear to you, if you'd been brought up in a society where sex was commonplace recreation and no one ever got jealous, you'd be like that too!"

Vanessa folded her arms firmly, shaking her head. "They did something to you, Sandy. Something in the foundational tape, or something in the brain structure, I don't know. Damn it, you see why I didn't want to bring this up?"

"Did something to me?" Sandy's head was spinning. She wasn't used to living on this level of her emotional spectrum for any length of time. She felt like someone afraid of heights, leaning on the rooftop railing of a mega-high-rise. "Did something to me how? You're saying that . . . that somehow, because I don't think like you, it must be because I'm an . . . an *android*?"

"Do you love Ari?"

"Do I love Ari? What the hell kind of a question is that? Of course I love Ari . . . I love you too, although you seem to be having a real hard time believing it . . ."

"Do you find yourself daydreaming about him?" Vanessa was pressing it home hard, now. She was like a predator with a fresh kill when she got like this, Sandy knew, having seen it inflicted upon others from time to time. Being now the target herself made her extremely nervous, on top of her other disorientations. "Does the very thought of him make your insides feel all gooey? Do your knees feel weak when he approaches? Does a kiss feel like heaven? Do you impatiently count the seconds until you can see him again?"

Unexpectedly, Sandy felt tears spring to her eyes. When she spoke, her voice was tight with new emotion. "That's not fair," she said. They both knew what she was like. Vanessa knew better than anyone Sandy's focus, her unerring concentration, her rigid mental compartmentalisation. It was a part of her psychology, the foundational fabric of the very person that she was. "That's your definition of love. I'm different to you. Just because it doesn't hit me like it does you, that doesn't . . . it doesn't give you any right to say . . ."

"Sandy, I'm . . ." And this time Vanessa grabbed her, tightly by the arms. "I'm sorry, I'm not trying to hurt you. I'm not saying you love any less, I'm . . . I'm not saying your feelings are any less significant than mine. They're different, as you say. And somehow, with you, and I suspect with Rhian, Ramoja and others too, you just don't feel love like straights do. It doesn't weaken you. It doesn't . . . Jesus, it doesn't fuck with your head and make intelligent thought difficult. Somehow, they did that to you, either intentionally or as something that just happens, with the way you think, the way your thoughts are structured.

"I'm trying to tell you that you can't know how I feel. And that . . . that even if you were capable of being attracted to a woman, sexually, you still couldn't return it. And you can't know how much it hurts, Sandy, to love someone that much and . . . and to know that they'll never, ever be able to give it back to you. Especially if that person's also your best friend, and you see them every day, and when they wake up in the mornings, and you have to just pretend you don't feel what you feel because you share a job together that's just so important, and because you desperately don't want to damage this amazing friendship even though sometimes it hurts to be around them . . ."

She broke off, tears flowing, barely able to speak. Sandy hugged her, and held her close, feeling that surely her arms had never held anything so precious in all her life. She buried her cheek against Vanessa's hair, and tried to blink back her own tears.

"I'm so flattered," she whispered hoarsely. "Honestly, I've never been so complimented in my life."

"Don't be," Vanessa replied, a familiar edge of humour in her voice, struggling for daylight. "It's just a biochemical reaction."

"At the end of the day, we're all just biochemical reactions," Sandy murmured into her hair. "It doesn't make us any less real."

# CHAPTER 12

"**F**rom about when, did she say?" asked Ari. The cruiser descended in a slow hover toward the yellow-striped transit zone beside the Columbo Park, past streetlights and lush foliage. Below, zone markers flashed warning lights, warding pedestrians along the parkside, strolling or jogging along the puddled path in the busy, early evening.

"I don't know," Sandy replied in mild frustration. "We didn't talk about that." Mentally aligning the cruiser's CPU com-systems with her own uplinks, a semivisual scrawl of flashing numerics and graphics across her innersight. She was having trouble finding a transmission package she liked, one that was compatible with her encryption and Ari's carrier boosters. With a bump of wheels, the cruiser touched down. Navcomp displays on the dash switched to road-navigation, the lights on the zone markers stopped flashing, and the cruiser eased forward on automatic, along the one-lane departure road that cut into the park's perimeter. Behind, the next cruiser was descending, and the zone markers began blinking once more as the local air-traffic grid guided them in.

"Then what did you talk about?" Ari persisted, implacably curious.

"We just talked! About . . . stuff."

"Stuff."

"Girl stuff," she said pointedly. She almost never invoked that particular piece of gender-territorialism. Take a hint, Ari.

"'I'm in love with my best friend but she doesn't want to sleep with me because she's straight and artificial' girl stuff?"

Sandy restrained exasperation with difficulty. "Look, just because you have this puerile, masculine fascination for lesbian sexuality . . ."

"Gee, Sandy," Ari deadpanned, "what are you saying? That I'm heterosexual?"

"This is very serious to me, Ari! It's not a game."

"I . . ." Ari blinked in consternation. "I never said it was a game, when did I say it was a . . . ?" He broke off as navcomp abruptly slammed on the brakes—a careless jogger running across the road, Sandy saw immediately, registered at once by the cruiser's ranger and road sensors. "Fucking pedestrians," said Ari matter-of-factly as the cruiser re-commenced, "some people in this city should be required to get a licence just for stepping out the fucking door."

The Fast Curry outlet was jammed with traffic, of course—aircars packed nose-to-tail along the left lane where the one-way road became two lanes, and ten more queued behind. Canvas awnings were stretched across half the road, the far right lane left clear to rejoin the main, parkside highway up ahead. On the opposite side of the low, one-storey restaurant buildings, many diners sat at tables beneath similar awnings, eating before a view of beautiful, rain-wet gardens and lawns, and passing pedestrians. Several cars departed ahead, and the lane edged slowly forward. Sandy glanced over her shoulder as the next cruiser behind boxed them in.

"Wonderful ambush spot," she remarked.

"Yeah, well I'm hungry enough to risk it. I just wish the takeaway joints could put themselves up the top of tall buildings or something, so we don't even have to land to pick up dinner. We'd just fly through."

"And get our curry splattered all over the windshield?"

"Yeah, I wasn't thinking at three hundred kilometres per hour, genius. We'd hover."

"I don't think a curry house could pay the rent eighty storeys up," Sandy remarked, happy that the conversation had moved along. "Unless they charged about sixty Feds per meal."

"Hmm." Ari considered that. Drummed briefly on the steering grips with his fingers. "So d'you think she's jealous of me? Or of us, I mean?" Sandy scowled at him. "What?" Ari protested. "It's important, right? I'm asking!"

The queue bumped up another space, then another. "I don't know, Ari, I honestly just don't know."

"I mean, I guess that must have hurt, huh?" Ari appeared quite intrigued at the prospect. "Although we don't . . . you know . . . we don't carry on together like some couples I could name . . ."

"She's not the jealous type," Sandy said firmly.

"You're certain? I mean, how would you know?"

"Ari!" Sandy stared at him, her eyes hard. "I don't want to talk about it! Understand?"

Ari sighed. Sandy resumed fiddling with the com-systems until the cruiser reached its spot in the queue beneath the awning, then lowered the window as an Indian girl on skater-blades zoomed from a building door with a tray stacked with containers. Sandy paid with her civvie card, and Ari followed the cruiser ahead out and down the road. Sandy unpacked the meal onto the plastic holders always given to airborne customers, and finally lined up a com-sequence that worked for her.

"I got it," she said, "patch me in."

Ari touched a few markers on a display screen, aligning his own carrier boosters . . . on internal visual, Sandy could see the cruiser's CPU com-matrix reconfiguring for long-range transmissions. Ari dialed up the destination and in a flash, the signal sorted and multitranslated through a dozen encryption and security walls to connect with CSA HQ's own central com network, with an ease and precision that even Sandy had to respect. Ari's codework was as eclectic and individual as Ari himself—impenetrably so, she'd heard many fellow codeworkers complain. On some subconscious level that very few straights or GIs could access or analyse, Ari's conceptual brain simply worked differently to everyone else's. As a GI, she possessed far greater raw processing capability than Ari ever could. But as a straight, if impressively augmented, human, Ari's consistently baffling mental processes gave him an edge that very few GIs could hope to match—in individuality, and uniqueness.

"It'll take a few seconds for the relay-satellite to acquire *Mekong*'s receptor dish," he warned, brow furrowed with concentration as his intent eyes studied the display screen. The cruiser took a left turn on automatic, away from the main highway junction, and on toward the next transition zone. "The Third Fleet's been a little jumpy lately, I hope they haven't been fiddling with basic access codes or we might not get in . . ."

Sandy handed Ari his tray, opening her own and cracking the lids. The smell of steaming curry filled the interior. She broke off a piece of pappadum and munched, waiting. The signal connected.

*"This is* Mekong *com-three, please identify?"*

"Hello, *Mekong*," said Ari, "this is CSA special operative Googly. I believe Captain Reichardt is expecting my call."

There was a few seconds' pause for transmission and encryption-processing delay. Then, *"Hello Googly, please hold."*

The cruiser pulled up behind the one in front, which was in turn behind three more aircars waiting at the transition zone—on weekday evenings, takeaway fly-ins were always crowded.

"Hey," said Ari in dismay, gazing down at his meal, "I ordered lamb kashmiri, not rogan josh. The most sophisticated goddamn infotech city in the history of humanity, and still they can't get a fucking takeaway order right."

"Would you prefer butter chicken? I like rogan josh."

They swapped, as Sandy knew they would—Ari loved butter chicken. The cruiser bumped up a space as ahead an aircar rose into the air and past the parkside treetops. Wheels retracting into the underside before accelerating off toward a busy overhead skylane, soaring black dots against a brilliant sunset of towering, orange and pink cumulous cloud. Sandy's uplink clicked back to life.

*"Hello, Googly, this is Captain Reichardt."*

"Oh, um . . ." Ari swallowed his mouthful of butter chicken fast, ". . . hello Captain, I have Snowcat here to speak to you."

*"Commander Kresnov?"*

"I'm here, Captain," said Sandy, "you'll have to excuse the poor speech clarity, we just stopped to get some dinner and we're starved."

*"I was under the impression that you were keeping clear of uplink networks, Commander?"*

"Yes, sir, I was, but that problem seems to have been solved for the moment. Besides, I've got some help in making this a particularly secure line." With a glance at Ari, who was eating again—quickly, in case he was once more required to speak. "Captain, I understand that Director Ibrahim has been in contact with you regarding certain contingency plans of mine."

There was a pause from the other end that lasted too long to be just transmission delay. She took the chance to shovel another mouthful, and chewed quickly.

*"Yeah,"* said the Captain. His Texan drawl seemed suddenly stronger to her ear, and she could almost hear the pained wince in his voice. *"Well . . . I gotta say, Commander, you've got a pretty interesting notion of what 'contingency' means."*

"The Fifth Fleet has committed an illegal, hostile act, Captain. We only seek to protect what is ours."

Reichardt's reluctant sigh was clearly audible over the link. "*I followed you down this road once before Commander, you might recall. Didn't work out all so beautifully now, did it?*"

"On the contrary, Captain, it worked marvellously. There were of course personal consequences for yourself, and your career . . . and doubtless what I ask of you this time will have similar ramifications. If that matters to you."

"*Don't even go there, Commander. The fact is, it's not just me up here. I have other captains, and I'll need to consult. This is one call I simply don't have the authority to make alone. And I'll need proof.*"

"What kind of proof, sir?"

"*Proof that Duong's murder was all a setup, as your people claim. Proof that the Fifth is clearly in league with the setup, and deserves what's coming to them. They might be arseholes, Commander, but they're* our *arseholes. We're not going to call down bad things upon their heads on the sayso of some bunch of downworld foreigners, beggin' your pardon, ma'am.*"

"I understand entirely," Sandy said calmly. Fleet loyalty, he meant. She was asking the Third to be complicit in a military action against their brethren. Reichardt's people and the third Fleet might be as politically opposed as two groups of people were likely to get, but still, she had no illusions of the scale of what she was asking for upon any Fleet man or woman's conscience. "We're in the process of acquiring that proof now."

"*Better make it real good, Commander. I'm a clever man, but I ain't no miracle worker, you understand?*"

CSA operatives found Enrico Kalaji shortly after midnight, shot through the head in what appeared to be his safehouse apartment in downtown Mananakorn District. The shot had awoken neighbouring residents—the bullet had passed through the corridor beyond and several adjoining rooms, just missing a man asleep in bed. Ari wasn't happy.

"Damn it," he muttered as they climbed from the cruiser atop its rooftop pad, "we nearly had it. Just another thirty fucking minutes and we'd have had it."

Sandy nodded tiredly, gazing about at the view from a mere eight storeys up, atop the Mananakorn residential building. Since dinner that evening, they'd been constantly on the move, acting on pieces of information, codes, suspicions and guesswork that had taken them right across Tanusha and back several times over. They'd paid visits to two of Ari's friendly underground code breakers to analyse bits of Kalaji's gear taken from the State Department network that neither Ari nor Sandy were familiar with. Then there'd been a blackmarket weapons expert (in a noisy bar down a dark alley, of course), then a suburban family man they'd dragged from dinner with promises to tell his new fiancée about the previous conviction and probation for smuggling if he didn't explain certain key details about the loopholes in Callayan customs it seemed Kalaji had dealt with in order get the rocket launchers through shipping inspections.

And so on, constantly cross-referencing their latest discoveries with the hundred-plus CSA operatives also searching, hoping for new clues and directing regional police to search those locations they didn't have the manpower to cover. Ari, as Sandy had already seen, knew Tanusha inside and out, and had avenues to so many irregular sources of information, she couldn't help but wonder how he found the time to maintain contact with them all. Or maybe, she'd found herself figuring at about 10 PM, all these shady figures deferred to him on reputation alone. Some of them clearly expected favours . . . which as far as she knew the CSA operating manual, were illegal to grant to anyone, least of all convicted or suspected felons, as the majority of his contacts appeared to be. Which cast new light entirely upon Ari's unpopularity among certain more formal, starch-collared segments of the CSA hierarchy . . .

The building they'd now arrived on reminded Sandy somewhat of her and Vanessa's old home in Santiello—a modest eight-storey residential building, with a skyport on the roof with awnings to keep off the worst of the Tanushan rain and hail, and garden boxes aligned decoratively about the railings. About them, the suburbs slept, streetlights smothered beneath the profusion of semitropical trees. The air smelled heavy with recent rain, their boots splashing on rooftop puddles as they walked. Distant lightning lit the horizon with discontented rumbling, a sharp, dark outline of towers against brilliant flashes of blue.

The crime scene was a square of space by the edge of the rooftop, where a narrow gap between a decorative bush and a rising wall afforded a clear view toward the Mananakorn central business district, slightly less than one and a half kilometres away. About that small square, scanner wands had been erected, sweeping near walls, bushes and puddles with searching lines of light. Elsewhere on the rooftop, CSA agents swept with handheld devices, or entered data into compslates, or stood about and watched, or talked with colleagues. One man stood at another gap between bushes, and gazed out at the rising cluster of Mananakorn towers, alive with light.

"Anil," said Ari, leading the way over. Sandy detoured slightly to the "crime scene," vision-shifting through multiple spectrums in the vain hope of seeing something the wands couldn't. Agent Chandaram turned to greet them, eyes refocusing from distant thought. "That where it happened?"

"We lined up all the holes in the apartment," Chandaram said wearily, "and the trajectory points straight back to there." Pointing at the crime scene. Sandy stopped behind the sweeping wands, gazing out through the gap between bush and wall. Her eyes found the residential building in question, then zoomed upon the target window—twenty-five storeys, second from the left. Her visual zoom was impressive, but she still couldn't see the bullet hole, fifteen hundred metres away. "There's no apparent platform upon which to rest a tripod or other support. Just the railing."

The railing around the rooftop perimeter was wet and narrow. Sandy shook her head. "No use if the shooter was a straight."

"Our trajectory matches aren't entirely perfect over this distance," Chandaram continued, "but they appear to indicate the shot was fired by someone standing upright."

"With no brace support with a heavy sniper rifle," Ari murmured. "Hell of a shot." And he raised an eyebrow in Sandy's direction, questioningly. Sandy looked for a moment longer at the trajectory. Considered the weapon in question from Investigations' initial ballistics report, and the prevailing conditions. And nodded, once.

"There's four people in Tanusha I know of who could make that shot," she said. "Me, Ramoja, Rhian and Jane."

"You have an alibi," Chandaram said drily. Sandy gathered from his expression that he was not about to leap to conclusions. Plenty in the CSA, it seemed, didn't trust Major Ramoja and the League Embassy contingent either. "Not the other League GIs in the embassy?"

"No." Sandy shook her head. "Not high-des enough."

Chandaram frowned. "A GI's designation affects accuracy? I didn't think intellect and physical capability were linked?"

Sandy shrugged. "Just does. I'm not a psych, I couldn't tell you why."

"There are root strands of lateral processing capability that meld with basic motor functions," said Ari. Sandy gave him a blank look . . . she should have known Ari would know more about GI neuroscience than she did herself. "You see it in straights too—most of the great athletes are smart. Great soldiers too, look at Major Rice. Physical performance is partly a function of spatial processing—the, um, awareness of a body's position and motion within a three-dimensional space. The broader an intellect, in terms of raw neuroprocessing capability, the broader the perimeter field and thus the, um, more minuscule, precision adjustments required to shoot or run or . . . or whatever."

"The Parliament massacre," said Chandaram, nodding slowly.

Ari nodded. "Yeah, sure . . . Sandy versus forty lower-des GIs is really a little unfair on the regs, they never had much of a chance."

"I knew their patterns," Sandy said quietly, gazing out at the view. "I helped *write* some of their patterns. It wasn't raw ability, it was knowledge and memory. If the League had trusted lower-des GIs enough to impart a bit more knowledge upon them, they'd be that much more effective. But then, maybe my defection proves that they're right not to."

"Hang on," said Chandaram, "it's still a static sniper shot. Surely a lower-designation GI can hit a still target just as well as a higher-des?"

"This is the eighth storey," said Sandy. "The target's on the twenty-fifth. It's a rising trajectory, the windows were waist-height, that means there was no chance to hit the target sitting down. He'd have been standing, and with Kalaji being so jumpy, standing means moving, or pacing, more likely. The windows were reflective, the air's humid, and the shot had to be a head shot to make certain. Too many variables. The real difference between a high- and low-des GI is the ability to process multiple strands of information. The rest is minor— that's the big difference."

"But Rhian Chu has the right designation?" Chandaram asked.

"Rhian's not a sniper," said Sandy. Lying through her teeth as she said it. Ari would know. Chandaram wouldn't. She hoped. "She could do it, but it was never a specialty or preference, and her spatial processing isn't as good as mine. At this range, in the dark, she might miss. Ramoja's a perfectionist, he'd never have taken that chance with her. He'd do it himself." If the League had a cause to execute Enrico Kalaji, that was. Recent experience in these matters had taught all concerned never to rule anything out. To Chandaram's side, Ari's expression never altered. "And besides, we had a deal. If anything strange went down, she was going to contact me. She'd never have taken an order like this without telling me first."

Chandaram looked at her curiously. Rhian, it occurred to Sandy, hadn't killed anyone for quite some time. Not since Dark Star, anyhow. As always with Rhian, it was difficult to know exactly how these things affected her. Possibly Rhian wasn't aware herself. Sandy suspected personally that that absence of death from her old friend's life had done wonders for her new growth and depth as a person. Death required justifications. Rationalisations of why it was all proper and necessary. Rationalisations that held a person back, forcing them to believe things that weren't necessarily true, for the sake of continued mental stability. She doubted, now, that Rhian could even do something like this, whatever her orders. Surely she would flinch. Surely she would ask questions, and wonder at the morality of what she was being ordered to do. Or maybe that was just wishful thinking, and Rhian's morality continued to revolve around the old soldiers' creed that all morality came from following orders, and nothing else mattered.

Damn, she hated leaving Rhian in their hands. They could destroy her, or corrupt her irreparably. Force her to do something that her new, awakening conscience would punish her for, for the rest of her life. And if they hurt her, or otherwise damaged her with their Machiavellian bullshit . . . well, Jane was not going to be the only high-des GI in Tanusha with cause to fear for her safety.

"We've been monitoring the League Embassy around the clock," said Chandaram. "Ramoja hasn't left . . . but then, he's snuck out before without us knowing, he might not have even been there in the first place."

His expression remained curiously unreadable. Most senior CSA types tended to swagger. Particularly the Indians, who maintained the very cool, suave demeanour at large in that subculture at the time— along with breezy sports jackets, open-necked shirts, swept-back hair and glossy moustaches. Even Sandy's old buddy Naidu went for that—

Director of CSA Intelligence and more than a hundred years old, so it wasn't something sparkling new and Tanushan, evidently. Chandaram wore a plain, grey suit (none of the popular cream or even banana-yellow that had come recently into style), displayed no showy silver chain beneath his open collar, and disdained even the moustache. To the best of Sandy's knowledge, he remained single at the age of forty-seven. Rumour had it that his last steady partner had left him two years ago, during the last major crisis, when he hadn't come home for a week without calling. Rumour also had it that he didn't sleep. Sandy didn't believe that. Even *she* had to sleep . . . if just for a few hours.

"The one person who *did* leave," Chandaram continued, "was Rhian Chu. Unaccompanied. She walked, she seems to like public transport." Of course she did, thought Sandy—more colour and movement to enjoy. Fresh air to smell and shop windows to look in along the way. And the other reason of course . . . "We lost her after about fifteen minutes," Chandaram continued. A faint smile appeared at his lips for the first time. "We always lose her. You'll have to show me how you guys do that."

"I will," said Sandy. "Rhian's been getting a lot of jobs lately. She's a less recognisable courier for one thing, and she likes being loose in the city."

"And you haven't mentioned the person who actually did it," Ari said pointedly.

"The key suspect, Ariel," Chandaram replied, with a raised eyebrow in his direction. "I discount no possibilities. League activity both in the Embassy and connected to it has been intense of late, as you know. We can't rule out some involvement in the whole Kalaji affair."

Sandy frowned at him. "What the hell would they have to gain by setting the Fleet at our throats? They've wanted Federation power out of the hands of Earth for as long as the League's existed."

"Or maybe they simply wish to sow disharmony," Chandaram replied coolly. "A Federation civil war could finish the job they started, without costing them anything. Anyhow, it's not my job to speculate, only to join the dots."

"I think they're looking for Jane," said Ari, lips pursed as he gazed out at the lights with faint frustration. "It fits the search pattern." Chandaram's look was questioning. "I, um, had some of their seeker functions intercepted and analysed by some friends," Ari explained. Anita and Pushpa, Sandy was willing to bet that meant. "It's the kind of pattern that they'd use if . . . well, I'll explain later."

"We found one of Kalaji's safehouses an hour back," Sandy added for Chandaram's benefit. "It'd been broken into . . . maybe League codes were used, I couldn't be sure, they're better at disguising how they penetrate the databases now they know I'm around to analyse whatever you guys pick up. Ari thinks Ramoja was trying to find Kalaji just as we were."

"Maybe he did," said Chandaram. Nodding toward the Mananakorn towers.

"Or maybe he was just hoping to get Jane's whereabouts from him," Ari added. "If Kalaji was Jane's coordinator."

Chandaram shrugged. "And maybe he did that too." Find Kalaji, and wait for Jane to kill him, Sandy realised he meant. Thus finding Jane. Or would he?

"It's too easy to be a sniper in this city," Sandy disagreed. "Even GIs can't see sniper bullets. He wouldn't know where to look . . ." She broke off, feeling suddenly cold. A red tinge descended upon her vision. Time slowed, and the dark landscape of sprawling city lights transformed to a mass of multispectrum colour and motion-highlighted traffic . . .

"Sandy?" said Ari, recognising that look. Sandy stared at him, seeing only a humanoid, face-shaped blob of heat-colouring and fine textures. Blood thumping in his jugular as he became himself alarmed. Eyes darting in small, involuntary motions as minor muscles twitched —a most un-GI-like phenomenon, involuntary muscle spasms . . . "Sandy, what's wrong?"

"Get off the roof," Sandy told him. "You too, Anil. Get off now. Don't hurry, just walk calmly."

Ari didn't question, but merely put a companionable hand on Chandaram's shoulder, and began walking. Sandy took up position on Chandaram's other side. From a distance, she hoped, it would look innocent enough. They walked to the upper entrance lobby, through the sliding doors that were being kept open for investigators, and inside. Only when they were down the stairs, and standing in the hallway of the eighth floor, did Sandy allow herself to feel safe. And furious.

"Goddamn fucking stupid," she muttered to herself, taking the pistol from her jacket pocket for the simple comfort of feeling its weight in her hand. "I should have thought."

"You . . ." Ari looked puzzled. "You don't think . . . ?"

"She's a goddamn ruthless bitch, Ari. We were standing right there, right where she'd have known we'd come to. And I just let us fucking stand there, in full view of any number of sniper-nests for several kilometres around . . . Jesus!"

"That's a big risk," said Chandaram with a frown. "Even if she fires, we've got any number of airborne vehicles in the region . . . even the mobile scanners can get some idea of trajectories on a moment's notice."

"I don't want to get into a chase with her, Anil." She stared at him from point-blank range. "No chases. She'll kill innocent people just to ward us off, I know her!"

"With all respect, you only met her once. You don't think you're maybe just mad at her?"

"Sure! Sure I'm fucking mad at her, I'm furious! And when she goes down, she'll go down in a nice, quiet little ambush somewhere. She won't know what hit her. That's the only way I'm prepared to do this because it's the only way that won't endanger countless innocent bystanders, do you get me?"

"Sure," said Chandaram, eyeing her cautiously. "I understand."

A bleep in Sandy's newly activated network receptor informed her of an incoming message. She held up a hand to forestall further conversation, indicating to her eardrum and taking several steps aside in the hall. "Kresnov," she said aloud.

"*Hi, Cap,*" came a familiar, mild voice in her ear.

"*Rhi,*" Sandy formulated silently. Depending upon the content of the conversation, she wasn't yet sure if she wanted Chandaram to know who she was talking to. "*How's things?*" Ari and Chandaram resumed conversation, in terse, low tones . . . Ari insisting that Jane was the most likely culprit, and Chandaram agreeing, but refusing to rule out any possibilities. Sandy wished she could follow multiple conversations as easily as she could process multiple data-streams, but thanks to the vagaries of neurostructure, it didn't always work that way.

"*Things are fine.*" Rhian certainly didn't sound very bothered by anything . . . but then, with Rhian, that was as normal. "*I suppose you know I went out from the Embassy? The CSA had several people following me . . . or I assume they were CSA.*"

"*They were,*" said Sandy. "*Where did you go?*"

"*I was given an errand to go and talk to some underground person. One of the old League network contacts here, one of the ones the CSA didn't catch yet.*"

"*Oh,*" said Sandy. Rhian's patience in getting to the point could test a less-patient person's nerves. "*Was that an interesting errand?*"

"*No, actually. It was extremely boring. This person doesn't appear to be connected in any way to recent events. In fact, I can't see why I was sent on this trip at all.*" She paused. Sandy could feel it coming—she knew Rhian that well. "*Which is why I didn't go on the trip. I followed Major Ramoja instead.*"

"*You tailed your superior?*"

"*Yes.*"

"*Um . . . why?*"

"*Because he seemed to be going somewhere much more interesting,*" said Rhian. "*And because I suspected I was being sent on this other trip in order to keep me out of the way. I think Ramoja knows there's a limit on things where he can trust me, where Jane is concerned. So I guessed he must be going somewhere interesting, if he was trying to get rid of me."*

It was a very frank admission, even by Rhian's standards. Despite her faith in Rhian, Sandy couldn't help but feel her trepidation rising. *"Where did Ramoja go, Rhi?"*

*"I don't know, I lost him."* Sandy repressed a snort of exasperation. *"But before I lost him, I got the distinct impression that he was heading toward Canas."*

Major Ramoja, the senior League intelligence officer on Callay, headed for Canas? Maybe he had an appointment . . . but if so, would he have gone with so much covert sneaking around? No, if one of the bigwigs in Canas wanted to bring Ramoja over for one of the usual covert chit-chats, they'd have sent a car themselves, and not left anything up to Ramoja at all—after all, it was the Callayan bigwigs who would pay the political or purely popular price if news got out of such secret dealings with dastardly League GIs who should have remained safely contained within their embassy grounds.

*"Cap,"* Rhian continued, in much the same unfazed, contemplative tone as before, *"I heard that Enrico Kalaji was murdered just now?"*

*"That's right,"* Sandy said cautiously.

*"Well, I was thinking,"* said Rhian, *"that maybe Jane's cleaning up after herself. I mean, Earth obviously planted certain people in Tanusha to help her with her mission. But if those people got caught, they'd spill everything . . . and, I mean, you're looking for evidence right now, aren't you?"*

*"That's exactly right,"* Sandy agreed. Unwilling to interject anything else at this point, least she break Rhian's surprising momentum.

*"So Kalaji was coordinating Jane, and now Kalaji's dead. But who was coordinating Kalaji?"*

*"No,"* said Sandy, *"we've got his direct superior Samarang in custody, he's already confessed . . ."* and she stopped, realising where Rhian was going even before she interrupted.

*"And who coordinated Samarang?"* said Rhian. *"I mean, Secretary Grey*

*didn't even need to be directly involved, did he? He could still prove useful in helping the CSA track everything back to Earth, simply because he's the only one who knew what Samarang, Kalaji and anyone else in the State Department was doing at all times, and how they operated."*

"Rhi, thank you very much. I'll be there as soon as possible."

She disconnected, and turned back on Ari. Ari and Chandaram broke off their conversation, seeing her expression.

"Ari," she said, "we got a situation."

*"Could you be a little more specific?"* said the head of S-2 Security over the cruiser's speakers.

"That's all I can tell you at the present time," Sandy replied. "I'm recommending a red alert, but keep it low profile. No visible guard rotations, no shifting your regular schedule, nothing."

They were inbound now, toward Canas, in one of the low-altitude emergency lanes, speed nudging six hundred kilometres per hour as towers and suburbs fled by to the sides and below. Sandy had the Ranchu-15 assault weapon Ari kept for contingencies in her lap, frequency adjusted to her personal interface uplinks.

*"It's kind of difficult to implement a red alert without it immediately becoming visible,"* retorted the S-2 chief. *"If I knew what kind of threat you were talking about, it would make it easier for me to counter."*

Sandy threw a look at Ari, who dealt with bureaucrat-oriented security probably more often than she did, and had done so over a much longer period. Ari shrugged . . . which meant he didn't think they were any more likely than any other unit to panic and fuck it up if she told them. Sandy's return look was darkly sardonic, and not entirely comforted. "Hello, Chief," she said after that pause, "my information includes the possibility of a high-designation GI in close infiltration position. The suspected target is the Secretary of State."

Now it was the S-2 chief's turn to pause before replying. Then, *"Uh, thank you, Snowcat. Will . . . uh, look forward to your arrival."*

"Roger that, our ETA is just over a minute. Don't do anything stupid, this one's *very* intelligent, do you understand me?"

"*Copy, Snowcat.*" The connection went dead. Sandy flipped the cruiser's dash screen onto the secure S-2 feed from Canas—it showed Secretary Grey's residence, complete with a multitude of automated and manned security posts and devices, all in real time. She touched the screen, widening the field of view to the near Canas neighbourhood, repressing her irritation that she could no longer use her uplinks with any degree of security. If this was Jane, and Jane knew she was coming . . . well, the only thing that prevented Jane from using the killswitch codes was that she didn't know where Sandy was.

"I've got a good feed," said Ari from the driver's seat, eyes slightly unfocused as he concentrated upon the mental picture.

"Lucky you," muttered Sandy, trying to make out the limited, two-dimensional display upon the dash.

"The barrier elements look secure, I can't see any sign of branching." His eyes flicked briefly back to the cruiser's controls, as the CPU began to reduce velocity, the descent-path down to Canas curving away ahead. "I bet S-2 didn't see that coming. Every security agency in the city just started to think no one was targeting our senior figures any longer."

"Well, for a while there, they were right." Sandy tried holding the Ranchu in her left hand, and winced with irritation as the cast-bound fingers and thumb refused to properly grasp the handle. Well, so long as it didn't slow her loading magazines . . . "What do you think about Grey? Wilful compliance, or basic stupidity?"

"I think the first implies the second, doesn't it?" Ari replied with heavy irony. "But I never had him pinned as that pro-Earth. Pathologically anti-League, maybe, but that's something else entire . . ."

"What'll he do," Sandy asked calmly, "if the bullets start flying?"

"My best guess . . ." which was what Ari knew she was asking for, ". . . would be simple survival. No tricks up that guy's sleeve, he's not smart enough."

"You can always underestimate a man."

"Yeah, ahem . . ." Ari mock-cleared his throat, sarcastically, ". . . in this city, amongst politicians, I find the reverse is more usually true."

The descent brought them in toward a roadside transition zone just outside the tall, brick Canas perimeter wall. They landed between roadside trees under the watchful eye of the northern gate security post, then pulled out to rejoin the perimeter road's traffic as soon as Central allowed. The security post checked vehicle ID and scanned faces and irises at the gate, while the road and wall-implanted sensors swept the entire cruiser from all angles for anything suspicious. Then the metal gates swung aside, and they cruised onto a narrow, cobble-stoned street between familiar, picturesque stone walls.

"Shit, how would she get in?" Sandy murmured, half to herself. Just leaping the walls was impossible—when they said all airspace above Canas was impenetrable without authorisation, that meant right down to millimetres above the perimeter walls, triple redundancy with three different kinds of detection technology.

"She had an inside source at the State Department," said Ari, "it's long been suspected they had more access to Canas security codes than they ought." The cruiser's suspension did not enjoy the cobbles—aircars were heavy, and not designed primarily for ground transportation anyway. Ari drove on manual between narrow walls, pulling aside once as an oncoming vehicle edged over to let them past. Picturesque creepers overgrew stone walls in the yellow wash of a streetlight. Then a little shop and a bar-restaurant that Sandy recalled having enjoyed a nice meal and flamenco music at several weeks ago . . . unexpectedly, she found herself missing her house, and her previous relatively peaceful, orderly evenings as a Canas resident. Then Ari followed a navcomp direction, up an even narrower street overhung by a ceiling of tree branches and bending all the way.

"Oh, this is fucking lovely," Ari muttered, leaning forward as he drove to peer ahead and upward in trepidation. "Blind corners, no other escape routes . . . gee I love this neighbourhood, doesn't it just make you feel so secure?" Ari, Sandy knew, had a somewhat different perspective on Canas's picture-postcard charms than her.

"You just don't like any security you haven't organised yourself," she reprimanded him.

"I'd feel safer letting the Beetle shoot an apple off my head." "The Beetle" was CSA Assistant Director N'Darie, whom Ari did not get along with at all.

"It's so pretty, though."

"So's lightning." As if on cue, the sky above lit in a racing blue flash beyond the treetops. Ari bit back a curse in what Sandy reckoned would have been Hebrew, if he'd let it come out properly. Ari professed to being neither religious nor superstitious. Sandy repressed a smile.

Around a bend on the left, broad gates opened upon the cruiser's approach. Ari paused them at another checkpoint, where a pair of S-2 security checked IDs (and gazed curiously at Sandy, and her new brunette look) before waving them past. The drive was long through lush gardens, and ended in a circle about a central fountain, with a wide apron to allow large VIP vehicles to park and unload multiple passengers and security.

Ari parked the cruiser short of the apron, and they got out. Boots crunching on the driveway gravel, Sandy slowly scanned about as they walked, while Ari's gaze remained distant, focused on his network uplinks. The Secretary of State's private residence was of course as much government facility as house—a grand mansion of stone and latticed windows, enveloped within a veritable jungle of lush, wet greenery. Sandy remained unsure about the foliage—the theory was that tight, enclosed spaces reduced the greater threat of long-range attack with high-powered weapons, and increased the risk to the theoretical attacker by forcing them to get close, right in where security, and lethal defences, were tightest. Against most attackers, Sandy reckoned the theory was sound. But there were some types of soldiers in the world, she knew from personal experience, who did their best work up tight and close. Flitting from shadow to shadow.

"I think maybe we need a jungle warfare specialist," Ari muttered at her side as they left the crunching gravel and strode up the paved path to an engraved wooden door.

The S-2 security chief—a squat, sturdy man named Sundaram—met them in the stone-paved hall. He looked nervous past his tough exterior, eyes darting with barely concealed anxiety. "What can you tell me?" he said with hushed earnestness, looking hard from Sandy to Ari. "I've tried to keep it quiet . . . I've isolated Secretary Grey in his central office, it's the most defensible room in the building, we've cut down unnecessary movement and limited staff access. The perimeter is one hundred per cent tight and the yard-grid is all fully activated. I don't see how she could get through that way."

Sandy didn't see a way either, but she didn't say so. She didn't want anyone to get relaxed in any direction.

"My bet is," said Ari, "if she's here, she's already breached the perimeter . . . she's got access codes and God-knows what else we don't know about. Can you track your staff? Do you know the whereabouts and identity of every person in the building and surrounds?"

Sundaram nodded shortly. "Yes, and I've had everyone double-checked visually, no false IDs. I've got people quietly sweeping storage spaces and rechecking delivery manifests. It's possible she got in a while ago and is just lying quietly somewhere . . ."

"Wait, wait, wait," said Sandy, holding up a hand. From the look in Sundaram's eyes, and the edgy looks on the faces of several of the S-2s behind him, she thought she could see where this was going . . . and it wasn't anywhere healthy. "Look, I think you've done a great job. Seriously. I know S-2 runs a tight ship, and with the measures you've put in place so far, I think you've got it all covered. We need to remain alert and ready, but let's not get carried away here. She's a GI. She's not a mythical spirit, she doesn't have supernatural powers, she's just a regular, run-of-the-mill GI like me. Okay?"

Sundaram nodded, not looking particularly happier at that declaration. Doubtless he knew only too well that there was nothing regular nor run-of-the-mill about CDF Commander Kresnov. But he appeared then, nonetheless, to surreptitiously take a longer, deeper breath. From the high skylight above the stonework hall, came the heavy, pattering sound of raindrops. "Maybe," Sundaram resumed, "if there's no immediate threat after all, we should just call in the heavy reinforcements."

With a questioning look at Sandy in particular. Doubtless he had a couple of heavily armoured flyers in mind, with a full complement of troops to match.

"No," said Sandy, with a slight but firm shake of the head. "We can't be sure yet. Let's leave it for a while longer, then reassess when we know more."

"Sure." Sundaram took another, longer breath. "Keep it flexible, we can do that. You two have the run of the place, just stay uplinked to the network so we don't mistake you for infiltrators . . . I know, Commander, it's not safe for you to be uplinked right now? That's okay . . . just stay close to Mr. Ruben, if you please?"

"I'll do that," Sandy assured him. Sundaram nodded again, gratefully, then strode off, taking one of his juniors in tow. Sandy and Ari walked on, the raindrops upon the skylight ceiling overhead growing to a thunderous din, punctuated now by a booming grumble of thunder.

"Very diplomatic," Ari complimented her as they entered the broad space at the hall's end. Quiet, as the door to the hall shut behind. A bar-kitchen bench to the right, then a step down to broad windows leading onto a balcony that overlooked a courtyard surrounded by the lush gardens. Stepping up again to the right, where a dining room table overlooked those gardens from a higher vantage. "Great, more fucking windows."

Ari drew the pistol from his shoulder holster, keeping close to the bar as he peered out at the garden foliage, rapidly becoming drenched in the downpour.

"It's okay," Sandy assured him, "I count three visible security, and more sensors than a gnat could fly through without having its testicles counted."

"The, um, rain won't affect that?" Waving a hand in that general direction.

"Not unless Tanushan technology is shoddy crap, which I know it's not." A staff woman in white shirt and dark pants hurried from a door with a tray of empty glasses and small plates. Paused in surprise to see Sandy and Ari with weapons, and then did a double-take to recognise Sandy, despite the dark hair. Flashed her a nervous smile, hurrying quickly to the bar to begin unloading cups and plates. Sandy beckoned Ari onward, down to the sunken lounge, then up three steps to the raised dining room. Ari followed, eyes continuing to dart anxiously toward the windows.

"Fuck," Ari muttered quietly when close at her side, "did you see how jumpy Sundaram was?"

"He's okay," Sandy replied, just as quietly, as her gaze continued to sweep the dark, rainy gardens. "I was serious, I think he's doing fine . . . and he'd be stupid not to be nervous. He's sure a hell of a lot more cooperative than some other security types I could mention. I'm not going to start busting his balls now."

"Sandy," Ari said warningly, "what are you planning?"

"I'm not planning anything," she said mildly.

"Oh sure, right . . . I know that look, Sandy. You're going to set a trap for her, aren't you?" Sandy made no comment. "Sandy, S-2 is positioned and trained to protect the Secretary of State, they're not a combat unit . . ."

"We might not get another chance," Sandy said simply.

"Look . . ." Ari raised both hands, expressively, ". . . I understand this is personal between you two, I understand you don't like her, that you think she's an . . . an affront to all civilised GI-kind . . ."

"That's bullshit," Sandy said shortly.

"Is it? Is it really? Shit, Sandy, look, don't insult my intelligence and don't insult your own. You're always accusing *me* of ideological leanings, why don't you look in the mirror one day?"

"I'm with the Callayan Defence Force, Ari." Sandy's gaze never left the windows, the snub-nosed assault rifle effortlessly poised in her good hand with clear field of fire over the dining room table. "I'm defending Callay."

"I'm not a GI, Sandy." Pointing earnestly to his chest, with the beginnings of genuine temper. "These people aren't. If we can scare her off without a confrontation, we should do it—we try and execute one of your Dark Star traps here, we're liable to get good people killed!"

"Ari, the longer we let this bitch wander Tanusha on her own, the higher the final death toll will be. This one kills people by the day, d'you understand that? We need to cut her operating time short, and that means now."

"Yeah?" For one of the few times Sandy could remember, Ari looked genuinely, seriously pissed at her. "Well . . . well fuck it, I disagree!"

Sandy fixed him with a cool glance. "It's a combat scenario. I rank you." Ari took a deep breath through his nose, looking like he'd just smelled something extremely unpleasant. "Now get me a sweep of the network and main floor keypoints, I'm going to check the perimeter and get a few things worked out with our S-2 friends. Can you do that?"

He didn't reply immediately. Sandy merely waited, counting the seconds. "Yeah," Ari said finally, his tone hard. Just two seconds before the limit she'd set as her deadline. "I can do that."

"Good." She made off quickly down the three steps, headed for the door to the outside balcony. Ari stood in her wake and fumed.

CHAPTER 13

**A**n hour later, they were waiting in an upstairs bedroom. Sandy sat by the French doors that led onto an outside balcony overlooking the main rear courtyard and surrounding gardens. Ari sat on the bed, gazing at a wall with a familiar, distant expression that meant he was uplinked and monitoring the network. Rain fell steadily, a constant silvery mist in the fall of houselight across the courtyard. Lightning periodically lit the sky, illuminating the outlines of several neighbouring mansions amidst a profusion of trees. After a moment, Ari's gaze flicked to Sandy. Studied her profile, the rarely blinking, unerring gaze across the courtyard. Illuminated, now, by a racing flash of blue across the sky. For a long while, he said nothing.

"When did you realise that it was all wrong?" he said finally.

"What was all wrong?" Sandy's gaze never shifted from the courtyard.

"The war. That you were fighting for the wrong side."

"I don't know. It was a combination of many things. I slowly began to discover my own view of the universe, and my own sense of what I believed in. And it just gradually dawned on me that the League's position on many things was problematic. And after a while longer, that made my position problematic."

"But there must have been one single moment," Ari insisted sombrely. His tone was more serious than usual. Sombrely, moodily thoughtful. "A time when it really hit you. A revelation."

Sandy shook her head, faintly. Not liking this new mood of Ari's. She preferred his sprightly, if somewhat cynical enthusiasm. Found it comforting, when things looked bleak, or confusing. She was the one with reason for moody introspection. This reversal wasn't fair. "I don't think so," she replied, trying not to sound evasive.

"My mother took me to a protest march once when I was little." Sandy refrained from giving him a curious glance. Ari didn't talk about his family often with her. "They had them here too, even in Tanusha . . . you had to go searching, sure, but after Valdez Station was destroyed in the outer system encirclements, you had that, plus the reports of famine where the food supplies failed, that got even some Tanushans out on the streets. And I remember all the slogans and chanting, and wondering what it was all about. My mother said that if they didn't stop the war where it was, it might end up here."

Ari shook his head, and shot her a curious, dark look. Thunder rumbled, and separate panes of glass within the French doors vibrated. "I still remember thinking how selfish that sounded," he said. "I mean . . . I remember . . ." and he repressed an exasperated smile, ". . . I remember telling her a few years later, when I'd grown up a few millimetres . . . or shouting at her more likely . . . 'you don't really care what happens to them, do you? Just so long as they don't die in your general vicinity.' She, um, didn't find the implication very amusing . . . to say nothing of my sisters. God, my sisters.

"D'you know I got a message from Daria—that's my eldest sister, the one that's five years older than me—just the other day, in fact. She said that if I ever became disillusioned with the CSA, given the enormous mess it'd helped dig the planet into, and . . . and needed a place to stay, well, her home would always be open to me." He ran a hand through his untidy hair, exasperated. And, Sandy thought, troubled. "I guess it was her way of trying to make peace. She's an artist, you know, Daria."

"You told me," Sandy affirmed.

"Did an exhibition a few months back in one of the small, private places on the subversive circuit . . . called it 'the silent soul.' All the usual stupid shit about how technology and bureaucracy have killed everything that's worthwhile about humanity . . . all these humanist types are like that. Filled with romantic adulation for things that never existed. They were at the big demonstration in Tihber two weeks ago, both my sisters . . . you know, the big anti-CDF rally?"

"They weren't the only ones," said Sandy. A gust of wind blew raindrops in a flurry against the glass. "The way the Indian humanist community here reveres Gandhi, I'm not surprised the pacifist marches get plenty of people out."

"I never signed on to be a soldier, Sandy." Sandy risked him a quick, sideways glance. He looked more distant, and more troubled, than she could remember seeing him. "I mean, tape-teach taught me to fight, and it turns out I'm pretty good at it . . . but this . . . I mean, guns and everything . . ." he gestured absently with the pistol in his right hand, ". . . it's not what I'm about. It never has been."

"You didn't have such a problem two years ago," Sandy reminded him. And gazed back out the window.

"Yeah, and I've seen a lot of corpses since then."

There was a silence, as the last of a distant roll of thunder slowly faded away. Only the rain, falling steadily through the trees, and the omni-present hum of the city itself.

"Do you want to go on the next protest march with your sisters?" Sandy asked pointedly.

Ari's look was faintly incredulous. "No! You fucking crazy?"

"Why not?"

"Because the goddamn pacifists, they don't know what they're for! It's so fucking easy to be against something if you've got no clue about possible alternatives . . . life's not like that! They've got no damn alternative—they know they don't like war, but they've got no clue how else to defend the things we've got if other people come and try and take them by force. 'You know, well,'" and he took on a mock intellectual, protester's voice, "'I got this real problem with gravity, I don't think it's morally correct for people's feet to be permanently bound to the planetary surface . . .' so fucking what? Do they think the universe cares?"

"Ari," Sandy said as patiently as she could, "what's your point?"

"My point is that you don't become a killer overnight and not wonder if it's worth it." Shortly, his eyes dark with intensity. "Maybe you can. Maybe your brain already handles that because it's all you've ever known. I'm just a network punk and compulsive socialiser who one day decided he was actually going to be *for* something, you know? To actually do something rather than just watch other people do it, then bitch about it with friends over coffee. That's all. I didn't think it'd ever come to . . . to this."

"I promise you something, Ari," Sandy told him, "if we do go up to take the stations back, you're staying here."

Ari stared at her for a long moment. Then gave a faint frown, as if in consternation. "What, you don't want me along?"

"For one thing," said Sandy, "you're not a soldier. But besides that, I just won't let you. It's enough that I'd have to tolerate Vanessa risking her neck. I'm *not* having you risk yours too."

Ari blinked. A corner of his mouth twitched upward. "That's . . . that's really sweet, Sandy. Thank you, I'm touched." Then he frowned, and gazed away at a wall, as something else occurred to him. "Only now my masculinity's been offended."

Sandy smiled calmly, seeing him only from the corner of her peripheral vision. "Deal with it."

An entire five blocks of Canas security network chose that moment to abruptly disappear . . . Sandy had been receiving uplink feed by relay from Ari, whose eyes widened a fractional moment before hers did.

"I don't fucking believe that . . . !" Ari exclaimed, concentrating hard to try and refind the lost network . . .

"Get me com relay!" Sandy demanded. "Keep the channel open, I need to know what's going on!"

A flood of harsh, panicked voices assaulted her right ear as Ari's feed came through, Sundaram's orders securing the perimeter and confirming crossfire zones along all the predesignated approach routes . . . and Sandy could see, in a flash, any number of ways in which a GI of her own designation and capability could come through the shadows, limiting threats to a pair at a time and eliminating them faster than any merely human opposition could coordinate a response . . .

"No, you don't, you fucking bitch," she snarled, snapped open the French doors and went out into the rain, ignoring Ari's exclamation. She got a foot onto the rail and leaped, straight up to the apex of the sloping rooftop.

*"Commander Kresnov's on the roof, that's her on the roof,"* she heard Ari's voice in her ear, *"don't fire, she won't register on your grids . . ."* She was, Sandy realised, totally out of the local tac-net loop, unable to uplink directly, reliant solely on Ari's indirect feed, and hoping the panicked S-2s didn't shoot her by mistake when she did something that no straight human could possibly hope to do. Flat atop the roof apex, rapidly soaking in the rain, she had a good view of the two sections of the mansion's approach that bothered her most—the driveway from the main gate, and the rear gardens about the courtyard. Her vision made out the telltale outlines of security personnel, strategically positioned and mostly IR-shielded beneath synthetic, waterproof coats, but even that recent innovation for Tanushan security wouldn't fool Jane's eyes any more than it did hers . . . although it might gain any target an extra half-second's life.

Lightning flashed, turning gardens, rooftop and surrounding wet foliage to brilliant flashing blue. Her vision shifted reflexively, then back, seeking that telltale flash of motion amidst the cover. But doubtless Jane would see her the same moment she saw Jane . . .

"*Sandy,*" came Ari's voice in her ear, "*I'm into the Canas network now . . . there's been an internal security override, looks like your friend had access to codes I didn't even know existed. She couldn't have initiated that by remote, she'd have to input with a direct feed. The best point of direct access looks to me to be the number twelve property to the north . . .*"

"*Yeah, and how the hell did she get in there?*" Sandy formulated in reply, vision-zooming in that direction through the blanket of obscuring foliage, barely able to make out the surrounding property wall, let alone the mansion on that northward property.

"*Well, it's registered to a Union Party rep named Naji Aziz, who I happen to know is a good friend of Secretary Grey's, and the rumour mill had accused of improper knowledge of State Department secrets regarding covert communications with FIA representatives . . .*"

"*Sure, sure, I believe you.*" Sometimes the speed at which Ari's brain made those subtle, not-so-obvious social and political connections was downright scary. He processed underworld subterfuge like she processed an armscomp calculation. Damn useful though, in the right hands. But risk her neck, on one of his hunches? If Jane got onto the property before Canas specialists could get the network back online, a lot of brave S-2s—and probably unarmed residence staff too, knowing Jane—were going to die.

That realisation made Sandy's mind up for her before she'd even made a conscious decision to move. She got up and ran, crouched along the spine of the rooftop, as thunder boomed and rumbled nearby. Along the top of the northward wing, dodging a communications array, then hurdling a skylight, she slid to a tight crouch behind a chimney upon the northern edge of the roof. Rifle braced upon her cast-bound left hand, she scanned the stretch of garden in front of the northern property wall at full, multispectrum intensity. Saw movement, abruptly, and shot the location back to Ari . . . who, in that agonisingly slow, stretching moment, cross-referenced the location against his tac-net feed, and shot back to her an unfolding tactical image that demonstrated . . .

Too late, the target fired, but Sandy was already ducking back as the stone chimney's north side disintegrated under a volley of high-powered fire. Fire ripped back at the source from multiple locations, alert S-2s replying with admirable precision as the target evaded with one final shot . . . but Sandy was already moving even as the grenade launcher fired, sliding sideways down the sloping roof, tracking fire one-handed to that last location before Jane could think about mowing down S-2s . . . boom! as the chimney exploded, and the gardens ripped with crossfire and disintegrating foliage.

Sandy's sideways slide ceased as her boots hit the gutter, rifle silent for a millisecond as she scanned for a target amidst the chaos. And saw one, dark and nearly IR-invisible, moving wide around the courtyard where the foliage was thickest . . . a flare-strobe erupted before her index finger could move, momentarily blinding, and she lost the target. Took the opportunity to drop from the roof to the paving surrounding the courtyard, since Jane would also be blinded. She ran to the right, where the verandah fronted onto the courtyard, rifle scanning ahead but unable to sight movement through the thick gardens, as the flare-strobe spent itself, and arced dully toward the ground.

The firing from house and garden paused, a cacophony of terse yells in her ear as S-2s reconfirmed status and position. Doubtless the tac-net was shifting also but she was in no position to see and Ari couldn't download anything that size through his relay. She ran forward at a crouch along the mansion's side, refrained from firing at a sudden low movement ahead, where she didn't think Jane would be—it was an S-2, crouched low and invisible not far from where Jane must have passed seconds earlier . . . and a damn clever, self-preserving move *that* had been.

More fire and yells then from the east wing, and Sandy snapped her rifle around the corner, seeing fire ripping along a garden path and a decorative archway losing pieces . . . and still Jane refrained from firing, having lost her initiative and now unwilling to disclose her location. It wouldn't last. Sandy sprinted across the smallest gap from mansion to foliage, and heard Ari's voice yelling her location and movement to the S-2s—he must have been watching from the bedroom window where she'd left him . . . which was about to go out-of-view as she dove into the tangled greenery and eastward.

The S-2s must have been paying attention, because no one shot at her, and she ducked and wove between trunks and undergrowth with a sudden impulse for a spot in the corner that her memory told her had a partial view of the eastward wing, and was in moderate fire-shadow from the flanks. She zigzagged toward a large, broad tree with a complicated root system, falling and rolling to a braced firing position past the trunk . . . and ducked back in the millisecond it took for her vision to process the shape of a rifle, in the suspected location, snap directly her way. Shots sprayed wood in shattered chunks, then a rush of footsteps as S-2 pinned that location from the mansion, rounds zipping and cracking devilishly, filling the garden with flying earth and splinters.

"Hi, sis!" Sandy yelled as the firing died down, and Sundaram's voice could be clearly heard in her ear, asking for Commander Kresnov's position with evident concern. "It's me, Sandy! Do you like gambling?!" There was, of course, no audible response. But no audible movement, either, and S-2s guns fell silent, so evidently they didn't have a target. "Tell you what—you better start liking it, 'cause right now I wouldn't give you one chance in twenty! It's no fucking fun when they all know you're coming, is it?! And now they all know roughly where you are, so you can take them out a few at a time, but there's so many guns pointed at you now, one of them's bound to get you if you start firing regularly!

"And now I'm here! Remember what I told you before, about

being a good little girl and behaving yourself?! You broke the agreement! That means I'm going to rip your fucking entrails out! So unless you like the idea of dying slowly, I'd just turn around and run for the walls, if I were you!"

Water fell in heavy drops from the leaves and branches, running cold rivulets down her scalp and neck. Super-enhanced hearing made out frogs croaking, and bats chattering to themselves in the higher branches, under cover from the rain. Doubtless scared witless by the recent noise. Jane could move silently, but S-2 had enough visual enhancement to spot slow, gradual motion. A fast dash provided greater safety . . . and would be heard. Jane would wait. Would wait for . . . a brilliant blue flash, there it was, forking and dancing across the overcast northward sky. Across sixteen to seven kilometres of range, Sandy's visual reckoning calculated, which meant the small matter of seven seconds until the barrage of sound began. Jane would go for the wall, she judged. Fearless, professional Jane, who lived for her missions and never shirked from a challenge, would suddenly arrive at possibly the first moral calculation of her short life so far— that this particular assignment wasn't worth her own, needless demise. Not a great victory for the moral conscience, perhaps. But proof, at least, of selfishness . . . and thus, perhaps, humanity. Maybe.

Thunder crashed and boomed, and Sandy paused that fractional extra half-second in case she'd been wrong . . . crack! came a shot from the mansion, followed by the unmistakable thud of bullet hitting combat-myomer, and a body rolling on loose earth. Sandy sprinted, and heard the footsteps resume in a rush beyond the descending rumble from the skies. Headed straight for the wall, and Sandy's mind saw immediately the nearest direct line from that last shot, to a leap over the wall behind the shelter of a particularly thick tree. She darted left, opening that projected angle for a shot on the reckoning that Jane, being Jane, would pause for a parting shot or two as she cleared the wall, to remove several S-2 heads and be gone, just to prove she could

. . . the footsteps ceased with a final spring, and Sandy fired a blind burst through the foliage as she ran, at where that trajectory ought to be . . . and thought she heard the thud of a second bullet strike, and an untidy, tumbling thud on the wall's far side.

It was only a little surprising (but extremely annoying) to hear the footsteps resume once more on the wall's far side, with no apparent lessening of pace. Sandy reached the wall herself, and knowing better than to leap headlong over a blind obstacle, she paused. The racing footsteps continued, and she realised it was going to be an enormous disadvantage if Jane could uplink to a complete local map, and she couldn't . . . no sooner had she thought it than Ari's uplink connected with an urgent download, which she accessed with a painfully slow assemblage of incoming data. It finally arrived and decoded within a half-second that felt like an age, and suddenly she could see the basic layout beyond the wall—a garden, a workshed, a swimming pool nearer the mansion before a grand patio.

She ran several steps along the wall, then tensed and leaped, angling for a low clearance and descent behind the work shed . . . shots erupted from the patio as she sailed narrowly over the wall, snapping past her legs, then fracturing tiles upon the workshed's roof as she landed with a crunch—atop a small fruit garden with plants climbing short metal stakes that would have impaled her, had she not been a GI. So much for topographical intelligence.

The familiar thud of the launcher came as she sprinted for the corner of the shed . . . the round smashed a window and exploded against the rear wall, which blasted flaming debris over the vegetable garden. Another thud, and she fell flat and away from the shed's corner before it too exploded, shrapnel peppering her clothes in a series of sharp, pain- less stings. Rifle shots then peppered that same corner, exploding stonework walls into puffs of dust and splinters—Jane knew basic tac- tics all too well, and saw Sandy's best firing points in advance. The tra- jectory of the shots shifted as the source moved along the patio, attempting to open up Sandy's position behind the wall. Sandy flattened her back to the wall, right arm extended, rifle poised, as the shots whipping past that corner drew steadily closer as their angle decreased . . .

There came then in the air the thrumming whine of an aircar, a powerful spotlight swinging across the yard toward the patio . . . it vanished in a thunder of shots from Jane, and the cruiser rocked wildly. Sandy was already moving, an explosive acceleration toward a leftwards garden wall, unleashing fire upon Jane's position . . . but Jane was already gone in anticipation, fallen flat and rolling behind a marble balustrade as Sandy's fire kicked pieces and fragments in all directions. The cruiser's desperate pilot struggled to pull his machine away from danger . . . too late, as the launcher thumped again, and the underside of the front field generators exploded. Sandy hit the garden wall with her left side, rifle braced, eyes fixed only on Jane's position, out of sight behind the balustrade foundation as the cruiser spun wildly away, shedding pieces with a shrieking, vibrating whine of failing lift.

Jane would try crawling on her stomach, she knew. The balustrade went upslope along the paved side of a path above the patio. This was the stalemate of GI-versus-GI combat at this high designation—if one had firing position, the other could not expose herself without taking fire. If Jane so much as exposed a length of her finger, Sandy would blow it off well before Jane could hope to get her own shot off. A grenade was a better option, if she had one, but again, if she exposed an arm in the throwing, she would lose it, and the grenade most likely fall in her lap . . . or be blown from the sky milliseconds after leaving her hand. But ditto if Sandy ran to a new position that exposed Jane's cover, the advantage lay with Jane to get the first shot off. Maybe. No better than a fifty-fifty proposition, at least . . . and GI reflexes being what they were, it was entirely likely they'd kill each other at the same instant. But Jane had been hit at least twice, and maybe more. It must have slowed her, just a fraction of a second. At the speeds Sandy's brain operated in combat, a fraction of a second was an eternity.

Still the cruiser spun, a sideways, airborne pirouette. The grenade had only struck three seconds ago, and the fragments were still falling. But already, to Sandy, it seemed an awfully long time to wait in one location, watching Jane's guessed-at position and waiting for the fool of an aircar to hit the ground . . . hopefully in the neighbouring property, which it seemed to be angling for.

Her uplinks automatically received Ari's next transmission, and . . . wham! as the attack codes sliced through her newly repaired defensive barriers, Ari's desperate yell ringing in her ear as she flung herself back behind the narrowly angled cover of the garden wall. Even as the secondary barriers engaged, halting the killswitch codes just short of their goal, Sandy's index finger depressed rapidly, spraying fire across the balustrade as she fell. It bought her an extra half second, then Jane's rounds were ripping the wood-planked garden wall to pieces as Sandy covered in a tight, defensive ball, trying desperately to reorder her uplink barriers as the graphical complexity overloaded her vision, a wall of visual network shifting and flickering as codework attempted to counter the penetrators coming through, delaying enough for yet more modulated barriers to reform behind . . .

A grenade hit the wall on a shallow angle barely a metre short, burrowing into flayed wood before detonating with a crash of exploding planks and pouring earth. The shockwave knocked Sandy rolling, struggling to bring her weapon to bear, and refocus away from her network chaos before Jane could move across and acquire a clear line of sight . . . There was a flash of motion, and more shooting from a new angle, a dark rush as Jane leaped away upslope, then crashed through the window of the mansion. Suddenly the attack barrier faltered, its direct link broken. Sandy saw her secondary barriers surge, a swirling mass of rapid-calculating colour and motion. Primary barriers remodulated, adjusting to the threat as they'd been programmed. They resolidified behind the stranded attack program, surrounding it, and slowly strangling.

Network functions abruptly restored themselves as her defensive barriers got on top of the problem, and no longer required the input of external functions—eyesight recovered, then hearing, then a rush of overwhelming sensation as suddenly, she could think clearly again, as if a crushing weight had been removed. She snap-rolled to a firing crouch, shoulder to the shattered planks as dirt continued to pour through the torn hole, and dust clouded the way. A new dark shape streaked across the upper patio, beside where Ari's feed had informed her the swimming pool would be, and covered beside the shattered window into which Jane had disappeared.

Rhian, she saw with a zoom of vision, and ran forward, feet digging up clods of earth with the traction as she accelerated. Took a low, flying leap up the garden embankment, over the balustraded path, hit the patio beside the swimming pool and smacked into a controlled collision at sixty kilometres per hour against the wall opposite Rhian . . . who, she saw, was holding her pistol left handed, with a bullet-sized hole in the right forearm sleeve of her black jacket.

"Fast, isn't she?" Rhian murmured. Typically, they would establish a tac-net and fight as such, tactically linked and coordinating as a single, two-track unit. Now, that was impossible. And speech, in these circumstances, was painfully slow. "I got her twice, but she's wearing armour."

Against which a mere hand pistol, obviously, would be useless. Probably Rhian's right arm had been the only visible thing to hit around whatever cover Rhian had been using . . . and Jane had hit it.

"Careful of the residents," Sandy warned, and they ducked through the broken window together. Broken glass littered the living room, Sandy and Rhian covering opposite sides around the lounge chairs and coffee table, covering opposing doorways by silent reflex. It occurred to Sandy, in a time-stretched flash, that she had no idea who the assigned resident of this house was. All lights were off, normal for this time of night, residents most likely sleeping, safe in the knowledge that

Tanusha's most impenetrable security network would protect them from any eventuality.

Rhian cut through the kitchen, wordlessly heading for the far side of the ground floor in case Jane had gone straight out . . . only now there was a new sound reverberating overhead, the familiar, rhythmic thrum of hypersonic-bladed fans atop support thrusters. A-9 combat flyers, which meant CDF. Someone must have called.

There came a scream from upstairs, and Sandy shot to the stairwell, hurdling one flight, then rushing smoothly up the next, rifle poised down the tiled hallway beyond. Another scream—a woman's scream, coming from several doors down. Then sobbing, Sandy's hearing caught the words . . . ". . . please . . . don't hurt him . . . don't hurt . . ." Then a thud of rifle meeting skull, and a second of a body hitting the floor.

"Tell the flyers to move away!" came that cool, familiar voice from down the hall. A new sobbing began—a child's sobbing. Then the screaming wail, perhaps a three-year-old, restrained by an armed stranger, and seeing now his mother (Sandy guessed) lying unconscious on the floor. Sandy moved closer, gliding on silent feet that held her torso as smoothly poised as if on rails. The rifle sought an angle through the walls, ears and mind in hard calculation to try and pinpoint Jane's location within the room by the sound of her voice alone. The fans grew to a harsh roar, surely deafening to unaugmented hearing. Doubtless they were in contact with Ari, and thus trying to contact her.

Ari's signal, then, in her inner ear . . . and she took her time, letting her receptor codes analyse and break down the signal key, not wanting a repeat of Ari's last communication attempt. Movement behind her, then, but preceded by Rhian's faint call of "me," Sandy's hearing automatically placing the vocal patterns as authentic. The child's screams grew louder, seeming to shift within the room ahead . . . Sandy immediately pictured Jane, weapon in one hand, child in the other arm, moving from window to window for a view.

"Cap," said Rhian as she arrived alongside. "She's got a child." Rhian's tone betrayed more tension than usual for any GI under combat conditions. Stating the obvious was not usual, either. Unless one were Rhian, faced with a predicament from her very worst nightmares, and needing to articulate . . . something.

"You've got ten seconds!" Jane shouted. "Otherwise, I'll do it slowly!" Sandy smacked her left arm cast across Rhian's chest before anything suicidal happened. Rhian stared at her, desperately. Sandy accessed Ari's link, and it unfolded with a strange, unpredictably shifting pattern of uniquely tailored encryption that was not regulation at all, but entirely Ari . . .

"*Sandy! Look, the line's secure for now, I'm sorry for last time, I didn't know she could . . .*"

"*I know,*" Sandy formulated silently. "*Ari, tell the flyer to move away from the house immediately.*"

"*Doing that.*" Outside the house, the flyer's engines changed pitch to an ascending roar, then faded as it pulled away.

"Good," said Jane above the screams of her hostage. "Now I want a cruiser, on autopilot, to come hovering next to this window."

"*You hear that?*" Sandy formulated to Ari, having patched her audio through to the uplink.

"*Got it. You want me to comply?*"

"*Yes.*"

"*Sandy . . . the CSA doesn't look kindly on generous negotiations with hostage takers . . .*"

"*I know what the handbook says. Just do it. I need events to unfold, Ari. I want things happening.*" Because when they happened, as she'd explained to him before, she was presented with opportunities. All of her combat strategy was based upon that simple philosophy. Keep it moving. Movement makes angles, angles make chances.

"*Doing that,*" Ari confirmed.

"It'll take a few minutes to get here," Sandy called to Jane. "If you kill that kid, you'll follow." Just in case Jane was unfamiliar with how hostage situations worked.

"That's why I'll do it slowly," Jane replied, with something that sounded like feigned patience. "I know you're not allowed to let him suffer." It was all a technical exercise to her, Sandy realised. That was not unexpected. That she herself could feel such cold, murderous fury, however, while still fully immersed in combat-reflex, was utterly surprising. God knew how Rhian felt.

Rhian made several handsignals to Sandy—she would go downstairs, and up the second staircase, to see if there was a second door into the child's room from the adjoining hallway. Thus preventing the need to dart across the open door directly ahead. Sandy nodded, once, and Rhian vanished without so much as a squeak of floorboards.

"Your friend's not as high-des as us, is she?" Jane commented above the screams. "I can tell. She's just a little bit slower, a little more predictable. She could have shot for my head, but she didn't seem to guess I was wearing armour. Not very imaginative."

Rhian had a hand pistol with limited range, Sandy thought in reply, and couldn't be sure she had the firepower to penetrate and kill any GI from where she was. She'd been trying to distract as much as kill, and put Jane off her aim by knocking her over, thus firing into the centre of mass.

If Jane got a cruiser, and kept the hostage with her, she'd be immune . . . and they couldn't shoot down a cruiser over populated regions anyway. Of course, a cruiser could hardly hide, being so easy to trace through urban skylanes . . . but then, given the degree to which Jane had demonstrated she could manipulate Tanushan networks, Sandy wasn't prepared to bet she couldn't find a way to escape once airborne. Either way, the hostage would be expendable, from Jane's point of view.

"Why kill the Secretary of State, Jane?" Sandy called. Jane seemed in a talkative mood. Perhaps she'd spill something. "Unless he knew what you were doing, bringing the Fleet down on our heads? Unless he knew you were going to kill Admiral Duong?"

"Where did your friend go?" said Jane, as if the questions had never been asked. "I can't hear her out there."

"*Sandy,*" came Ari's voice in her ear, "*I'm into the house network—it's occupied by a cousin of the Trade Minister, apparently she's under protection after extremist threats of some kind . . .*" And she'd chased every Tanushan's worst nightmare straight into her home. At another moment, Sandy might have sworn and kicked something. "*I'm . . . hang on, I'm patching into the bedroom . . .*"

"She's gone around to the other door, hasn't she?" Jane continued. The child's screams resumed with renewed urgency. "I wouldn't advise that, I might have to start breaking limbs in here. Maybe I'll start with the mother."

Another portion of Ari's uplink feed showed the automated cruiser on its way, nearly a minute distant. And the pair of CDF flyers, holding position half a klick distant—easily within pinpoint weapon range, and too heavily armoured to be bothered by any armament of Jane's, but unauthorised to fire in heavily populated areas unless entirely certain of a clear shot.

"*She's maintaining shielded uplink to the room system, Sandy, I've got some CSA people onto it but I doubt they can hack her . . .*"

"We've got you crossed, you bitch!" came Rhian's voice from around the corner, perhaps several metres down the adjoining hall. "Give it up, you can't shoot both ways at once!"

Sandy's mind, which had been processing several fluid possibilities at once, abruptly froze. There was harsh, desperate emotion in Rhian's voice. Damn it, Rhi, what are you doing?

"I can too," was Jane's reply.

"So let the child go!"

"Cassandra!" Jane called warningly. "Your simple friend is making a big mistake, and it will be on your head."

"Ten seconds!" Rhian shouted. "You can't get us both, let him go now!"

"Cassandra, rein her in or I'll start shooting!"

"Five!" yelled Rhian. The boy howled, as if in anticipation.

"Rhi . . ." Sandy began, and a single shot cracked within the room. In a flash, Sandy moved, hearing Rhian and Jane moving simultaneously. Another shot, as Sandy rounded the doorframe and dove, but already Jane was gone out the window, glass and frame exploding in her wake even as Sandy's rifle blazed fire that clipped her departing heels . . . and Rhian, in that mesmerising, time-frozen moment, was toppling slowly to the floor, a bullet hole in her forehead, just below the hairline. Sandy rolled past the bawling little boy, past the end of the double bed, and rebounded off the wall beside Rhian's collapsing body, diving explosively for the window. Propped and braced, but Jane had already dropped out of sight below the rooftop rim. Sandy's hand grabbed the window frame and prepared to throw herself out and after . . . and then it hit her.

She spun back to Rhian, who had fallen half across the unconscious mother's legs, bare beneath her nightgown. Blood dripped on the floorboards beneath her lolling head. Her eyes were closed, and body motionless. And Sandy felt the combat-reflex calm dissolve in a rush, as she flung herself to Rhian's side, and grabbed her.

"Rhian? Rhi!" Tears and panic came in a flood, and a horrible, crushing pain that she'd thought, had hoped, had been banished from her life. "RHIAN!" Cradling the slim, limp body in her arms, supporting her head, staring with stricken agony at the lifeless face, eyes searching desperately for any sign of life . . . but a GI's pulse was not visible at the jugular, as all blood supply to the brain went through the spinal column.

And Rhian's eyes flicked open. Sandy's artificial heart seemed to skip a beat. Several beats, as Rhian gazed at the ceiling, looking slightly puzzled. Then at Sandy. Seeming to realise, then, that she was supported in Sandy's arms, and Sandy was crying.

"It didn't penetrate," Rhian admonished her, mildly. "I ducked. I didn't think she'd be *that* fast, and I knew you were coming in behind, so she wouldn't have time to finish me."

As if she'd had it all planned, and Sandy was just overreacting again. Sandy tried to catch a breath, feeling the simultaneous, overwhelming urge to laugh, scream and cry. Stared at the wound beneath Rhian's hairline—blood welled thickly, but nothing like a straight's scalp-wound would, trickling slowly to her brow. Beneath, she could see a faint hint of ferro-enamel bone . . . tough enough to stop many projectiles, but not from a high-powered assault rifle at point-blank range. Unless one were ducking at the time, and moving very fast, and the round struck at a diagonal angle like so . . . and then she could see the little flap of skin from the ricochet, just behind the main wound.

"Jane's getting away," Rhian pointed out. "Can't let her take another hostage."

The truth of *that* hit home also, as did Ari's clamorous signal in her ear, and the middle-distant roar of hyperfans—doubtless her flyer pilots had seen Jane leave and were after her, seeking permission to fire. She kissed Rhian hard on the cheek, leaped to her feet and sprang through the window.

Rhian watched her go, with a faint, affectionate smile. Then put a hand to her head, feeling dizzy. Alongside, the little boy stood at his mother's side, wailing and sobbing in helpless distress. Rhian moved swiftly to check on the mother—she was bleeding beneath her hair, but the skull seemed intact, Rhian noted with relief. Jane hadn't wanted her killed, desiring a second hostage. Of course, if that had not been so, there wouldn't be a head left to examine . . .

"Oh, here now," she told the little boy, "please don't cry." Checking his mother's vitals as she knew how, with straights, rolling her onto her side and checking that the airways were unobstructed. "Mummy's going to be fine. She's just sleeping, that's all."

She pulled the cloth she always kept for cleaning her pistol from her jacket pocket, and held it to her bleeding scalp with one hand, then gathered the little boy in the other arm, sitting him in her lap as she sat beside his mother. There was a single bullet hole in the floorboards directly beside the mother's head, Rhian noted with satisfaction. So it had worked. In combat-focus, all GIs were threat fixated. Anything not a threat, would hardly register. Attack had put Jane on the defensive, and she'd been forced to nearly ignore the hostages completely . . . while continuing previous strategy, to keep both hostages alive, and thus useful, for possible later contingencies. One shot into the floor, to provoke a charge, thus regaining the advantage. Maybe, Rhian thought, those years under Sandy's command in Dark Star had rubbed off. But Sandy herself had been more cautious. Why?

"I'm sorry," she told the little boy, in that voice she'd learned to speak with, when talking to small children. *Enjoyed* speaking with, enormously so. "We gave you a big fright, didn't we? My friend Sandy and I, we came in here so fast, and then all that nasty noise? I know, it's very frightening. I was frightened too. But it's over now, and the nice ambulance people will be here in a minute, and they'll take care of your mummy, and then she'll wake up again and give you a *big* hug."

The little boy's hysteria was fading now, partly through exhaustion, but partly, it seemed, that he instinctively knew that safety had arrived. That pleased her. He clutched to Rhian's jacket as she held him, crying miserably, but at least no longer panicked and terrified.

"And don't you worry about that mean, nasty woman," Rhian told him smugly. "My friend Sandy's after her. My friend Sandy's the most amazing person in the galaxy. That mean, nasty woman's going to wish she'd never been made."

Sandy didn't need to risk an enhanced data-stream from the flyers via Ari to know where Jane was. She just followed the sound of engines in the sky ahead, and the occasional glimpse of armoured flyer through the trees and rain.

*"They're trying to get permission to fire,"* Ari told her as she sprinted across a garden, then leaped a flying ten metres through the air to land boot-first atop the property wall, shoving off once more to hurtle past foliage, crash land and roll across a paved path then come up running. *"CSA's onto it but there's TV watching, someone's got some telescopic feeds and I think a few politicians are putting a word in."*

"It's an A-9, damn it," Sandy formulated as she regained velocity, boots skidding on wet grass as she tore across another wide property garden. Passage down the sides of the house itself looked a difficult maze of paths and garden fences, so she leaped for the roof. *"I know that armscomp's capabilities, they should get a clear target."* Hit the sloping top of the two-storey roof and held balance with difficulty, racing up the side. *"If they get a shot, tell them to fire."*

The next stretch of Canas properties were not so large, midsized houses with smaller yards, nestled amidst a profusion of trees. Sandy leaped directly for the next rooftop, crashed through foliage, then rolled across the sloping surface with a clatter of displaced tiles. Cut nimbly across that downslope, leaped to plant a foot on an upper-storey balcony, and used it to shove explosively toward the next rooftop, which was mercifully flat.

*"I've got a pilot's feed right here, Sandy,"* Ari told her. *"They've got motion fixed, but no heat and hardly any visibility. I think she's wearing opto-cam."*

Well, that figured. She leaped from that flat rooftop onto another, then angled toward the cobbled road and jumped, sailing over the stone wall and barely holding her balance upon impact with the slippery cobbles. Then she ran, flat out along the winding street toward the retreating sound of flyers ahead. Jane would avoid the roads, cutting across yards and over rooftops. If the road stayed straight for long enough, she would gain on her . . . but Canas roads never did. Rain slapped her face as she ran, and the bends between wet, creeper-covered stone walls were too slippery to take at full speed.

Good opto-cam was not full invisibility, but it was damn close. It didn't fool multispectrum visual capability entirely, save blocking heat, outline, colour and brightness differentiations . . . which left a dark, formless shape that blended into any background, and softened the sharpness of motion-sensation. It explained why Jane had been quite so difficult to see in the gardens . . . although if she'd had a direct line of sight for longer than a fractional second, Jane would have been dead, so it was not surprising she hadn't noticed. It was one piece of operational hardware that Sandy did not have much experience with—opto-cam was a weapon for thieves and assassins, not soldiers, who operated on the assumption that direct line-of-sight *would* be acquired by heavily armed opponents, techno-camouflage or not, and thus preferred armour.

*"If it's opto-cam,"* said Sandy as she powered at speed through another slippery bend, *"then they can't fire, not in this neighbourhood. Where the fuck is she?"*

*"Approaching the perimeter wall . . . hang on, we're almost there, we'll pick you up."*

Pick her up? She refocused her hearing, and found a third CDF flyer approaching from behind. Another bend in the road, and suddenly there was a groundcar emblazoned with Canas security insignia blocking the way ahead, two uniformed security officers crouched behind with weapons levelled. Sandy skidded to a halt, as both officers yelled at her to stop . . . damn security was out of the loop again, uninformed as to her identity and location. She ignored their shouts to drop her weapon, focusing instead upon the faint, broken visual feed from the first flyer . . . it looked like an aircar, zooming in low where no ordinary, civilian aircar should be able to fly. One pilot acquired weapons lock, but had no immediate cause to fire, and unwilling to knock down several tons of airborne machinery over residential housing.

Then the third flyer arrived over Sandy's head with a blasting downdraft, engines howling as both security officers ducked and held onto their caps. The A-9 Trishul slid into a drifting hover five metres above the narrow cobbled road, nearby trees thrashing in protest, the cargo door descending at the rear to reveal the dim hold lights within. Sandy waited until it found the right position, then leaped, boots smacking upon the metal plates as she grasped an overhead handline and ran forward past the harness-locked cargo master. Immediately the door began closing, and the flyer nosed forward and climbed.

Sandy squeezed between the six armoured soldiers in the rear, and found Ari jammed in beside the command post behind the cockpit, peering at the display screens. The occupant of the command post cast a glance over his shoulder as she approached—it was Hiraki, Sandy noted with little surprise. He always seemed to get himself in the right place at the right time for a fight. He moved to get up.

"Stay there," Sandy told him, grabbing an overhead support and bracing. The display screens showed that the unidentified cruiser was now hurtling away from Canas, two CDF flyers in flanking pursuit. "Damn, she got on board?"

"Yes," said Hiraki, and flipped to speakers, considerate of Sandy's inability to uplink. One Trishul pilot was challenging the cruiser to stand down. Another was in terse communication with CSA HQ, who were trying to hack into its CPU with apparently little success. "If we let her have everything, there won't be enough left to hit the ground."

Sandy shook her head. "There's always enough left to hit the ground."

"We need her dead," Hiraki remarked, his businesslike tone as cool and calm as any GI's. "It's cost-versus-gain, I say we come out on top."

"If we kill civvies on the ground," Sandy replied, "the CDF loses its popular mandate. No popular mandate, no CDF. That's a loss, Hitoru."

"So wait until she's over a river," said Ari.

"Now you're talking," Sandy told him. "Get me an armscomp track plotted, a single STP at the rear field-generators."

"Copy. But I think she might be aware of that." Pointing at the display screen, which showed the cruiser staying low, zooming just above the treetops of suburban Tanusha, weaving between the larger buildings in utter disregard for mandatory Tanushan skylanes.

"Must have removed the navcomp controls," Ari muttered. "Who's flying that thing?"

Hiraki handed Sandy a headset, which she fitted, then connected to her insert socket . . . and the data wall hit her with a rush far more intense than she'd been receiving through Ari's relay feed. The flyer's internal network was separate and secure—unhackable, at least in the short term, unlike the broader Tanushan network. Suddenly Sandy had full access to the airborne tac-net, a massively detailed three-dimensional picture of Tanushan airspace and the evading cruiser's low-altitude trajectory.

"Can we get a telescopic visual from another angle?" she asked.

"Tried it," said Hiraki. "Too much window tint, we can't see inside."

Traffic Central was doing a good job of diverting local airtraffic out of the way, although most was well above the minimum ceiling that the cruiser was currently violating. They were headed east now, one flyer on each flank, holding back several hundred metres and slightly above, with Hiraki's command flyer in the middle, directly behind.

"Where the fuck does she think she's going?" Ari muttered incredulously. "Out to sea?" Lightning flashed, disrupting the visual. Then the cruiser's rear, side window shattered, and a large, tubular object appeared, held in the five hundred kilometre per hour slipstream with inhuman strength.

"Incoming!" Sandy announced at the same time as five other voices. "Countermeasures!" The starboard flanking Trishul broke away in a rush, transmission breaking up completely as massive countermeasures disrupted all neighbouring electrics . . . the missile fired, streaking back from the cruiser, then flashed harmlessly past the flyer's main engine nacelle to detonate alongside.

"*Provocative little bastards,*" Sandy heard the pilot of that flyer murmur, and realised it was young Gabone, who she'd flown to Parliament with the day of President Neiland's impromptu press conference upon the Parliament roof. Transmissions flicked back to normal with a crackle of dissipating static.

"*Lieutenant,*" called the weapon's officer, "*I have a river approaching, no visible boat traffic.*"

"Commander?" said Hiraki. Anyone firing high explosive projectiles within Tanushan airspace made their removal from that airspace an immediate civic security requirement. Doing so while violating all traffic codes, having just launched an assassination attempt upon the Callayan Secretary of State, even more so.

"Go," said Sandy.

"If you get the shot," said Hiraki into his mike, "take it."

"We should kill her," Ari warned. Sandy saw the river approaching, one of the numerous branches on the forested Tanushan delta. The cruiser's trajectory appeared to be cutting directly across, not leaving much margin for error. Full sensor scans compiled upon tac-net from all three flyers plus river traffic central told that there were no rivercraft on the water that would be put in danger.

"We need evidence," Sandy replied simply.

"She'll survive and we'll regret it," said Ari, staring hard at her from his cramped corner. "Blow her apart." Tac-net showed the cruiser making a wide, banking course between midsized apartments that loomed thicker as the river approached, the tall, blazing lights of central Asad district ahead. Sandy met Ari's stare. He was, she knew, watching exactly the same feed as her, on his own uplinks. The cruiser passed the point of no return, and he exhaled hard with disgust.

Gabone's weapons officer fired, a single, high-velocity, self-terminating projectile from one of the unfolding underside racks. It closed the three hundred metres range in slightly less than two seconds, and blew the rear of the cruiser into thousands of flaming pieces. The cruiser appeared to buck forwards, frozen momentarily against the gleaming vista of city lights, then tumbled and rolled through an arcing, shallow dive . . . cleared the riverside trees and hit the precise centre of the river with an enormous explosion of water, showered seconds later by flaming wreckage from the explosion.

"Gold six," said Hiraki, "maintain a covering position. "Gold four, dismount on the east bank, gold one, dismount upon the west."

Affirmatives came back, Hiraki's pilot pulling them up into a wide, howling turn as the river approached, engine nacelles angling forward in a broad flare that pressed all occupants hard to the deck. Sandy stood firmly braced, secured only by her cast-bound left hand, rifle braced in the right, staring at the displays on command screens and her own tac-net link. The spray was dissipating, waves from the impact rushing toward the far bank, and crashing against the retaining wall. Flames burned upon the heaving surface of the dark water, and along the east shore of the riverbank, several stunned pedestrians were pausing on a walkway, staring and pointing in disbelief.

Air rushed and swirled through the flyer's hold as the rear doors opened, the pilot losing speed fast as he came in over the river, sliding sideways toward a green space of private property around an apartment building, where a break in the trees provided an available landing zone. The six soldiers in the rear unhooked their restraints, double-checking weapons and gear.

"This is the Commander," Sandy spoke into her headset mike, "take me directly over the crash site, I'm going in immediately."

Hiraki deactivated his mike. "There's no visibility in that water, you could be ambushed."

"GIs aren't invulnerable, Hitoru," Sandy replied, deactivating her own. "That impact must have hurt. I'm betting she's trapped and probably unconscious." On the other side of Hiraki's seat, Ari was unhooking himself. "You're not armoured, Ari, you stay here."

"Bullshit," said Ari. But reconnected his harness, with dark frustration. The flyer sank with a final, fast slide to a hard landing, soldiers leaping from the rear as Hiraki cleared his seat and went to join them. No sooner had he cleared the hold than the grass, trees and apartment buildings fell away once more, replaced by dark river waters, and the rippling flames on the surface. Ari gave Sandy a final tense, worried look before she turned and made her way along the short hold aisle, then paused at the exit.

*"That's the spot, Commander,"* said the pilot. Below, bubbles and froth stained the dark surface white amidst the flickering, rain-doused flames and floating wreckage. Sandy removed the safety from her rifle, and dove off the edge.

She hit the water head first and with rifle poised, lashing out with left arm and both legs as soon as the water closed on her, driving herself downward with great, propulsive thrusts. The silty dark overwhelmed even a GI's vision, and she could make out nothing beyond several metres down. But the river could not be more than eight metres deep, and the current was not strong . . . suddenly she could see the cruiser's roof, torn and mangled at the rear. She twisted and dolphin-kicked toward a firing position through what remained of the front windshield, but could see nothing within the cabin but crumpled seats. The entire front of the aircar had caved in on impact, forward field gens smashed back toward the passenger compartment. Sandy kicked downward, twisting upside down for a firing angle straight through the compartment. Nothing was visible, and the entire rear of the cruiser was missing. An easy escape route, for any survivor.

She stayed down for a full two minutes, her headset continuing to feed flickering, distorted data from the hovering Trishul overhead, stretching that short-range subnetwork to its limit and considerably impressed at the headset design that somehow managed to continue functioning underwater. There were troops now spread right along the riverbank, weapons trained upon the rainswept, brown surface, looking for any sign of movement. A flicker of tac-net voices revealed even that some of the late-night pedestrian wanderers were volunteering to keep watch, spreading up and down the banks even as another two flyers arrived on scene, and disgorged more troops onto the banks, and more flyers began moving up- and down-river. And Ari's voice, then, telling several questioners that a GI could hold breath for better than ten minutes if needed, thanks to a variable bloodstream chemistry that was highly self-contained when needed, and thus able to withstand all kinds of unfavourable environments.

Sandy went several hundred metres up and downstream herself, exhaling most of the air from her lungs as she went to reduce buoyancy, but found nothing. No lost weapons, personal items or articles of clothing, no recent impression on the bottom to disturb the soft, weed-ridden mud, no faint trace of GI plasma staining the uniform brown of the water. And when she finally, despairingly informed all along the riverbank on the tac-net that she was about to surface, it was with the dark, sinking feeling that she'd made a great and terrible mistake.

# CHAPTER 14

S andy stood amidst the blasting jets of water and rising steam, and fumed. Further along the soft-floored shower berths, fellow soldiers gave her looks that were filled with caution, beyond the usual intrigue at seeing the Federation's most famous GI naked. Sandy dialed the touchpad up to maximum heat and force, and let herself practically disappear from view.

It was six thirty in the morning, and she hadn't slept. Reports had been flooding into CSA HQ endlessly, piecing together the events of that night. It all seemed to go back to the State Department—the codes that brought down the Canas security grid, the registration of Jane's getaway aircar, everything. Agents had the entire department wing shut down indefinitely, by order of Director Ibrahim. Benjamin Grey was under investigation, and no one seemed to be giving him the benefit of the doubt any more. A breach of that magnitude either had to be incompetence on a massive scale, or complicity. And Ari, being

Ari, had pieced together numerous personal and technical details no one else had thought connected, and was now leading an investigation into the possibility that Grey had somehow been placed under hypno-trance. The media knew it as "brainjacking," and the more modern techniques drew the effects out indefinitely by infiltrating the target's uplinks with code that echoed modern VR enhancements in design. Advanced network uplinks and even VR entertainment worked by inducing a hallucination. Ari said the hypno-trance was based on a similar concept . . . except that the target wasn't aware the "reality" wasn't real. Technologically induced schizophrenia, he'd called it. And was rounding up the relevant experts, among other things, to inter-view staff, and review briefing tapes, to search for symptoms.

In the meantime, there was no sign of Jane. Krishnaswali was furious, and had chewed her out for a solid half hour. Had accused her of pursuing her personal, interventionist, militaristic agenda at the expense of local security. She'd been so busy looking for evidence with which to persuade Captain Reichardt of her cause, that she'd allowed Callay's single greatest security threat to escape when she should have shot to kill. Even Ibrahim had not been happy. They'd have had evi-dence enough from her corpse, he'd suggested. They'd have raided her uplinks, removed information, data connections . . . all likely to have survived the body's death. Proof of who Jane had talked to, and where she'd been.

Sandy turned her face into a jet blast that would have been painful to a straight. Trying to blast the frustration from her skull, perhaps. Jane had proven herself every bit as immoral and callous as she'd feared and Takawashi had suggested. She'd nearly killed Rhian. She'd nearly killed Vanessa. Sandy couldn't believe that she herself, with the cold, steely hatred she felt toward everything that Jane represented . . . a hatred that penetrated well into the depths of her soul . . . had subcon-sciously made a decision to spare Jane's life, for no apparent good reason. She'd evolved a lot as a person of late, both during her last years in the League, and particularly during her last two years on Callay. She was wiser, smarter, and more appreciative of all life's vast complexities. But still, as she'd acknowledged herself on numerous occasions, she was no pacifist.

She'd killed so many people during her early years of life, whom hindsight informed her hadn't deserved it. And now, she'd been given the chance to take the life of one who clearly did deserve it, and refrained. She didn't understand why she'd done what she'd done. And now, she had trouble looking her comrades, who had lost friends at Jane's hands, in the eye.

"Commander." Vanessa's voice, to one side of the shower row. Sandy glanced sideways through the blasting water and steam. Vanessa was in casual fatigues, her beret tucked into a thigh pocket, looking somewhat less tired than she ought—after the State Department raid, she'd returned to sleep on the fold-down bed in her office, and no one had had the heart to wake her. Last Sandy had heard, just an hour ago, she'd still been asleep. "I've some news."

Sandy refrained from a wry remark, in the presence of underlings, and keyed off the shower with a sigh. Took a towel from the wall dispenser and towelled down her hair as she walked on the puddled floor, down a row of lockers to her own. It was an egalitarian arrangement, by Sandy and Vanessa's own design, just a simple metal locker amidst the others, with no preference for rank. They, and Krishnaswali, all had private showers in the bathrooms adjoining their offices. Krishnaswali, spending more time at his desk than his two next-most senior underlings combined, showered there, when needed. The men's and women's general locker rooms were down on the ground floor, alongside the weapons and PT sections for convenient access. Sandy had heard her guys talking, when they thought no one could hear, making sarcastic remarks about Krishnaswali not even knowing where his general locker was. Which wasn't fair on Krishnaswali; it really *wasn't* convenient for him, given the different nature of his job . . . but still, Sandy knew that soldiers would say what soldiers would say, and there was nothing anyone could do to stop it.

"What's up?" Sandy said when they were far enough away from company. Stopped before her locker, letting the red light scan her iris. A click as it opened, and she reached for her clothes. There was no immediate reply, and she glanced at Vanessa. Vanessa stood, arms folded, contemplating her naked form. One characteristically arched eyebrow said more than any words could. "Oh," said Sandy, sheepishly. And quickly began towelling herself down. "Sorry."

Vanessa seemed to be biting back some great amusement, lips pursed with effort. Rushing to get into her clothes, Sandy was pulling her ops jumpsuit to her waist before she finally noticed. And frowned at her. Vanessa's amusement broke in a stifled laugh. Sandy smiled in puzzlement.

"What?" she said. Vanessa shook her head, a hand raised in apology, still unwilling or unable to speak. "What?" With mounting indignation.

Vanessa sighed. "Oh come on, like this isn't the most absurd thing you've ever seen." Sandy pulled on her T-shirt, still smiling uncertainly, and zipped the jumpsuit over it. Sat down to begin pulling on socks and boots.

"What's absurd?" she ventured after a moment. Uncertain whether she'd misunderstood, and not wanting to make another mistake.

"Us!" Vanessa laughed. "You, suddenly nervous about being naked in front of me. I bet you've never been nervous about nudity before in your life. You looked like a ten-year-old, scrambling for a towel when her brother's friends burst into the bathroom."

"You're exaggerating," Sandy retorted, pulling on a boot. "And besides, it's not my fault I'm suddenly concerned about the effect my bare arse might be having on you."

"It is your fault," Vanessa retorted. "You're gorgeous."

"That's not my fault, it's the League's fault. Fuck, it's probably

Takawashi's fault. I'm probably the spitting image of some old girl-friend of his, the one he still thinks about when he jerks off. If he still can jerk off."

"Well thanks, that's spoiled my mental image entirely."

Sandy half-grinned. "Good." She finished with the other boot, strapping the fasteners with typical lightning speed. Then stood, and looked Vanessa directly in the eyes. "Ricey. Are we okay?"

"We're okay," Vanessa said firmly, her gaze unwavering. "I don't make a good drama queen, Sandy. I'm not going to go storming off because I can't get my way on something. I just . . . haven't been single for a while, and it's been two years since the divorce, and I didn't think I'd still be single. And it just . . . started getting to me. With all this stuff going on. I started wondering about my future. Our future."

"You want kids?" Sandy asked, with a flash of insight.

Vanessa shrugged. A little evasively, Sandy thought. "Maybe," Vanessa conceded. "But not on my own. With this job, I couldn't handle it. I'd need some long-term help."

"And who's the lucky sperm?"

"I'd thought . . . I'd thought maybe a donor bank. I mean, my taste in men is terrible. I can't imagine sharing a kid with someone like Sav, it's a complication I *really* don't need in my life. My taste in women is far better." With a faint smile.

Sandy rolled her eyes, and brushed damp fringe from her eyes. "That's debatable. Never thought of adopting?"

"Call me selfish," Vanessa replied with a shrug, "I want a kid who's at least half me. The gene-screens are pretty thorough, I could make out the father to look like anything I wanted." Sandy shook her head with faint disbelief. Vanessa frowned. "What? You don't think that's a good idea?"

"No no, nothing like that. It's just more Federation hypocrisy. Every time you see photos or footage from a few hundred years ago, you notice there's much more variety of facial features and body shapes.

I'd say there were far more ugly people, if that weren't such a subjective judgement. And an unfair one. But despite all the Federation's bitching about the League technology taking over the species, we've still managed to weed out a huge range of genetic variety over the last few centuries. Just with gene screening, which is supposed to only select for disease and health purposes, but of course it doesn't."

Vanessa shrugged. "Every living, organic creature is battling against its own genes from the day it's born. Why should we be any different?"

"I'm not saying it's a bad thing. It's just hypocritical. There's something more . . . I don't know . . . romantic, about a random selection, don't you think? Guessing what the kid's going to look like?"

"There's nothing romantic about cystic fibrosis," Vanessa said flatly. Sandy grimaced, remembering having read about that, from before it was eliminated more than three centuries ago. "Or getting abused all through school because your nose looks like a vegetable. What about you?" With a curious smile. "Has Rhian's decision rubbed off on you yet?"

Sandy shook her head, calmly. "No."

Vanessa's smile faded. "No? But someday, surely?"

"Only if I change my mind. Maybe one day I'll want a kid. But right now, I think never."

Vanessa looked genuinely dismayed. "Seriously? But that's so sad!"

"I know," said Sandy, with a faint smile. "It'd be tragic, for the kid. Rhian might get away with it, she's low profile. But me, with my job, and all the attention . . ."

"You could manage!" Vanessa insisted. "Hell, Krishnaswali's got three!"

"I don't want to be the mother of the child of a killing machine," Sandy said sadly. "I don't have the right to inflict the fears and dangers of my life upon anyone so innocent. I don't want him or her to have to live the rest of their life in the shadow of my legacy. And I won't put all this guilt on anyone else's shoulders."

Vanessa just stared at her, in great dismay. Looking like she wanted to argue, but somehow, couldn't think of any counterargument. Sandy smiled, and put a hand on Vanessa's slim, uniformed shoulder. "But if you have a child one day, I'd love to be friendly Auntie Sandy, who calls in frequently to corrupt its innocent little mind."

Vanessa's eyes gleamed. "I'd like that," she said. And took Sandy's hand off her shoulder, giving it a tight squeeze.

"Now, you said there was news?" Sandy prompted, thinking that this particular encounter had gone about as well as she could possibly have hoped, and wanting to end it before things could degenerate again.

"Yeah," Vanessa said with a sigh, releasing her hand. "Takawashi left. He went on an attached shuttle, registered to the League freighter *Corona*. There was a security lapse—remember the customs report last month saying there was too much emphasis on entry, and not enough on departures? Well someone got a visual on Takawashi's party *after* they'd gone through the checks, just before boarding. One of that party, Intel's pretty sure, was Jane."

Sandy waited patiently outside the League Embassy front gate, the raincoat hood pulled over her head, hands in pockets. At her back, cars hissed upon the wet street, gleaming beneath the streetlights. Simple concrete blocks lined the street edge, an age-old precaution against car bombs. Two years ago, there had been requests to block off the entire road, but local residents had protested. Nowadays, violent Callayan activist groups were more angry at Earth than the League, and the Embassy security no longer had quite so many reasons to be nervous. But still, a simple, enhanced visual sweep through the metal rails of the fence showed the crouched, dark shadows of snipers upon the roof, and scanner grids overlaid across the broad, grassy garden.

The Embassy itself was pleasant on the eye—a two-storey white building with Corinthian pillars, very much in the style of eighteenth-century English colonialism. An instantly recognisable style, in Tanusha, with its prominent Indian influence that recalled such architectural influences readily. A long driveway curved in a U, meeting the Embassy's main doors beneath the front pillars. There was little decorative lighting to advertise the building's existence to the outside, and no sign on the fence. Everyone who was interested in such things knew what the building was, of course, but no one inside found a need to announce the fact to casual passersby.

After twenty seconds of waiting, a police officer climbed from the van at one end of the street barricades, and walked toward her. His raincoat was transparent, clearly displaying his blue uniform beneath. He arrived at Sandy's side.

"Excuse me, ma'am, do you have some business here?" Sandy looked at him, fully showing her face beneath the hood. The policeman's eyes went wide. "I'm sorry, ma'am . . . I mean Commander. We weren't informed."

"That's okay, Sergeant, I didn't inform anyone."

The sergeant gave a quick look across the Embassy's broad, wet lawns. "Did you inform the Embassy?"

"No."

"I see. Is there anything we can do to help?" Hopefully.

"Just continue what you're doing, Sergeant. And watch for any unusual activity within the grounds."

"Yes, Commander." The sergeant nodded formally, then hurried back to his van. Sandy returned her attention to the Embassy. If the security people watching her now had any doubts of her identity, the sergeant's reaction had surely dispelled them. A moment later, the front doors opened, and a woman in a raincoat came out. The walk up the gravel footpath to the front pedestrian gate took more than thirty seconds. Sandy could see within the first few steps that the approaching woman was a GI, and was armed beneath her raincoat upon the left side. Probably a machine-pistol, or a snubbed assault weapon. The female GI came up to the gate, and Sandy stepped close. Thunder muttered and grumbled, distantly.

"Please state your business," said the other GI. The tone was expressionless. Her eyes were alert and aware, but somehow there was something missing. A depth.

"I'd like to come in," said Sandy. When dealing with regs, it was wise to keep things simple.

"Make an appointment," said the reg.

"I'm the commander of the CDF," Sandy replied. "I don't need an appointment."

"Procedural protocols say you do."

"Fuck procedural protocols." The reg frowned, apparently not knowing what to make of that. It was nice to know these regs were capable of frowning, Sandy supposed. She'd known some who weren't. In combat, they'd done plenty of damage, but not always to soldiers, and not always the enemy's. Their own life expectancy, during a heavy period, had been not years or months, but weeks. "Either you open the gate, or I'll jump it and walk in."

"The Embassy is legally League territory." Sandy doubted the reg knew what that really meant, but had been instructed to say it when required. "We are allowed to use lethal force."

"I'm not going to attack you. I'm just going to walk to the Embassy."

"You're not allowed."

"So stop me."

Now the reg was becoming confused. "We'll restrain you."

"You're aware of my designation. You know what happens when you try and fight a designation like mine." If this GI had ever gone hand-to-hand against Ramoja, she'd know. They'd need at least ten to stop her.

"Then you will be attacking us," reasoned the reg.

"No, I'll be defending myself."

"On League territory."

"So I'm not allowed to defend myself if ten or twenty GIs rush me?"

The reg took a deep breath, looking more disconcerted than ever. "It would be much easier if you made an appointment," she said.

"Forty seconds, and I'll jump the fence," said Sandy. The reg did not reply. From her slightly desperate look, Sandy reckoned she was asking for instructions . . . but she couldn't tell for sure without her uplinks. It ought to have been safe to do so, with Jane gone. But in the proximity of the League Embassy, it wasn't a risk she was prepared to take.

The metal gate clacked unlocked, then hummed open. The reg stood aside as Sandy walked in, looking about as relieved as was possible for a reg to look. Relieved not because she'd been fearing a fight, that wasn't in any reg's nature. But relieved to be freed from such an unsettlingly complicated problem of suitable responses. Regs were happier when things were black and white. In Sandy's experience, the battlefield was rarely that. And she simply couldn't believe the attitude of people who would send such mentally simple creations into combat. Regs—indeed, all GIs—had been an invention of desperation from a smaller power looking to even the odds against massive numerical inferiority. But now the war had ended, and still the League persisted with a backbone force of low-to-mid designation GIs. Inevitably, they'd become dependent. And worse, being League, they'd become infatuated with GIs' more obvious physical and technical advantages.

But create an entire army of high-des GIs like herself? Like Ramoja, or Jane? That was to risk creating an enormously powerful weapon that could not be controlled. And so they persisted with blunt instruments like this one. It wasn't fair to the regs, and it certainly wasn't fair to any civilians in proximity to a hypothetical combat zone . . . to say nothing of what it meant for the gradual disintegration of any League concept of human rights, to even have regs in the first place. Sandy felt herself fuming with old angers as she walked up the crunching gravel path in the moderate, steady rain. Her thumb ached within its cast—a good sign, that the nerves were regenerating. And a bad sign, for the tension it indicated.

To her little surprise, Major Ramoja met her just inside the front door.

"Commander," he said mildly, as the reg shut the door behind. Sandy unbuttoned her raincoat. "Don't take it off, you won't be staying that long."

"Is that right?" Sandy said flatly. Removed the raincoat, shook it out, and offered it to the reg standing at her elbow. The reg did not take it. Sandy shook her head. "The service in this place is simply not what it used to be." She tossed it to the floor, against the wall by the door.

"What do you want?" Ramoja asked. He stood in the middle of the broad entrance hallway, on polished floorboards before an expensive Indian carpet. Paintings on the walls, and a large overhead chandelier maintained the eighteenth-century ambience. A carved wooden table at the cross-corridor behind held a vase containing a brilliant plume of peacock feathers. To Sandy's maxed hearing, the Embassy seemed remarkably quiet. On her previous visits, there had been much bustle and activity, Embassy staff going about their routine chores, and serving drinks or meals for the various official activities that seemed to continue on a steadily rotating schedule. Now, she could hear barely an echo of compressed floorboards, nor a murmur of distant conversation. The security outside, however, had been as intense as always. Doubtless they were all still here. Equally doubtless recent events had brought the typical daily cycle to an abrupt end.

"I want answers," Sandy told him. "I want to know everything you know about Renaldo Takawashi. I want to know exactly what he was up to in Tanusha. I mean what he was *really* up to. And I want to know exactly which League faction authorised Jane's recovery, and how."

Ramoja raised an eyebrow. He wore military pants and jacket, with many pockets and obvious weapons. Lately, in quieter times, he'd taken to wearing suits. Doubtless he'd found it enhanced his newly discovered dapper self-image. Today, things were evidently different. "You already seem to know all the answers," he said mildly. "Why don't you tell me?"

Sandy shook her head. "You don't understand. Ibrahim's preparing an order to close down the Embassy."

Ramoja nearly frowned. Nearly. Sandy knew a GI's reflexes well enough to recognise the onset of combat-reflex. Ramoja was highly alarmed. "Why?" he said flatly.

"Suspected complicity with a direct threat to Callayan and Federation security of the highest level. Suspected complicity in the assassination of Admiral Duong, and with the attempted assassination of the Callayan Secretary of State. Neiland's authorising him for any measures necessary. He's not just going to send home the Ambassador, he's going to close down the Embassy. By force, if you don't meet his timetable. His timetable, in case you're wondering, is the next thirty minutes. Either you talk, or you're all gone."

Upon which she folded her arms and waited. Somewhere above, a door slammed. Then footsteps, multiplying as they echoed down hallways and across rooms. Some echoing voices. Ramoja seemed to be waiting, lips pressed to a thin line, arms folded tightly. From the hard look in his eyes, Sandy guessed he was processing a terse, uplinked conversation.

Then . . . "I said *I'll* handle it!" he snarled aloud, to that silent interlocutor. The approaching footsteps continued, and then Ambassador Yao himself arrived in the hall, appearing somewhat less collected than Sandy could ever remember seeing him. He strode quickly across the carpet, a somewhat rounded, inoffensive-looking Chinese man with his tie uncharacteristically askew.

"Commander, please, you must tell the Director that we had nothing to do with . . ." And he broke off as Ramoja spun to face him, stepping firmly across his path.

"I said I'll handle it," Ramoja said in a dark, tight voice. Yao blinked at him. Ramoja stood no taller than Yao, and despite an intensely muscular build, probably weighed less too. Yet his sheer physical gravity seemed to suck all presence out of the Ambassador, and render him transparent by contrast.

"Major," Yao managed to blurt after a deep intake of breath, "I am the Ambassador here, and it is my responsibility to . . ."

"League security is in question," Ramoja replied, tautly. "It just became an ISO matter. I rank you."

It evidently wasn't a question he wanted discussed in front of the CDF Commander—who ranked who in the Embassy, and when, was a matter of speculation still within the CSA. Well, she was now a little wiser. For whatever good it would do, if she didn't get what Ibrahim considered a reasonable set of answers. Yao blinked furiously, evidently thinking fast. Which was what he was best at, by all reports. But none of his conclusions appeared to give him a way past the bundle of lethally coiled synthetic muscle that currently blocked his path, and so he stood aside, and waited in anxious silence. Ramoja swung on his heel, and faced Sandy once more.

"Takawashi's mission was to recover the FIA's GI," he confirmed, shortly. "He appears to have been successful."

Sandy just fixed him with an unimpressed stare. "Do better," she told him, just as shortly.

"It was authorised a long way up the chain. The Embassy was instructed to provide cover, but not direct assistance."

"We in the business of Callayan security don't have the luxury of making that distinction," Sandy remarked sourly.

"I protested the instruction."

"Well, good for you," said Sandy, with much condescension. Ramoja's eyes narrowed beneath dark, firm brows. "I'm so glad to see you're developing along your moral continuum."

"Takawashi was dubious of the need for our assistance," Ramoja continued. "He felt that Jane would be open to persuasion."

"Persuasion?" Sandy exclaimed, with raised eyebrows. "Jane?"

"He felt that she would wish to meet her maker." There was now a trace of dark irony in Ramoja's voice. A scepticism toward Takawashi and his intentions. From Ramoja, the clean-cut, every-League-officer's-favourite GI, it was unexpected. "He told me that she was confused. That she would jump at the chance to be where she belonged, and to broaden her horizons."

"Yeah, she's a real compulsive socialiser, huh. Maybe that or she's got a killswitch in her brainstem too, and he's got the trigger."

Ramoja made a "maybe" motion of his head. "She did display an instinct for self-preservation."

"What have the FIA said about Takawashi stealing back his prize?"

"No, no." Ramoja shook his head, some of the usual, familiar smugness returning. "You don't understand. Jane was not stolen from Takawashi by the FIA. She was a gift."

Then she *did* understand, having already suspected. But she said nothing. Ambassador Yao coughed, nervously, and wet his lips. "Actually, Major, I'm not sure that you should be speaking of . . ."

"Takawashi's pathetically self-serving mission is over," Ramoja cut him off, hard. "We've been forced to jeopardise our broader mission enough with his foolishness. League relations with the entire Federation are now at stake, thanks to his little escapade, and now we must return to our true priorities." Yao nodded quickly, lips pursed.

"The war was ending," Ramoja continued to Sandy. "Takawashi's greatest perfection of his life's work—us—was complete. Yet GI production was ending, the old government was falling, and with it, all support for him and his research projects. He wanted to give his creations life, but was not allowed. There was an order to destroy his prototypes, yet he refused. I cannot prove what happened next, but suffice to say that I do not find his evidence of their destruction convincing."

"Why the FIA?" Sandy said suspiciously. "What did they offer?"

"As far as I can discern, they offered nothing. Merely the chance to give Takawashi's baby life. It took much preparation, though." And

Ramoja's eyes narrowed. "Some of the required information could only be gleaned by close examination of a physical subject. And Takawashi had no prototype of the advanced design available. Except for one, who had wandered off. Directly into Federal Intelligence's web."

Sandy stared at him, unblinkingly. Then, in a low voice and as calmly as she could manage, "You're saying that Takawashi set me up, two years ago?"

"I can prove nothing," said Ramoja. "I only know that Takawashi was disappointed in you."

"He expressed otherwise," Sandy said darkly.

A corner of Ramoja's mouth twitched upwards. "Oh, he was pleased enough that you had shown such . . . initiative. But your defection to the Federation did represent a definite failure on his part. Renaldo Takawashi was once a simple researcher, as he often says. A shining star in the independent, nonpolitical League science community. But however reluctantly he joined the League's military development projects when it seemed to League policy makers that war would become inevitable if the League were to fulfil its manifest destiny, he quickly changed his tune. He would deny it, of course. But for at least fifty years now, Renaldo Takawashi has grown accustomed to his immense political influence within the League, and his enormous research budgets. Not to mention a lavish lifestyle that verges upon the obscene. That ship in orbit, the *Corona*, to which he is currently headed? It is listed as owned by the Cognizant Corporation, the holding company to which Cognizant Systems is affiliated. What is not well known is that Takawashi effectively owns a controlling stake in Cognizant Corporation, through various roundabout methods. And the *Corona* is effectively his private starship."

As many wealthy people as there were in the Federation and League combined, there were very few who owned private starships. For those who did, it remained the ultimate statement in wealth and privilege.

"Your disappearance greatly damaged Takawashi's prestige within the

League government and military," Ramoja continued. "He had warned that it was a possibility within your first ten years of life. After that, however, he firmly expected that your loyalty toward the League and its principles would be firmly entrenched. When you left, he lost face, and the powers that be lost confidence with his predictions. I believe that Jane had been merely one of several side-projects up until that point. Afterwards, however, he felt compelled, by ego as much as the technical challenge, to work toward a solution to the problem you posed."

"A GI's loyalty," Sandy muttered.

"Exactly. And to control her loyalty, you first must control her mind. I believe he donated Jane to the FIA because he knew they would use her. That they might use her against the League would never have bothered him—Takawashi was always far too bound up in his personal quests to waste time with such pointless distractions as patriotism. He knew the FIA would use Jane, and doubtless he was curious to see her effectiveness. He maintained covert links to the FIA with which to monitor her activities, that being a condition of the deal. Which was how he knew she would be here. Perhaps the FIA even agreed to hand her back after two years, I cannot say."

"Maybe there's more than just Jane," Sandy remarked. "Maybe Takawashi gave them several. Maybe lots. Maybe Jane's just the first."

Ramoja nodded. "Clearly possible. Cognizant's records are more closely guarded than many branches of the ISO. We have no way of knowing just how many prototypes were made."

"He couldn't hide Jane away before," Sandy said with suspicion. "Why does he feel he can do so now?"

Ramoja took a breath, and shoved both hands into the pockets of his army pants. "League recruitment has largely survived the immediate purge of the new regime," he said, with an expression that hinted at unhappy resignation. "Cognizant has been building facilities in systems far removed from easy scrutiny. They have worked their way into the new government's favour as they did with the old."

"Wonderful system you work for," Sandy remarked sourly.

"Perfection of the system is not a prerequisite for loyalty," Ramoja said sharply. "If it were, neither of us would choose the jobs we hold. If the system is flawed, then fixing it is merely another part of the job. Our loyalty comes from our commitment to the values that underpin the system, not the system itself."

"Or because someone high up in League military command decided they wanted a GI who would believe exactly what they wanted her to believe," Sandy remarked, eyes hard with anger. "What a fucking joke. Another great chapter in the League's commitment to the rights of its synthetic citizens. The war's ended, and we're still just a fucking commodity to them. A military asset." Ramoja stared away at a wall, his jaw set hard. Ambassador Yao looked at his shiny shoes upon the floorboards.

"I hadn't thought it was possible," Yao ventured timidly. "I mean, I'm just a layman . . . but to create a GI of the level of intellect that you two possess . . . and to control her personality and brain function from the first day onwards? Surely that control would . . . would destroy the very creativity that is her . . . and your . . . greatest asset?"

"It would seem to fly in the face of all established psych theory," Ramoja said tautly. "Jane may yet evolve, I suppose. But to be where she is now, at barely a year-and-a-half's age, is worrisome."

"If Takawashi were to abruptly meet with misfortune," Sandy said blankly, "it would all die with him." Yao blinked at her. Ramoja frowned, incredulously.

"And this is your official position, is it?" he asked. "In your new role as an enlightened, democratic authority sworn to uphold human rights and the rule of law?"

Sandy fixed him with a hard stare. "This is mind-control, Major. It's illegal in both League and Federation to apply it to straights. Somehow though, the League doesn't have a problem applying it to GIs. What if it progresses?"

"Tape-teach doesn't work on straight humans like it does on GIs," Ramoja contradicted firmly. "Straights are naturally evolving. You can't just brainwash an organic mind indefinitely, it doesn't work."

"It wasn't supposed to work on GIs either," Sandy retorted. "Not this way. Either the people behind this have to be exposed, or it's got to be ended. One way or the other, this is just too dangerous right now."

"Commander," Yao protested, "the technology isn't the problem, so long as the regulatory mechanisms are functioning . . ."

"Yeah, I know the usual League spiel, Ambassador. And how wonderfully are the League's regulatory mechanisms working now?"

Yao swallowed. "I will not discuss an ultimatum from a simple Federation functionary—no disrespect intended—to interfere with matters of League internal policy in exchange for the continued functioning of the League Embassy on Callay. Furthermore, I can't believe that Director Ibrahim would include such a tangential demand into his list of requests in sending you here."

"He didn't," said Ramoja, studying Sandy with contemplative eyes. "She's just voicing her opinion. Again."

"Yeah, well at least I care enough to have one," Sandy retorted. "I want full documentary evidence. All the dealings this Embassy had with Takawashi. All the communications files, all the intel you received from ISO back League-side. That *is* a part of Ibrahim's demands."

"You'll get as much as you need to convince Captain Reichardt and his people of what really went on," Ramoja responded calmly, his manner as impenetrable as his arms-folded stance. "That's all Callay's security requires. Director Ibrahim and President Neiland will be happy enough with that. The rest is League property."

"I'll decide what's enough here, thanks . . ."

"I'll tell you," came a new voice from down the adjoining hall. Rhian appeared at the corner, as Ramoja gave a frowning look over his shoulder. Rhian's head was bandaged, and she wore a loose, grey tracksuit, very unlike her usual, glamorous self. The front was unzipped, in the manner of someone recently out of bed, and her feet were bare. She steadied herself against the corner, and gazed at the small group gathered in the entrance hall. Her gaze, Sandy thought, appeared slightly unsteady. "I got into their files," she told Sandy. "There's lots of stuff about Takawashi. It wasn't the Major's fault, Cap. Nor Mr. Yao's. They were under orders. But they knew Jane was going to kill Admiral Duong, and couldn't stop it because Takawashi's faction had instructed them not to."

"That's enough, Lieutenant!" Ramoja barked. Behind her left shoulder, Sandy could all but feel the female reg begin to tense.

"Takawashi was very excited about Jane," Rhian continued, walking upon weary, bare feet across the expensive Indian carpet. "He said she appeared to exceed any of his expectations. Apparently his superiors were very excited. I got the impression they said something that referred to mass production and new League rebuilding strategies, but I couldn't be sure. Maybe someone in the CSA can tell."

Rhian stopped in front of Ramoja. Ramoja gripped her shoulder with a firm hand. "Lieutenant Chu," he said. The effort in his voice, to keep calm and controlled, was evident. "You've been shot in the head. You're still under partial sedation. I think you should go back and lie down. The doctor said your skull had been well and truly rattled. Do you understand?"

Rhian blinked at him, almost dreamily. "Do you remember what you said to me a few days ago, Major? That you knew my loyalty was divided, and how you thought I should take some time to think about it? Well, I've thought about it."

Sandy simply watched, barely able to breathe. Combat-reflex was attempting to impinge upon her vision, and the throbbing ache in her thumb was receding.

"Rhian," said Ramoja, in a softening tone. There was real affection in his voice, whatever the evident strain. A comforting surety. Charisma. "Rhian, I know how much you like Tanusha. I know how much you love Cassandra. Truthfully, I've always expected that you would wish to join with her in service of Callay and the Federation one day—honestly, I'll show you my reports to ISO command, I predicted that one day it would happen. But now should not be that day, Rhian. This is the wrong moment. This would cause complications. And you owe us more than that, Rhian. You owe us more, for everything we've given you, for all the tolerance we've shown in letting you keep on in our service despite knowing that your true loyalties were shifting. You can't do this to us. It wouldn't be right."

Rhian frowned at him for a long moment. Slim and apparently vulnerable, before her CO's athletic, square-shouldered build. That, like so much about Rhian, was deceptive. Then she looked at Sandy. Sandy just waited. She knew she could not intervene. She had recruited one of her old team mates into Callayan service before, so eager had she been to be reunited. That eagerness had killed him. Of course, Vanessa insisted otherwise, but . . . well, she just knew that she could not intervene again. The choice had to be Rhian's. Nothing else would work.

"Wouldn't be right," Rhian repeated, as if to herself. "What's right?"

Ramoja smiled. "Ah, Rhian. Always asking the right questions."

"I'm serious," Rhian persisted. Ramoja's smile faded. *That* wasn't like Rhian, to challenge so directly. "What's right? Is it right to treat GIs as a tool to win wars? I like being a soldier. I'll fight for a cause I believe in. But now Takawashi's faction want to make GIs who don't have *any* cause? Who just do what they're told?"

"That's always been the case, Rhian," Ramoja said warningly. "You know that. The League's survival has depended on it, however unpalatable the policy."

"Well, sure," Rhian conceded with a faint shrug, "but I mean, regs are regs." With a faintly anxious glance at the reg standing behind Sandy's shoulder. Sandy doubted she was offended. "We're *so* much better at fighting than them. I remember you saying once that we had a responsibility to protect everyone back in the League. But don't we have a responsibility to protect everyone here too? And everyone everywhere else? I don't see how an army of ten thousand Janes makes anyone safe, here or there. I think there's just a few people doing this to serve themselves. I think they need to be stopped."

"And we can do that, Rhian," Ramoja soothed, putting the other hand upon her opposite shoulder. "I agree with you. But we can do that from here. Within the system, where we have access to those who matter."

Rhian shook her head, adamantly. "No. I'm a soldier. I don't like diplomacy much. I think you stop people by stopping them. Like this." And she made a wall with one hand, and a fist with the other. Smacked the fist into the wall, definitively. Her eyes searched Ramoja's face, in search of understanding, but found only concern. "I don't mean killing them. But if that's all they understand, you have to at least threaten it. It's like a bluff. Like in a game of cards. If you don't mean it, then it's not worth doing. I've seen the diplomacy here. I don't think it's working. No one stopped Takawashi, did they? I want to stop him. I think I can do that better with Sandy than I can here."

Ramoja took a deep breath. "Rhian, you made an unauthorised access of Embassy storage. I can't let you walk out of here with that information. That would be stealing League secrets, and I know you know that's wrong."

"And we helped get Callay blockaded," Rhian replied calmly. "So where does that leave us?"

"I won't allow it, Rhian."

Rhian took Ramoja gently by both wrists, and removed his hands from her shoulders. Ramoja performed a fast reversal, but in a blur of motion Rhian was faster, and retained a grip on his forearms. Ramoja stared in consternation.

"Mustafa," said Sandy, in the slow, profound stillness of combat-reflex. "Don't do it. ISO commissioned you. You're a good soldier, but you're Intel, not Dark Star."

"Major, please!" Yao backed two steps along the wall, bumping into a decorative cabinet. "Let her go, we can discuss the protocols later . . ."

"Rhian," Ramoja said reasonably, "I'll let you go if you first void your memory storage of the data files you stole."

"It's Callay's right to see them," Rhian replied, just as reasonably. "It's well within Callay's natural security parameters."

"You're not a lawyer, Lieutenant. That's not yours to decide."

"You're not a lawyer either."

The GIs' respective stances were unmistakable, feet subtly positioned and posture squared. Undrugged and healthy, Sandy would have bet on Rhian any day—tape-teach was supposed to negate the need for practice, but Sandy knew better. Experience in any skill made a huge difference, even for GIs, and particularly in free-form, unpredictable skillsets like combat. Rhian's combat experience was vastly superior to Ramoja's, despite their similar (Sandy suspected) ages. But Rhian *was* drugged, and dazed.

There came then the light, fast thudding of footsteps. GIs—too fast and lithe to be straights. Sandy recognised the tactical disadvantage immediately, with a reg at her shoulder, and made three rapid feints of shoulder, foot and head within a split second, tangling the reg's more predictable reflex responses. The final left elbow struck within that blur of motion, the GI's head snapping back with a force that would have decapitated a straight, then crumpling to the ground unconscious. And, reg or not, Sandy made a mental note to apologise later—she simply couldn't afford that presence at her rear when her front required full attention.

Neither Ramoja nor Rhian so much as moved an eyelid, gazing at each other with a strange silent intensity. Rhian's slim hands held Ramoja's forearms. Ramoja made no attempt to remove them. At GI speeds, starting postures were hardly crucial. What mattered was what happened next. Five GIs in plain fatigues appeared from the cross-corridor, weapons levelled down the entrance hall. One darted forward to pull Ambassador Yao back, out of the firing line.

"No weapons," said Ramoja. "No one is going to fire in here. I forbid it." The GIs put their weapons away without a moment's hesitation, so as not to hinder their movement. That, the nuances of posture, plus the way their eyes took in the scene, told Sandy that they were all regs. Sandy opened an uplink to an external, presecured network point, and opened a shielded channel. Made contact, gave a simple command, and disconnected.

"Rhian," she said then. "Let's go."

"Cassandra," Ramoja said mildly, "I am warning you." Ramoja fancied himself a hotshot soldier. Which he was. He'd disarmed her once, on their first meeting, in the attic of an organised-crime gambling den—she'd been overenthusiastic and underprepared, and he'd been waiting. Given what she was, he'd been very pleased with himself. She walked up to him now, slowly, and stopped alongside.

"You're not holding any cards here," she told him, very calmly. "You know there's only one way to stop us from leaving."

"I know," he said. And from there, further words were pointless.

It happened almost too fast for even a GI's brain to register, except that one moment everyone was standing dead still, and the next everything was a blur, Ramoja and Sandy grappling through a series of rapid holds, reverses and counterreverses, balance shifting through an uncontrolled spin as each sought the advantage. They crashed into a wall, Ramoja using the impact to shift grips, which Sandy anticipated with an angled slide of forearm to forearm as her foot slid and body weight shifted . . . and suddenly she had the leverage. She swung, crashed Ramoja headfirst into the wall, the grip sliding easily to a momentarily uncontrolled arm which she brought down across her knee with enough explosive force to snap anything.

Following the loud crack! she spun to confront the rest of the entrance hall . . . and found Rhian dropping the last, unconscious reg with a spin-kick to the head. Four other bodies lay sprawled across the floor, two still conscious but with fractured limbs. Wall plaster was cracked and holed in places, and the wooden table at the hall's end was upended and broken, the porcelain vase smashed on the floor in shattered pieces about the peacock feathers. Somehow, that sight, more than anything, filled Sandy with an overwhelming sense of regret.

One of the injured regs was reaching for a fallen weapon. "No shooting!" shouted Ambassador Yao desperately, from the safety of his corner, having wisely backed well away. "You heard the Major, no shooting!"

The reg relented, forestalling Sandy's reach for her own pistol. She looked at Rhian. Rhian now *did* look dizzy, her right hand rigid with discomfort—no doubt from Jane's other bullet wound. But her friend's gaze held steady enough when their eyes met.

"Flamboyant," Sandy remarked, meaning that last spin-kick.

Rhian shrugged. "I never knew where all that combat drill had come from until I came here." Kung fu, she meant. Rhian had discovered it shortly after her arrival on Callay, and quickly become fascinated. "So *that's* where it comes from," she'd said with amazement, meaning her basic, strictly practical Dark Star training. And Sandy recalled her own amazement, upon first becoming a civilian, that food could be "cuisine," and clothes could be "fashion," and sex could be "love making." *That's* where it comes from, she recalled realising, with similar amazement.

And she smiled. "Let's go," she said. But Rhian paused, moving on soft, bare feet to where Ambassador Yao stood stunned and helpless. To his credit, he did not flinch when Rhian stood before him, regardless of the display of inhuman power that had preceded. Whatever his faults, Callayan-style GI-phobia did not number among them.

"I'm sorry, Mr. Yao," said Rhian. "I didn't want to do it this way. You deserve better." And she kissed him on the cheek, then padded to Sandy's side. Ramoja was levering himself upright, moving to block the way. He held his right arm with the left hand. The elbow was badly hyperextended, and the entire forearm flopped uncontrollably, the fingers dangling. From the look on his face, Sandy reckoned the pain had not yet penetrated the combat-reflex.

"Don't be stupid," Sandy told him. "You couldn't beat me with two arms."

"You won't get past the yard," Ramoja said impassively. "The defences will stop you."

Sandy ignored him, walking past without bothering to guard her back—with her and Rhian, and Ramoja's one arm, he'd never touch her if he tried. She opened the door, and went to the top of the short steps that led down to the driveway parking, beneath the Embassy's front pillars before the door. Behind those pillars and across the gardens, she was not surprised to see the dark shapes of more GI security, automatic weapons levelled at the doors.

Some of those guards turned, then, as the sound of flyer engines grew louder above the usual background airtraffic hum. And then, emerging above the roof of an opposing, low building, there appeared an A-9 flyer. Another appeared further to the right, hovering low past the beautiful spire of a Hindu temple, its intricate carvings alive in a wash of light from below. A few early-morning pedestrians stared upward at the menacing shapes overhead, engines howling, unfolded weapons bays and underslung cannon directed with obvious intent toward the Embassy grounds.

Sandy turned to confront Ramoja, as he emerged from the doorway behind, eyes sweeping the scene. "We've got camera feeds recording all of this," Sandy told him, above the howl of engines. "It'll go straight to the news networks if you fire or stop us. Rhian is now claiming asylum. Under the Federation security Act, any League military figure claiming asylum will immediately come under Federal forces protection. Even GIs." Since very recently, anyhow. Her case had achieved that much amendment to the regulations, at least.

"You're standing on League territory," Ramoja replied impassively, clutching tightly at his useless arm.

"Attempting to keep Rhian in custody against her will effectively makes her a political prisoner. We don't tolerate the holding of political prisoners in League embassies." The look on Ramoja's face told her the obvious—he knew it was bullshit. But the overriding security imperatives had to be justified somehow, even through acts of clear hypocrisy. So long as it got the job done where required, Sandy didn't care. "If you restrain us, we'll shut down the Embassy. If you shoot us, we'll flatten it. Callay's grown up, Major. Bureaucratic protocols don't stop us any more. We do what we need to. You get in our way, we'll crush you, protocols or no protocols. And you know I don't bluff."

Ramoja gazed at the hovering, deadly Trishuls beyond the perimeter fence. No doubt his vision was attuned enough to see the underslung cannon centred precisely upon his chest. Preprogrammed and accurate to GI-standards, it alone could take out half the GIs in the yard in a matter of seconds. His partner, no doubt, would take out the other half, coordinating via tac-net to avoid wasteful overlap. Each was too heavily armoured to worry much about small arms, and the Embassy's defensive personnel were not allowed anything heavier.

Sandy turned, and walked down the stairs. Rhian kept to her side. Together they walked across the driveway parking, beneath the Embassy's front pillars, and then along the central path across the front lawn, beneath the beautiful, shadowing branches of native trees.

"You think he'll shoot us?" Sandy asked Rhian, casually as they walked.

"The League needs this embassy," Rhian said thoughtfully, her bare feet soundless upon the wet gravel beside the soft crunch of Sandy's boots. Still the rain was falling. And she'd forgotten her raincoat. That was stunning . . . or would have been, in any other mental state. Probably it was right to leave it behind, it would have gotten in the way—but still, she could not recall having actually outright forgotten anything before in her life. Ari, no doubt, would be intrigued. Takawashi too. "Would Callay really shut down the Embassy?"

Sandy nodded. "For a few years at least. No League access to the Federation capital."

"He won't shoot us then," Rhian said confidently. And sure enough, at the end of the path, the GI guarding the gate actually opened it for them manually. "Thank you, Cristophe," Rhian told the reg, pleasantly. "And good luck to you."

Cristophe's return gaze was uncomprehending.

"They're not that bad, you know," Rhian said to Sandy as one of the Trishuls manoeuvred above the road, and began to lower itself down, the rear bay door slowly opening. Traffic along the road fronting the Embassy had mysteriously ceased, but given the CDF's integration into central Tanushan networks, a simple traffic reroute was hardly difficult to perform. "The regs there. They're smarter than regs I've known. Cristophe actually laughed, once."

"I wish they'd made him so he could laugh all the time," Sandy replied.

"Me too." They walked along the centre of the wet road, becoming steadily damper in the falling rain. The growing howl of engines drowned regular conversation, but a basic tone-filter adjustment allowed them to hear each other, at least. Upon the sidewalk to the left, a couple of elderly women, with transparent raincoats over colourful saris, stood staring at the Trishul, hands over their ears. Despite all Tanusha's noise regulations, no one had yet figured out how to make a hovering Trishul quiet. Sandy waved to the two women, in the vain hope they wouldn't file a complaint. Tanusha being Tanusha, she doubted it would work.

"Did you mean what you said back there?" Rhian said as they walked up the ramp at the rear, wet hair blasted with the instant blow-dry of the rear stabilising thrusters.

"Which bit?"

"About Callay crushing anyone who got in its way."

Sandy signalled to the crew chief within the cramped hold, who said something into his helmet mike. Sandy and Rhian took overhead holds, braced for familiar movement. "Did I say that?" Sandy asked with a frown.

"Yes, you did."

Sandy made a glum half shrug. "Maybe I did."

"Did you mean it?"

"Why do you ask?"

Rhian thought for a moment. The flyer's engines thrummed with power, more of a roar than a howl, here within the relatively sound-proofed interior. Clouds of blasting water vapour swirled past the open hold door. "I suppose it just sounds very military," Rhian replied. "I hadn't thought civilian societies worked like that."

"Some think they shouldn't," Sandy replied. "Some think people shouldn't. They say that we should turn the other cheek." The flyer lifted from the street, then banked gently to the left, picking up speed. For a long moment, they had a perfect view of the Embassy gardens, and the steps behind the front Corinthian pillars. Atop the steps, holding a limp right arm with the left hand, a dark figure stood in silhouette against the bright doorway behind, and watched them leave.

"One time, back in the League," said Rhian, eyes fixed upon that lonely, receding shape. "When I learned you'd left. I thought you might have agreed with them. About turning the other cheek."

"Maybe for a little while I did," said Sandy. The flyer nosed down, picking up speed and altitude, and the cargo door whined upward to close. "Ultimately, I think it's a balance. There are many paths. We have to choose which to take, and every choice is different."

"Choosing is hard," said Rhian. More quietly, and more sombrely, than Sandy could ever remember her speaking. "I'm so used to being sure. Now, sometimes . . . I just don't know."

Sandy smiled, sadly. Reached with her cast-bound left hand, and tipped Rhian's gaze her way with a touch at her jaw. "And that's what makes us human," she said.

President Katia Neiland stood before the broad windows of her Parliament office, and surveyed the grounds. Ground lights illuminated paths across the vast, grassy surface, and lit trees into beautiful, ghostly outlines. A typical summer lightning storm danced and flickered across the horizon, brightening the sharp silhouette of towers. The drink in her glass was strong—an off-world whisky, sharp and angry upon her tongue. A present from one of the foreign ministers, although she forgot which. Upon the signing of a deal, to join his world to the pact that would overwhelm the old powers of Earth, and force the relocation of the Grand Council on the terms of the Federation majority, not just the homeworld minority.

She took another sip, watching a convoy of cruisers departing overhead, running lights blinking, some important VIP or other heading home for the night . . . wherever home was. She thought of her son, Reese, now living in the Canas hacienda where the security was tighter. It was a serious inconvenience for an independent twenty-year-old. He'd always supported his mother's political ambitions. Had enjoyed having the President for a mother, in fact, having inherited from her a similar-sized ego, as well as the dark red hair. Well, it wasn't so convenient now. It interrupted his social life, his studies, and his penchant for arriving home at four in the morning. And having twelve special security operatives hanging off one's elbows only impressed the chicks for so long.

He'd wanted her home, this evening. He'd been cooking. So that was *one* good thing to come of this present, dangerous mess. Two good things, in fact, as Kacey was helping him. Kacey the steady girlfriend. Both the cooking and the girlfriend had been features of the hacienda for the past few months. The food was surprisingly good, and the girlfriend surprisingly smart and agreeable. Reese had known her for some time, apparently, but merely as a friend. She'd been interested (of course) but he'd been too preoccupied with the chase to bother about the possession. Now, chasing girls in crowded, popular nightclubs had become somewhat hazardous for the President's only child. Security forbade it, for the most part. And so, stuck at home, he'd sat still long enough to discover his buddy Kacey.

Katia shook her head, smiling faintly, and took another sip. She didn't even want to *think* about how closely that entire behavioural pattern fitted her own, at his age. It was uncanny. And more than a little worrying. Maybe Kacey would be a feature long enough to iron him out a little. Kacey had blonde hair, worn shortish, but with style. The inspiration, she freely admitted, was Commander Kresnov of the CDF. She positively *gushed* about Sandy. How brave, and how courageous, to have overcome the odds of her creation, and become something special. Somehow Katia doubted that Sandy would appreciate being regarded like a handicapped child who'd only recently learned to walk . . . but then, as she'd said, appreciation of any kind beat the hell out of the alternative.

She was pleased Sandy was okay. Truly relieved, when she admitted to the plaintive demands of her conscience, during weaker, quieter moments like this. Of course, Sandy being Sandy, it was always unwise to bet against her. But then, as Ibrahim had reminded her on several occasions, even Sandy was not immortal.

Well, it had worked. Ben Grey and the other rats in the State Department had been flushed out. *That* was sad, too, for she'd long considered Grey to be a friend, whatever his various inadequacies. But then, her sources had also told her that he'd long been dabbling in corners with people he shouldn't have been dabbling with, and so it was really no surprise when Ibrahim had come to her, one fine morning six months ago, with evidence of an FIA mole somewhere in the State Department.

To try anything big, in undermining Callay's security and helping the Fifth Fleet's designs, they would need to penetrate Callayan defences, Ibrahim had told her. Once, that would not have been difficult. Now, there was the CDF . . . which although showing signs of promise, was not yet an effective institution from top to bottom, and relied heavily upon the input of its senior officers, Commander Kresnov in particular. Remove her, and you opened a gaping hole.

Katia took another, longer sip, waiting for the pleasant, warming numbness to take effect. It had been taking longer and longer, of late. Too many drinks, Reese warned her. Alcoholic presidents were common enough, but damned, he'd said, if he was going to tolerate an alcoholic mother. Well damn him too. It was all going to be over soon, one way or the other . . . or this little, dramatic phase would be, anyhow. Then she'd revert to green tea. But not yet.

They *should* have warned Sandy. Even now, her conscience demanded so. Ibrahim had agreed . . . in principle. But where information to Sandy was concerned, there was now the matter of Ari Ruben . . . who had a knack for finding out *everything*, eventually. And without whose steady input of additional clues, Ibrahim would never have been able to suspect the State Department mole in the first place. Ruben had too many friends in the wrong places—precisely what made him so valuable to the CSA. But also precisely why they couldn't warn Sandy. The trap would have a better chance of success, Ibrahim had stated, if she and Ruben were ignorant. He hadn't liked it either. But where Shan Ibrahim was entirely, consistently reliable, it was in doing what he thought was in the best interests of Callayan security.

No one had known about the killswitch. That had been Ruben's discovery alone. Had she known . . . Katia shook her head, and took another, longer sip. Lightning sped across the horizon, forking and spreading like a blanket of blue fire, then gone. Had she known just how much danger the bait would then be in . . . maybe she wouldn't have let it all go ahead. It was only politics, after all. She could have closed down the State Department anytime, technically. But the political ramifications within the left of her own party, to lose one of its shining lights so ignominiously and without proof, to say nothing of the upset to ongoing State Department negotiations with various other Federation worlds . . .

It could have destabilised everything she'd been working for, these last two hectic, frightening years. So she'd lied to Sandy, and to Major Rice, in that last meeting at the State Department. Put on a good performance, pretending to be angry, pretending she hadn't known anything about the State Department mole, nor her own culpability in using its desperation to remove Sandy, to give her the excuse she needed to shut the whole thing down. Flush the entire State Department, if necessary, and all connected to it. And if she'd tried that, without party room backing . . . God. Her own wonderful, loyal, praiseworthy colleagues would have torn her to pieces. She'd needed proof. And Sudasarno, bless his honest, naive heart, had been innocently played right along with the rest of them.

Probably Sandy would discover the truth eventually. Indeed, with Ari Ruben sharing her bed, she'd bet on it. She'd answer those questions when the time came. Right now, she needed her world's sharpest, most lethal weapon entirely focused upon the job at hand. Take the stations. Truthfully, she hadn't been as concerned at the plan as she'd let on at the last meeting either. Sandy was right—there was very little choice, if Callay, and more broadly, the Federation were to become what they had all toiled in the hope of making it become. But she'd wanted to confront her senior military leader with all her darkest fears and doubts, and see that look in her eyes. That look of unerring, certain confidence. Sandy was no "yes man." She never had been, and she never would be. That look in her eyes would help the President sleep tonight, her belly full of her son's experimental cooking, and hopefully no nasty side effects from either, the following morning.

It was a long way to come, for a small world upon the periphery of Federation politics. And for a technocrat president previously more interested in communications law reform than transforming her world into the epicentre of human power in all the universe. One way or another, Callay and its president were about to come of age. She just hoped that the cost, for either, would not prove too great a price to bear.

## CHAPTER 15

"**L**ooks like they're really leaving," said the scan tech, gazing at his screen. Captain Verjee observed over the scan tech's shoulder, lips pursed. A distrustful frown creased one eyebrow as his experienced eyes followed the two dots on the nav screen, automatically translating the two-dimensional graphics into three-dimensional time and space. Callay, its five small moons, a remarkably civilised G-4 sun, twelve outerlying worlds and countless system settlements and intersystem traffic. A busy system, but nothing compared to Earth. The traffic within the Jovian system alone was heavier than the Callayan system in entirety. Although once Callay became the Federation's capital world, God forbid, that might change.

"*Pearl River* and *Kutch* are both Chandaram-class," Verjee replied. "That's some of the most mobile firepower in the Fleet, and I don't trust two-hour-old V-signatures for a second. Keep an eye on them, let me know the moment they finally jump."

"Yessir," said the scan tech.

And where could they be going, Verjee wondered as he straightened and surveyed the Nehru Station bridge. He knew Captain Marakova too well to easily believe she'd abandon her old friend Reichardt . . . not without at least chewing his ear off in an attempt to change his orders. There had been any number of opportunities to send for help with departing freighters. Probably he should contact Captain Rusdihardjo about it—Admiral Rusdihardjo, he corrected himself—except that she doubtless knew already, and had been watching developments on board the *Euphrates*. God only knew what she'd been doing in there the last Callayan week since Duong had been killed. Hardly anyone had seen her, save the constant stream of staff from Secretary General Benale's new station office—which had been established directly opposite the *Euphrates* Berth Four, unsurprisingly enough.

Verjee wished she'd let someone else in on the party. He hated station bridge duty, but ever since they'd been forced to lock up the uncooperative stationmaster and his bridge crew, Fifth Fleet crew had been forced to substitute with their own staff. And from the bridge of his own ship, he would be that much better positioned to keep an eye on that traitorous fool Reichardt, whose warship and crew were far too impressive to be left unwatched for any period of time, and whose actions were notoriously unpredictable.

Verjee's eyes flicked to a dock monitor screen, across which Reichardt and his small marine contingent had walked a minute ago, on their way to a captains' meeting in the rooms upon the other side of bridge-section. The meeting, ostensibly, was to begin discussions on the partial transfer of station command back to the Callayan authorities. And it was about time that the Third Fleet had finally started to realise the operational reality. The Fifth needed to resume Nehru and the other three main trade stations to at least fifty percent of their previous efficiency, both in order to free up their own personnel, and to make some kind of reduction in the size of the growing queue of freighter traffic that clustered now in high polar orbit, awaiting an increasingly rare station-slot. With the troublesome dockworker unions smashed, their ringleaders either imprisoned or otherwise disposed of, there wasn't an awful lot of traffic moving through any of the stations right now. With Reichardt signalling that the Third Fleet representatives were finally ceasing their ideological obstinacy, the chances looked good that the Callayan administration would recognise the hopelessness of their situation, and begin discussions on separating Fleet Command from the new Callayan Grand Council.

With their fledgling military hopelessly outgunned and without any space capability to speak of, their influence with the Grand Council limited, Fleet HQ unwilling to oppose the Fifth's actions, and their economy losing billions each day from lost trade, it didn't appear that the Callayans had any choice in the matter. Ultimately, one day, these soft, pampered civilians would realise that it was those with the most firepower who decided the course of history. The Fleet remained unrivalled. And Earth, thank God, controlled the Fleet. God willing, it always would.

A signal light flashed above the bridge's main security door. Verjee saw one of the marines on guard signal to him, and walked over, down the central aisle of chairs before multigraphical display screens. The first blast door opened, then closed behind him. Then the outer door, with a massive hiss of hydraulics. Reichardt was waiting in the metal hall beyond, lightly armoured and with a sidearm at his hip. It was less armour than Fifth Fleet personnel were wont to wear about the docks these days—snipers had accounted for five soldiers so far, one of them an officer, although none of the injuries were serious. Despite repeated sweeps, and extensive interrogation of suspects, they still hadn't found all the culprits. Soft Callayan civvies or not, they were proving remarkably stubborn once aroused, and reports indicated the other three stations were no better.

"Captain," said Verjee, with a nod. Reichardt returned it. Sometimes there were salutes, between captains of equal rank. And some-times not. Now, it hardly seemed appropriate. "What can I do for you?"

"Stop being an arrogant puss-head and change your mind."

Verjee smiled, tiredly. Glanced about at the fully armoured marines guarding the bridge doors. Reichardt's own small contingent from *Mekong* waited several metres down the corridor, fronted by Lieutenant Nadaja. Nadaja was known by reputation from several major battles during the war. Her broad, African face was neither attractive nor expres-sive. Verjee had seen bulkheads that radiated greater warmth. The marines too wore light armour, with breastplates and webbing, but no faceplates or powerpacks. That too was defiance—it openly differenti-ated Third Fleet from Fifth before all the station's people. The Third Fleet had nothing to fear from Callayan locals, it meant. And thus con-demned them, in the eyes of many captains of the Fifth, as traitors.

"Change my mind about what, Captain?" Verjee replied finally, glancing wearily up at him. Reichardt was too damn tall to be a Fleet carrier captain. God knew how he fit into his command chair, let alone through the numerous smaller hatches. He was also a sandy-haired, coarse-mannered, undisciplined, arrogant American with an appall-ingly irritating Texan accent. Verjee could not help but respect Reichardt's formidable combat record. But the man clearly didn't like him, and he saw no point in bothering to conceal his own opinions.

"You know."

"You know, William, I really don't." Verjee shrugged, expansively. "There's nothing left to discuss. It's over. The Fleet will get its way. As if there was ever really any doubt."

Reichardt winced slightly as he scratched an itch on his scalp. The man didn't even bother with a helmet. "That's your final position?"

"What are you even doing here?" Verjee said in exasperation. "You've got a meeting down that hall, the others will not leave their ships until you're in the room, I suggest you go there and sit down before someone decides to have you rounded up and put there forcibly."

That was security too—none of the Fifth Fleet captains wanted to be sitting together in a meeting room without Reichardt sitting there first. If he tried something, or had the room rigged somehow with the rebel terrorists he was doubtless in communication with, it would happen to him too.

"I don't suppose that would be you making that decision, would it, Atal?" Reichardt remarked wryly.

"Captain," Verjee replied, with mock sincerity, "you know I hold you in the highest esteem."

Reichardt smiled at him, grimly. "That's what I thought," he said. And he pulled the sidearm from his holster, and shot Verjee in the head.

The next two rounds went straight through the guard's visorplate at point-blank range. It shattered in a spray of blood, the armoured body collapsing with a crash as Nadaja's fire took down the second. Alarms rang, deafeningly, Sergeant Pollard leaping across one body to the access panel as the armoured outer door slid rapidly closed. Reichardt stepped back as Nadaja leaped past, headed for the corridor's opposite end as Twan did the same in the other direction. Pollard fed a card from his portable unit into the access slot and began feeding in code as the outer doors crashed closed. Private Anwar provided cover at his side.

The corridor abruptly rang with the thunder of Nadaja's rifle fire, then screams from further down above the racket of alarms. Then from Twan at the other end, multiple bursts and a grenade that detonated with the familiar sharp crack of an AP round, and more screaming. Pollard stared at his handheld screen, apparently oblivious, watching the patterns and numbers count down. Then, with a hiss, the sirens silenced, and the bridge doors hissed open.

Reichardt pulled a grenade and flattened himself to the side bulkhead. The second door opened, and fire ripped from within, hammering the corridor wall even as Anwar fired a rifle grenade through the gap, fading left before the fire could reach him. An explosion tore the bridge even as an answering grenade hit the corridor wall,

Reichardt, Pollard and Anwar ducked and covered as the explosion blew them sideways and peppered their armour. Reichardt recovered and on reflex threw his own around the corner. It detonated with a heavier, concussive thud, followed by a lot of white smoke. Anwar charged in, Pollard following, visors in place and rifles blazing with sharp, precise bursts, spreading chaos before them.

Reichardt followed, immediately aware that Nadaja and Twan were planting their mines and falling back at speed. Wincing through the blinding smoke, Reichardt went straight to the inner hatch access, not even bothering to raise his pistol or make out targets as Pollard and Anwar's rifle fire continued. He found the access panel and began punching in his own, new code, as more explosions and rifle fire erupted from the corridor outside. Nadaja burst in as the first doors began to close.

"Twan's dead," she said, and covered the doors as they whined closed once more. Within the bridge, firing had stopped. Someone was gurgling and moaning horribly, somewhere within that choking white smoke. The doors thudded closed, sealing them in. A single shot from somewhere along the central aisle, and the moaning stopped. That would be Anwar, Reichardt reckoned. Twan was his friend.

Reichardt strode down the central aisle, wincing through the smoke as he stepped over more bodies. Found the central docking post, hauled a body from the chair and dumped it aside, then called up specific berths upon the main screen—Berths Twelve and Seventeen. *Mekong*, and the recently docked freighter *Jennifer*, and deactivated the control overrides that kept the main hatches locked. Then he called up Berth Two, where *Amazon* was docked, and Berth Four, which was *Euphrates*. And began shutting down all air, water and other umbilical systems, and locking the docking jaws into place. At the neighbouring com post, incoming lights blinked furiously. A loud, negative beep emitted from the blast door access, as someone outside fed in the wrong code.

"Better work," murmured Pollard at his side, meaning the door. The smoke was beginning to clear now, fans humming in the ceiling corners.

"League code," Reichardt replied as he worked. "Embedded into the subroutines for emergency overrides two years ago. Kresnov said she wrote it herself."

"Better work," said Pollard. And Reichardt knew exactly what he meant.

When the *Jennifer's* hatchway opened, Vanessa led the way. Fully armoured and environment-sealed, she didn't feel the deep chill of the passage, nor smell the distinctive, metallic tang of dockside air that she recalled from her first off-world trip, when she'd been a little girl. Tac-net was not yet established, and she didn't have a feed from the bridge, but there was no time to waste. She burst from the main access and found herself on the elevated entrance platform upon the docks, with vast, curving expanses of steel stretching away to either side. And, true to their word, friendly dockworkers had stacked numerous shipping crates about the entrance for cover.

It didn't stop the two patrolling marines directly opposite from firing, and she dove in a crashing roll down the steps as shots hit the station wall behind. At dock level she came to her feet with a grenade in hand, primed for impact fuse and lobbed over the sheltering crates . . . she half spun about one corner, predicting the fast run for cover, and nailed one marine with a vicious volley that sent torn armour spinning and shattered the shopfront windows against the far wall. That marine fell, the grenade exploded, and the next Callayan trooper— Cal-T, the newly christened abbreviation was—nailed the second as the blast knocked him over.

And then they were pouring out onto the docks, a clatter of armoured footsteps and terse, sharp commands upon local tac-net . . . the uplink signal arrived from station bridge, and Vanessa patched her suitcom into the local station network. Tac-net established itself with a torrential inflow of information, rapidly building a 3-D picture across her visor even as she ran across the docks to cover on the far wall where she could get a good look along the neighbouring berths. The station alarms were blaring, warning people to get off the docks, but the massive section seals were yet to descend from the ceiling to divide the station into pressurised segments. Rapid movement would assist the attackers and hurt the defenders.

Tac-net then linked the feed from *Mekong* through the bridge, and suddenly she could see the entire, doughnut shaped station, the positions of all the ships, and now the new flood of Third Fleet marines pouring onto the docks from the *Mekong*'s position.

"Watch your spacing!" a sergeant was yelling as Cal-Ts established firing positions about the docking crates, then raced across the open docks toward the inner wall. "Don't bunch up, watch your spacing!" Along the inner wall, the few civilians allowed on the docks during the Fifth Fleet's curfew quickly scurried into doorways. Several spacers were sprinting toward their berths, for the safety of their ships. Well, Vanessa thought as she watched the CDF's first major combat action in its history unfold across the tac-net, at least they had the first element achieved. Surprise. And then she had com with the bridge.

"*Bridge is secure,*" came Reichardt's voice upon the command channel. "*I reckon you've got twenty minutes until they get the equipment up and cut through these doors.*"

"We'll be there," Vanessa replied. "I'm not getting a feed on station systems yet, what can you tell me?"

"*We're still accessing it . . . we've got just four people here to run bridge systems and none of us are experts. Section seals we can't guarantee, nor the other emergency overrides, a lot of them are activated by local emergency systems in case of fire, decompression or GBS. But if you move quick, we reckon we can get you where you need to go.*"

"Speed's our plan, Captain," said Vanessa, as soldiers clattered past her, headed into dockside doors and through the passages beyond. All were on tac-net, and saw what she saw, but tac-net only knew what was fed into it, and those sources were always less than perfect. A shot cracked past from somewhere up the curving slope ahead—and was returned instantly, rounds zipping just under the low overhead, striking on a down-angle amidst a cluster of shipping crates and transport flatbeds. "Give us a fix on the other captains as soon as you can if any of them are off their ships, and keep an eye on *Corona*. We'd like to get Takawashi too, if we can."

*"Just take the damn station first, Major, then we'll worry about the details."*

Still the Cal-Ts came, in pairs at several points across the dock, supported by sporadic covering fire. Tac-net showed squads forming up within the corridors, then moving out in tight, coordinated formations. Just like Sandy had trained them. Vanessa gritted her teeth and stayed low in the cover of her window. Her own squad were well back in the departure order from *Jennifer*, and tactical doctrine said that effective second-in-command could *not* lead the main formations into the station's guts, however determined she'd been to lead them out, for morale alone. In the corridors, pointmen were always first to hit the GBS, as Reichardt had put it—marine slang for General Bad Shit. CDF majors were not, she'd had it forcibly explained to her, expendable.

Upon that thought, tac-net highlighted a particular red dot coming across the docks, and she turned her head to watch a tall, loping suit of armour come to a crashing halt beside one doorway, covering as his squad went through behind. Then General Krishnaswali followed his troops in at speed. Some damn argument *that* had been. But if second- and third-in-command were going in, there was no way in hell anyone was going to be able to tell the General that he had to watch it all from an armchair in Tanusha.

As for the acting third-in-command, who had so valiantly delegated her command position to Vanessa . . . well, Vanessa reckoned she ought to be making a move right about . . . now.

The shipping crate's seal exploded outward as Sandy and Rhian's armoured feet hit it simultaneously. Cold air flooded in, or at least the armour suit sensors said it did, and Sandy rolled quickly from her cramped containment and swung a rifle about the edge and down. Two young men stood frozen in the below-docks gloom, staring first at the quarter-ton side of metal that had boomed to the decking before them, and then at the mean, visored figure levelling a rifle at their heads.

"Commander?" one of them said, recovering faster than his friend. A tall, broad young man in his late teens. "Hafez Bhargouti. My friend, Simon." With a gesture to his companion. Sandy rolled from the crate and thudded neatly to the ground two metres below. Rhian did similar, facing the other way.

This portion of the lower-decks cargo space was a long conveyor of overhead grapples, holding crates suspended along a gloomy passage of bulkheads, exposed pipes and internals. It was chillingly cold. Beyond Hafez and Simon loomed the huge scanner paddles, four metres tall on either side of the conveyor, peering into the contents of every container as it passed. Unmanned for now, its marine contingent fled topside now that the shooting had broken out.

"Where are they?" Sandy asked, rifle levelled past the two young men.

"There's a guard," said Hafez, eyes more urgent than scared. He couldn't have been more than sixteen, Sandy reassessed, despite his size. But immediately she was impressed. Given the reputation of his father—Mohummed Bhargouti, leader of the Nehru Station dock-workers' revolt and unseen since the Fleet had thrown him and most of the station crew into confinement—that was hardly surprising. "One section across, you'll run into him if don't know where."

"Stay between us," Sandy told him, "someone might come to check out that noise." She edged past and advanced at a walk, rifle levelled. Her suit uplinks found the local network nodes, and locked in . . . tac-net unfolded in a rush, the assault shown well under way, CDF thrusts penetrating rapidly into the station bowels, headed for the captured bridge, the rail transit system, key local control nodes to secure life support and other systems in their sector, and into the station's main three-arm, the only way up to secure the station hub, and thus the powerplant.

In fact, it all looked extremely familiar. *Mekong*'s troops were out on the docks too, five berths down from *Jennifer*. Defensively, that entire section of docks was solid. But Nehru Station was the central hub for the Fifth Fleet occupation, and currently docked two carriers and four other, smaller contingent warships. Maybe 1050 Fleet marines, plus a hundred spacer personnel who might fight, if they couldn't make it back to their ships. CDF stealth shuttles had docked with the *Jennifer* three days ago, on approach from a far-side trajectory and unnoticed by Fleet vessels, which were more worried about potential Third Fleet reinforcements than CDF launches from the ground. Let alone CDF launches from Deccan, the third continent, upon the far side of the planet from Tanusha. *Jennifer*'s captain had not been happy at the forced conversion to the CDF's trojan horse, but it *was* a Callayan registered vessel, and if its owners wanted to keep their licence (and not get thrown in prison for obstructing Callayan security) they were strongly advised not to protest. *Jennifer* had held 245 of the CDF's best troops, crammed into its various holds. *Mekong* provided another 300. The numbers were not on their side. But as she'd always told those under her command—it wasn't what you had, it was what you did with it. And what help you got along the way.

Hafez directed them past where the conveyor rail doglegged toward main storage. They ducked under suspended, unmoving containers, then edged quickly through a narrow serviceway alongside massive fuel pipes that ran to the berth umbilicals from the station's own storage tanks. There was no gunfire or general activity to be heard above the whine of generators and section pumps, a familiar, industrial white noise that permeated everything, like the dim fluorescent light. From the worn state of their heavy jackets, boots and dockworker overalls, Sandy reckoned Hafez and Simon were familiar enough with the environment. Some station kids grew up in orbit above planets they'd never even visited, nor wanted to. These two looked like dock rats through and through.

Sandy followed Hafez's directions up a service ladder, along a cramped walkway above the fuel pipes, avoiding turnoffs and crawl-ways that tac-net told her would serve, but Hafez insisted were rigged with Fleet sensor gear the dockers had somehow noticed without detection. Then they ducked into a cramped metal engineering space that Sandy was sure would have smelled of lubricant grease and bad ventilation, if such things could have penetrated her faceplate. Under more pipes, then, and into a crawlway, within the mouth of which waited another teenager—a girl this time—looking pale and scared, to assure them that the coast was clear.

Crawling in armour through a cramped metal crawlway with a weapon in hand was not an easy thing to do silently, even for a GI. Sandy knew, as she concentrated on that task, precisely why her guides were all children. Most of their parents were either locked up, or missing, having refused to work under Fifth Fleet control, even when threatened at gunpoint. Some, reliable reports from inside had indi-cated, had been beaten. Or worse, many feared, in attempts to root out the remaining rebels, who were hiding in the dark, cramped places like this, places that engineers and dock rats knew well, but suits and top-siders rarely ventured. Although many of the suits hadn't fared much better, and were even protecting and assisting the rebels . . . or were rebels themselves. Indeed, word was that relations between topsiders and dock rats had never been so good, two disparate, mutually dis-dainful cultures united by a common threat. And if that wasn't a good metaphor for much of Callay at this moment, Sandy reckoned, then she didn't know what was.

A narrow service well climbed up to dock level. Sandy pushed the manhole aside and found herself in yet another engineering space in a narrow access corridor. She climbed swiftly out, murmured "Stay here," to Hafez and Simon, and stalked down the corridor to a main hatch. Tac-net told her that it opened into the rear of a dockside restaurant, of all places. She opened it, weapon ready, and surveyed a gleaming, stainless steel kitchen that looked far too clean and unused for any such establishment she'd frequented in her spacer days. Business couldn't have been good lately.

She ducked out, swept it quickly, then did a fast visual out the doorway at the restaurant beyond. It was deserted, tables arrayed in an orderly fashion before broad windows that looked onto the docks. And now, for the first time, she could hear the clear, staccato crackle of gunfire. Could tell the type, range and direction of fire just by the sound. Tac-net showed her some of the dots, where friendly forces, and sensors, had a read on the opposition, here in front of the *Euphrates'* berth. A lot, she knew, would not appear on tac-net. But she'd fought Fleet marines for the majority of her life. She knew their patterns, defensive or offensive. Knew how they thought, how they operated, how they talked, moved and reacted. She knew their weak points. And she knew their greatest fears . . . mostly because they were also her own.

She turned back, and found Rhian waiting patiently against the kitchen wall, and the two kids nearby. Hafez seemed eager to see what lay outside. Simon seemed eager to be elsewhere. Obviously the junior of this pairing, he appeared to have come along mostly to cover his friend's back—it would have been very dangerous to move alone, as one pair of eyes barely covered half of all there was to see. She could only admire the bravery.

"You two," she told them, "turn about, and get as far away from here as possible."

"But we want to help!" Hafez protested.

"If you stay here, you'll get killed. I can nearly guarantee it." The visored stare and stern, metallic tone must have done the trick, because Hafez seemed to reconsider. Simon tugged at his arm. "And thank you," she added as they departed.

Tac-net indicated a light, defensive formation about Berth Four, but offered little information on Berth Two, having no sensors or IFV, as regular tac-net users called it—Integrated Field of View. Sandy got down on her hands and knees, and crawled out along the restaurant floor between the tables, Rhian following. Once at the windows, Sandy leaned against the corner potplant, and extended the helmet eyepiece out, to peer above the lower window rim. More light cover about defensive positions, many shipping crates and other vehicles positioned for cover about the gantries and elevated hatchway.

Tac-net took milliseconds to analyse the image, and then a new set of red dots arrayed themselves across that section of the dockside. Anyone on tac-net now knew that someone had IFV on Berth Two. Most of the two Third Fleet carriers' marine complement had been outwardly deployed, manning all the station posts the local station workers had refused to fill. Now, the reserve rotation had also deployed, following the initial alarm. The defences that remained were easily strong enough to guard open docks against regular assault. But GIs were a different question.

"Twelve immediate points of fire," Sandy observed in a low voice. "Thirty total. I've got the right, you go straight and clear out."

Their own, private subchannel sorted the details, a rush of data that illuminated primary and secondary targets, fields of fire, projected trajectories, fire-shadows and multilayered kill zones. This, more than anything, was what GIs were designed for. Open combat, multiple targets, fast motion. Corridors were a leveller, and gave smart opponents a good chance . . . or better, against regs. Out here, with surprise and fire support on their side, even twenty-to-one odds weren't bad.

At some other time, in some other mood, Sandy might have felt that some intimate, personal gesture to Rhian might have been in order. Now, as they prepared weapons and double-checked armscomp interface, it barely occurred to her. They'd done this before. The future did not exist. There was only the present, and nothing else mattered.

"G-squad," Sandy announced on directional com as she and Rhian traded places so Sandy could cover the more distant right flank, "request status on fire support."

*"Any time you're ready, Snowcat,"* came Lieutenant Bjornssen's reply. Already there was limited fire engagement with *Euphrates'* perimeter, lots of noise and heads being kept down. Smoke grenades sprewed a thick, white wall between opposing forces, giving Fifth Fleet troopers some cover.

"Ready in three, two, one, go."

She and Rhian leaped, and exploded through the window in a simultaneous rush. Reflex pulled her rifle's muzzle toward preestablished targets behind cover off to her right, a rapid volley of six bursts as bodies more than a hundred metres distant toppled in near unison, high-velocity rounds punching through faceplates that were the only parts of the *Amazon* marines visible. Sandy ran on an arc out from Rhian's right, aware of Rhian's fire upon the *Euphrates'* positions toward which they ran, aware of explosions amidst those positions as Cal-Ts shot grenades into their positions. There was very little return fire. Startled *Amazon* marines tried, and were killed as soon as they entered Sandy's line of fire. She pumped a couple of grenades into choice locations to flush out the cover, then simply stopped forty metres from the Berth Four cover positions, confident of her back as Rhian dove in amongst the smoke and chaos behind, gaining a better field of fire across the entire docks, up along the possible points of cover along the upward-curving inner wall.

She walked backwards, calmly dropping another two marines through the smoke and confusion, then a third who poked his head around a doorway another fifty metres up the inner wall, only to get it blown off. The precision was automatic, a simple matter of identify the target, match her laser-sight onto the target, and pull the trigger. That process took barely a tenth of a second, and remaining *Amazon* marines were now wisely keeping out of sight. Behind her, tac-net was rapidly erasing the last *Euphrates* marines from its display.

Grenades started flying from amidst the carnage of Berth Two as she reached a flatbed, positioned as cover, and ducked behind into a low, running crouch toward the hatch rampway. Rhian took cover behind the main ramp as explosions tore the defensive perimeter— *Amazon* marines evidently loath to fire directly into their mates' positions lest any were still alive. Rhian snapped fire at a couple of targets that dared show themselves, then pumped two grenades back on a lower trajectory, as Sandy hurdled the raised railing, and rolled into the open main hatchway.

"Inner hatch is closed," she announced on a direct comline to the bridge. Shots cracked off the hatch's metal rim, then an explosion tore the deck to hell and showered her with fragments. Sandy barely blinked, wiring her suit's unit into the hatch access and trusting Rhian to make sure nothing came too close. The hatch before her was tightly sealed—it shouldn't have been, if Reichardt had full control of bridge systems. Except that Fleet captains were known to be paranoid about security, and could have overriden it earlier.

"*Sorry, can't help you,*" came Reichardt's reply. In the background, Sandy could dimly hear the buzzing howl of industrial cutters, doubtless trying to break through the bridge doors. "*We've got it all wide open. If it don't work, it ain't my fault.*"

"Hang on," Sandy remarked, redundantly, as her suit wired in . . . and suddenly she could see the software pattern unfolding upon her inner-visual. It looked recently familiar, and sure enough, after a rapid sorting through various Federation-specific security patterns, she found something of Ari's that matched, and the door hummed open. She disconnected and moved aside with the door, rifle about the edge to search for targets without exposing herself, but saw nothing.

Tac-net showed Bjornssen's squad now advanced close along the outer wall, well positioned to hold off any advance from *Amazon*'s surviving marines upon their rear. Rhian came without having to be told, a quick leap into the open hatchway, and together they ran through the narrow passage and into the cold chill of the umbilical tube. Around the bend, and there was the carrier's scarred chilled metal hatch, closed and undefended. On this side, at least. Doubtless by now all aboard would know, from *Amazon's* marines, that two GIs were at the hatch. Luckily, disconnecting the umbilical was controlled by station bridge . . . and full armour was as good as a spacesuit anyhow.

Rhian took up position partway along the tube, with a good line of fire past the curve, covering the way they'd come. Sandy set about removing the shaped charges from her armour webbing, now shredded in places from that last grenade blast, but she hadn't lost any. The palm-sized disks fitted in a roughly circular arrangement about the rectangular door's centre, exploiting a relative structural weakness that only a person who'd spent much of her life concerned with such matters might be aware of. Tac-net showed no advance upon the docks outside, *Amazon* marines still pinned down by Bjornssen's fire.

Rhian retreated to join Sandy, and they put their armoured backs against the hull to the hatch's side. Sandy connected the final uplink to the charges' triggers, and extended a fist to Rhian. Rhian tapped it with her own. Not much of a gesture, for all their years together, and everything they'd shared. But, in the life they'd been granted, it was all they could afford. Sandy charged the triggers, the hatch exploded in a blast that tore much of the umbilical tube to shreds and open space, and the two GIs charged in through the flames, debris, and the howl of escaping air.

"Did they get past the doors?" Captain Rusdihardjo demanded from her command chair, staring at her screens. The *Euphrates* bridge was in pandemonium, com stations attempting desperately to contact marine units through nonresponsive channels, long and short range scan posts scrambling to cover skimmer traffic and out-system movement respectively, and now engineering yelling that the main hatch was gone, and they'd had a forward decompression, now contained.

*"I don't know, Captain!"* came the shout over com. *"I'm not getting anything from forward posts!"*

"Find out!" the captain demanded.

"Captain," said Chipelli from helm, "if those were GIs, it had to be Kresnov and maybe one other!"

"So what?" Rusdihardjo snapped, calling up the internal emergency frequency. "Lieutenant Yin, why aren't you responding? We have a forward intruder alert."

*"Captain, this is Private Khazan, fourth platoon."* Breathless and frightened. *"I can't contact Lieutenant Yin, he was forward of third head arranging a defensive excursion, and now I can't find him . . ."*

"Private, calm down. Who's my senior marine?"

*"That'd be me, Captain,"* came a new voice, that her screen identified as Sergeant Raphael. *"I'm headed up from armoury, I'll try and get you some . . ."*

Yells and gunfire erupted from an unidentified location, then an explosion. Internal tac-net lost a source, then two more, in the blink of an eye. More shouts, Sergeant Raphael shouting terse commands, as the clear realisation spread that they had intruders aboard. Rusdihardjo looked up, and met Chipelli's stare. Chipelli looked pale. Rusdihardjo felt her own gut tighten involuntarily.

"It's just two intruders!" she snapped furiously. "We'll deal with them!"

Chipelli nodded, hastily, and turned attention back to his screens. GIs on deck. Dark Star GIs. Regs were one thing. Dark Star, another entirely. There were nightmare stories, tales Fleet spacers and marines spun to keep each other awake on off-shifts. Of ghost ships found drifting and not a soul left on board, save the marks of a forceful docking, bullet holes in the walls, desperate barricades erected in haste, and bloodstains on the decking.

Reichardt had done this, Rusdihardjo thought, with a fury that defied description. He'd better hope he won. Because if he didn't, and Fifth Fleet got their hands on him, each and every one of them would desire a little piece for a personal trophy.

A priority signal was coming in from *Amazon*, and she flicked it open. *"Admiral, this is Lieutenant-Commander Tupo."* Only off-decks called her Admiral. On decks, there was nothing ranked higher than a captain. Rusdihardjo was old fashioned about such things. *"Request your status."*

"Two intruders," she replied. "We're dealing with them. Tupo, we are firing up engines. We might need to break dock and bring weapons to bear on Third Fleet vessels."

*"Admiral, Fleet engagement protocol prohibit firing upon vessels at dock with inhabited facilities . . ."*

"I know the regulations!" Rusdihardjo retorted. "Prepare to break dock! That's an order!"

*"Aye, Admiral."*

Rusdihardjo leaned back in her well-worn command chair, and stared at her screens. The other stations had reported back, and none were under assault. This action appeared to be focused entirely upon Nehru Station, as the centre of Fifth Fleet occupation strategy. Third Fleet vessels, heavily outnumbered, remained docked safely at station, where regulations prohibited them from being fired upon. But the Fifth Fleet retained control of space, and retained numerical superiority upon the docks. CDF soldiers might pass muster for planetary security forces, but they were no match for Fleet marines in their familiar environs. No, if she played to her strengths, and forced the opposition to play to their weaknesses, the result was not in doubt. She needed serious firepower in open space, away from station, to cover the approaches. And then she'd . . .

"Captain!" yelled the chief scan tech from across the bridge. "It's *Pearl River* and *Kutch*! They're coming back!"

*"I have two down!"* Lieutenant Bhavan was saying with commendable calm, voice only raised to be heard above the racket of weapons fire and explosions in the background. *"There's at least five marines holding sections*

*B-4 through to B and C-7, heavy electro-mag fire plus I lost Cao to a limpet mine. Gold squad five tells me they've cut the escapes at E-4 through 9, I'd like to try flanking left but I need cover topside."*

"Okay," Vanessa replied, utterly absorbed in her tac-net display, "Lieutenant Levkin, topside manoeuvre, get to level three, catch and hold, then manoeuvre on the mark."

*"Copy, Major,"* came Levkin's reply, and tac-net showed a rush of dots along schematic corridors to respond. Vanessa zoomed out, graphical vision darting along corridors, changing angles as Cal-Ts manoeuvred, fired, and countermanoeuvred through the enclosed, tight spaces of Nehru Station. It wasn't as fast as she'd have liked—Fifth Fleet marines had been spread out from one side of the station to the other. Here, concentrated about Blue sector, attacking forces had enjoyed both surprise and numerical advantages, and Reichardt had been making reinforcement from elsewhere difficult by locking strategic hatchways and section seals from the bridge. But Fifth Fleet marines fought hard and well, and her guys were taking casualties. If they didn't reach the bridge soon, Reichardt and his team were dead, and the attackers would lose their major strategic advantage.

She knelt in a level one corridor, back to the wall and weapon buttdown on the decking. The bodies of two Fifth Fleet marines lay sprawled across the cross-corridors alongside, armour holed and seeping blood. The body of one of her own troops had been removed to a more secure location. Vanessa barely noticed any of it. She was more accustomed to small scale actions, thinking and fighting simultaneously. This was effectively generalship. Movement and engagements happening simultaneously across a broad front, and if she wasn't careful, her brain would overload with the effort to micro-manage every encounter. She kept the tac-net vision broad, trying hard to focus on the broader patterns, and not use the zoom too much.

Twenty metres down the corridor, a door opened and a head peered out . . . Sergeant Major Zago fired a shot past his nose, eliciting a yelp of fear and a panicked retreat. "Stay the fuck inside!" Zago yelled in his wake. "Are you fucking stupid?!" The door hummed shut. "Fucking civilians." His section of four ignored it, braced and covering about the cross-corridors.

"*Major,*" came Reichardt's voice in her ear, "*they just broke through the outer door. I reckon they'll be through in five minutes.*"

"Keep your pants on, Captain," Vanessa told him. "We'll be there." *Amazon,* tac-net showed her, was breaking free of the station, despite the bridge's attempts to leave the docking grapples in place. When a warship wanted to leave, it left, and did a lot of damage to the station in the process. Following Admiral Duong's demise, Lieutenant-Commander Tupo was acting captain on *Amazon.*

"*That Tupo's one unpleasant sonofabitch,*" Reichardt remarked offhandedly, above the howling din of laser cutters in the background. "*I'd truly recommend you kill him before he starts shooting up the station.*"

"Yeah, we're doing that." If the whole ridiculously expensive, secret, troublesome damn system worked, that was. Upon tac-net, Lieutenant Bhavan achieved his objective, and a whole section of Fifth Fleet flank from level one to four began to unwind. Vanessa redirected com in a hurry. "Gold squad four and three, flanking assault! Get around, hold and fix, then manoeuvre in pairs! Go, go, go!"

She gestured to Zago, who waved his squad forward, Vanessa falling fourth in line with Zago and another bringing up the rear. Zago slapped a magnetic sensor into a doorframe corner as they went, to warn tac-net if anyone moved in their wake.

Sergeant Raphael braced one armoured foot against the corridor corner to prevent a slide down the sloping deck. Here at dock, *Euphrates'* crew cylinder was locked stationary, and most habitable areas in transit were now fixed at a crazy angle, or totally upside down. It would not, he knew, prevent a GI from moving through it. Engineering was behind him, and he could not let the intruders in that far.

"Wiki," he said into his helmet mike. "Wiki, what's your situation?" There was no reply from Wikramasinga. "Wiki?" His rifle fixed unerringly along the corridor, floor angled at forty-five degrees, armoured backside supporting his braced stance. Tac-net showed Wikramasinga was still alive. So were his team. They just weren't moving. "Wiki, what the hell . . ."

An explosion tore through the next cross-corridor, smoke spilling downward with gravity, obscuring his vision. Gunfire erupted from above his position, and he stared up to see Reiner, propped at the entrance of his corridor where the deck curved upward even more sharply, blazing away at something unseen. Further up still, two positions abruptly vanished from tac-net amidst yells and shooting.

"Shit," Raphael muttered, shouldering his rifle and grabbing the guide line that ran up the sloping corridor. Between that, and grasping holds upon the inner wall, the armour gave enough power to haul him up the ever-increasing slope. He passed Reiner, whose corridor seemed empty, then transferred his weight to the inner wall ladder rungs, now deployed in dock. Further along, he paused and peered over the rim. Two marines lay sprawled, armour torn and riddled in precise locations. Topside, someone was calling for clarification.

"Shut your yapping and figure it out!" Raphael snarled on the net. "We've got two of 'em loose in here! Engineering is sealed, and they're trying to find a way through! Now, so long as we all cover our positions, and watch each other's backs, they're blocked off, right?" He scrambled to crouch beside the bodies, unslinging his weapon and peering through the drifting smoke. His feet were upon a hatchway that would normally be a door, the ceiling lights on what was now the right "wall." "They're just machines, people! Keep it straight, use your brains, and we'll get these fuckers, they ain't no match for us."

Tac-net showed him the full circumference of this rear portion of *Euphrates'* habitation ring. His guys had it sealed all the way around, a marine covering each corridor, a weapon on each passage. Tac-net showed every doorway, every local system. If something activated without a marine or spacer crew in proximity, it would flash red. Even GIs wouldn't try to get to the bridge—it was amidships, with just one way in or out, easily defensible and currently sealed behind multiple blast doors. From engineering there were accessways to the ship's spine, and back to the engines. There was nothing like a full complement, with most of the ship's marines caught onstation when the attack began . . . but thirty-five would have to do. Or thirty-three, he grimly corrected himself, considering the two bodies before him. Well, the one way to make things easy for any GI was to stay immobile and defensive.

Raphael stepped gingerly over the bodies, careful of the clang of armoured boots upon the corridor wall. Armscomp tracked through the drifting smoke, seeking targets, straining to identify errant sounds above the omnipresent ship white noise. A muffled thump, then, from somewhere above. Then a metallic rattle. Raphael froze, staring upward . . . tac-net showed nothing.

"KD, is that you?"

"*Sorry, Sarge. Dropped my mag.*"

"Well, watch where the hell you . . ." A burst thundered, directly above. A clatter behind, and Raphael spun in time to see an armoured body fall past the corridor's end, then a crashing tumble as the body skidded down the curving slope toward neutral gravity below. Raphael ran toward the far end, grasped the edge, glancing first down, then up, rifle ready and braced. The main access corridor was an empty, vertical drop, curving gradually out of sight. Raphael stared, rifle braced upwards one-handed, the other steadying against the corridor rim. Could a GI run up the damn vertical surface like a . . . like a bug?

More firing echoed further around the rim. Tac-net identified the source as Corporal Vass, firing blind.

"Vassy, you see something?"

"*I . . . I dunno, Sarge . . .*" The fear in her voice made Raphael's skin crawl, his heart suddenly galloping in sympathy. "*I thought so . . . I'm just gonna . . . gonna take a look . . .*" Raphael crouched upon the lip of that vertical drop, licking dry lips. With KD dead, the corridor above him was unguarded. Obviously one GI was in there, planning its next move. Damn it, he had to go up there. Couldn't just sit here and wait for the attack, in an empty corridor with no one to guard his back . . .

"Vassy?" he pressed, trying to keep the wobble from his voice. He was a Fleet marine sergeant with ten years of combat service. He bench pressed three-twenty kilos augmented, was tape-trained to eighth-dan wing chun style kung fu, and bore the tattoos and rings to prove it. When he walked into dockside bars on leave, civvies stopped talking and made way. He didn't need this shit. "Vassy, are you there?"

No reply. The fear was plainly audible on tac-net now. You could hear it in the silence.

"*Sarge,*" someone said then, "*KD's not dead. Hit him straight in the sweet spot, knocked him cold.*" Full kit helmets had a spot on the forehead that would stop just about anything . . . but give your skull a right rattle. Everyone knew it.

"*Goddamn it,*" someone muttered. "*They're playing with us.*"

Fuck it, Raphael thought, shouldered his rifle and flung himself onto the inner wall ladder. If someone appeared above or below with a rifle, he knew there was nothing he could do . . . but ascending one-handed with rifle ready wasn't going to deter any GI, you simply couldn't out-shoot them, and he preferred the speed two hands afforded. Nearing the corridor above, he slowed, and unslung the rifle. Activated an eyepiece, which separated from the helmet to peer above the corridor rim. The corridor seemed empty.

Raphael hauled himself up, rifle ready, and crept forward. A shuddering vibration seemed to pass through the corridor wall beneath his feet . . . a station shudder, he reckoned, not from the ship itself. God only knew what was happening out there—it was beyond his tac-net parameters. He stepped over a doorway, scanning for any sign of a discarded cartridge, some sign of where that last shot had been fired from, and how they were moving around . . .

There was a sound from above and he swung the rifle upwards, only to have it snatched cleanly from his hands, and thrown away with a clatter. And then there was an armoured face directly before his own visor, suspended upside down, hanging by its knees from the open hatchway above. Raphael dimly realised that the hatchway hadn't been open a second before. It must have been opened silently, somehow. A stupid, demeaning way to die. Except, the second thought occurred to him, that if this was a GI, it was taking its sweet time about killing him.

The visor portion of the faceplate hissed open, eyepieces unhinging to reveal a pair of incongruously pretty, pale blue eyes, upside down and regarding him with an expression that was difficult to read. Spacers might have found it easier, maybe. Marine or not, Raphael preferred his feet to know which way the floor was, and for facial composition to make familiar sense. The GI had only a pistol in hand, her rifle clipped to her back. The pistol hovered unwaveringly at Raphael's throat, beneath the chinstrap. Above the collar seal, there was no armour at all.

"I'm sorry about the two down there," the GI said, her calm voice muffled beneath the faceplate. "They surprised me. I don't take Fleet marines lightly." Raphael just stared at her. His mike would hear anything he said. He could call for help. She could shoot him, just as easily. Worse, she'd shoot anyone who answered. He remained silent. "I'm Kresnov. The experimental one."

Her eyes seemed to be seeking some kind of comprehension. Still Raphael said nothing.

"It was pretty easy to get this far," she continued. "If you had anything like a decent complement here, you'd have a chance. As things stand, it's just a matter of time. You guys have done some real nasty things to the local dockworkers the last few weeks. I don't mind killing you all if I have to. But given another option, I'll take it."

Surrender? No *Euphrates* marine had ever surrendered. Numerous times, they could have. Several times Raphael recalled personally, either trapped, ambushed or otherwise overwhelmed, fighting against terrifying odds. He'd survived then, when many others hadn't. And he had the scars to prove that, too.

"What are you even doing here?" the GI continued. There was a faintly incredulous note to her voice. "This is Callay. Your capital. The Federation capital. This insignia here on my shoulder? That says Callayan Defence Force. This is what I do—defend Callay. So how the hell did we come to this?" The eyes hardened, with cool determination. Penetrating. "I came to the Federation to get away from the League. I came 'cause I didn't want to fight you guys any more. I started thinking you were the good guys. So by all the stoned, crazy prophets, man, what the fuck are you doing here?"

# CHAPTER 16

**P**lans to hold in reserve only lasted until Fifth Fleet, who'd bypassed Third Fleet barricades from *Mekong*, began a counterassault through the lower cargo bays that quickly had Blue Squad falling back in strategic withdrawal. That exposed Red Squad flank, halting their advance about the lower, dock side of the bridge defences. At which Vanessa drew herself and Command Squad out of reserve, sprinted along a length of engineering accessway above the breakthrough, and thanks to a coordination of Blue Squad defences and some very snappy Intel overlaid upon tac-net by Lieutenant Singh, simply fell upon them from above.

It was the last thing an experienced *Amazon* marine platoon, in full pursuit of a rapidly retreating and obviously inferior opponent, had expected. Command Squad troops fell from the cargo-conveyor space's ceiling, crashing down amidst a thunder of exploding grenades and rifle fire. Vanessa dropped from an overhead walkway, past a suspended shipping container and into the erupting smoke and confusion of multiple grenade blasts. She hit and rolled with a power-assisted crash, shooting past decking pipes at shadowy shapes that fell, staggered, tried to adjust in the confusion that fell upon them from above.

She shot one marine point blank as he tried to get up, ducked as something hit the bulkhead, spun as a marine alongside tried to tackle her but staggered in a spray of blood that spattered her visor. She spun beneath the leg supports that held several massive pipes suspended, and shot another marine at point blank range in a thunderous burst that sent him crashing off the bulkhead. Fast motion erupted to her left and she restrained fire with difficulty, a Cal-T taking cover and firing, tac-net warning her just in time . . . a shot cracked off her chest armour and she dove for the cover of a bulkhead . . . and found a marine crouched there amongst the smoke.

He fired, she sprung aside and forward, slamming her weapon against his and driving a forearm under his chin to slam the head back . . . he countergrasped and slammed her into the wall. Vanessa dropped the rifle entirely to reverse grips on the arm at lightning speed, then something massive exploded and she was spinning, crashing to the decking. The armour must have shielded her from the worst of it because she barely even blacked out, recovering in a rush of enhanced adrenaline, hand grasping for a secured secondary weapon as she came up to a crouch . . . a Cal-T was staggering, missing an arm and screaming. Flames exploded in hellish orange from a ruptured pipe, engulfing a suspended container, burning the walls. Shots ripped past, and she rolled beneath the piping, feeling it shudder . . . her recent combatant was there, somehow, stunned and slowly recovering. Vanessa shoved her pistol under the chinstrap and blew his brains all over the visor.

Saw her rifle nearby in the midst of fire, and suddenly several Cal-Ts were at the nearest bulkhead, firing ahead in a hail of tracer, then ducking back as grenades exploded. Tac-net didn't make any sense now, Vanessa rolled into the dissipating smoke, recovered her rifle, rolled back under the pipes and began running along beneath in a low crouch that only someone of her stature could have managed. Ahead to the left were two marines covering behind abandoned cargo, facing the wrong way. She hit one with her second-last grenade, sending him flying and the other apparently scattering in several directions at once—the first was hit by a storm of fire from up ahead before she could fire again, armour shredding, broken pieces of ceramic and flesh spattering the walls at all angles.

And then the formerly retreating Blue Squad were hurdling the bodies and racing past her, withholding fire as they plunged through Command Squad and onward, yelling furious, howling obscenities that would have made an ancient Viking warrior's blood run cold. Vanessa rolled out from under the pipes, and was abruptly confronted by Lieutenant Arvid Singh, visor smoke-stained and armour battle-scarred, asking if she were okay. Then exclaiming something at her in Hindi that she missed entirely before running off in pursuit of his blood-lusting mob. She took a moment to blink at that surreal image. Her little Arvid, from old, long-disbanded SWAT Four. The practical jokester, the irresponsible, fun loving, cheerful one, who had somehow blossomed when the CDF was formed, and had become—to her and Sandy's mutual agreement and astonishment—one of the CDF's best squad commanders. The universe was crazy.

And wondered again that she could ponder such things, with bodies all about and flames gushing from a ruptured fuel line, like a small sun attempting birth within the station's bowels. Fading now as the emergency cutoffs engaged, and she strode forward to recollect her troops and her breath. The one missing the arm was Enrique, now mercifully unconscious and pumped full of suit drugs and IV to keep her blood pressure up, attended to by several others. Dravid and Habie were also wounded, though less seriously. Wong was dead, as was Poloski. As, she discovered, was her old friend Zago, the only loss from her personal Command Section of five plus herself. She wanted to take time to look at the body, but couldn't, there were commands to issue, people to organise, a broader tactical scenario to plug herself back into. Control to be reassumed. Private Deitrich seemed to think differently, so Vanessa grabbed her by both shoulders, and stared the young, tear-streaked private in the eyes.

"Hey!" Vanessa got her attention. "Fight now. Cry later." And gave the young woman a smack on the helmet as she departed, other Cal-Ts fanning ahead to scout the stairwells back up to dock-level. Tac-net, she realised, was informing her that *Amazon* had broken dock, taking a large number of docking grapples with it. She narrowed her com band to tactical com, relayed back to Callay via *Jennifer* and *Mekong*. "*Amazon's* out," she said as she walked, ducking beneath the dwindling blaze from the ruptured fuel pipe, stepping past bullet-riddled bodies, bulkheads and shipping containers. "Do you have the fix?"

The reply took a few seconds to come back. Then, "*Copy, Tac-two, we have the fix.*"

"Take that stupid fucker out of my sky."

"Engineering!" Captain Rusdihardjo was yelling at her com now, in blind fury. "I want a reply! How the hell have we lost power!"

At the bridge engineering post, an ensign was poring helplessly over his screens, double- and triple-checking every indicator. "There's no reply, Captain!" he shouted back, desperately. "I'm not getting anything! I have to think the spinal feed's been cut!"

Sergeant Raphael was not responding. None of the remaining marine contingent were. Spacers tucked into duty stations were unwilling to venture into the corridors. Familiar ship odours were now flavoured by something new. Fear.

"Mid-ships," she commanded into her com, "I want a detail to go and check on that spinal feed! I want engines back on line, and I want them now!" She was utterly unwilling to countenance the possibility that her grand warship, veteran of so many battles against the League, had been crippled at dock by a boarding party of two . . . all her intel had insisted that the CDF was nothing *like* this capable. The Fifth had subdued the station population, Callayan Parliament had finally begun to cool in their frenzied denunciations, Secretary General Benale had been slowly growing an ear-to-ear smile at all his briefings . . . things had been slipping into place. Soon, word was to have come from Earth, and additional ambassadors, to assess the latest situation. Third Fleet, and Captain Reichardt, had seemed increasingly resigned to circumstances. Where had it all gone wrong?

"Mid-ships!" she yelled into com.

*"Captain,"* a crackling voice came back, *"we're not reading real clearly, I think the com's been damaged. Could you repeat the last instruction?"*

Rusdihardjo nearly exploded with rage. In all her military career, she'd *never* had her crew pull that old trick. It was Fleet-versus-Fleet. They'd assured the lower ranks that it would never come to fighting. The lower ranks had followed on that trusting assurance. But they'd been on board. They'd believed in the cause. Marines had been picking fights all over station, and sometimes even on Callay, with those who disagreed. Now was no time to be changing minds, with so much at stake.

She stared at the tactical display, separate to station-side tac-net— *Amazon* was now pulling away from the station, joined by the cruiser *Berlin*, with *Tehran* and *San Diego* making fast preparations to follow. Inbound at fractional-V, *Pearl River* and *Kutch* were well away from Callay's gravitational strictures, free to manoeuvre and reposition rapidly with jump-fields giving capabilities far beyond simple propulsion. Sitting at station, content in their numerical superiority, no one had considered the possibility that the two Third Fleet warships would turn around to surf the gravity slope back toward station orbit. Outerlying picket vessels would not realise *Pearl River* and *Kutch* had moved for another half hour at soonest, as the light wave reached them. And the light wave from both vessels was itself forty minutes late. Tactical was rapidly calculating a likely approach vector along the probability cone, attempting a guesstimate of the ships' true location. It was possible that they'd already fired. At fractional-light velocities, any warship hit by so much as a deep-space pebble was in serious trouble.

Even as she considered the situation, she could hear Lieutenant Commander Tupo issuing an ultimatum to *Mekong*, ordering unconditional surrender. *Mekong* gave no reply. A separate channel opened on com, parallel to the highest command channel, and she opened it. The channel unfolded from bridge com, transmitting to every Fifth Fleet ship.

"*Captain Rusdihardjo,*" said a vaguely familiar female voice in her ear. "*This is Commander Kresnov of the Callayan Defence Force. CDF forces have control of the station bridge. I have personally disabled your ship's engines. Your vessels have lost the strategic high ground. Any further hostile action on their part will ensure their destruction. On behalf of the people of Callay and the free Federation, I demand that you cease your unprovoked hostility toward my world and my people.*"

Rusdihardjo's hands grasped so tightly upon her chair restraints that she nearly buckled metal alloy. "Get off my ship, you mechanical bitch!" she hissed.

"*This reply is not acceptable,*" Kresnov said calmly. "*You underestimated this world, Captain, as you've underestimated the will of the entire Federation. I'll give you one last chance to save the lives of your people.*"

"Get the fuck off this channel!"

"*Wrong answer.*" The connection ceased.

"Priority!" yelled com. "Two marks, intercept trajectory . . . !" Rusdihardjo's screen lit with multilayered graphics, plotting an emerging course on a direct line toward *Amazon* . . .

"Oh by the Prophet . . ." Rusdihardjo murmured as her eyes followed the trajectory trail back to its origin.

"It came from the planet!" yelled Tactical. "Northern continent, grid reference 144 by 381!"

From out in the vast Callayan wild, there came multiple strike-missiles, accelerating at forces that could only mean a modern reaction drive, for a projectile that size and mass. But they'd tracked all imported materials and systems to Callay for years! There was no way they'd imported such a sophisticated weapons system directly under watchful Federal Intelligence eyes. Unless . . . unless they'd built one themselves? Equally impossible—from Callay's neophyte armament industry status to cutting edge in two years? It just couldn't be . . .

*Amazon* applied main engines too late, a silent roar of bone-crushing power that surely smashed any unsecured bodies to pulp and drove breath from the lungs at close to ten-Gs . . . both missiles struck before the pilot could rotate to bring defensive armaments into line. *Amazon* disappeared in a huge, pyrotechnic flash, nav-signal fracturing in a million directions, close-zoom visual blanking out completely . . .

*"The planet is live!"* someone was shouting on com. *"They've got it rigged, that trajectory was directly across station orbits! We're going to have to assume the entire orbital access is covered . . ."*

Should have scanned, Rusdihardjo thought dazedly. Should have scanned from orbit. The construction activity should have been visible, if nothing else. It had not even crossed anyone's mind that Callay could build such systems so quickly. Two years to prepare for this moment, and no one had thought to check. With two serious warships on high-V approach, they needed to get vessels undocked and burning for out-bound velocity to meet the threat. But anyone who undocked was a target . . . defensive systems could counter some planetary assaults, but doing so forced evasive manoeuvres that would throw outbound burns wildly off-course. They were trapped.

Vanessa strode the corridor outside the bridge, stepping carefully to avoid bodies, bits of torn metal from walls, ceiling or armour plate, and discarded equipment. The thick smoke made it difficult to see—life support on this level had broken down, and much of the lighting was out from shrapnel or bullet strikes. They'd passed CDF wounded on the way up, being evacuated to emergency medical teams in safe zones on lower decks. Now, she stood aside as the same was done for several Fifth Fleet wounded. The dead remained where they'd fallen, mostly marines, but including another three Cal-Ts. The tally was nineteen so far. Sometimes she hated tac-net's precision.

The smoke was flowing into the bridge through the damaged blast doors, a sure sign that the bridge's separate life support systems remained functional. Vanessa strode in past Third Fleet marine guards with *Mekong* clearly emblazoned upon their shoulder armour, and found Captain Reichardt supervising bridge posts filled with temporary crew, a mix of his own marines and partially qualified Cal-Ts, watching the systems. To one side, bodies were piled in a grisly tangle of arms and legs, clearing walking space the only way possible. There was blood all over the deck, spattered upon chairs and control panels among bullet and shrapnel holes.

"Show me," she said to Reichardt, coming to stand at his side as a *Mekong* marine stood respectfully aside. Reichardt pointed to the display, manned by another marine sans-helmet . . . damaged bridge systems and inexperienced bridge crew meant that some readings were not uplinking to tac-net as they ought.

Vanessa flipped up her visor, and peered at the station display. It showed the broad station wheel, with a particular focus upon the central hub. The station reactor glowed multiple shades of red and orange. Coolant flows were tracked up and down the station arms, technical grapics to one side indicated a range of temperature and magnetic readings that would surely make more sense to a fusion technician . . . except that some of them were flashing red, and displayed alongside other numbers that appeared to indicate the optimum reading. The figures did not match, and the mis-match appeared to be increasing.

"How long?" she asked Reichardt.

"Twenty-eight minutes before it goes critical," Reichardt replied grimly. "I think it's a marine Lieutenant Colonel named Bhatt."

Vanessa winced, trying to recall that particular briefing. "What's he like?"

"Arsehole," Reichardt replied, predictably. "He's not responding. We thought he might be around here . . ." pointing to another part of the station, ". . . over in red sector, supervising the station maintenance schedules after all the mech-shop folks refused to keep working. Well, now we reckon he took an elevator up the arm and commandeered the reactor. The elevators are all sabotaged, we've got one of our teams headed up the three-arm, but your guys in the two-arm are closest."

Vanessa nodded, and opened her link. "General? Captain Reichardt estimates twenty-eight minutes before we lose the reactor."

"*I copy that, Major,*" came Krishnaswali's reply. He sounded faintly out of breath, the rhythmic thudding of footsteps in the background, as if he were moving at speed. "*We're nearly halfway up to judge from the gravity, we're receiving sporadic small arms fire from the top, firing straight down the arm.*" A loud, unmistakable thud. "*Grenades too. We are laying suppressing fire where possible, but we've already taken two wounded and will undoubtedly take more as we get closer.*"

"We could do a vacuum assault," Reichardt said in a low voice to Vanessa's side, off-net and not audible to Krishnaswali. "Undock a ship, we'd just make the deadline."

"Too much risk and not enough time," Vanessa replied, momentarily off-net. And reconnected. "General, the containment mechanisms on that reactor ensure it won't go thermonuclear no matter what they do to it. A failure is survivable. If you feel the casualties aren't worth it, best that you back off—we're in the process of gaining control of the space lanes, we can evac all station personnel off on ships or escape pods before the emergency batteries drain and we lose life support."

"*Major,*" Krishnaswali replied with a note of familiar, stern reprimand even past the exertion, "*this reactor will take months to replace or repair. I will not allow some fanatical fool to put this planet's primary trading station out of action for that period. A damaged economy will cripple everything the government is attempting to achieve vis-à-vis reforming the Federation. I assure you it shall not happen.*"

He disconnected. Vanessa restrained a low mutter. And looked up at Reichardt—a long way up for her, even in armour. His lean, angular face was deadpan, almost nonchalant. As if he'd barely noticed the dried blood from a cut upon his jaw, nor the surrounding carnage, nor the acrid smell in his nostrils. Sandy had described some of the station actions during the war to her. Descriptions that gave some insight into the mindset of Fleet soldiers of any insignia. Reichardt had seen worse than this. They all had. Reichardt seemed to be more than just acting calm. He was calm. Combat-reflex, it seemed, was not exclusive to GIs.

"Damn fool's determined to get himself killed," Vanessa said darkly.

"Cut him some slack," Reichardt remarked. "Can't be easy taking orders from a major. He's got his hero moment, let him take it."

"Officers getting themselves killed is one thing," she retorted. "Getting my troops killed is another. If he's got a problem with taking my orders, he should have spent more time building his combat competency instead of his management style. He didn't *have* to come along, I told him that."

"I bet you did. Can he do this?" Nodding to the screen.

Vanessa exhaled hard. And gave a sharp shrug, mostly hidden within the armour. "Shit, I don't know. Maybe. That's Spec-Lieutenant Mutande up the three-arm?"

"Yep. One of my best."

"Well, let's make sure they keep talking." It was amazing how calm she felt, considering everything that had just happened. Colours were sharp, smells distinct, sounds crisp and immediate. The whole thing felt curiously out-of-body. Somehow, she was not particularly self-aware—not of her body, her various aches and pains, her fears or concerns. There was just the situation, broad, varied and fast-moving . . . and somehow, in an utterly impersonal manner, that situation included herself.

She saw something else upon a neighbouring screen, and frowned at it. "*Corona's* still here. Any idea why?"

"A lot of people weren't on their ships when the GBS went down. I don't think Takawashi was. I've no idea about your buddy Jane."

"It's a damn wonder they didn't leave days ago . . ." as she linked to another specific channel. "Sandy? Captain Reichardt thinks maybe Takawashi wasn't on *Corona* at zero-hour. If he's stuck somewhere in the fighting, there might be a chance we can grab him. Maybe Jane too."

*"For God's sake don't let anyone try and take Jane,"* came the familiar reply in her ear. *"If she goes looking for him, she's mine."*

On the tac-net, one particular dot on board *Euphrates* began moving, its constant companion staying close to its side.

"That's personal, I take it?" Reichardt remarked to Vanessa.

"Could say."

"Well I hope she makes it. I'm gonna need some people to write to me in my prison cell when this is over."

Vanessa snorted. "I'll send you a cake with a GI inside."

"Will she jump out naked and dance for me?"

"Could be arranged."

"Well now, that'd be dandy."

Sandy took off running down the dock from Berth Four, headed down-spin toward *Amazon's* abandoned Berth Two. Rhian followed close behind, leaving the stricken *Euphrates'* main access guarded by an advance perimeter-defence squad of *Mekong* marines, plus a CDF AMAPS that had waddled into position behind a cargo flatbed, twin rotary cannon arms scanning the docks for any sign of trouble. Warning lights flashed, lighting the broad, metallic expanse with strobing red, and a klaxon echoed from the overhead. Smoke drifted lightly in some places, remnants from exchanges of fire, though it seemed nothing combustible had ignited upon the docks.

Sandy and Rhian ran past the bodies of fallen *Amazon* marines in front of Berth Two, hugging the outer wall and weaving amidst the available cover of the containers. Tac-net showed a promising picture, immediate strategic objectives achieved and perimeters established. Now it was the Fifth Fleet marines forced to regroup from their initial, scattered locations, and figure their next plan of attack. Now that *Mekong* marines had reached the engineering bays that had been reconfigured for use as mass detention cells, that was going to be a whole lot more difficult.

Reports indicated hundreds of very angry Nehru Station dockworkers moving quickly to help establish defensive barricades with welding and electrical jury-rigs. Some top-side women were setting themselves as human shields, linking arms across hallways and daring marines to shoot their way through. Dockworkers had infuriated Fifth Fleet marines enough lately that they might be tempted. But white collar, urbane Callayan femininity was something else entirely. A visual Sandy had accessed from a nearby Cal-T showed a line of elegant saris and other gowns, dark hair in crimps and braids, and a lot of flashing jewellery. She hadn't recognised what they'd been chanting, but the name of Gandhi-ji had been mentioned, unsurprisingly . . . although the problem now seemed to be that they were threatening to blockade *all* combatants, be they Callayan, Third or Fifth Fleet. Well, fine, she thought as she ran in pounding, armoured steps along the deckplates—just so long as no one breached those lines.

The dock ahead seemed clear of soldiers or civilians as they passed Berth One and headed for Berth Thirty. *Corona* was at Berth Twenty-five, just beyond the lowest point of the ceiling horizon ahead.

"Cap," Rhian remarked, "*I don't understand those women. Don't they want the station back?*"

"Not by force they don't." Sandy pulled in beside the raised platform beside the Berth Thirty docks, angling for a good fire position and wary of blindspots ahead behind the space-wall gantries. Heavy pipes wrapped around the massive brace reinforcements, anchoring one end of the docking grapples outside. Rhian raced past, headed for the next available cover—a wall-mounted hose that plunged through the decking. No warships here meant no conveniently arranged containers for cover.

"*That's an ideology, huh.*" Sandy had been trying to explain ideologies to Rhian, on and off. Among other oddities.

"Yes, it is." She hurdled the platform railing, dodged through the security desks and detectors there and jumped the other end, passing Rhian with her weapon ready for surprises. It was a League vessel they were approaching. Jane might not be the only GI they had to worry about. "Remember I told you about Gandhi? He's big on Callay."

"*History again.*"

"Culture, more like. It's the same thing." She kept running until she hit the next major air hose against the wall, and braced.

"*You don't agree with them?*" As Rhian started running.

"Course not."

"*So why tolerate them? We're in charge here.*"

"Right now they're helping as much as anything." As Rhian dashed past, headed for the Berth Twenty-nine platform. "And besides, where would civilisation be if people weren't idealistic?"

"*Even if the ideals are stupid?*"

"Who decides what's stupid?" Rhian skidded into cover, and Sandy took off.

"*Democracy again, huh?*"

"Sure. A conflict of ideals. The stronger ideals win."

"*So everything's a conflict. Doesn't that kind of prove your point?*"

"Now you're getting it."

Across on one of the other stations, the Fifth Fleet cruiser *Stockholm* had pulled free. Already two reaction-warheads had been launched, accelerating all the way. If *Stockholm* didn't manoeuvre real soon, there wasn't going to be a lot left. *Pearl River* and *Kutch* were coming back *fast*, a strike run if ever she'd seen one. The kind of approach that was to FTL space warfare what the high ground had once been to open-ground infantry warfare, before infotech and modern weaponry had rendered mere spatial considerations insignificant. Their new flagship out of action, their old flagship mostly destroyed, the Fifth Fleet were wavering, trapped between the conflicting demands of maintaining station occupation on the one hand, opposing the incoming Third Fleet assault on the other, and avoiding destruction by planet-based missile systems on the third. No military commanders, in Sandy's experience, had three hands.

She raced in behind an abandoned flatbed laden with smaller dock-side cans, peering about the wall-side end as Rhian came sprinting up behind . . .

"Cover!" she announced, fixing upon a sudden appearance from an inner wall hatchway another hundred metres up the curve, directly opposite Berth Twenty-five. Rhian saw immediately what she saw, and kept the flatbed between her approach and the object of Sandy's atten-tion—a squat, bald man in dark glasses and a suit, an automatic weapon in one hand. Not a GI, Sandy reckoned with a visual shift to IR, to judge from the body temperature. Clearly he was covering the approach to Berth Twenty-five. Just as clearly there would be a corre-sponding guard at the outer wall, covering the entry. A quick flash through cybernetic memory files found no visual match for the face.

"If he's League," Rhian said a moment later, having taken cover at the flatbed's opposite end with a good visual on the target, "then I can't find any match. And I updated all my files a week ago."

"How comprehensive are Embassy files?" Sandy asked, keeping her rifle lowered to present the minimum profile. More proof that he wasn't a GI—he hadn't spotted them yet. Or didn't appear to have.

"I'd recognise the face if he were ISO." Rhian was still nominally ISO. At least until the paperwork came through, anyhow. "Or if he were a part of Cognizant's security party—they were all listed. He's not there."

The man ducked back into the hatchway, located between an Indo-nesian restaurant and an entertainment parlour, windowfronts awash with garish neon. Probably he was waiting for someone. From his movements,

Sandy reckoned they were overdue, or he was impatient to be gone, or both. She snap-stored the image, dialed a new connection, and achieved a time-delay on the link back to Tanusha, via satellite relay now that the other stations' coms had been shut down by Fifth Fleet occupiers.

"Intel," she said, "I need an ID on this man." And sent the image with little more than a thought.

"*Hold on, Snowcat,*" came the reply, after several seconds' delay. "*It's not on the available database, let me check . . .*"

"*Sandy,*" came Ari's voice over the top, unsurprisingly, "*that guy's FIA. I don't have a name, just trust me, he's FIA. I got a separate list that's not on the main database. You're opposite Berth Twenty-five?*"

"Yeah. Looks like Takawashi's been talking to Federal Intelligence. That would explain why *Corona*'s still here."

"*Goddamn Fifth Fleet occupation's become a haven for FIA remnants,*" Ari replied after a two-second delay. "*Should have guessed . . . look, this is good shit. Can you get some of these guys alive? If we prove the Fifth was in bed with the same FIA guys who've been fucking us the last few years, we'll be clear.*"

"Jane's my priority, Ari," Sandy replied with mild reprimand. "We can't let her escape."

"*I thought the priority was to retake the station?*" Rhian remarked doubtfully. Which was the first time in memory Rhian had ever questioned her operational tactics. One of these days she'd have to start keeping a diary, to keep track of all these momentous developments.

"Yeah, well I'm reprioritising."

"*Sandy, get this,*" came Vanessa's urgent voice, "*a captured Fifth Fleet marine says Takawashi and several aides were intercepted and detained up on level four in your sector for acting suspiciously. They were put in detention with about forty other civilians in one of the rooms there. We were just reviewing security tape from around Berth Twenty-five, we see Jane and several others leaving* Corona *just a few minutes ago. I think they went to go get him . . . com's been shielded in your sector, it might have taken them this long to figure out where he was.*"

"I don't want Jane rampaging anywhere near some group of civilians," Sandy replied. Tac-net flashed before her vision, a fleeting rush of station schematics, then highlighting the level four lounge in a residential district. "If she gets into a firefight with guards there it could be a bloodbath . . . Rhi, one pair advance, let's go."

She levelled her weapon about the end of the flatbed. Waited several seconds, and then when the FIA man did not appear at his hatchway, set off running. Rhian covered that target, her own rifle tracking left toward Berth Twenty-five . . . another man in a suit was crouched there beside hatchway railings, rifle moving as he spotted them. Sandy shot him in the arm. Another two peered around container rims, and she shot them too, an arm and a leg, without breaking stride. Halfway toward the hatchway, the FIA man appeared ahead with weapon in hand, and Rhian clipped his skull with a rifle round that sparked off the doorframe as he thudded limply backward.

Rhian led in, Sandy covering the docks . . . tac-net showed her Rhian's view of an empty hallway beyond, and she backed her own way in. From there it was a fast, two-person-shooter manoeuvre along the hall, through several hatchways, then into a broader, more decorative administrative area with carpet on the floor and occasional paintings on the walls. They passed offices with doors flung open, tables and chairs overturned within, coffee and half-eaten meals spilled upon the floor. Then up a stairwell, tac-net giving no reading whatsoever on possible enemy activity here, having no eyes nor ears to access, save their own.

Up four floors, then out into another hall. A display upon the wall gave directions . . . it was an exclusive business zone, it seemed, as they passed an open office with transparent dividers and a broad display screen alive with the latest Tanushan news and business stories at loud volume despite the utter lack of audience. A junction then, and what looked like an elevator lobby, with an abandoned service desk and holographic display screens offering a choice of entertainment section, gymnasium or meeting rooms. Graffiti upon the wall opposite spoiled the tranquil order—"Fuck the Fifth," in hasty, black letters.

An explosion, and shooting in reverberating rapid bursts nearby, Sandy and Rhian flattened themselves against available walls. Screams and yells, muffled and of indistinct range, from somewhere ahead. Then a rush of movement, civilians bursting around a corner, suit jackets flying, sprinting to get clear. A woman, feet bare, still clutching her heels as she ran . . . one saw the two armoured figures ahead and might have panicked, except that Sandy yelled at them to come, waving a free arm and pointing them onwards to empty hallways she knew were safer.

They rushed past, Sandy and Rhian unplastering themselves from the walls and gliding forward in a balanced, weapon-braced rush. Another two civilians rushed past, barely seeming to notice them. Another, colliding off the corner and falling in his haste, then scrambling back to his feet and continuing. Sandy braced her back to the corner of the T-junction, Rhian to the opposite side, each peering out to clear each other's blind-spot, each seeing instantly what the other saw. Tac-net showed the way toward the shooting, and so Sandy spun about the corner and dashed, Rhian close behind. Several more fast manoeuvres around corners, a smoke alarm blaring now, corridors turning a wash of red, emergency light.

Then a big, important double-door, shattered off its hinges, decorative wood splintered and blackened across the hallway, still smouldering. Several civilians stood coughing and bewildered in the thick smoke, hands pressing cloths over mouths, one crouching to throw up. Sandy and Rhian pushed through the wrecked doors and found pandemonium—a broad, circular table arrangement within a large room, holographic display suspended from the central ceiling, filled with smoke and sprawled, coughing people . . . at least twenty, Sandy reckoned at first glance.

"Need a medical team here ASAP," she remarked to tac-net,

knowing someone was monitoring her visual and location, and would figure the rest themselves. She and Rhian fanned out in opposite directions around the room . . . against one wall a woman in Muslim headdress had cleared a space and was treating several wounded, tying rags of clothing about bloodied parts, giving directions to frightened helpers. She looked up as Sandy approached, recognition of the CDF insignia dawning past the initial fear at the armoured, visored monster stepping through the smoke.

"I need medical help here fast," the woman said sharply, "this one here has a punctured lung and maybe a kidney, and this one . . ."

"It's coming," Sandy assured her. Unclipped and handed off her emergency medical kit from the front of her armour webbing. Turned and caught as Rhian tossed her own across the room, without needing to be told. "Maybe five minutes, just hold on."

Rhian had already reached the rear doorway, this one apparently kicked open rather than blasted. Sandy hurried to join her, and together they moved into the hallway beyond.

"*Docks are covered,*" came Bjornssen's voice in her ear, and sure enough, tac-net showed his squad now occupying her and Rhian's previous position. No one was going to be running straight across to Berth Twenty-five, then. Even Jane couldn't outdraw a Cal-T with rifle already levelled and finger on the trigger. The carnage in the meeting room hadn't been as bad as it could have been, Sandy found time to reflect as she and Rhian continued moving through hallways, angling for the nearest stairwell. Maybe Jane was learning moderation. Or maybe she'd simply been concerned about hitting Takawashi, and any of his FIA friends in attendance. Concerned? Why would Jane be concerned? A suspicious, gnawing sensation tugged at the back of her mind. The feeling that there was something significant going on here that she was missing.

More shooting then—more muffled than before, apparently from several levels down. She accelerated, risking the next couple of corners before smashing open the stairwell door and skidding down at speed, peering through the narrow gap within the central well to scan below . . . still nothing registered on tac-net, clearly it wasn't any friendlies being engaged. Shooting seemed loudest on level two, and she kicked the steel door off its hinges, peering a telescopic eyepiece around the corner . . . and got it shot off. So she knew she was in the right place, anyhow.

"Jane!" she yelled, pumping the suit mike up several notches for greater amplification. "It's me! Time to give up!"

A grenade thumped, and she ducked back, crouching to a ball as the explosion tore the outer doorframe, showering her armour with fragments.

"Maybe next time with less sarcasm?" Rhian suggested mildly, still three steps up the stairway with that effortless calculation of an AP grenade's effective radius that all close combat vets acquired in time. Sandy mentally set a delay fuse on her next two grenades, then fired both at where tac-net displayed a bare length of wall, one high, one low. Each ricocheted and exploded in turn, without exposing her gun muzzle to Jane's fire . . . amplified hearing made out footsteps and the clatter of an evasive roll, and Sandy spun about the corner, Rhian immediately at her back, covering the opposite direction within the cramped doorway.

"Go," said Sandy, and ran, Rhian running more backwards than sideways, trusting Sandy to deal with Jane. A reply cracked off the corridor wall ahead, then exploded over their heads as both Sandy and Rhian hit the floor. Sandy's rifle never wavered even in falling, and fired at the first sign of Jane's movement, clipping the rifle barrel. The gun muzzle vanished, then rapid footsteps retreated down that corridor. "One pair," Sandy observed, as they rushed back to their feet in unison. "They're splitting up. I've got Jane, you get Takawashi. Don't hurt him."

Rhian dashed off down that cross-corridor, Sandy heading for the next, and Jane's route of departure. Flattened herself to that corner as she arrived, watching Rhian's position dart down the adjoining corridor, and wondering if it were a ploy to get Rhian isolated and deal with her separately . . . except that she'd gone the wrong way, away from the docks, where Rhian had gone toward them, down Takawashi's most obvious route. Trying to lure Sandy away. Which still meant she had to think Takawashi's protection had a chance against Rhian. The bodies of several Fifth Fleet marines were sprawled upon the decking—the evident source of the earlier shooting.

"Watch for traps, Rhi," she remarked as she risked the rifle muzzle around the corner. Armscomp saw nothing, and she moved around in full. "Just get between him and the docks and don't let him past."

"*I have it,*" Rhian replied. There was a tone of mild reprimand in her voice. Meaning that she knew exactly what was going on, and Sandy should know better than to think she didn't. Deep in those regions of the brain that were repressed under combat-reflex it didn't stop her from worrying.

Rather than following Jane down that corridor, Sandy ran on along her present one. Follow-the-leader through tight spaces was tiresome. If Jane wanted to play escape and evasion, she'd let her. It only became an interesting contest when neither player knew exactly where the other was. She snapped a tac-net sensor into a doorframe as she went. It never hurt to have more coverage.

Upon the broader tac-net display, *Stockholm* vanished in a blinding, pyrotechnic display. Either the captain hadn't been able to implement defensive manoeuvres properly, or he'd seriously underestimated Callayan technology. The missiles' reaction-drive manoeuvring/propulsion system not only pinpointed targets less than two-metres diameter, she'd been informed by an eager starship-component-manufacturer-turned-weapons-maker, it actually anticipated the target's evasive patterns according to a new, multispectrumed quantum integrated logic system (QILS, in military parlance), perfect for the kind of over-the-light-horizon warfare found in high-velocity space combat. Fleet could say what it liked about Callay on other matters, Sandy had often reckoned, but when it came to raw technology, Callayans *ruled.* Two years for an untested, cutting-edge, antiwarship, planet-launched missile system? No problem—from blueprint to final, secret testing within eighteen months, in fact. Fleet's main Earth contractors couldn't have done it within three years. That Callay could evidently hadn't occurred to them. But as always, big companies lagged small ones in only knowing what they *did* do, not what they *could.*

She moved fast, down a narrower corridor, then paused to listen before doubling back through a side room, out the far door, and along another passage. Too much thinking did not help. She knew the layout. Jane did too. Each knew the other's capabilities. Manoeuvring was instinctive, like breathing. Too much thought only brought self-doubt. She moved on automatic, letting the lines and angles of the tac-net schematic wash over her. Feeling for the rhythm, for the inspiration of motion, knowing only that Jane was trying to draw her away from Takawashi, and allow him to escape. Why that should be so, she did not have time to fathom . . .

Movement as she rounded a corner, leaping as she fired, return fire thundering past, an explosion of sparks and metallic impacts against the wall behind. Sandy flattened herself to the corner, aware that Jane had ducked back in time to avoid most of her own burst . . . difficult to maintain accurate fire *and* dodge behind a corner simultaneously, lest the weapon hit the wall. Further along, decorative wall panelling tore further under its own weight, ripped by Jane's fire and now hanging across the corridor, exposing cold steel and cabling beneath.

"Takawashi's bodyguards are no match for my friend," Sandy called, double-checking her rifle's mag-charge, naturally cautious of a static-jam. Switched it to her left hand, and undid the strap on her pistol, attached across the chest of her armour webbing. "If you're trying to protect him, you're not doing a real good job out here."

"You've no legal reason to pursue him," came the reply from around the corner. Calm, as always. Doubtless rechecking her own equipment. Sandy pulled a grenade from another pouch, and set the timer with a flick of the soft-tip of her armoured thumb. "He's a League citizen. He hasn't broken your laws."

"You have." Jane was quoting *law* to her? If she'd had the time, and her helmet visor wasn't commanding so much of her attention, she might have shaken her head in disbelief.

"Fine," came Jane's reply. The sound was coming from the open doorway of a room, before an adjoining corridor. Jane would dare not duck around that corner. But tac-net schematics showed a spot on the walls of that room where a structural doorway had been deemed unneeded, and walled over with the same panelling that was hanging loose across from Sandy's position. Jane's schematics were doubtless as thorough. "Try and take me. But leave Renaldo alone."

Renaldo? "That sounds suspiciously like concern for a fellow sentient being," Sandy remarked. "What did he promise you?"

"More than you can."

"Considering I'm offering you a choice between violent death or imprisonment, that's not saying much. The man's a megalomaniac. So sure, maybe he's perfect for you."

"I'm a GI," Jane retorted. For the first time, Sandy thought she could detect the faintest trace of emotion in her voice. "I seek my creator."

"So go to church."

"Be serious," came the mildly scornful retort. "Religion is for the lost. I know who I am."

"You'd be the only one." Sandy stepped far enough forward from the wall to clip the rifle to her back armour. "Creating us doesn't make him worthy of whatever it is you think you're looking for."

"I seek only my own kind. I'd thought perhaps that meant you. Clearly I was mistaken. Renaldo knows me. He respects what I am. Together, we find a commonality of purpose. He treats me as I deserve."

"Hey, bitch—*I* know you. And I know exactly what you deserve." Hands now free of the rifle, she took the pistol in her left hand, the grenade in her right.

"Your analysis lacks precision," Jane replied. "You have become ragged and uneven. A flawed tool. It shall be your downfall."

"Tell it to someone who cares."

"I'll tell it . . ." and broke off as Sandy flipped the grenade about the corner, on a low trajectory, then went high and left-handed with the pistol. Jane shot the grenade in midflight, but was simply not quick enough to target the simultaneously emerging pistol as well—Sandy fired an explosive volley, tearing the rifle from Jane's hands, then charged, holstering the pistol and ripping the rifle from her back in milliseconds, discharging two grenades through the open doorway through which Jane had vanished.

They detonated with a crash, followed by a volley of fire as Jane softened the weak wall panelling, then a crash as she dove through into the adjoining corridor . . . Sandy pulled up short as a second volley whistled through where her head would have been had she stuck it around the corridor corner. She ricocheted a grenade off the wall instead . . . it tore wall panelling rather than bouncing cleanly, so she risked a peek with her rifle muzzle only to snap it back as Jane put a bullet through the grenade launcher, then several more. Then nothing, light footsteps springing up an adjoining corridor, and Sandy dashed in armoured pursuit.

The array of grenade debris told her that Jane must have taken fragments, probably from all blasts . . . she switched hands approaching the next corner, and shoved the rifle butt out instead of the muzzle. Two shots hit it, the burst cut short prematurely as she *heard* the pistol go empty, and stepped around the corner into calm, plain sight, with a swing of the rifle to underarm-level like a cricket batsman stepping up to the crease. Jane was already running, but fast as she was, she was two metres and forty-five hundredths of a second short of the next corner, and wearing no armour.

Sandy fired low, shots striking thighs and calves. Jane hit the decking and rolled hard for cover. Sandy ran after, hearing more shots ahead as Rhian engaged Takawashi's group just short of the docks. Targets appeared on tac-net, only to vanish, panicked yells and Rhian shouting at them to stop or else. She gave the next corner a wide berth, seeing blood on the deck plates . . . and realising that somehow, she'd fired low. She couldn't remember making that conscious decision at all. A single burst between the shoulderblades would have solved everything. But now, the corridor was empty, and the engineering door was forced open. Damn it.

She ducked within, eyes and rifle muzzle darting within the dark metallic space. Two closed hatches along the right wall, and a larger one through a reinforced bulkhead straight in front. Sandy kicked through it with a resounding wham! that proved nothing was hiding on the door's far side. Beyond, a dark, narrow space of low overhead pipes, and the reverberating hum of aircon and station systems. Sandy moved forward at a low crouch, tracking multiple places where a body could hide up ahead, and eyeing the occasional blood spots on the decking that she knew could be deceptive . . .

A grenade flashed to her side, blinding, and Jane was on her barely before the shockwave had finished smashing her into the wall, tearing the rifle from her grasp and sending her flying headfirst into a pipe brace, the visor imploding to shattered white. Her countermove swept arm and leg simultaneously, predicting Jane's counterbrace and switching to a simple, right-fisted punch that sent her crashing backward. Sandy's next blow went straight through the pipe as Jane whipped away and rolling, steam erupting as Sandy ripped the pistol from her webbing.

Jane came up and grabbed it faster than even a high-des GI had a right to, considering the state of her legs . . . Sandy simply let her have it, releasing the pistol and punching her in the face with that hand instead. A straight's head would have smashed like a melon. Jane's snapped back, in that fractional, time-frozen moment, eyes wide in desperate, rapid-time processing as her brain tried to catch up with events. Disbelief, Sandy saw. Shock. Sandy's kick smashed her into the wall, an armoured elbow smash bounced her artificial skull off the pipes, and her overhead hammer-blow drove her straight into the deck . . . where she grabbed Sandy's legs and pulled her feet from under her.

Sandy twisted and kicked on the way down, but only succeeded in imparting greater velocity upon Jane's new dash for a side exit. Sandy stayed long enough to retrieve her pistol, then scrambled after. Down the cramped side passage was a metal ladder descending through a manhole . . . she heard the movement below, grabbed a hold and slid down one handed, the other hand aiming the pistol as she hit the deck below. Fired a shot that clipped Jane's arm as she fled stumbling through yet another side door. Sandy ducked rolling through that one, darting a look both ways past the blur of her shattered visor. Jane was headed dockward in a flashing, strobing wash of red emergency light—jacket flying, legs straining to control the limp as synth-alloy myomer calves and thighs screamed in protest, contracted to steel-density and impact-shocked, and now struggling to loosen for running. Sandy took aim between the shoulder blades, as Jane approached the final corner, and let her have a full ten rounds in a half second.

Jane's head snapped back, hair flying as her body was thrown forward, back muscles erupting to super-hard density under compression, contorting her entire posture. She hit the ground and rolled into the corridor mouth, a straining hand held desperately toward the sign and arrow on the wall, pointing toward Berth Twenty-five. Sandy advanced at a walk that felt no faster than slow motion in knee-deep mud. Jane did not look back, her desperate, wide-eyed stare focused instead up the hallway, toward the docks. Body rigid, arms outstretched, fighting the agonising tension of bullet-strike on unprotected muscle. Arms and legs tried to lock out, fingers straining like claws, teeth bared in an animal snarl.

Then, she began to get up. Like some broken puppet, attempting to rise on its own once the strings had been cut . . . an awkward, staggering motion of stiff legs and precarious balance. Sandy's finger hovered over the trigger. Somehow, she did not fire.

Jane staggered off, limping forward like a wounded automaton, eyes fixed only upon her goal. Further up the hallway, Sandy heard commotion, and Rhian's voice shouting for someone to keep still. A cry of anguish, surely Takawashi's. Then Sandy rounded the corner herself, Jane staggering frantically ahead, making no inconsiderable pace despite the horror of her injuries. Desperation, Sandy realised. Beyond, she saw Takawashi, a gaunt, ghostly figure in a silvery robe. Arms outstretched to Jane, advancing toward her. Rhian behind, several bodyguards crouching nearby with hands wisely on heads, several others sprawled in bloody ruin having failed to do likewise. Rhian was yelling at Takawashi to stop. Takawashi did not seem to hear, eyes only for Jane. Somehow, Sandy could not seem to hear the words.

"JANE!" she yelled. The pistol was not assault-rifle calibre, to which Jane owed her briefly continuing life. But another burst, in the same spot as the last, would surely, finally penetrate. "You surrender now! I don't need another excuse!"

Jane did not stop. Takawashi surely had a weapon under those robes. And besides, the moment had been a long time coming. Sandy fired. Jane lurched, and crashed forward like a falling statue. Takawashi cried out in anguish, trying to run on aged, slippered feet, but managing no more than a rapid, agonised shuffle.

He reached Jane's side as Sandy approached, pistol ready for any sudden movements. Slowly, and with great, shuddering effort, he managed to turn Jane onto her side. There was blood in her mouth, Sandy saw, and she breathed with difficulty. The eyes were stunned, seeking only Takawashi, who knelt at her head and clawed helplessly at her shoulder. One brown, skeletal hand found hers, and clasped. Even in Jane's state, she could have crushed it. Drops of blood stained the shimmering white kimono. Her bloody lips struggled to move.

"I . . . I'm sorry," she breathed to him. "I failed you." Sandy unclipped the helmet faceplate with one hand. The breather came away, then the shattered eyepieces lifted. Cold air filled her lungs, tinged with acrid smoke.

"No!" Takawashi had tears in his eyes. A gnarled hand stroked at Jane's cold, pale face. He smiled through the moisture. "You were magnificent! You nearly matched your sister, despite all her advantage of years. There is no shame, my dear. No shame at all." A thumb and forefinger pulled Jane's eyelids apart, peering at her irises. "You have exceeded my wildest expectations."

"She's better than me," Jane murmured. Takawashi felt for the back of her torn, bloody jacket, fingers seeking the location of the holes. "You told me. I didn't want to believe it. But she is."

"Now, now, what did I tell you? We all learn our greatest lessons from our failures, not our successes. Your problem is that you have been *too* perfect! You never failed, and so you never learned."

Further down the hall, Rhian had approached. Watching curiously, her expression invisible behind the helmet's visored mask. The three suited guards crouched against the wall might have been hopeful, with her back turned . . . except that somehow, Rhian's left hand kept the rifle levelled dead-straight, even behind her.

None dared move.

"I would have liked to have seen Ryssa," Jane managed to breath. "I've never . . . belonged. It would have been . . . nice to belong. With you."

"Come come, my girl," Takawashi retorted, a new, firm purpose restoring itself over his emotions. "I won't have defeatism, do you hear me? Come on, we're going to get up. Up, do you hear? You're not finished yet, I command you to rise!"

He struggled to his feet, grasping helplessly at her arm. Jane tried. Sandy stood, and stared, watching her try. Feeling . . . numb. It was hope. Plain, desperate hope. And it was the last thing she'd wanted to see. Takawashi waved desperately to his cowering guards, as Jane tried to get a knee beneath her, and then a foot. The guards exchanged nervous, sweating glances.

"Come on, come on you fools!" Takawashi snarled, straining breathlessly. "They're honourable soldiers! They won't hurt you!"

"*Cap?*" Rhian questioned by uplink as the guards slowly rose, keeping their hands in plain sight. Sandy didn't reply, watching Jane's attempts, dumbly. The guards edged cautiously past Rhian, her rifle tracking them all the while, then ran to Takawashi's side. Together, they lifted Jane. When half-upright, they linked hands beneath her for a seat, and lifted. "Cap?" Rhian repeated, audibly this time.

Takawashi turned to face Sandy. The guards carrying Jane waited, casting anxious glances back at her, now. Her eyes met Takawashi's, his gaze brimming with emotion. Noting her blank expression, and the lowered pistol, with tearful expectation. And he smiled at her, thankfully. As if this, in all the universe, was the greatest gift she could possibly grant him. She knew, past the numbness, that she didn't like it. It opposed everything she believed in, all that she stood for and admired. But, for the first time, she understood completely. God help her.

Takawashi put a hand upon one guard's shoulder, and they moved off, holding Jane suspended between them. Takawashi shuffled along behind, hovering like an anxious father, as if to be sure she did not fall. They passed Rhian, who stood, and watched the unlikely grouping in disbelief. Then she turned, and walked toward Sandy. Popped her own faceplate, to display the curious frown upon her face.

"Cap? You okay?"

"I'm okay." As she watched the little group retreating up the hallway, toward Berth Twenty-five, and *Corona*, and a long trip home.

"Didn't we, like, want to ask them some questions, at least?"

"Takawashi wouldn't talk," Sandy murmured. "He's a League VIP, he'd just sit tight until we had to let him go."

"And Jane?" With great expectation. "She looked like she might survive." As if the prospect were notably disappointing.

Sandy shrugged. And let out a long, tired sigh. "Jane's going home, Rhi. She's going home."

CHAPTER 17

The one nice thing about the summer, Sandy reflected as she paddled, was that there wasn't much wind.

To be sure, summer meant heat and humidity (she was informed, barely noticing such things herself), a profusion of biting insects (ditto), lots of rain, lightning strikes, and more than the usual numbers of crazy, mystical types running naked down streets proclaiming to be emperors of long-lost alien civilisations. But no wind meant no "afternoon rubble," as the locals called it—the surf collapsing from its still, morning perfection as the wind came up later in the day. So summertime, all surfers knew, meant great waves.

The next set rose before her, clear and sparkling in the midday glare, and even the curling, rising face seemed to be carved from blue, polished marble. She dug in her strokes, and accelerated her board comfortably over the lip, then over and down the next two in turn. To her right, a young grommet she knew to be named Pradan went hurtling down a wave with a howl of delight, skinny brown limbs in perfect balance, long, matted hair flying out behind. She smiled to herself and continued, toward where Rami, his cameraman and his producer were getting set up with their little support boat.

"Ready yet?" she asked as she paddled alongside.

"Uh, sure . . ." said her favourite Tanushan TV personality. "Just about." He looked a little nervous, with the inflatable rising and falling beneath him, with each passing swell. Although the water was much deeper out this far, just beyond the sudden rise in the seabed that brought each wave to its towering crest. And utterly smooth, save for the swell, the water gleaming a deep, luminescent shade of green. Rami's cameraman climbed onto his longboard with evident expertise, then reached as the producer handed over the camera, encased in a waterproof, black casing.

"How deep's the water here again?" Rami wanted to know, sitting on the inflatable's edge in his blue wetsuit. Only a small man, and quite unfamiliar with any body of water outside his bathtub, as he'd put it. But as handsome in real life as on a monitor, Sandy had been pleased to discover. And as pleasant.

"Far too deep, Rami," said his producer. She was a cheerful, red-haired woman with freckles—and a hat, shades and lots of sunscreen. An automated camera mount monitored the whole scene from the inflatable's bow, presumably for later screening of the most amusing bits. "It's such a long way down, you can't even see the bottom."

"Crawling with flatrays and razors," his cameraman added, sighting his lense upon Sandy and adjusting.

"Don't you mess with me, Angus!" Rami snapped, breaking into one of his familiar personas. "I'm the most powerful man in Callayan showbusiness! I tell you I have every flesh-eating carnivore swimming along this entire beach front *on contract*!" Snapping a closed fist against his palm. "Now I command this water to part! Part before me, ungrateful liquid substance, or you'll never work on my show again!"

He jumped in feet first, and proceeded to make a great show of floundering and splashing like a clown until finally reaching his long-board, dragging himself on board like a half-drowned animal, and collapsing.

"You're now wondering if this was such a great idea, aren't you?" the producer suggested to Sandy, who was seated upright on her board and grinning.

"You know," Sandy commented, "when you lie face down on the board like that—from below, to a razor, you look just like a floater squid. They eat floater squid."

Rami scrambled to sit upright in such a hurry he fell off, and spent another thirty seconds floundering and gasping, appealing to numerous Hindu gods that regular viewers would know he regularly lampooned—not always wise, as a Muslim Indian, but Tanushans were fairly sanguine about such things, and Rami was so inoffensive, and so egalitarian in his targets (frequently including himself) that he always got away with it.

Several minutes later, with Rami precariously balanced upon his longboard, and the cameraman and producer indicating all in readiness, the interview began.

"Now first of all," Rami began, "let me just say that I'm . . . incredibly honoured that of all the thousands of pathetic little media parasites that have been chasing after you for the past two years, hiding in bathrooms, bursting out of your closet in the dead of night, trying to grab an interview with the Federation's most famous artificial person . . . you chose me." With a hand on his chest, smiling disarmingly. "May I have the pleasure of knowing why?"

"You're the most powerful man in Callayan showbusiness," Sandy replied.

Rami laughed. "Well, yes of course . . . but seriously?"

"Well . . ." Sandy wiped a strand of wet hair from her brow, trying not to feel too self-conscious, with the camera focused unerringly upon her face. Her natural, familiar blonde hair, now that she'd had the dye removed. She did not, she was pleased to realise, feel particularly nervous. Nerves were not a natural part of her psychological state, under any circumstance. "For one thing, I was instructed by the powers that be to do just one interview . . ."

"Just to get everyone off your back?"

"Off the CDF's back, I guess. And, you know . . ." she shrugged, ". . . there's such a thing as public accountability."

"You'd be the only Callayan official who believed that."

"I'm still gullible enough to believe it, maybe," Sandy replied with a smile. "And I chose you because I knew I wouldn't like any of the usual stuffy, formal interviews. I knew you'd give me something different." She gestured to the ocean about them, and the waves breaking upon the sandy beach beyond. "And I was right."

"I should, um, explain this to the viewers," Rami added, with a gesture to the camera, "especially considering there'll be a lot of people watching this beyond the . . . five or six who normally watch my shows. Some guests I have just aren't studio guests . . . or at least, I just don't think of them as studio guests. You know, sometimes you get actors, or other performers who just belong there, naturally. Somehow, with you . . ." and he winced, trying to articulate what he saw, ". . . I just couldn't conceive of you there. I mean, trying to turn you into a celebrity, something you seem to have been trying your level best to avoid the past two years. And it just seemed so stupid, and so fake, that I decided that I'd ask you if you wanted to do the interview someplace you felt most comfortable. And silly me, I thought maybe you'd pick the CDF grounds, or a firing range or something . . ."

Sandy made a face. "That's not me. That's just what I do for a living."

"So Cassandra . . . surfing." He patted his board, a little gingerly, as if willing it not to upend and tip him off. Again. A swell brought them rising up, then sinking down again, as the hump moved on toward the beach, where it transformed into a wave, and then a curling, breaking crest. "What does this place mean to you?"

"Oh . . . freedom, I suppose. Happiness. All that good, corny stuff."

"Considering what you are, a lot of people wouldn't naturally see freedom and happiness as being immediately important to you."

Sandy smiled. "And what am I?"

Rami looked incredulous. "You mean you don't know?"

He was kidding, but Sandy decided to take it seriously. "No," she replied, shaking her head somewhat glumly. "No, I don't. I don't think anyone does, about themself. Not really. Not if they're honest with themselves."

"Know thyself," Rami said with a tone of mock-wisdom. "A wise man once said. Is that why you come out here? To know yourself?"

Sandy shrugged. "Sure. That's a part of why anyone does anything, I suppose."

"And it's a part of why you left the League in the first place?"

Sandy smiled. This was the other reason why she'd made the unlikely choice of Rami Rahim to do her first Callayan TV interview—behind the clownish persona lurked a man of insight and intellect. His best humour she found amusing because it cut its subject straight to the bone. He wouldn't fall for the cliched rubbish much of the media liked to spout about her. "Of course," she replied. "That was me growing up. Children have to leave home sometime. I just had further to travel when I left. And much more to run away from."

A large swell carried them higher once more. Several kilometres to the south lay Turgesh Heads, one of numerous rocky formations along this stretch of coast, northeast of Tanusha. Further south, the Shoban Delta began to break up the firm, straight beaches with a network of river mouths and shifting sand banks. There, the ground became swampy with marsh trees and root networks. Here, a rocky foundation held the ground intact, and steered the river mouths southward. The beach here ran straight and long between the heads, a little too gravelly and rocky to be paradise, but the waves made up for it. Some people lived here, and only visited Tanusha when they had no other choice. Most commuted. Some spots were crowded, but the coastline was long, and those with access to flyers could reach the southeastern beaches too, south of the delta. Today, there were people scattered at random across the sands and the waves . . . but for most Tanushans it was a work day, and there was nothing approaching a crowd. Much of the CDF now had time off. Which was welcome, yet felt somehow unnatural.

"Now, the last time the Callayan public saw you," Rami continued, "you were at the memorial ceremony for those who died taking Nehru Station. The turnout was just enormous . . . did that surprise you?"

"Surprise me? No, not really. I don't think anything the Callayan public does surprises me any longer."

"I know exactly what you mean," Rami deadpanned wearily.

"I'll tell you what *impressed* me, though, was the manner of them. There wasn't any false triumphalism. People were positive; they weren't gloomy or depressed or anything . . . but there was a weight there, you know? As if people had realised that things have changed, and they're not wildly excited about it on the one hand, but not terribly depressed on the other. They're thoughtful. That's the feeling I got that day, anyway."

"I got that too," Rami agreed, nodding as she spoke. "It has been a big change for a lot of people, it's given them a lot to think about."

"I know," said Sandy. "But I think too that Callayan people sometimes haven't given themselves enough credit. All these clichés about decadence and superficiality . . . there's some truth in every cliché, of course, but I haven't been seeing any of that lately."

"Does it make you proud?"

"Yeah . . . you know, it really does. But then, I was proud before, too. I think this place has a lot to be proud of . . . and can do so without having to resort to hollow jingoism. I like that."

"There's been some other talk lately," Rami continued, "about General Krishnaswali and whether he's been hogging too much of the credit for the victory. Some people have leaked information to the effect that he wasn't actually in charge of the attack, and that you and Major Rice in fact deserve most of the credit."

Sandy smiled broadly. "Rami," she said reproachfully. "You should know better than to go around dealing in scuttlebutt."

"Are you kidding? I love scuttlebutt. Scuttlebutt has made many a great media career before, and will do so again."

"General Krishnaswali did a fine job," Sandy said firmly. "He was wounded during a very brave assault upon the station hub, and pressed on regardless to capture the reactor and keep the station online. He's a first class general, and I'm very proud to serve under his command in the CDF. As far as I'm concerned, everyone on that station was a hero, and not just the CDF. We couldn't have done it without the civilians who helped us either."

Rami grinned. "Darn it, I thought I had you."

Sandy just smiled. Damn right Krishnaswali was hogging more than his share of the credit. Damn sure people were pissed at him. But equally damn sure she wasn't about to undermine the CDF and Callay's achievement in a fit of political backbiting over the spoils. Politics was politics, and would always be so. And you either dealt with it, as calmly and rationally as possible, or it dealt with you. Besides all of which, when Krishnaswali had emerged from the two-arm elevator with his squad, exhausted, sweaty and cradling a wounded arm, having against all the odds secured the reactor core with no further fatalities, she'd pumped her fist in the air and yelled with all the rest of them. If Krishnaswali wanted the credit, let him have it. Of the CDF's three senior commanders, he was the only one who actually wanted it, anyhow . . .

"So tell me," Rami pressed, moving to lean meaningfully forward upon his board . . . and almost losing his balance as the board tipped. Sandy restrained her amusement. "Whose stupid idea was this anyway?" Rami muttered as he recovered.

"That would be yours," Sandy told him.

"Ah." He resettled the board between wetsuited legs. In the bright midday sun, the wetsuit was becoming quite hot . . . yet the water here was verging on cold, with strong northerly currents hauling it down from the poles. Cold by warm Tanushan standards, anyhow. Sandy's artificial muscles preferred heat to cold, and she always wore a wetsuit while surfing, whatever the sunlight, least she stiffen and cramp for days to follow. And besides, she was determined that people the day after this interview was broadcast would be talking about the content of her words, and not the proportions of her figure as revealed by the kind of skimpy swimsuit Rhian favoured.

"You were going to say?" she reminded him.

"Going to say what?" Rami looked baffled.

"I don't know. What?"

"What what?" He double-blinked, looking more baffled. Sandy repressed a grin. There was something in the delivery, with comics. They made anything funny. "Oh yes. The memorial service. Some people were very emotional. *I* got very emotional, I don't mind admitting . . . and I don't consider myself to be militaristic in any way, nor the kind of flag-waving patriot we're starting to see crawling from the woodwork. How *should* we respond to what happened, do you think?"

Sandy recalled the memorial service, just six days ago—two weeks following the departure of the remaining Fifth Fleet ships. It had taken place in a broad park, out in the new Herat district, within sight of the enormous domes and construction cranes of the new Grand Council buildings. Previously intended as a general purpose recreation area, some rapid redesign had paved a pedestrian avenue between existing gardens and trees, with the names of each of the thirty-six Callayan soldiers who had died engraved upon small headstones along the way. It all led to a monument within a raised, paved circle—not a stone or other carved edifice, but a native banyal tree, with enormous spreading branches and thick foliage. This one was already two hundred C-years old. The good ones lived to be a thousand, on average, and frequently much more.

Sandy recalled reflecting upon the symbolism, as the CDF honour guard had assembled beneath its shady branches following the entire force's march from the Grand Council buildings to the memorial. They had planted something that would grow, not merely protected something already old. A future for a Federation run by its own people, not ruled by special interests from afar. It did mean something to her, and as she'd gazed out upon the tens of thousands of Callayans gathered in a human sea across the park, it was clear that it meant something to them, too. More than the uniforms and the chestful of shiny new medals. Something that would last for generations. Centuries, in one form or another. A legacy, in the truest sense of the term, to be enjoyed by billions of people across countless light years. And for the first time in her life, she'd felt truly, unashamedly proud of what she was, both as a soldier, and as a person.

She cast a gaze now toward the beach, as she considered Rami's question. Vanessa was seated over there somewhere, watching these proceedings with interest. Sandy wasn't sure that Vanessa felt quite as she did. Vanessa had always been proud of her role in Callay's security, and had nothing in her past to be ashamed of. Rather than being an uplifting moment, the battle of Nehru Station had come down on her rather hard. The loss of Zago and Sharma from old SWAT Four in particular had struck with force, although many others, too, she had known well and helped to train, in recent years. She'd been strong, despite several nights of unashamed sobbing—getting it out of her system, she'd called it, and had seemed somewhat better the following mornings. But somehow, standing to attention beneath the banyal tree's branches before the gaze of Federation-wide media, Sandy hadn't been able to escape the feeling that Vanessa's uniform hat sat somehow too high upon her head, and the collar too loose, as if the polished dress uniform were refusing to fit her properly . . . or she, it.

As for Rhian and Ari, well . . . if she trailed her eyes along the shoreline, she could catch a brief glimpse, in a break through the rolling waves, of Rhian playing in the shallows with Vanessa's niece and nephew, Isabelle and Yves, five and seven years old respectively. Jumping the broken wash as it rolled the final few metres toward the sandy shore, and sometimes trying to bodysurf, with Rhian's assistance and encouragement. Rhian, as Vanessa had observed, was indestructible. Nothing seemed to get her down for long, and where others saw clouds, Rhian saw only silver linings. No wonder she identified so readily with children . . . and children, so readily with her.

Ari of course remained, in his own words, "unbeachable." Probably he was somewhere with friends, below ground or otherwise far from sunlight's treacherous reach, discussing some latest network configuration, or the processing speed of the latest nano-routers. The Fifth Fleet's departure had allowed him some return to those other aspects of his life to which Sandy continued to feel somewhat remote, despite his enthusiastic attempts to convey its obvious fascinations to her. She'd seen enough technology in her life, and lived in enough gloomy, artificial places, that she really didn't need that whole scene right now. And so she continued to see Anita, Pushpa, Tojo and others, as chance and scheduling would allow . . . but right now, she wanted sunlight, space and natural beauty whenever possible. Just the other night she'd dragged Ari along to an open-air concert in a beautiful, garden amphitheatre. CDF privileges had obtained front row seats for them, and Ari had actually seemed to enjoy it, despite his initial reluctance. So maybe there was hope for him yet. And hope for them, together, as an ongoing concern. Time, as always, would tell that story.

"I can't speak for other people," she replied at last to Rami's question. "I only know what *I* feel. I think the new patriotism is warranted. I think some people are probably overdoing it . . . but you'll get that anywhere. But the most important thing is that people are now thinking and talking about stuff that previously wouldn't have crossed their minds. And when that happens, it makes everyone safer, in every way."

"There are a lot of pacifists," Rami countered, "as you'll know, who said we should never have ended the blockade with force. That there were other ways, and it needn't have cost those lives."

Sandy shrugged. "Inaction can have awful consequences too. Earth conservative elements were becoming emboldened by their apparent success. If they'd kept pushing, we could have had a full blown civil war at some point, with God knows how many deaths. Now, that's not going to happen. People die during periods of instability. That's just a cold, hard fact. The best policy is to limit those periods of instability to the shortest timeframe possible, because that's the best way of limiting the total number of casualties."

"So you think we did the right thing?"

"I do."

"And the charges that you've succeeded in militarising a civilised, Gandhian utopia don't bother you?"

Sandy shrugged again. "In civilised society, ideologies do battle. We figure which ones are best by watching how they can be applied to changing circumstances. There are people today who are unhappy because their ideology was proven relatively ineffectual. Maybe, in different circumstances, their ideology would have worked better. In this one, it didn't. That's life."

Rami smiled broadly, as some private humour occurred to him. "You know," he said, "this does feel slightly surreal. Sitting out here, talking with you about such serious, philosophical things . . ."

"I'm quite impressed," Sandy remarked, swishing her feet in the cold water, attempting to keep the creeping stiffness at bay. "You've been more or less serious for the past two minutes straight."

"Well, it's serious stuff," Rami protested offhandedly. "I'm a Callayan, and I'm concerned like . . ." and gave a start, staring downward into the shimmering green water. "Something brushed past my leg. Something brushed past my leg!"

"Of course it did," Sandy said calmly.

"Of course . . ." he shot her a rapid, alarmed look. "What do you mean of course it did?"

"I mean it wouldn't go after me. I'm artificial, I wouldn't taste good."

"It?" With wide-eyed hysteria. "What do you mean it?!" And to the invisible razorfish, doubtless circling somewhere nearby, "I'll sue! Do you hear me, you big, ugly, stupid critter?! One bite of me and I'll sue your arse off!"

"You know the best defence against razors?" Sandy added conversationally.

"No! No, what?!"

"Make certain there's at least one person in your group who's a slower swimmer than you are." Rami stared at her for a moment. Then the eyes widened as he realised the implication.

"You're a GI?" Pointing nervously to Sandy.

"I am."

"And you're a regular swimmer?" Pointing to his cameraman.

The cameraman nodded, moving the lense up and down so any viewer could see. "That's right."

Rami plunged for the inflatable, splashing frantically, yelling and cursing of conspiracies and treacherous underlings, while everyone fell about laughing. It took another minute to get things settled back down again, and for the interview to resume. This time, with recent, serious stuff out of the way, the mood was lighter. They talked for a while about personal tastes, what kind of music she liked, what kind of places she'd been to across Callay, her opinion on various light, inconsequential, Callayan things. Sandy was unsure how much of it would end up going to air, but thought it would probably be a lot, given the anticipation for this interview. She kept her answers brief where possible, and didn't try to compete with Rami for amusement value.

After a while, Rami smiled, and said, "You seem like a really nice person." With a very warm sincerity. "How is that possible? Given what you are, and what you were made for?"

Sandy smiled back. "I realised the alternative," she said. "That's all."

"You have some friends over there," Rami said, casting his eyes across to the shoreline. It was slightly closer now, the current having pulled them in a little. The next swell heaved them higher than the last, but they remained a safe distance from the break zone yet. "They came out with you today with a few family members and a couple of very noisy children I met earlier, who didn't seem to believe I was a famous media personality . . ." sounding very miffed. Sandy smiled, scratching at a salt-itch above one eyebrow. "How important are friends to you?"

"Oh . . ." Sandy made a face, considering. "They're pretty much everything, I think."

"Why?" It seemed an honest question. "I mean, some people need friends because they're insecure, others because they just love company and people, and others because they've been lonely a lot in their lives, and value relationships more than other people might?"

"The latter, mostly," Sandy conceded. "Although it's more than that. There's no such thing as absolute self-knowledge. I think the only way to know anything, including about ourselves, is by relative comparison. Relationships hold up a mirror to ourselves. They tell us who we are. And so I think what my friends give me, aside from love, is just . . . the sure knowledge that I'm something more than just a bundle of parts. Somewhere along the line, they've become my anchor. And I just can't imagine living without that."

A glance across to the shore showed Rhian now bounding from the water, the children in tow, headed for Auntie Vanessa with mischief on their minds. There appeared to be a jellyfish involved. Vanessa sprang from her towel and retaliated, which resulted, inevitably, in noisy children being grabbed, restrained, and tickled mercilessly.

"And besides that," she added to her previous answer, "there's just love. And even rational, stuffy old me doesn't have a sensible explanation for that."

"And so now," Rami said, with some theatrics, "we come to the great, climactic, money question. This is the one where I demonstrate all my intellectual acumen as a probing interviewer of great repute, and not just the silly bugger who makes a fool of himself in front of a planetary audience . . . trust me, this question will really blow your socks off. I was up all night working on it . . ."

Sandy's attention, meanwhile, had been drawn toward deeper water, where a particularly large, building swell was just screaming for attention as it approached. She pivoted her board on an impulse, pointing toward the shore. "Sorry," she interrupted, "can it wait just two minutes?"

And began paddling with fast, explosive thrusts of her arms, accelerating at a speed no merely human surfer could ever hope to match.

"Wait!" Rami yelled after her, in great indignation. "What about my question?!"

"I'll be back!" Sandy shouted over her shoulder, powering toward the break zone ahead. The swell reached the inflatable, lifting it, Rami and cameraman gloriously high above the neutral water mark. "I just have to catch this wave!"

## ABOUT THE AUTHOR

Joel Shepherd was born in Adelaide, South Australia, in 1974, but when he was seven his family moved to Perth in Western Australia. He studied film and television at Curtin University but realised that what he really wanted to do was write stories. His first manuscript was shortlisted for the George Turner Prize in 1998, and *Crossover* (the first Cassandra Kresnov novel) was short-listed in 1999.

Apart from writing, Joel helps in his mother's business, selling Australian books to international schools in Asia and beyond. This has given him the opportunity to travel widely in Asia and other parts of the world. Joel also writes about women's basketball for an American Internet magazine.

Joel currently lives in Adelaide.

451